01-15

COST OF A KILLING

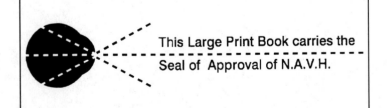

This Large Print Book carries the
Seal of Approval of N.A.V.H.

THE LIFE AND TIMES OF JESTON NASH

COST OF A KILLING

RALPH COTTON

THORNDIKE PRESS

A part of Gale, Cengage Learning

GALE
CENGAGE Learning·

Farmington Hills, Mich • San Francisco • New York • Waterville, Maine
Meriden, Conn • Mason, Ohio • Chicago

LIBRARY OF CONGRESS CATALOGING-IN-PUBLICATION DATA

Cotton, Ralph W.
    Cost of a killing : the life and times of Jeston Nash / by Ralph Cotton. —
Large print edition.
        pages ; cm. — (Thorndike Press large print western)
    ISBN 978-1-4104-6693-8 (hardcover) — ISBN 1-4104-6693-0 (hardcover)
    1. Billy, the Kid—Fiction. 2. Outlaws—Fiction. 3. New Mexico—Fiction.
4. Large type books. I. Title.
PS3553.O766C67 2014
813'.54—dc23   2014018451

Published in 2014 by arrangement with Ralph Cotton

Printed in Mexico
1 2 3 4 5 6 7 18 17 16 15 14

FOREWARD

Three times in my life I had occasion to meet Henry McCarty, alias William Bonney, alias Billy the Kid; and on each occasion, due to the striking resemblance between me and my cousin, Jesse Woodson James, the Kid always thought that Cousin Jesse and I were one and the same. That's not to say that the Kid was easily fooled, or thick and slow-witted as some might imply, because over the years many people made the same mistake. Cousin Jesse and I not only favored in appearance, but we also rode with the same bunch out of Missouri during the final days of the great Civil Conflict, and for a long time after — robbing banks, railroads and such.

It always amazes me, looking back at all the ole boys I knew who became legends, because at the time I knew them they were no different than the rest of us — doing what they thought they had to, just to get by. I'd never speak ill of Billy Bonney, but I do have to say that as outlawing goes, he was never more than a back alley thief . . . a nickel and dimer who never had the presence of mind to go on to bigger and better things.

Billy got blamed for everything from train robbery to passing counterfeit money, but mostly all he did was steal cattle — and he never made much money at *that*. His buyers knew the cattle was stolen, so they took advantage of him at every chance; and the way the Kid must've figured it, was since he'd paid nothing for the cattle, anything he made off them was clear profit. I don't think he ever stopped to consider that he'd put his life on the line every time he rustled out a few head — don't think he ever saw what it would cost him in the final tally. But there's a cost to everything you do in life, from the cost of doing business to the cost of being what you are. If he ever learned it, it might've been right there at the end when he saw the flash of a pistol split the darkness. Right then he might've seen that all the bills in his life had finally come due. Who can say?

The Kid idolized Cousin Jesse, as did most rowdy young men of that place and time, although, the person he always thought to be Jesse James was really just me. There's something sad about it in a way — the fact that Billy the Kid went to his grave thinking he'd met his idol, made friends with the most famous outlaw of all times; but then, the Kid went to his grave with a head *full* of misunderstandings, so I reckon one more didn't make any difference once the hammer fell. I tried many times to tell him who I really was, but he *could* not, or *would* not hear of it. So finally I just let him think it, for who among us doesn't at some time fashion reality to fit our liking, and leave *truth* to swirl in the sands of time. Perhaps it is from *that* self-same premise that legends are born.

There was only two ways to regard the Kid, you either loved him or hated him. Those who loved him were the ones to whom he'd give the shirt off his back, and of course, the ones who hated him was the ones he'd stolen the shirt from in the first place. Some called him an angel — a Robin Hood of the badlands — and if that's the case I'd have to say: *He stole from the rich and gave to the whores.* Others called him vile, lowdown and loco — a devil's monster straight up from hell, and I can see how either side was right, depending on which day of the week they caught him on, or whether they found themselves in front of or *behind* his double action Colt.

Myself, I always liked Billy, and always felt sorry him for some reason. Maybe that doesn't speak well for me to some folks way of thinking; but even before he thought I was Jesse James, he stood beside me and my partner, Quiet Jack Smith, and faced off a bunch of Nuevo Mejico thugs when the odds were long against any one of us finishing the day standing up. That was the first time I met him, when he was around sixteen, and I'd best describe him then as a marble rattling in a Mason jar.

But once a man has sided with you against long odds, it's easy to overlook any craziness or meanness in him. Of course after we'd fought off the thugs, the Kid did manage to steal a thousand dollar riding mare right out from under me. But he did it more or less on a lark, and he did it so slick and easy like, I couldn't really foster a grudge over it. No matter what the Kid ever done, he never took it too serious, and for that reason I reckon I didn't either. It's hard to stay mad at a person like that, the same as it's hard to stay mad at a fox for raiding a henhouse. It's just a nature that can't be changed. Nobody's perfect.

The second time we met was in the dusty

little town of Fort Sumner where Quiet Jack and I had been shooting at cans and bottles with some of the Kid's amigos; but actually, the events leading to my meeting him there had started in a roundabout way a few weeks earlier in the back room of a gambling hall in New Orleans. That was the night I met the contesa, and anytime I think of the Kid, I always think of *her;* and anytime I think of either of them, I still picture that clock standing against the wall of the billiard-room, looking wise and patient, ticking slow and steady like the heartbeat of a powerful beast.

I remember seeing it out the corner of my eye and hearing the brass pendulum pass back and forth, slicing through time, leaving eternity to dangle on either end of its swing. That was the night of the great storm when the eyes of God and the hand of the devil moved as one — the night I heard the message of a dying man, and the night I began to learn the *cost* of a killing.

CHAPTER 1

It was sweltering hot in the room, and the air above French Quarters had drawn its breath and held it, awaiting the storm that boiled low above the sea somewhere southwest of the city. The game was Nine Behind the Deuce, and I'd never shot such excellent pool in my life. I could do no wrong. The game was played only by the highly skilled or the very reckless. Ordinarily, I was neither. But that night I was both.

The game was played fast, for high stakes, with nine balls shot in rotation, the money riding on the two ball and the nine. We'd started out betting ten dollars on the two and twenty on the nine. Of course if you made the two but didn't end up making the nine, you paid the other player double. The stakes and the tension had swollen gradually as the day wore on.

By dark we'd upped the wager to a thousand on the two and two thousand on the nine, and had started making thousand dollar side bets on nearly every shot. A game could now be worth as much as twelve thousand — a heady amount by anybody's standard — and my concentration was that of a thoroughbred wearing blinders. Nothing existed except the field of green felt in my narrowed vision, and there was no sound, save for the soft tap of the cue, the gentle click of ivory, and the hollow plop of a ball into the woven leather pocket.

We'd been playing all day, well past dark, there in the small room off the main casino, just the two of us, and I still didn't know his name. The only other person in the room was my friend, Quiet Jack Smith, who stood leaning against the wall beside a narrow table, sipping rye and watching.

No one had spoken for the longest time, only a glance of acknowledgement at the end of each game, as money slid across the felt from one powdered hand to the other. A bead of sweat ran down my forehead, stopped on the bridge of my nose and hung there. When I dared raise my forearm to blot it away, I did so slowly, grudgingly, fearing that any change of movement or even of *thought* might break my winning spell.

When I lowered my forearm, I saw his eyes searching mine from the other end of the table. He raised the rack for the next game; a smile twitched, then vanished. "Getting tired," he said. It was not a question, but an observation, or perhaps wishful thinking. Thunder grumbled low in the distance.

Without answering, I reached forward, gathered the stack of money and held it out for Quiet Jack to hold. He took it and leaned back against the wall. I'd never seen Quiet Jack so *Quiet.* In spite of his name, most times he could drown out an army bugle. Tonight he seemed in awe, as if he couldn't believe the shots I made. To be honest, neither could I. Winning seemed predestined. All I had to do was go through the motions. It was eery.

"Let's up the bet," the big man said. He hooked the rack on a wall peg and faced me, raising and dropping his cue stick on the toe of his dress boot. Again, a smile twitched and vanished. "Say . . . *five* thousand on the two, *ten* thousand on the nine? Maybe get a little bolder on the side bets?"

He watched my eyes for the slightest flicker of doubt; and I saw that he was trying to push me past my edge — get me to the point where my nerves would rattle. He saw I was riding a powerful streak. His only hope now was to floor me, overpower me with the weight of money.

"Why not," I said, sliding a stone-faced glance across Quiet Jack, then back to him. "It's only money." Lightning flashed purple and gold through the open window. I reached out and rolled the cue ball into position with my fingertips, doing so gently, careful not to offend it. I formed a high, closed bridge with my left hand, and had rested down for the break when I heard the beaded curtain rustle behind me. Then I stopped, raised slightly, and looked around as a darkhaired woman stepped through the parted beads and stood watching us.

I saw Jack straighten up against the wall and offer a courteous nod; but she didn't seem to see him. She gazed past him, past me, and riveted her dark eyes on the big man. "What are doing here?" he said. His voice was low, menacing. Again, thunder grumbled, this time closer, rolling across rooftops.

"This is a public hall, is it not? I am free to watch, si?" Her voice carried the hint of polished Spanish, not the barroom and border Spanish I'd grown accustomed to. She glanced away from him, to me, as if asking my permission.

"I've no objection, mam," I said, not wanting to speak, move, or even *think* of

14

anything right then except the smooth stroke of wood between my fingers. I turned my gaze to him, waiting.

"Then *watch,*" he said to her. A smile twitched again on his lips, but this time it did not vanish. It twisted down into a thin sneer, and he turned his eyes to mine and said: "Why don't we turn this one into a gutting match . . . give the little lady something to look at."

I straightened up from the table and glanced back and forth between them. Something was at work here. I didn't know what it was, but I felt it, hot and dangerous, a fire just beneath the surface, ready to spill out and consume them. I let out a breath and glanced at Jack. He saw it too. He slipped the cork into the bottle of rye, patted it with the palm of his hand, and sat the bottle on the table beside him. "Call it a night," he said. His expression went blank, but I saw the warning in his eyes.

Lightning glittered. I saw it lick across the brass pendulum of the clock as I looked away from Jack and ran my hand down my trouser leg. I couldn't let it go, not now, not while my winning streak was still burning a hole in my belly. I looked up at the big man and only nodded. He raised his brow and said: "How much you holding?" I barely made out his words beneath a crash of thunder.

"Fifty thousand, give or take," I said. I glanced at Jack. The warning was still in his eyes, but he nodded and took the stack of winnings from inside his shirt. I'd started with only five thousand. It helped, knowing that was the most I could lose.

"You're covered," the big man said. "Nothing on the deuce, nothing on the side. The nine ball does it all. Shoot 'em up." He took a step back from the table, staring past me and at the woman.

"Hold it," I said. "You see my money. What's yours look like?"

He slipped his hand inside his linen jacket and pulled out a long leather wallet. "Check it," he said, flipping the wallet onto the green felt. As I reached for it, he pulled out a folded paper and flipped it down also. "This will make up for any shortage."

Behind me, I thought I heard the woman gasp. But I didn't look around as I reached out a finger and turned open the paper. "A deed?" I looked up at him and shook my head slowly. "I have no use for land . . . only money." I fanned the cash from the wallet. "You've got enough for a couple of games at ten thousand, just like you asked for. We'll shoot for that or call it quits —"

16

"What?" His face glowed red; his hand squeezed tight around the stick. "Do you have *any idea* what that land is worth?"

"Evidently, it's only worth a game of pool, to you," I said. I eased the money back into the wallet and slid the wallet and the deed across the felt toward him.

"Wait, señor," said the lady behind me; and she stepped around and laid her hand gently over mine before I could draw it back. "If he must do such a thing, I will cover his wager against the deed. My home is near there, near Silver Basin in Little Sand Hole."

I shot her a glance, then back to the man. "What's your interest here, mam? I know there's something going on between —"

"What does it matter? I will put up fifty-thousand for the land. If you win, I will give you money and take the deed. Is that not fair?" She raised her hand from mine, and I let my hand drift back from the wallet and the deed, over to the cue. I picked it up and stared into it as if consulting a crystal ball, rolling it back and forth with my fingertips, considering.

After a moment, I looked at the big man, saw his eyes riveted on hers. "Is this satisfactory to you?"

"Sure, why not," he said, staring straight

17

at her. "I'll burn in hell before I lose *this* game!" Lightning glittered behind him.

"Alright then," I said, hearing the thunder closer now, almost directly above us. I had no interest in the land or what it was worth. Even the fifty thousand was no longer of great importance. What was important was to see this winning streak run its course, ride it until it headed into the barn, then get off at the last second, slap it on the rump and close the door behind it. I faced her: "Where's *your* fifty thousand?"

Her hands swept beneath her hair and un-clasped a necklace of diamonds and rubies set in a bib of tooled gold. I just watched as she laid them on the table. Tossing back her hair, she took off the matching set of ear-rings and let them roll down her fingertips. "I thought we were talking about cash here," I said.

"You hold these until tomorrow. Have them appraised. If they are not worth over *one hundred-thousand,* you keep everything. is that not fair?"

"And you take the risk of the deed being real or encumbered?"

"Si . . . I mean *yes,* of course. I know it is real. And that will be of no concern to you —" As she spoke to me, her eyes went back to his. Lightning flashed again. "— Just beat him. You will have your money."

I looked at him and nodded toward the half opened window as I laid the cue ball back on the felt and rolled it with the tip of my finger. Thunder exploded overhead like cannon fire. "Want to wait until it passes?" I asked. The woman stepped over near the wall, beside Jack. I saw Jack raise a boot behind him and lean back against the wall on his boot heel. He hooked the bottle of rye from the table beside him.

The big man wrapped both hands around his stick and twisted them back and forth. "Only if you're afraid of storms."

"I'm used to 'em," I said, leaning forward again, onto the felt, forming a bridge with my fingers. Behind me, Quiet Jack chuckled under his breath; and I heard the muffled pop of the cork and the slosh of rye whiskey.

I broke the balls with a smooth, solid stroke, not too hard, but hard enough to pull out the seven, bank it off two rails and drop it into the side pocket. The rest of the cluster spread out in a nice shooting pattern, all but two of them that rolled to the far end of the table. I'd used low *side* on the cue ball — what some players were starting to call *English* — and it spun in place no more than two inches from where it had struck the cluster.

The one ball slowed to a stop three inches off the rail and a foot from the left corner pocket. An easy cut shot. But the deuce was one of the two balls that had ran back up the table — it and the six. I saw that I couldn't make the one ball with enough *English* to pull the cue ball back up the table where I would need it. So I made the one and left the cue ball behind the nine, half-way between the spot and the far rail, play-ing it safe. His only shot at the deuce would be to bank off the side rail, go across the table and kick it into the corner pocket. *No way,* I thought.

But he did it! Her being there had brought something to his game. Whatever dark drama was at work between them seemed to have sharpened his eye and steadied his hand. Now he shot with a vengeance, force-ful and exact. It was not a vengeance di-rected at me, yet I felt the sting of it in his every move.

Even as the deuce dropped, he stepped around the table holding his stick across the front of him, snatched a cube of chalk from the rail on his way, held it in the palm of his hand, and twisted the tip of his stick back and forth against it, grinding it. Chalk dust fell in a fine mist. Before the cue ball had stopped rolling, he was in place, ready to shoot the three ball down rail. An easy shot — one that would leave him straight across from the four in the opposite corner pocket.

I shot Jack a glance; he looked away, threw back a shot of rye and let out a whiskey hiss. The man shot hard. The cue ball slammed against the three, sent it down rail, and as it fell, he chalked again, quickly, and leaned out to shoot the four. This time he looked up, and across the table at the woman, even as the tip of his stick banged into the cue ball. He smiled, not even bothering to see if he made the shot. The four ball fell.

"I owned the land when I came here," he said, stepping around to shoot the five back across to the side pocket. "And I'll own it when I leave."

She took a step away from the wall and toward him. "If there is a God in heaven you will never see a moment of peace —"

Her lips moved, but her words were swallowed up by a heavy clap of thunder as the five ball hit the pocket so hard, it spun around the rim before it dropped. "— And the soul of an animal!" Her words came back as the thunder rolled away. I turned to Jack and could only shrug. *Why me?* The sound of heavy rain pelted the half opened window like a handful of nails. I felt my winning streak sink like a stone.

"Maybe he'll fall on his stick and poke an eye out," Jack said just above a whisper. I watched the six ball make a long fast run the length of the table and drop into a corner pocket. With the seven ball already down, the cue ball spun over like a soldier following orders, kissed the eight ball just enough to pull it off the rail, then fell in behind it for a perfect shot into the side pocket. From there, even a beginner could nail the nine across corner. I felt like hanging up my stick.

He walked around the table slowly now, chalking his tip, taking his time. His eyes glittered in the bolt of lightning that seemed to linger outside the window, twisting and curling like a tortured snake.

A dark laugh spilled from him as he leaned out behind the eight ball. "You can win all day —" Without even looking, it seemed, he dealt the cue ball a hard punch. It slammed the eight ball and jumped back. The eight ball hit the side pocket with the sound of somebody slamming a trunk shut, bounced three inches above the rail and shot down into the pocket. "— You can win all night," he added.

He grinned now, walking around the table to shoot the nine across corner. He chalked up again and leaned out behind the nine. "But no matter how many games you win," he said, glancing at the woman who stood holding her breath. Then he glanced back to me, grinning, already gloating. "There's only one game that counts in a gutting match." He stroked the cue stick back and forth, leaned low and sighted in. He started to shoot, but then stopped, taunting me, dragging it out as long as he could. "And after tonight I think you'll know what game that is, eh?"

"Just make your shot," I said through a tight jaw.

"It's the *last* game, young man," he said with finality. And with a tremendous punch of the stick, the cue ball struck the nine like a sledge hammer, turning it into a yellow blur as it shot into the corner pocket with a loud thump. My heart sank with the sound of it.

I glanced away, heartsick. Then I heard Jack say: "Look at this . . . look at this . . ." And I glanced back at the table just as the woman gasped; and I watched the cue ball rolling back as if it had been shot from the other direction. It struck the rail as the big man stepped back with his arms spread. Then it seemed to speed up coming off the rail.

"No!" he bellowed. But as his eyes widened, the white ball rolled silently and accurately across the table and dropped into the corner pocket with a soft and fatal *plop.* "No!" he bellowed again.

"SCRAAAATCH! You lose!" I yelled so loud, my voice echoed out through the main casino. A hush fell over the crowd beyond the beaded curtains. The woman stood staring across the table at him with a strange, dark expression on her face.

"I'll be *damned* if I lose! You suckered me into it!" He dropped his cue stick, took a step back from the table and threw his linen coat open. I saw the dull shine of a pistol in his belt, and was a little surprised by it. When Jack and I came in earlier, we'd checked our pistols at the door just like the sign said. But luckily, I'd kept another forty-four under my shirt, tied around my neck by a strip of rawhide. Jack had his fancy thirty-six caliber La Faucheux stuck down in the back of his belt. Somehow I'd felt we had the only guns in the place.

"I didn't sucker you in, mister," I said without taking my eyes off his. "You *scratched,* fair and square! *Life* mighta suckered you, but I didn't. I just happened to be the one holding the stick." I stepped to the rail and closed my left hand over the money

24

and the deed. He wrapped his hand around the butt of his pistol.

Beyond the beaded curtain separating the billiard room from the main casino, I heard someone cry out: "They've got guns!"

"Watch them," I said to Quiet Jack without taking my eyes off the big man; and I heard Jack step over to the beaded curtain.

"You're not taking that deed," the big man said.

"Got a sheriff coming this way," I heard Jack say behind me. "Got a bartender raising a shotgun — Uh-oh! Got two bystanders in suits pulling pistols." I heard him chuckle under his breath. "Whole damned *place* is armed. These people have no regard for signs."

"Here's the sheriff," Jack said. I heard him step back.

"What going on in here?" I heard the rattle of the beaded curtain as he stepped into the room.

"No problem, sheriff," said Jack. "Just a little misunderstanding. All settled now."

"Then I'll just take a look for myself," I heard the sheriff reply. I shot him a glance and noticed he was a tall, serious looking man with a dark mustache. He stopped beside me.

"Good thing you're here, sheriff. These

sons-a-bitches just tried to skin me out of my land!" The man across the table stepped around quickly and started to put his hand on the deed. I grabbed his wrist and shoved him back.

"Everybody hold it!" the sheriff yelled beside me; but the man reached for his pistol as he stepped back.

I jerked open my shirt, reaching for the pistol around my neck. But before I could draw it, the young woman snatched the bottle of rye from the table and busted it sideways across the man's jaw. He landed on the floor like a pile of dirty laundry.

"Jesus!" I brushed whiskey and broken glass from my coat sleeve. I heard Jack laugh behind me. The sheriff stepped around and leaned down over the man. Beyond the beaded curtain, someone whistled and the crowd roared.

The sheriff stood up, shook his head and turned to me. His hand slid near a long barrelled pistol inside his waist belt. "Who are you, mister?"

"I'm Beatty . . . James Beatty," I said quickly. "I'm a horse dealer out of Missouri. I'm only here for the dealer auction tomorrow. Then headed back up to Shreveport."

His eyes slid from me to Jack. "And you?"

"I'm with him," Jack said, nodding toward me.

"But what's your name?" The tall sheriff stared at him. Jack stared right back, but offered nothing more.

A tense silence passed until the woman stepped forward and said: "I am the Contesa Animarciclo Cortez, sheriff. These men have done nothing wrong. I will attest to it."

The sheriff looked at her and had started to speak, when on the floor the man opened his eyes and groaned. "I'll kill you . . ."

The contesa stepped toward him. "And this one is a pig! A worthless, losing pig." She spit down on the man, tried to kick him, and sliced off a few words in heated Spanish.

"Easy, mam," I said, taking her arm firmly but gently just as the sheriff reached for her. "Sheriff, she offered to buy his bet just to keep down trouble. I can see why she's a bit upset."

The sheriff glanced from the contesa to Jack and back to me. "Alright. I believe ya. But I want this mess settled, right now."

"Thanks, sheriff." I nodded toward the jewels, the deed, and the money on the table. "Señorita, I have no interest in the jewels. Maybe we should go work this out

27

—" I glanced around at the crowd beyond the beaded curtain. "— Somewhere a little quieter?"

"Of course," she said. "But I must first have the deed to the land —"

"That's my land!" The man tried to grab her leg but she kicked at him. The sheriff stepped between them.

"The deed?" She smoothed her dress and smiled, but I saw the slightest trace of eagerness in her dark eyes.

"Yes," I said. "As soon as he signs it, we'll go settle up somewhere."

She hesitated for a second as if in thought, then held up a finger. "You are right," she said in a soft voice. "We have raised too much attention. Keep all of this —" she gestured toward the table "— until morning. We will meet for breakfast and finish our business. Where are you staying?"

"At the Three Sisters' Inn." I also gestured toward the table and the glittering jewels. "But this is a lot of valuables here. You don't even know me."

She smiled. "You said your name is Mister Beatty. Is it not so?"

"Well . . . yes." I felt my face redden. My real name was Jeston Nash; I was wanted for murder under the name Miller Crowe, had been for years. I traded horses under

28

the name James Beatty. Names were something I changed more often than some folks changed socks.

"And, you are a caballista, a horse dealer, yes?"

I shrugged, "Yes." But trading horses was more of a sideline. At that time I still made my living riding with my cousins, Jesse and Frank. "Still, you don't know me well enough to trust me with all this." Maybe I was telling her I didn't trust myself.

She flipped a perfumed handkerchief from her bosom, pressed into my hand and nodded toward the jewels. "Gather them. I will send my carriage for you in the morning." She smiled and leaned near me. "Be hungry when you come." I smelled the warmth, the heady sweetness of her; my pulse quickened. Her lips pursed slightly, "And take good care of the deed and the jewels until then."

"Now there goes a mighty trusting lady," Jack said, with a curious expression, watching the contesa as she turned and left.

"Lots of class," I said. And once she'd left, I wrapped the jewels in the perfumed handkerchief, tucked them safely inside my jacket, and along with Jack and the sheriff dragging the man by his shoulders, we stepped out into the main casino.

The sheriff spread the deed out on the

bar. At first I thought there might be a problem getting it signed, but the sheriff hovered over the man's shoulder as he wiped his face with a wet rag and completed the deal with a fancy ink pen. His eyes burned into mine as he handed the deed to the sheriff for inspection.

"I'll be damned." The sheriff breathed in a low voice as he looked at the signature. "You've just beat none other than Quick Quintan Cordell."

"Boy-oh-boy!" I heard Jack say behind me. I took the deed and glanced at the name, trying not to look too impressed. Quick Quintan Cordell was a legend among gamblers, especially among the billiard sharks. Last I'd heard, he'd gutted a railroad man up in Montana and retired a millionaire. No one had seen him in years. But I reckon gamblers never completely retire.

"Then I'm disappointed in the way you've acted here tonight," I said to Quick Quintan. I folded the deed and slipped it inside my lapel pocket. "I've always heard you were a stand-up man . . . a real sport in any game."

"What do you know about anything, you little weasel-eyed bas—"

He'd started to lean toward me; the sheriff stopped him with a hand on his shoulder.

30

"Maybe you better go somewhere and cool down, Quick Quintan. The lady says this fellow beat you fair and square."

"Where is that lying hussy?" Quick Quintan glanced about the casino.

"Hold on now," said the sheriff. "She left. But I won't have you blackguarding her."

"Yeah? Well, all of you can go to hell!" He jerked from under the sheriff's hand, slung himself away from the bar and stomped out the door. The sheriff's deputy stepped forward with his hand on his pistol, glanced at Quintan Cordell's back, then at me, then at the crowd in general. Then for some reason, he fixed his gaze on Quiet Jack and said to the sheriff: "Want me to rough somebody up, boss?" I suppose he couldn't stand not being involved.

"No . . . but thanks, Gosset." The sheriff gestured toward their table and the deputy backed away, brooding, still staring at Jack. He couldn't have picked a worse person to hone in on. Jack would close the deputy's eyes quicker than a snake could shake its tail.

"Thanks for your help, sheriff," I said, trying to play down any further disturbance. "Things got a little out of control there for a minute." I smiled and took two cigars from my pocket. I offered the sheriff one;

he took it, sniffed it and grinned. "Maybe I can buy you a drink?" I asked, gesturing a hand toward the row of bottles behind the bar.

"I'd be honored," the sheriff said. I noticed the deputy's stare soften just a little, but it stayed fixed on Jack. Jack chuckled behind me.

As I turned and raised a hand to a waiter, I caught a glimpse of something near the door. "Look out!" I heard a woman scream.

I spun toward the commotion just as Quick Quintan Cordell stepped in raising a shotgun toward me. "You rotten son of a ___"

In reflex, I jumped sideways ripping open my shirt and drawing my forty-four. But before I could fire, I heard Jack's La Faucheux explode twice, saw the bartender's sawed-off belch a streak of fire, and heard two other pistols explode from among the crowd. Quick Quintan's shotgun blasted a large chandelier on the ceiling as he reeled backwards, jerking like a man stung by several wasps. I started to shoot him before he hit the wall, but a whore drew a four shot pepper-box derringer from beneath her dress and emptied it in him before I got a chance.

"Lord-have-mercy!" I stood stunned and

watched him slide down the wall, leaving a smear of blood beneath the No Firearms Allowed sign; and he fell face forward on the thick Persian carpet. I felt a hollow sickness jolt low in my stomach. For a second, the crowd fell deathly silent. Then, a murmur stirred through it like a breeze through a wheat field as every gun disappeared except mine and Jack's.

"The man didn't have many friends here —" Jack whispered beside me. "— None that can *read*, anyways." His La Faucheux still smoked in his hand. I spit out my cigar and faced the sheriff and his deputy with my pistol raised slightly.

"Sheriff," I said quickly, "You saw the whole thing. I never even fired a round." I watched his hand twitch near the pistol in his belt then ease away slowly.

"Yeah," he let out a breath, "but your *nameless* friend here did." He glared at Jack.

"It was self defense, sheriff." I gestured my pistol toward the crowd. "Hell, everybody here shot him *some.*"

The sheriff still glared at Jack. "I know, but you'll have to explain it to the local constable. I have no jurisdiction here. I just happened to be here — trying to keep down trouble. Now both of you hand over your

33

guns. You'll be treated fairly. You've got my word." Gosset the deputy stood tense and staring. I returned his cold stare. I thought I saw a string of saliva run down his lip.

We had them covered. I wasn't about to give up our advantage, and I sure didn't want the law asking me any questions. "Sorry, sheriff. We've got no time for treatment, fair or otherwise." I backed away toward the doorway with Jack right beside me, flashing my pistol back and forth across the crowd, the sheriff and his deputy. Gosset was ready to explode. "Think about these folks' lives before you pull iron. As many guns as there are in here, we'll all end up with our brains on our shoes!" I said it loud enough for the crowd to hear. It worked.

"For God-sakes, sheriff, let 'em go," said a trembling faro dealer. "This ain't Dodge City! We'll all die!" Every hand in the place went inside a coat, or under a dress, or into a handbag, or down a boot. The sheriff saw it and raised a hand.

"Let's get to shooting!" Gosset the deputy said, stepping forward. The bartender's hand went under the bar and stopped.

"No! Everybody freeze!" The sheriff bellowed; thunder crashed above the building, jarring it. "Let them go, for now." He shot

34

me a hard glance. "We'll meet again some-where. I'd bet on it."

We'd been backing away, and now as I stepped over Quick Quintan's body in a pool of blood, I glanced down at his face and saw a flicker of life in his eyes. "Somebody get him some help," I said, stepping farther away, still watching the lawmen and the crowd. "He's still alive."

Quick Quintan's body jerked. I thought it was a spasm; but before I backed out to the main door, I saw him turn his head slightly and damned if he didn't try to laugh. I stopped for a second as Jack stepped around me and out. I'll never forget the look in his eyes as he raised his face an inch from the puddle of blood. "Now it's you're turn," he'd said in a fading voice. Then his face relaxed against the floor, back in the puddle of blood, as if snuggling into a warm eternal pillow.

Chapter 2

Outside the gaming parlor, rain blew sideways in wavering sheets as Jack and I outflanked a gathering crowd beneath the canvas awning and heard the shrill scream of a constable's whistle somewhere up the street. "They've got guns," someone yelled. The canvas bellowed, slapping up and down in the wind.

I shot Jack a glance. "Everybody *here* has a gun! Why do they keep pointing us out?" Lightning twisted and curled above us.

"Don't ask me." Jack nodded toward an alley at the end of the block and we ran to it beneath a loud growl of thunder. I saw Jack stumble, heard him cuss; I caught him by the arm and he ran on, limping.

"Are you alright, Jack?" My breath heaved in and out of my chest. In the shadows, around the corner of the alley, we pressed our backs to a brick wall and listened to the pounding of leather boots along the wet sidewalk.

"Stumped the hell out of my big toe," he said. "I think it's broke."

I held my pistol near the side of my face, peeped around the corner and saw the flash of two badges head into the crowd. Above the crowd, I saw the sheriff's tall Stetson hat bob back and forth, searching both directions. "Damn it!" I glanced up and down the narrow alley, then at Jack. "Any ideas?" From the far end of the alley another whistle shrieked.

"Yep," he said, checking his pistol. "Shoot till we run out of bullets, then run till we run out of road." Lightning glittered, licking along the barrel of his pistol like a serpent's tongue.

"Are you able to run?" I glanced down at his foot.

"Have I got any choice?" He peeped around me with the La Faucheux raised near his face, and shook his head. "Why do you *always* have to end a game with a gunfight?"

"I don't *always*, Jack. It's just when I win. When I *lose*, seems like everybody's real happy with me." I glanced around the corner of the building. Three more badges ran up as the sheriff and his deputy stepped from the crowd. I saw a stately trimmed

37

coach turn onto the street and head toward us, the team of horses bowing their heads sideways against the rain, their backs glittering wet in flashes of purple lightning.

"Here we go, Jack!" I pressed against the wall and nudged his arm as the coach rolled closer. "When it starts past, let's grab it and make a run." But as it came closer, it veered toward us, turned into the alley, and drew to a stop. The door swung open. I threw my pistol out, arm's length and cocked. I heard voices and running footsteps from the street.

"Quickly, señors," said the Contesa Cortez, glancing at my gunbarrel then into my eyes. I hesitated a second, felt Jack shove me forward, then tumbled into the coach and heard the door snap shut behind me. The contesa's dark eyes watched me closely as I leaned across her and peeped back toward the street. The sheriff, his deputy, and four constables stood in the street staring in both directions, but without a glance toward us as the coach ambled up the alley and turned toward the auction barn near the levy. The horse's hooves clacked steadily on the wet cobblestone.

"Thanks," I said, leaning back, letting out a tense breath, and uncocking my forty-four. I yanked my shirttail from inside my trousers and wiped the pistol dry. Beside me, Jack slapped water from his hat and dried the La Faucheux on his sleeve. The contesa observed with interest from her seat facing us as we attended our shooting gear. "How did you happen to come along when you did?" I looked into her eyes, saw her watch as I holstered the pistol under my arm.

"I had just gotten to my coach when I heard shots," she said, watching Jack dry and holster his weapon. Then she leaned near me. "I knew it was that pig, that —" She caught herself and sighed, "You cannot know what an animal he is . . . low, disgusting." She lay her hand on my arm. "I do hope you killed him, Señor Beatty. Please tell me you did."

I stared at her in silence for a second, then cleared my throat. "Well," I said quietly, "he's dead, that's for sure." I glanced at Jack and saw him study the contesa in the dim glow of the coach lantern as we rolled along.

"Good," she said softly, closing her eyes briefly as if giving thanks. I glanced at Jack and saw a nerve twitch in his jaw. He'd crossed his ankle over his knee and sat staring at the contesa as he squeezed the toe of his wet boot.

When we neared the livery barn, the door swung open, spilling light into the dark rain;

and an old Mexican stepped back, letting us roll inside, then closed the door quickly behind us. "Let's move out," Jack said, stepping from the coach and limping quickly toward our horses.

"Señorita," I said, taking my time and offering her my hand. She stepped from the coach and said something in Spanish to the old man by the door. He nodded, turned, and kept an eye on the street through a small window.

"So," I said, "you knew that was Quick Quintan Cordell?" I took a pair of riding gloves from my hip pocket and pulled them onto my hands as I looked into her eyes — eyes that drew me closer. I saw Jack lead our horses out of a stall; my chestnut stallion reared slightly and Jack checked him down. "I mean . . . he must've done something pretty bad to you . . . for you to want him dead —"

"He stole my horse. He had to drug the stallion just to be able to steal him and bring him here . . . that *pig*!" She spit at the ground as if it were his face, then looked back at me, composed herself and smiled. "Now, the deed, señor. Under the circumstances, I must ask you for it now, before you leave."

"Hey!" I heard Jack call out. "Let's get

40

going." But I held up a hand toward him and saw him shake his head and turn to the saddle rack.

"There's just one problem," I said. I took the deed from my pocket and unfolded it before her. "There's no more room here for me to sign it over to you."

"What are you saying?" She took the deed and looked at it carefully.

"Evidently it has changed hands lately," I said. We'll have to cut a new one for me to sign. I took it back and glanced at it, saw the name Cortez above Cordell's and stared at it with a puzzled expression.

"Yes," she said, reading the look on my face. "It was mine until that pig took it from me. But now I must have it back. It has belonged to my family for many generations . . . until he stole it from me."

"Stole it?" I shook my head. "Stole your horse? Your land? How could he have —"

"Come," she said, taking me by the arm and leading me to the door of a large stall. "Look at my stallion, Morcillo. Then you will know why he stole him from me."

"So —" I heard Jack call out as she reached out a hand to the stall door. "— I guess we're about ready to ride, huh? My toe's really thumping here." I glanced over my shoulder at him, held up my hand, saw

41

him stare down at his foot: "Damn thing's starting to swell," he muttered.

I'd started to speak when she swung open the stall door, but my voice stopped in my throat as I saw two red fiery coals flash in the darkness and heard — and felt — a heavy hoof jar the ground. I felt a presence of rage and heat permeating the large stall, and imagined something angry at my intrusion, as if to say, how dare I enter. "Easy, boy," I said as I stared up at the glowing red eyes, higher than I ever recalled looking up at a horse before.

The old Mexican crept in beside me. I picked up a bucket of water and held it before me; and I reached around to the old Mexican for a scoop of grain without taking my eyes off Morcillo the stallion. I stepped over slowly to one side, poured the grain into a feed trough, sat the bucket of water on the floor beside it, then stepped back and watched the red coals move toward the slash of light through the open door. "That's it, boy," I said in a low voice, "let's take a look at you . . ."

Morcillo stepped slowly into the light and turned facing me. I stood breathless. Before me stood the picture of every horseman's dream. He stood at least four hands higher than any stallion I'd ever seen, blacker than a bucket of greased-midnight, with every muscle perfectly defined as if sculpted from a slab of glittering onyx. "My God," I whispered softly, as soon as my breath would allow, "you sure are a beautiful thing."

The big stallion tossed his head up once, slinging back his mane, then lowered it and walked toward me with his ears back. "Come out, señor, please, quickly . . . before it is too late," the old Mexican coaxed.

"I can't," I whispered, and I meant it. I was riveted to the spot, watching him move closer. I had to see him up close . . . had to touch him, feel his muzzle, and run my hands down his neck and up across his tall withers, just once . . . just to see if he was real.

"Sante-Madre, señor . . . I will go get a whip!"

"A whip? Stay where you are," I said quietly. I watched Morcillo step closer, reach his long neck down toward the grain trough, sniff it, then straighten up and stand before me with his ears still back, as if ready to pound me into the dirt. "Easy," I whispered. I raised my hand to him carefully.

He sniffed me up and down, nudging me, blowing out his breath and nipping at my shirt. I stood still with my hand out and near his head as he raised back up to face level and stopped.

"Señor," the old man said, as if witnessing something sacred. "He has never let anyone but the contesa stand this close to him for this long."

"What I wouldn't give to ride this big stallion." My voice was a low whisper as I rubbed Morcillo's black velvet muzzle.

"Oh no, señor," said the old Mexican, "It would be imposs—"

"Of course you will ride him," the contesa said. "I have waited long for someone to ride Morcillo."

"We need to be leaving," Jack said from behind me. Morcillo jerked back at the sound of Jack's voice and circled to the far corner of the stall.

"Damn it, Jack." I started to step toward the stallion, but the contesa's voice stopped me.

"He is right," she said. "Go now. But you must come to me. I will have a new title drawn up for you to sign, and I will give you the fifty thousand."

"But what about the jewels? Maybe I better give them back —"

"No," she said. I'd reached inside my shirt for the handkerchief, but she stopped me.

44

"Hold them in good faith. Then I know you will come to me."

"Mam, there's something I oughta tell you —" I don't know what I was going to tell her, perhaps that I wasn't the kind of person to be trusted with such valuables. But I never got the chance to tell her. She dismissed my words with a wave of her hand. "The jewels will remind you that I wait for you. They will bring you to me." Then she turned and gazed into the stall at the two fiery coals in the darkness. "Come, and be the one who rides Morcillo for me, Señor Beatty."

I breathed in the heady sweetness of her, of desert flowers, warm sand and fire. Jack stepped beside me at the stall door, forcing my reins into my hand as I stood there unable to pull myself away from the aura about her. "We gotta go!" He shoved me, and I forced myself away. I stepped up into the saddle and looked down at her.

"Come to me *soon,* Señor Beatty —" She smiled and laid her hand upon my knee. I saw a spark of something deep in her eyes, something wild and exciting, that flashed, then disappeared. She squeezed my leg, once, then pulled her hand away. "— For I will lie restless at night until you do . . ."

■ ■ ■ ■

I couldn't quit thinking about the contesa, about her dark eyes, her aura, or the alluring scent of her; but when I thought of her, I couldn't help but also think of Quick Quintan's death and the last words he'd spoken looking up from the puddle of blood. Even though I hadn't killed him, I felt responsible in a way for him dying that night beneath the howling storm. Any man who has taken part in another man's death and says it has no effect on him, is either a liar, a madman, or a man without a soul.

I couldn't help wondering at what point the forces of heaven and hell must converge to bring about the killing of one stranger by another. It was something arcane to man's nature, I reckoned — too dark and deep for me to discern.

There was no doubt in my mind that Quick Quintan would've killed *me* that night had not everybody in the place commenced putting bullets in him when they did; but even though his death was the result of his own rash and intemperate actions, his last words played over and over in my mind all the way back to Missouri and for a long time after. Everybody must've seen it. I'd grown as testy as a mountain cat, pensive and restless, till one day it all spilled over onto the wrong person and came near getting me killed. We'd been sitting around the yard near the corral at the Samuels' place near Kearney when all at once Cole Younger stood up slowly like a man in a trance, looked across the yard at Curtis Mayhugh and said: "I'm gonna take that guitar, bust it over his head and feed it to him one piece at a time."

He took a step toward Curtis, but Curtis was so engrossed in his playing that he didn't even look up. His music *wasn't* the best, but I never thought he deserved to eat a guitar over it.

"Leave him alone!" I bellowed; and before I could stop myself from doing something so foolish, I'd jumped up, grabbed Cole by the arm and slung him away.

As soon as I did it, I realized it was something nobody had ever done and lived to talk about; but I knew it was too late to stop it as the yard fell as silent as a tomb, and Cole's face took on the blank-white expression I'd seen in the past right before somebody died.

"Well now," he said, breaking a tense silence. His hand poised tense near his holster and a stiff grin formed across his lips. "I see we have a music lover here."

I felt like raising a hand and saying the whole thing was a mistake — which it was, a bad one — but I knew it had gone too far the second I laid hands on him. Now that I'd made my stand all I could do was try to hold it. "I'm tired of you, Cole," I said. "Tired of your mouth and tired of your ways. Curtis is all the entertainment we have around here. If you don't like it, go to hell."

I saw the dark crisp shine in Cole's eyes as he took a step toward me and spread his feet shoulder width.

"Easy, Cole," I heard Quiet Jack say from his perch on the corral railing. I heard him slip down and into the corner of my vision with his hand near his La Faucheux, not tense and poised like Cole's hand, but loose and relaxed as if he already knew the outcome and saw no cause for concern. "I myself am partial to good music. Before you go busting ole Curtis up, you better learn to play something yourself."

"Ahh," said Cole, nodding slowly from Jack to me. "A little two on one. Nothing I like better." But behind him, his brothers, Jim and Bob stood up slowly, dusting the seat of their trousers.

Jack spit and chuckled: "Cole, you couldn't go to the jake by yourself without your brothers holding the paper."

Now Cole took a step toward Jack and I saw the whole thing was headed way out of control. I glanced at Curtis who'd looked up now and saw what was brewing. "I could tighten the strings up," he said in a nervous voice. Past him, all the way over on the front porch, I saw Jesse and Frank stand up and crane their necks toward us.

"This ain't between you two," I said, looking from Jack to Cole. I eased my hand up, slipped my shoulder harness off and dropped it on the ground. "Cole, I know you're a big gun and I can't outshoot you. But why don't you skin down and we'll settle this toe to toe." I reached down and started rolling up my shirtsleeves. Cole almost laughed out loud; behind him one of his brothers actually did.

Cole was a big strapping man, not only known for his shooting, but also for his ability to cut, stomp, and pound a man senseless with his bare hands. I didn't want to be the cause of him and Jack shooting each other; and I figured at least in a fist fight on a hot day, he might wear himself out on me and not beat me to death.

"Have it your way," he said; and he reached down, loosened his holster belt and let it fall.

"Good enough," Jack said. I saw the dark gleam in his eye as he stared at Cole. "And *I'll* fight the winner."

"Yeah?" I kept rolling up my sleeves. "What if I win? You gonna fight me, Jack?"

Jack looked Cole up and down, then shot me a glance: "There ain't one chance in hell you're gonna —"

"Thanks, Jack." I took a step forward.

"I could just play the harmonica," Curtis said. Cole also stepped forward, stretching, rolling his arms at his shoulders. His brothers stood grinning behind him. I swallowed hard and we crouched and walked sideways of each other.

"Hold it there!" yelled Jesse as he and Frank came running, sliding to a halt. Behind them a flock of chickens scurried in all directions, batting their wings and raising a low swirl of dust.

"What's going on here," Frank demanded in a tight voice.

I let down my guard slightly and took a step back, nodding toward Cole. "It's him. He can't let a day pass without bullying somebody around."

"It's that damned screeching, whining guitar," said Cole. He nodded toward Curtis. "I'll hear no more of it. I killed a man once for misusing a fiddle. Damned if I'll

50

be straddled with this idiot."

Curtis stood up scratching his head. "I know *other* tunes —"

"It's not your fault, Curtis," said Frank. "Now everybody hold it before somebody gets hurt." Frank had a way of stopping a ruckus just by staring a man in the eyes. "Now, what's your problem?" He stared straight at Jack.

Jack shot him a glance, then back to Cole, and smiled; but his eyes held the fury of a mountain cat. Nothing," Jack said quietly. He rocked back and forth on one boot and a bare foot. "Cole ain't shot nobody in a while. I reckon he can't stand it —"

Cole turned facing Jack with his fists still raised.

"Stop it! I won't have it!" Jesse bellowed loud enough that everybody flinched. "My poor mother is in that house right now, getting over losing an arm. You sons-a-bitches upset her and I'll kill you both with a pick handle." He turned to Curtis Mayhugh and his voice softened. "You alright, Curtis?"

Curtis scratched his head and stared at his guitar. "I told 'em I'd tighten up the strings . . ."

Jesse shook his head, walked right between Jack and Cole, and stared straight at me. "Cousin, you ain't acted right since you got

51

back from New Orleans. What's bothering you?"

"Me?" I spread my hands. Out the corner of my eye, I saw both Jack and Cole ease down. "Jesse, I didn't do a thing," I said. "But I ain't gonna sit there and watch Curtis eat a guitar."

"Eat a guitar," Jesse said in a flat tone, shaking his head. He shifted his eyes between Cole and Quiet Jack, saw they'd settled down, then looked back at me and nodded toward the house. "I've been wanting to talk to you anyway." He turned to Cole: "You and your brothers go torture a rattlesnake or something." Then he pointed at Jack, "And you —" He shook his finger. "— you go and . . . and soak that toe . . . or something!" He shook his head. Nobody ever knew how to handle Jack.

I growled something under my breath at Jack and Cole as I walked between them and followed Jesse and Frank to the house.

Curtis shrugged. "I told 'em I've got a harmonica. Maybe I could —"

"Shut up, Curtis," I spat, "or I'll kill you *myself*." I kicked at a chicken on the way.

Inside the door, I spun toward Frank and started to say something, but Jesse shoved me back a step, and said: "Have you lost what little sense you ever had? Cole would

52

step on you and just keep walking."

"I don't appreciate being called down like this. Cole's always starting something." I felt my face redden and realized I sounded like a schoolkid.

Frank raised a hand and smiled. "Alright it's over. But you better watch who you go jumping on."

"Frank's right," Jesse said. "Cole ain't the man to go messing with just because something's eating at you. Sorry I singled you out like this, but it was just a way to let everybody's blood simmer. You *did* start it."

I let out a breath. "Well, maybe I did. But I ain't afraid of Cole toe to toe. And if he keeps running his jaw, one day Jack's gonna blow him away. If he don't, somebody will."

Jesse laughed. "Someday somebody'll blow us all away, Cousin. For now, I meant what I said about upsetting Mama. She's been through enough."

"I know," I nodded. It'd only been a short while since a band of detectives had thrown a bomb through the front window. It'd torn off Ma Samuels' arm and killed her simple-minded son, Archie. Everybody felt bad about it.

"I'll keep my mouth shut from here on," I said. "I've just had a lot on my mind."

Frank and Jesse glanced at each other.

53

"We know you have. Fact is," Frank said, "since you came back toting that parcel of jewels, it's got everybody a little stirred up and restless. You're not the only one that lets things eat at them."

"What do you mean?"

"I mean that's a powerful lot of money if you broke them down to a jeweler. It's enough to make a man want to get his hands on them."

"She trusted me," I said. "Probably saved Jack and me from a lot of trouble. I can't explain it, but it don't seem right that I should —"

"Nobody's asking you to divvy them up. We know how you feel about it. But it's been awhile and you need to make a move one way or the other. Either find her and give them back or sell them and get shed of them. You know this bunch. It eats them up knowing those sparkling do-dads are just laying somewhere gathering dust. Can you blame them?"

"Naw, I reckon not."

Jesse grinned. "We *are* outlaws, after all."

I spread my hands. "I don't even know why I feel the way I do about it. Maybe it's because of ole Quick Quintan dying the way he did. I hated that. Maybe I feel like giving her back the jewels or else signing over the deed would clear me someway."

"You didn't shoot him, Cousin. And you and Jack did the right thing by hightailing it out of there. The law could've found out who you are and brought trouble down on all of us. There's been no news of a murder charge against you or Jack, or we'd have heard of it by now."

"I know. They had to call it fair . . . everybody shooting him like they did. I reckon I'm just trying to sort it all out in my mind." I couldn't tell him that even though I hadn't killed Quick Quintan, going there and collecting the money would somehow feel like collecting a reward.

"What is there to sort out?" Frank took a long stemmed pipe from his pocket, filled it and packed it with his thumb. "You give her the jewels, sign a new deed, and get your money. Fifty-thousand ain't to be sneezed at. There ain't enough sand and scrub grass twixt Cimmaron and Sonora to be worth fifty thousand."

I thought it odd, how to Quick Quintan the land was worth a game of pool, to the contesa it was worth risking a hundred thousand dollars in jewels. "I've got to get settled up. But I wouldn't know where to start looking for her."

Frank raised the pipe to his lips and lit it.

Gray smoke swirled upward, gathered and spread on the ceiling. I watched it as if it might give a clue. "She said she lived near Silver Basin — near Little Sand Hole. I suppose I could go there and ask around."

"Why don't you take Jack along," Jesse said. "It'll keep him and Cole from killing each other."

"I can see if he's up to it," I said.

"Good," said Jesse. "Maybe everybody can see a peace around here for a change."

Outside the house, Curtis and his guitar were gone; so was Bob and Jim Younger. I walked across the yard to where Jack and Cole stood passing a jug of whiskey between them as if nothing had happened. But their good spirits wouldn't last. The problem was that Jack could outshoot Cole, one-eyed, blind, or sideways. It was something nobody else could do, and Cole couldn't stand it, especially since Jack came from back east.

"That's what you get for butting in," Cole laughed. "I shoulda thrashed you for an hour or two."

I started to say something but decided against it when he offered me the jug. I took it, threw back a shot and passed it to Jack. Jack shot Cole a glance that could've been taken any numbers of ways, then smiled like a man biding his time and threw back a drink.

"I'm heading for New Mexico Territory," I said, wiping my hand across my mouth. "I'm tired of hanging around here listening to everybody growl at each other." I didn't feel like explaining the reason for the trip. The less said the better, I thought.

"Gonna rob something?" Jack's eyes lit as he passed the jug back to Cole.

Cole chuckled. "There's nothing worth stealing there except cattle. I'd like to see you two handle cattle. Work from daylight to dark. Grinding down on that bad toe."

"Only way I'll handle beef is if it's on a plate," Jack said.

"I'm just going to look at my land and decide if I want to keep it. I've no interest in cattle rustling." I thought it best not to mention the jewels. I looked at Jack. "Wanta ride along?"

"I ain't stealing no cattle."

"I told you, Jack —"

"Because I knew Clayton Hibbs before he started rustling. He stood near six feet tall —"

"Jack, I'm going to check on the land. That's all."

"— last I seen him, his back was bowed and his shoulders wouldn't hold his suspenders up."

Cole socked the cork in the jug and belched. "They say a cattle rustler can't piss past the toes of his boots. Their nuts draw up and turn hard as marble —"

"Is that a fact." I stared at them and bit my lip. Maybe I *really did* need to get away for awhile. Jesse and Frank were right. I needed to settle things up one way or the other with the contesa before I could ever put the whole incident out of my mind. "Well . . . I'm leaving come morning." I turned and walked toward the barn.

Jack fell in beside me, limping. "Just like that? You're gonna traipse off to New Mexico Territory?"

"Yep. That's what I'm gonna do."

"It ain't to look for that silk-tailed little contesa with them pert and pointy ya-hooes, is it?" He jiggled his hands at his chest.

"It's not what you're thinking," I snapped. For some reason I resented him talking like that about the contesa. "You're welcome to ride along —"

"I ain't handling no cattle. I mean it. Cole's right. Hibbs' boots are always splattered with dark spots."

I shook my head. There was no point in explaining it any further. "Are you up to going or not?"

"Yeah, I'm up to it. I'll have both boots on come morning. But I ain't doing no rustling. My back's straight and my boots are dry. I plan on keeping 'em that way."

"I promise, Jack, no cattle, alright?"

"Alright," he said; but then he took me by the arm and stopped me. "You know who rides that part of the territory, don't ya?"

I looked at him: "Who?"

"Billy Bonney, that's who."

His eyes searched mine for a second until I shrugged and started walking again. "So? I've got no problem with the Kid. If I did I would've settled it a long time ago."

"What if he don't *know* you've got no problems with him? What if he starts shooting as soon as he sees ya?"

"Aw, Jack. The Kid ain't like that, and you know it. He's just the same ole boy he always was. Probably still thinks I'm Jesse James —" I grinned. "— Probably still thinks you're Frank."

Jack chuckled. "I hope you're right. He's running with a wild bunch. You never know what changes a man can make over a few years."

"Well, I've got no problems with him. He did us a hell of a favor, far as I'm concerned. I heard he hangs out around Fort Sumner. I wouldn't mind swinging by and seeing him

— just say howdy. Just see how he's turning out.

Jack spit and ran a hand across his mouth. "He's turning out with a bad reputation from what I've heard."

"Well," I said. "Ain't we all?"

A silence passed as we walked on to the barn, then Jack chuckled and said: "Yeah, I reckon we are."

Early the next morning after a breakfast of grits and buckwheats, I put on my linen riding duster and a long-oval Stetson with a high Montana crown. Then I went outside and saddled up — tied down my saddlebags behind my saddle, shoved my Henry rifle in the saddle scabbard, slung a bandoleer of ammunition around my saddlehorn and stepped atop the tall chestnut stallion.

I'd packed a tote sack of dried shank and cornbread; and I tied it to my saddlehorn, reached down and smoothed my reins and gigged the chestnut forward.

Up the trail, I saw Jack round the bend at an easy gallop. Sunlight danced in the mane of his silver-gray gelding as he reined up, let the big horse toss his head and prance for a second, then headed down the path toward me. I met him halfway up the path and he turned the silver-gray beside me. He glanced over my supplies. "I'm not taking a rope," he said in a determined voice.

"Neither am I." I gazed ahead, knowing it would be a long ride.

"Just so's you understand." He glanced down at the toes of his boots as we turned and loped to the crest of the hill. I spun the chestnut stallion and looked back at my cabin in the valley for a second, then we gigged our horses and rode away west.

CHAPTER 3

"Let me make sure I understand," said Jack, the evening we followed the Cimarron out of the Indian Nations and pitched camp inside New Mexico Territory. "I was right when I asked if you were looking for the contesa? But it's not to pitch her heels in the air, it's to give her back her jewels?" He shook his head and poked a stick around in our low campfire. I'd told him the true purpose of the trip earlier that day. He'd harped about it ever since.

"I'm not asking you to understand. But yes, that's a big part of it." I took my glades knife from my boot, cleaned it over the flames and cut slices off the dried shank. "But I really *do* want to see the land. That much is true. Who knows, it could be worth keeping."

"Thought you had no *interest* in land?"

"Well . . . the lady sure wanted it bad enough. Quick Quintan was willing to die over losing it."

"Naw. Quick Quintan just wanted to die and be done with it. That just happened to be a sure way of doing it. I didn't wanta say it that night, but he could've beat you with one hand under ordinary circumstances." Jack spit and nodded his head.

"Thanks, Jack."

"It's the truth," he said. "You didn't beat him — he beat himself, scratching like that on the money ball . . . You shot a good game, but you ain't no pool *hog* like Cordell was. Another hour, you'd have come apart. He knew it. He would've won if the contesa hadn't showed up. Notice how as soon as she got there he started coming undone, got reckless, started talking crazy? Only a woman can push a man over the edge that way."

"Maybe," I said. "But I'd never let a woman —"

"Careful now," Jack chuckled. "Something about that little gal spells trouble to me. I thought it the minute she walked into the room. And what's a woman like her doing out there?" He swung his arm taking in the flatland reaching to the red-streaked horizon. "Out there, all you've got is scorpions fighting rattlesnakes over a dead lizard."

The vastness of the land was overwhelming, sparkling in the clearest sunlight I'd ever seen. Heat swirled up from earth the color of rich toast. Scattered pinon stretched their bony arms toward heaven; waist high clumps of grama grass cast gray shadows beneath a cloudless sky, a sky so wide it rounded overhead like the inside of a thick dome. I watched evening melt like red and blue lava, running down the far side of the distant mountain range. "— And I know how you are," Jack rattled on. "Once you settle up on the land and jewels, you'll wanta play a little touch and giggle with the *Contesa Animar*— whatever the hell her name is. I'd worry about you if you didn't, I reckon."

I gazed out across the empty space. "They call this the Enchanted Land." I breathed in the night air.

"It just looks like more Texas to me. Who calls it that?"

I didn't answer. I felt the first stirring of an evening breeze sweep across me and caught a faint scent of something heady in its arid sweetness. I thought of the dark and beautiful Contesa Animarciclo Cortez and realized it was something akin to her scent that drifted in the cooling wind. It was a presence belonging to her, and the desert, and the distant mountains in the red fading sky.

Even though I denied it to Jack, I could not help but wonder how it would feel to have such a woman, to hold her, to stroke her hair, her body, and to feel her dark warm skin against me in the desert night. Beside me, the big chestnut stallion raised his nostrils, probed the air, and tossed his head, stretching his neck southwest into the breeze.

"Probably wild mustangs in the air," said Jack, breaking into my thoughts of the woman and her *enchanting* land. "He'll be hard to handle if there's mares in season. Should've brought a gelding." The stallion let out a long neigh and stomped the ground. "You know this time of year a stallion's gonna lose his head over the call of nature." Jack stared at me with a knowing grin, then spit and chuckled to himself.

"It ain't about the contesa, Jack," I said. I got up dusting the seat of my pants, walked to the pack mule we'd bought from an old Cherokee three days before, took two sets of hobbles from our supply roll and walked over to the stallion. I pitched one set to Jack and kneeled down to my task. "What did you know about Quick Quintan Cordell?" I dusted my hands and walked back to the campfire.

Jack studied my eyes for a second before answering. "Not a whole lot," he shrugged. "I heard years back that he made a fortune gambling up and down the gold fields . . . monte, billiards, poker. He shot a good stick I'm told. Made big, lived big . . . spent big. Heard he had a real weakness for the ladies — that probably cost him a lot." Jack smiled, "But God bless 'em, they're worth every deal and dollar."

"Didn't he win a railroad once from a feller up in Montana?"

"He won the contract to lay rails, is the way I heard it. But I figure he probably contracted it out. Hired on a gang of Irish gandy-dancers and let somebody else run the show. Alls he probably did was take the profits. I reckon he was too busy shining cards and shooting billiards."

"Can't blame him," I said, "if he was doing that good at gambling."

"But he kinda dropped out of sight after that, I reckon. His luck might played out since then. Of course it took *you* to put the final brakes on his winning streak." Jack chuckled. "Never seen so many people shoot a man that way. Poor bastard."

"I reckon so," I said, seeing Quick Quintan's face in the low flame. "What do you

66

suppose he meant, telling me that now it's 'my turn?' " Night closed sharply around us as the sun slid down behind the mountain range; and the embers of our low fire stirred and flared. I felt a chill drift in on the cooling wind and I picked up my blanket and wrapped it around me.

"Who knows? Your turn at the wheel . . . the dice . . . the game. You know how gamblers are. They're always at odds with themselves. Always looking for the next *bigger* game . . . no matter what the cost. Reckon he found his that night." Jack took out his fixins and rolled a smoke. "Who knows . . ."

"But how could a man retire rich, then come back in and lose it all — right down to betting land."

"Something must've happened." Jack lit his cigarette from a twig of firewood. "Every gambler has one big weakness that they find out about in time. It usually gets them in the end. Maybe he thought he saw yours. Maybe he was saying 'let's see how you handle it.' Either way, something had him wanting to waltz with the angels, coming back that night . . . throwing down like that with a shotgun and all." Jack let go a long puff of smoke and watched it as if considering something.

"And since I was his last game, he just figured he'd take me along with him." I thought about it a second looking down at my boots, then I shook it from my mind, looked back up and watched the smoke curl from Jack's lips and drift on the breeze. "Well . . . I'm glad I ain't a gambler, except for sport. I sure wouldn't be wanting to die just over losing a game. I reckon a gambler like Quintan gets obsessed with it." I shook my head. "That ain't my way."

"Yeah." Jack leaned back against his saddle and tilted his hat down over his eyes. "But you're traveling over a thousand miles to give back a handful of trinkets to a woman you wouldn't have seen again in a hundred years. What do you call that?"

"You just don't understand." I shook my head and laid back in my blanket. I watched stars sparkle and dance in a dark wide heaven. Somewhere a coyote let out a mournful cry. In a second its cry was answered from farther out in the darkness. How could I possibly explain it to Jack when it still wasn't clear to me. To me, we were in the *land of enchantment* — to Jack, it was just more Texas.

We crossed Indian Territory and the Canadian River in good time, then swung down past Tucumcari and Saddleback Mesa where we picked up the Southwest Trail and followed it on toward Old Fort Sumner. It was late evening by the time we'd reached a low rise east of Fort Sumner, and we sat there awhile watching the flicker of lanterns glow dimly in the night before riding in. Our horses were spent, and so was our supplies, save for the last few trimmings of dried shank and an air-tight of beans Jack had brought along.

Our clothes and animals were covered with dust and grit as we rode past a sign saying: *Welcome to Residue Point — Wearing or carrying of firearms prohibited by town ordinance.* The sign was riddled with bullet holes, and Jack and I just glanced at it, then at each other. Ahead we saw light spilling through the open door of a quiet saloon.

"Thought this was Old Sumner?" Jack said.

"So did I." We looked around the town riding in slowly, low in our saddles, our hats down and our riding dusters still clinging damp against our backs from the day's heat. Far off in the west we heard the faint sound of gunfire.

Half-way up the deserted street, a man in a bright plaid coat and a well brushed bowler hat sprang out of the shadows from between two buildings and stood before us with his arms spread. I almost drew my pistol before I saw his hands were empty.

"Gentlemen?" he called out, running a hand down the front of his crisp white shirt and wiping the toe of a Wellington boot on the back of his calf. "May I ask you *one* question?" We reined up short and I saw that his eyes were swollen and as black as a raccoon's. He snapped both lapels of his plaid coat between his thumbs and fingers. His hands looked as clean as a preacher's. "The hell's this?" I spoke to Jack out the side of my mouth as the man walked toward us through the late evening haze. He stopped and looked at us from a distance of ten feet. "What's on your mind, Mister?" I said.

He raised a finger in the air. "Gentlemen. Let me ask you. If you were to die right *here* right *now* . . . on this very spot —" He pointed straight down. "— Could you say in all certainty that your loved ones would be well provided for?"

"What the — ?" I glanced quickly around at doorways and shadows, then back to him.

"Is that a threat?" I heard Jack's voice, speaking above the swish, click and cocking of his La Faucheux pistol. I glanced at him and saw the pistol out arm's length.

"Easy, Jack." I raised a hand.

The feller's swollen eyes opened wide above his blue crooked nose. His hands sprang out as if to hold back an oncoming train. "Oh, no sir! Please no! That is the furthest from my intentions! Let me assure you that was strictly a hypothetical question!"

I let out a tense breath and said: "I'll be damned. An insurance salesman."

"I prefer, *Final needs administrator.*" He flashed a broad smile and again smoothed his shirt. "But let's not quibble over titles when what's really at stake here is the security and well being of your loved ones. Isn't that correct? I'm Joseph Rafferty — call me Rafe — of the New England Life And Trade Insurance Company? I'm certain you've heard of my company and the fine service we provide? We are considered among the highest quality —"

"Don't need any," I said. "Never even *heard* of any." I started to heel my horse forward. Rafferty took a step back but stopped, blocking our way. I took a deep breath and let it out slowly.

"Perhaps we've gotten off to a bad start here, gentlemen, but believe me, I wouldn't be doing you a service if I didn't allow you a few minutes of my time to show you what a few cents a months will do for your loved ones in the event of — *God forbid* — your untimely demise."

"Want me to shoot him?" I heard Jack say in a low voice. "Just once, while there's nobody around?"

"Not just yet," I said, "but keep that thought." I stared down at Rafe Rafferty. "Mister, we're hot and tired, and all we want right now is something cold to drink. You oughta have better sense than to come upon strangers like that."

"You're absolutely right of course — I couldn't agree more — but you *will* thank me once you've seen what my company can provide you."

I reined my horse around him. He turned with me as I passed by. "Gentlemen, I don't simply *sell* life insurance. Let me make that clear. I offer peace of mind to you and your —"

"Come on, Jack," I said over my shoulder. But Jack sat there staring down at the man.

"Life insurance?" Jack slid his pistol back into his holster and crossed his wrists on his saddlehorn. "Never heard of it. You mean you pay somebody for getting killed, the same way they pay a ship for sinking?"

I saw Rafferty's hand streak in and out of his coat, and he flashed a business card up to Jack. "Precisely . . . but not quite. It works exactly the same way except it's entirely different. What I'd like to do is take just a few simple seconds to tell you how our coverage works —"

"It's too late in the evening for all this," I said. I shook my head and heeled my horse forward. "I'll be at the saloon, Jack. Whatever you do, don't *sign* nothing."

"— Why, for no more than you'd spend on, say . . . just one can of gun-oil . . ."

His voice trailed as I rode off; and I looked back at them through the darkness when I'd slipped down from my saddle and hitched my horse outside the saloon. Jack had dismounted and led his horse out of the middle of the street. I saw him lean against a post as Rafferty leaned near him, gesturing with his smooth clean hands as he spoke.

Inside the saloon a few bored looking faces turned toward me, then away. I took off my hat, slapped dust from my shirt, and walked over to the bar. "I ain't really supposed to serve ya if you're wearing a gun," said a one-eyed bartender with a black powder burn down the side of his face. Once again I heard gunfire in the distance. I glanced along the bar at pistol butts sticking up from holsters and belts, then back at him. He cleared his throat. "But what'll ya have?"

"Couple of beers," I said. "Good and cold. I've got somebody joining me in a minute."

"Ain't that insurance man, is it?" He shook his head. " 'Cause if it is, you'll never get rid of him 'less ya kill him. I don't allow killing in here."

I let out a breath, knowing he was probably right. "Better make that *three* beers," I said.

I turned to a grizzled old teamster standing beside me as the bartender jerked three mugs from under the bar. "I thought this was Old Fort Sumner?"

He cocked his head sideways. "Sumner's four miles on. This here is Residue Point. A place for them that want a little peace and quiet away from all the whooping and carrying on." As he said it, I couldn't help but notice he did so with a certain wistful longing in his eyes.

I nodded: "I see. I'm looking for the Cortez spread. Know of any Cortezes down around Silver Basin?"

"Weeeeel! Now let me see." The old teamster raised his hat and scratched his scaly head. "Cortez ya-say? Seems like I've heard that name." He turned to the gathering of dusty boots and dirty clothes lined along the bar. "Here that, boys? Wants to know if there are any Cortezes around Silver Basin." He cackled and swung his arms as if he'd been waiting all day to get a rise from the others; but only a dull attempt of laughter rippled along the bar, then faded and died. I shot the old teamster a cold stare. He dropped his arms and cowered back a step.

"He's funnin' with ya," said the bartender. "Why don't ya take him outside and bust him upside the head a lick or two?" A wet smile twitched in his lips. "Just don't do it in here. Fighting ain't allowed in here. *Kill 'im* out back if you want — but not in here."

I couldn't tell if he meant it or not. Faces turned toward us along the bar and fell silent. I stared back at them, looked them up and down. The old teamster swallowed hard.

"I understand —" I nodded to the old teamster. "— no harm done." He looked relieved. I glanced at the faces and back to the bartender. The faces seemed disappointed as they huddled back into a low buzz of conversation. "I'm looking for the Cortez family, somewhere around Silver Basin, near Little Sand Hole. Just wondering how much farther it is from here."

"It's still a good ways off." The bartender

nodded and brushed a hand toward the distance. "You won't ride it straight through. Cortez used to be a common name down there —"

"That's all I was getting at, Mister." The old teamster shrugged. "Just trying to have a little fun here, is all."

The bartender's eye sliced across him like a razor, then continued. "— But the bandidos have kilt off most of 'em past couple years." He turned his head and spit behind the bar. "Which Cortez ya looking for?"

I leaned closer against the bar. "The Contesa Animarciclo —"

"Whew!" The bartender shook his fingers as if he'd touched a hot coal. "Yeah, she's still down around there, I reckon . . . or was, last I heard."

"Good," I said, "that's who I'm looking for."

"Why?" His voice was blunt. I just stared at him. Residue Point was no more than a strip of a town made up of crumbling adobe, canvas, dust and flapping boards. I saw how living here for any length of time could do something to the mind and manners. He cleared his throat. "If you don't mind me asking, that is."

I pointed to the three mugs of beer he'd sat before me. They were greasy; one had a

76

dead fly stuck to it. "There's a dead fly here," I said, pointing at it, to change the subject.

"I see it," he said. "I ain't blind, you know." He tapped his cheek as he smeared away the dead fly with his thumb. "I see more with one of these peepers than most men see with two."

"I'm sure you do." I shrugged and slid that mug two feet down the bar — for the insurance man when he got there. "I'm a horse dealer out of Missouri. I heard the Contesa Cortez might be interested in some riding stock." I wasn't about to mention the land or the jewels. "I thought I'd stop by and do some business with her —"

"Don't try dickering her out of that black stallion, if you know what's good for ya," the bartender said."

"Que-pasa?" A stocky young Mexican wearing gauntlets and chaps jerked away from the bar with a startled look on his face. "Caballista? A horse dealer? You come to take that 'diablo caballo' . . . that 'potro' devil horse? Sante-madre!" He whipped off his battered sombrero and crossed himself, then stepped back looking me up and down.

"Damn-it, boy!" The bartender slammed his hand on the bar. The crowd stirred then went back to their huddle. "You're new here, so I'll say this once and once only. I don't allow Mex-talk in here. Causes more trouble."

"Arrepentido . . . I mean, *sorry,* señor. I will speak only Ingles." He stepped forward with the sombrero hanging in his hand. "You come for the "black blooded stallion . . . to take it away?"

"No," I shrugged. "I've come to —"

"Crazy Mangelo Sontag will keel you, señor. He knows that someday someone will come to take the stallion, and he has vowed to keel that person. He say that the stallion is his caballo —" He shot the bartender a glance and ducked his head. "— Sorry . . . I mean, his *horse.*"

Faces turned from the bar. This time they watched intently. "No," I waved a hand. "I'm here to see if the contesa would like to buy some horses. I'm *selling* . . . not buying."

"Sure, señor," he leaned close with a wise smile. "And where are these horses you bring to sell?"

I glanced around, saw Jack and Rafferty step through the door and walk over to the bar. Rafferty was scribbling something in a receipt pad. "Well, I'm just here to see if they want any. If they do I'll bring them some." I faced the bartender. "You misunderstood me."

"You better hope crazy Mangelo don't hear that you've come to take the stallion. The Mex here is right. He'll kill you, is what. I never met him, but he's a straight up killer."

I turned to Jack, handed him the other mug and gestured Rafferty toward his. "What's going on?" Jack glanced along the bar.

"They think I'm here to take somebody's horse." I watched Rafferty take a long swallow and blot his mouth with his coat sleeve.

"Crazy Mangelo Sontag's horse," said a big feller with a drooping mustache full of beer foam. He stepped forward. " 'Leastwise he thinks it is." He wiped a thick thumb across his mustache. "Can't say as I blame you, though. I hear it's a fine animal. But I wouldn't wanta die finding out."

"Now this is *exactly* the type of risk my company wants to insure you against," I heard Rafferty say beside me.

I looked at Jack; he chuckled and shook his head.

I threw back a drink, ran my sleeve across my mouth, and held up a finger. "Now everybody listen up. I'm not here to take anybody's horse, especially this Crazy Mangelo Sontag —"

79

"He called him *crazy,*" said a voice. A hush swept the bar.

"You *all* called him crazy," I said, spreading my hands.

"That's a little different, *stranger,*" said the bartender. "I hope you didn't come in to start trouble."

"No, I sure didn't," I said; and I just stared at him for a second until another volley of fire erupted in the distance. Then to change the subject again, I asked: "What's all the shooting about out there?"

"Oh! It is a fiesta, señor," said the Mexican. His eyes lit up, then he saw the look on the bartender's face and lowered them as if he'd fallen from grace.

"A party, huh?" I looked at him. "What's the occasion?"

"Ah, señor," the Mexican shook his finger back and forth with a wide grin. "A man who must have an occasion to *celebrate,* is a man who would not celebrate even if he *had* an occasion."

I grinned: "Makes sense to me."

"It is why I came here —" He glanced at the bartender; his voice raised toward the others along the bar. "— To welcome everyone to the fiesta!" He spread his hands in a grand gesture, but along the bar the drinkers only milled without looking around.

"Naw." The bartender swiped a hand. "We're all doing fine right here without all that Fort Sumner trash. Them kinda wild get-togethers always ends up in a shooting, or some kind of rig-a-ma-roll." He tugged at the garter around the sleeve of his dirty shirt. "Be glad when the Santa Fe Ring puts a stop to all that nonsense."

I glanced along the bar at all the sullen faces, then turned to Jack and shrugged. "What do you think?"

"Why not?" He grinned and killed off the mug of beer. "This place looks like it's getting ready to bury Aunt Mildred."

"Would you gentlemen mind if I ride along with you?" Rafferty the insurance man leaned toward us along the bar. "I've been waiting for the opportunity to go there myself." He lifted his shiny bowler, ran a smooth hand back across his perfectly parted hair, and smiled.

"Will you not talk about insurance?"

"I'll certainly try not, although it is something you should be thinking about." He adjusted his bowler back on his head and ran a thumb along the edge of the brim. He snapped the lapels of his dandy plaid coat.

"Alright then," I said. "I'll think about it. But you keep your mouth shut until I do. Deal?"

"Yes, deal," said Rafferty.

"See," said the bartender. "This is what I get. I run a nice respectful place here where you can drink in peace without all that laughing and loud music — But *no*! . . . All these newcomers want to do is hang around all the shooting and the whores and the carrying on." He shook his head in disgust. "I'll be damned glad when the Ring does something about it."

"I'd go myself," said the man with beer foam in his mustache. "Hear it's a fine affair." He ducked his head beneath the bartender's cold stare. "But I wouldn't want to die finding out."

CHAPTER 4

We rode four abreast along the dusty trail into Old Fort Sumner, our faces lit by the flash of skyrockets and fireworks streaming upward, exploding high in the night and showering down above us. Through the open main gates beyond the sun bleached adobe walls, colorful skirts twirled to the sound of Spanish guitars, accordions and castanets; and over the laughter and the roar of the crowd, pistol and rifle fire reined high above all else.

Inside the walls two young boys chased a spotted pig beneath our horse's hooves and we veered to the side, near rows of hanging meat, cheeses, and goatskins of wine set out by street vendors. Jack reached out, hooked a wineskin, threw back a long squirt and pitched an old Mexican a gold coin for it. The old man grinned and called out to us, but his voice was lost in the din of fiesta. "Can you believe all this?" Jack shouted at the top of his voice but even so I could barely make out his words. He had a strange gleam in his eyes, and he threw his head back laughing as he raised the goatskin of wine.

I leaned in my saddle and yelled to the young Mexican riding on the other side of me: "What's all the shooting about?" He looked confused until I asked it again, this time yelling it so loud it made my throat ache.

He nodded: "Aw, si, señor, that must be Billy Bonney and his amigos. I'm told they will be shooting at bottles and cans all night —" He spread a grin. "— Until they get too drunk to see."

I nodded in return and reined around a passing throng of laughing young girls. "I think I'll go find them," I called out to him, making a gesture with my hand to show him my intentions. I tapped my hat brim in a salute and nudged the chestnut stallion toward the sound of the gunfire.

"But, señor! It could be dangerous going around them when they are like this —"

"We'll be alright," I called out to him, knowing he probably couldn't hear me. I motioned for Jack to follow me, and began weaving my way to the edge of the crowd and toward the far wall. I saw Jack pass the skin of wine to Rafferty and they fell in behind me. I caught a glimpse of Rafferty raising the wineskin, and saw a stream of it squirt down the front of his white shirt. The young Mexican sat watching us for a second with a curious expression, then nudged his horse along with us.

"I could live like this —" Jack yelled as he reined up beside me and handed me the wine. "— Straight up, full time, for a hundred years . . . and never complain about dying."

I stopped my horse near an open fire pit where an old woman and a young boy stood turning a skewered goat above the flames. The aroma of sizzling meat filled the air. The boy looked up and grinned as I threw back a drink of wine. "Tienes vino por el cabrito, señor?" he called up to me. I saw his eyes light up in anticipation.

"What?" I glanced from him to Jack.

Jack laughed and yelled above the din of the crowd: "He wants you to squirt some wine on the goat."

"How do you know, Jack? You don't speak Spanish." I had to hold the stallion in check as a rocket screamed overhead and exploded in a dazzling spray of color.

"Si, señor," said the Mexican boy, jumping up and down on bare feet. "Por el cabrito, por-favor."

"See," Jack said, reining up at the sound of another rocket screeching overhead and holding his hat on with one hand. "Some things ain't that hard to figure."

"Sure." I shrugged and squeezed a stream of wine out on the slow turning spick of meat. The boy stuck his face in and gulped a mouthful. Beside him the old woman cursed, and quit turning the spick long enough to thump the boy's head with a long fork handle. The boy rubbed his hand across his mouth and ran away laughing. Jack chuckled and gigged his horse forward.

We stayed close to the wall until the crowd thinned; and the gunfire grew louder as we neared a livery station, watching streaks of powder flashes blossom and disappear as if a part of the fiesta fireworks. "You couldn't hit dirt shooting straight down!" said a voice. Laughter spilled across a crumbling adobe wall, and I reined my horse toward it. "Could too, if you'd shut up and let me shoot," came a reply.

"Hello the corral," I called out from twenty feet away. I saw hats turn toward us in the flicker of torch lights. A couple of men stood up from the crumbled wall dusting their trousers.

"Hello ya-selves," someone called out.

"Come on in and shoot with us if you got any money — unless you're the law." Twenty yards past the wall stood a row of whiskey bottles and tin cans, lit up by torches stuck in the ground on either end. Then another voice said: "Hell, even if you are the law, come on in. Lawmen can't shoot nothing no way."

"No lawmen here," I said, stepping down from my stirrup. I glanced back at Jack and Rafferty and saw them dismounting. The young Mexican lagged behind, watching, still atop his horse and looking back and forth across the faces of the shooters. "Just a couple of Missourians and an insurance man."

"Insurance man?" Somebody laughed as I stepped around the low wall and into the firelight. "I ain't never shot an insurance man." I saw a skinny young man grin beneath a wide hat brim, a bottle hanging from one hand and a pistol from his other. He glanced around at four other dusty young men strung out in a firing line. One took aim toward the row of bottles and cans. Three shots exploded from his pistol and three cans jumped and disappeared in the night. "Any ya'll ever shot an insurance man?"

"*Insurance man?* What's that?" said a

87

young man checking his pistol and rolling the cylinder.

The skinny man looked back at me, shrugged and grinned across broken teeth. "You'll have to overlook them," he said. "This is an unlearned bunch." His grin broadened and he offered me the bottle. "Missouri huh? Ya'll run outa something to do there? Had to come all this way just to shoot at bottles?"

Jack and Rafferty stepped in beside me, and the men along the firing line glanced at us, then away. "I'm here looking for a friend of mine," I said. "His name's Bonney . . . Billy Bonney." I looked along the firing line as they turned toward us again, this time looking us up and down much closer and speaking quietly among themselves. I looked closer at them as well, and all around, but saw no sign of the Kid.

"I've heard that name somewhere," the skinny man said, scratching his head beneath his hat brim. "Just can't recall where."

I passed the bottle on to Jack, then looked back at him. "I bet you have." I smiled and watched his eyes closely. "My name's Beatty . . . James Beatty. I met Mister Bonney a few years back, up around Cimmaron and Gris. Just thought I'd stop by and say howdy since I was in the area."

"Ah," he nodded his head. "Up around Cimmaron . . . Lambert's tavern?"

"Yeah," I said, watching him click the cylinder of his pistol as he checked out the shoulder harness inside my duster and eyed Jack's La Faucheux. "We had a run in with Ned Quarrels up around Gris—"

"I know you from somewheres," he said to Jack, cutting me off and eying Jack curiously.

"No you don't," said Jack. "I never been there in my life." He smiled, hooked his thumb in his belt above the fancy pistol, wagged the bottle back and forth and threw back a drink.

The man reached for the bottle and Jack handed it back to him. He smiled, threw back a shot, and said: "Well-sir . . . you're right. Come to think of it neither have I." He turned back to me. "But I haven't seen Billy Bonney for the longest time. Ya'll are welcome to stick around though. You never know who just might show up." He nodded past us toward the young Mexican still on his horse beyond the crumbled wall. "What's that ole boy's problem? He acts plumb unfriendly."

"Naw, I don't think so," I said. "He's just shy, I reckon."

After an hour of conversation and target

shooting, a meal of roast goat, sweetbread, tortillas and wine, I dozed off against the crumbling adobe wall, near the fire, even with the sound of pistol shots and laughter ringing in my ears and fireworks exploding overhead like muffled cannon fire. It was early in the dark hours of morning when I awoke, and I did so to the feel of a rough boot toe against my shoulder jostling me back and forth, and a voice saying: "Wake up, Missouri. Your pal's got some trouble here."

"What?" I propped up on my elbow, wiped my hand across my face and looked up at Tom O'Foliard — the skinny young man who'd welcomed us earlier. I glanced around, saw Jack talking to a tall Mexican and two other men on the firing line. The rest of the shooters had drawn back and stood leaning against the crumbled wall. "What's going on?"

"Your partner there has won everybody's money and now he's about to mix it up with some of Crazy Mangelo's gunmen. Thought you'd want to know about it." Tom O'Foliard shook his head. "Never seen nobody shoot like your friend there, drunk or sober. Is he always like that? Is he a little touched in the noggin?"

"He's got his ways," I said. "Thanks,

Tom." I stood up shaking sleep from my head. I looked around again and saw Rafe Rafferty sitting against the wall on his dandy plaid coat, with his shirtsleeves rolled up, counting a handful of dollar bills. Next to him the young Mexican looked up, saw me, got up and walked over cautiously.

"This could be bad, señor," he said shaking his head. "These are Mangelo's soldiers. The tall one is an officer . . . a very bad hombre. These men will keel your friend for no reason, and think nothing of it. Maybe we should leave?"

"Soldiers? An officer?" I glanced between the young Mexican and Tom O'Foliard.

Foliard shrugged and stepped back. "Every bandido from Old Mex thinks he's a soldier of some kind or other. They can't just be good ole everyday crooks like anybody else, you know. Say the word and I'll have Charley and the boys commence shooting a bunch of holes in 'em."

"Hold on," I said. I stepped past them and walked up to Jack and the tall Mexican on the firing line. Backing the Mexican, two hard looking Anglos stood with the feet spread shoulder width and their hands poised near their pistols.

"It don't matter to me," I heard Jack say to the tall Mexican. "All three of ya, far as I care. One-eyed or one-handed." His pistol spun into a blur that ended in his holster with his hand hanging loose beside it. "Throw down some money and take your steps —"

"Easy, Jack," I said, stepping up just as he took a step back. The tall Mexican chewed on a long thin cigar and grinned a sinister grin. His men behind him stepped one to each side, then readjusted their feet.

"Mi amigo," he said to Jack. "I only say to you, that it is always much easier to shoot at a bottle than at a man who is shooting back —"

"It ain't *what* you said, it's *how* you said it." Jack grinned right back. "So don't mealy-mouth around about it. If you think you've got something to settle, let's get to settling it here and now —"

"Shoot him," said a drunken voice from the wall.

"Hold it, Jack," I said. But even as I said it, I stepped back glancing around, at the two Anglos backing the tall Mexican, and I rested my hand on my chest near my shoulder harnessed forty-four. "This is supposed to be a fiesta here . . . a party. Let's not go spoiling it."

"Twenty dollars on the boys from Missouri," I heard Rafferty say through a wine slur. I glanced at him and saw that his bowler was caved in on one side, and his shirt tail hung outside his belt. The tall Mexican glanced at him also, then eyed the young Mexican standing beside him.

"These gringos are your friends?" he asked the young Mexican. "You side with them?"

"Devez en cuando," said the young Mexican with a serious look in his eyes. "Para atajar matanza, I do."

"Ah," the tall Mexican said, "for *now* you do. You speak like a politico, mi hermano — a bad politico . . . or else a coward. We will talk later, you and me." Then he turned from the young Mexican back to Jack. "But your amigo here is right —" He took note of my hand near my pistol, and he raised his gun-hand slowly and took the cigar from his mouth. Behind him, the other two men seemed to ease down. So did I. "We can talk of keeling another time. Tonight we keel only bottles." He turned his head slightly to the men behind him. "Isn't that right, hombres?"

"Si, otro tiempo," one replied in a Texas accent. Though the two looked to be American, they appeared to have been thrown to the wilds at an early age and raised by hawks and night critters. One's eyes were dark and hollow. The tall Mexican gestured over his shoulder with his cigar, then the three of them backed away slowly, him still grinning, his eyes fixed on Jack's until they turned and walked away to their horses.

I watched as they rode off into the grainy gray darkness of morning, then I turned to Jack and said: "Can't I leave you alone for a second?" I watched him wobble slightly. An empty wineskin lay at his feet surrounded by a pile of spent cartridges. "You gotta settle yourself down some, Jack. Damn it. We coulda both gotten killed there."

"You both *coulda*," said a voice from the darkness on the other side of the low wall. "But I doubt it. I had 'em covered."

I watched as a dusty gray gelding hopped over the wall and stopped; and I recognized the bucktoothed grin of the Kid beneath the wide brim of a worn and battered sombrero. He stepped the gray gelding over to us, raising the shotgun he held in his hand and letting down both hammers on it. "Every time I see you boys somebody's fixing to kill ya."

"How you been, Kid?" I said, taking the reins to his gelding as he stepped down.

"They said they knowed ya, Billy," said Tom O'Foliard. "I made them welcome as much as I could, but I didn't wanta take any chances on them being —"

"It's alright, Tom," the Kid said. He shook mine and Jack's hand. I noticed the strong smell of cattle, sweat and trail dust. Then he turned to the men along the adobe wall. "Bet ya's don't know who this is, do ya?" He let out a cackling laugh as the men stirred forward as if for a closer look.

"Come on," Kid," I said. "Don't start saying that again." I was sure he was going to say we were Jesse and Frank James, something he'd decided back in Cimmaron four years ago. But instead he turned to me, settled down and winked.

"This is *James Beatty* . . . slickest horse-trader I ever seen."

I grinned, saw Rafferty get up shoving the money in his coat pocket and stepping over to us. "Not too slick," I said, smiling. "You *sure* got me for a thousand dollar mare."

"What I wanta know," said a stocky young man in a ragged bowler hat, "is who's this gunslinging asshole, and why's he taken all our money?" He pointed at Jack; Jack wobbled.

"Hell, Charley," said the Kid. "You oughta know better'n match shots with a man wearing a La Faucheux. Ain't a dozen men in the world got the nerve to even carry one." He grinned at Jack.

"How's it going, Kid?" Jack grinned, wobbled again, reached out and tugged the Kid's sombrero down. "Doing anything with cattle?"

"Everything but fathering calves," the Kid said.

Rafferty pointed a trembling finger. "So, you really are — ? I mean, you're — ?" He pulled out a battered paper novel from inside his coat and waved it toward the Kid. "I've read about you, sir."

I snatched the novel from his hand and looked at it.

"Who's this yardbird?" The Kid pointed a finger back at Rafferty, took aim with one eye closed and clicked his thumb up and down at his chest.

"I, sir, am Rafe Rafferty of the New England —"

"He's an insurance man," I said, cutting him off. I pointed to the novel and read aloud: "Billy Bonney, *King Of The Bandits.* Damn, Kid. They're writing books about you?"

"Aw-hell, that's all bull." He swiped a hand through the air, and turned back to Rafferty. "What kinda alias is *Rafe Rafferty?* If that's the best ya can do, you'll never make it outlawing."

"But I'm no *outlaw.*" Rafferty shrugged,

looking confused.

The Kid grinned and said: "Neither am I. We'll just call you *Alias,* till you can come up with something better."

"But my name *really* is —"

"Shut up, *Alias,*" I said. "If you go around selling insurance, what do you expect people to think?"

The Kid laughed. "What brings you two over from Missouri? Ya'll hiding out?" He reached out and poked a finger in Jack's belly.

"Don't start that *stomach poking nonsense,* Kid," Jack said. And as the Kid laughed and ignored him, I recalled just how aggravating the Kid could be at times, always picking, always moving around, and always on the verge of getting real excited about something.

"Hope ya didn't come looking for that mare I borrowed from ya. She's long gone, you know. Got shot out from under me by a couple of Chisum's men. I've got all the big ranchers so screwed up they don't know whether to *wipe* their watch or wind their *ass.* We could go shoot a few of 'em if ya got time." His eyes lit up.

"Naw, Kid. I forgot about the mare a long time ago."

"So this is a social call? I'm honored." He

97

gestured a bow.

"Sorta," I said. "We're heading over to Silver Basin on some business. Thought we'd stop and see how you're doing."

"Another day you mighta missed me altogether," said the Kid. "I've been kindly asked to leave the territory. They're hiring a new sheriff out of Lincoln to run me off. So, I could be leaving here most any time."

"Hell," said Foliard. "Don't listen to him. He's been saying that for the past month and still ain't left."

"Well, it's kinda hard, getting chased from your home." The Kid's voice lowered, and he looked off at the thin streak of sunrise on the far horizon. Morning darkness shone in his eyes, and I thought I saw something akin to regret sweep across his brow.

"Dang, Billy," said Foliard, "you know as well as I do, nobody's gonna make you go nowhere you don't wanta go. Ain't that right? They might play hell a-trying!" Foliard let out a whoop and slapped his knee. But damn 'em . . . let 'em try!"

I saw the Kid's expression change again quickly, back to that of *The Bandit King,* reckless and wild; and he yelled something in Spanish as he spun, drawing his pistol and pulling off four rounds towards the bottles and cans. "That's right, Tommy boy, damn 'em all! *Love* all their beef and *eat* all their daughters!" His friends along the adobe wall cheered and came forward, circling him and forcing a bottle of whiskey in his hand. Nobody seemed to notice that of the four shots he'd fired, only one tin can fell.

We took breakfast that morning, just the Kid and me, on the porch of a feller by the name of Pete Maxwell who ran a trading post beside his adobe hacienda just out of the path of the all night party crowd. Jack, Rafferty, and the young Mexican had drifted off into the fiesta with Tom O'Foliard, Charley Bowdre — the stocky boy wearing the bowler hat — and two others who were still able to stand up on their own.

Once we were alone, I couldn't help noticing that the Kid had a lot on his mind. He was still the same restless, crazy boy I'd met back in Cimmaron, but his mood seemed to bounce up and down like a rubber ball. One minute he was as keyed-up and talkative as I remembered him to be; the next minute he would turn stoic and grim. So when a young Mexican woman laid out our steaks, peppers and beans, and walked away, I looked at him over a plate of sizzling steak and said: "I see something's bothering you,

Billy. Maybe we came at a bad time?"

"What — ?" He'd been gazing off, but he snapped his eyes to mine and grinned. "Bad time? *Hell* no." He seemed to perk right up, but I felt like it was just for show. "You couldn't have picked a better time." He waved a hand taking in the crowd and the sound of music, still going strong but looking a little frayed and sounding a little tired. "There's no *time* like party *time.*"

I smiled, sipped a steaming cup of coffee: "Yeah, but you don't seem to be taking as much part in it as I thought you would. Not like you would've back when we met."

"Guess you're right," he said. He let go a breath and shoved the sombrero back off his head. It stopped at his shoulders, held by a strip of rawhide. "Them was good times back then —" He nodded and raised his mug of coffee. "— Drinking, shooting up the Quarrels gang . . . smoking that ole Mexican brown-weed. Not giving a damn for nothing —"

"Stealing my *borrowed* mare." I laughed and forked up a fried pepper.

"Yeah, I knew you'd get a kick outa that."

I chewed the pepper, swallowed it, felt my eyes swell up and the back of my neck draw tight as a cinch. I cleared my throat and said in a strained voice as I reached for a tall mug of water: "So, what's changed for ya?" I felt like I was talking through somebody else's mouth, and I threw back more water. It didn't help.

The Kid saw my eyes water, laughed and called out over his shoulder: "Leche fria, pronto por-favor!"

"God," I said through a head of steam, "I hope you didn't order more peppers."

"Cold milk," he said. "It keeps peppers from burning your brains out. I like 'em hot enough to melt my belt buckle. Keeps ya from going to sleep on the jake."

"Gracias," I gasped, grabbing the glass of milk before the young woman even set it down.

"I don't know," the Kid said, going on with the conversation as if nothing had happened. "Seems like the more I try to go my own way, the more everybody else keeps hanging onto me." He carved a piece of steak, stuck a whole pepper on it and ate it down.

"Charley, Tom, all of them . . . they can't understand that maybe it'd be better if I did pull out and lay low awhile." He shook his head. "I can't see letting 'em down."

"Hey, Kid —" I pointed my fork at him for emphasis. "— You're your own man. Don't let your amigos talk you into getting

101

yourself killed. Friendship only goes so far, you know —"

"I know." He wiped a hand across his face and gazed away for a second. "But I'm the one they follow, even if I am the youngest. If I back out of here, it looks like all I've been for the past couple of years is water and wind. Ain't that how it would be with your bunch?"

I stared at him for a second, knowing that he still thought I was Jesse James. Since he did, I figured I might as well make good use of it. "If I *was* Jesse James — which I *ain't*. My bunch wouldn't crowd me into a corner. If they did, I reckon I wasn't quite the leader I thought I was. When it's time to lay low, I'd lay low, if I *was* Jesse James, which I —"

"Yeah," he swiped a hand. "I know I gotta do something soon. I'll just have to figure it out." He threw back a swig of coffee. "But that's enough of my goings on. What's this business you're up to in Silver Basin? You know there's nothing around there but some bad-ass Mexican guerilla ready to kill anything that moves."

Is that *Crazy* Mangelo's bunch? The ones I keep hearing about?"

"That's them. What business you got over there? If you don't mind saying."

"Horses, of course," I said, not about to mention the jewels or the deed to the land. "Met the Contesa Cortez in New Orleans. She said she's looking for some good riding stock."

"New Orleans, huh? I don't know the contesa." He cocked his head and shot me a curious look. "You didn't know ole Quick Quintan Cordell, by any chance?"

"Not well, I didn't. But I was there when everybody in French Quarters put a bullet in him. That's where I met the contesa."

"But you didn't shoot him, even a little bit?"

"Naw." I shrugged. "I would've, if everybody hadn't done it for me. We got into it over a billiard game. He came back shotgunning for me. Why?"

The Kid laughed: "And now you've come to sell the contesa some *horses*? You've got the balls of a blue bull!" He slapped his hand down on the table; I just stared at him.

"I don't get it, Kid. What's so funny?"

"What's funny? Ole Quintan ain't been in the ground a month and here you come, acting like you wanta *sell horses* to his grieving widow?" He winked and threw back a swig of coffee. "I *like* that, Jesse — *like* that a lot."

I just stared at him, not knowing what to say.

He stopped laughing and returned my gaze in silence for a second, then said in a hushed tone: "Are you telling me you didn't know? Didn't know them two was husband and wife?" He must've read my answer in the stunned expression on my face. "Boy oh boy," he said softly, pushing back his coffee cup with his fingertips.

"That's right, Kid," I said, turning my head back and forth slowly. "I had no idea in the world."

From the dusty street a drunken musician staggered over with a violin in one hand and the bow in his other. He swept off his sweat stained sombrero and said to the Kid: "Musica? Musica alegria por tu amigo?"

"Alegre, triste — lamisma," the Kid said with a shrug. He flipped the man a coin. I watched as the man snapped it from the air silently, effortlessly, catching it even in his drunkenness, even with his violin in hand, as if his life had molded itself around music and money and one could not exist without the other.

"Musica triste." He smiled, but with a puzzled expression as the coin slid from his palm, down the veins in his bony wrist as he raised the violin, and disappeared into his ragged shirtsleeve. "Pero, que es musica triste?"

"Vida," the Kid said as I looked back and forth at them. "La musica de vida."

The man looked at me, then he took a breath and began playing a snappy tune as he danced about, barefoot in the dust.

"What's that about?" I looked into the Kid's eyes, still stunned by what he'd told me about Quick Quintan and the contesa.

"Nothing," he said, and he flipped another coin. It landed in the dirt by the musician's feet. "He asked what kind of music we'd like to hear. I told him anything . . . anything at all."

I thought about the contesa for a second, and suddenly I felt foreign and ignorant here in the land of enchantment. I looked back at the Kid: "Are you *sure* that's what ya'll said?"

He turned from watching the musician, back to me. "It's close enough," he said; and he smiled his bucktoothed smile and threw back the last drink from his cup of coffee.

CHAPTER 5

I was stunned, to say the least, at what the Kid told me about the contesa being married to Quick Quintan. Even though I hadn't killed him myself, I felt now that I'd been played into some terrible game between them that had led up to his death. I recalled the look of pure hatred flashing in her eyes the night of the billiard game and later when she'd mentioned his name after picking us up in her fancy coach just ahead of the law. And now, even as the scent of her whispered on the warm Nuevo Mejico breeze, I had to force myself to think of her in a whole new light. I had a hard time listening to anything else the Kid said during breakfast. It was as if he spoke to me from a long ways off, through the sound of the Spanish violin and through the swirl of events dating back to that stormy night in New Orleans. When we'd finished eating, I told the Kid we'd see him again before

106

riding out that afternoon, and I set out looking for Jack among the tired but still partying fiesta crowd.

Even as I searched for Jack I had a hard time concentrating on what I was doing. I would catch myself drifting aimlessly from one makeshift cantina to another and from drinking crowd to drinking crowd, thinking of the contesa, and of Quick Quintan's last words. Only when I ran into Tom O'Foliard in a throng of people did I manage to shake the two of them from my mind.

"Tom," I said, grabbing his arm as he drifted past me. "Have you seen my partner anywhere?"

He turned to me with a bleary stare and grinned. "Seen him? Damn right I've seen him. That man's crazy I hope you know." He thumped a hand on his chest. "Even by *my* standards he's plumb —"

"Yeah, I know," I said, trying to cut through his whiskey haze. "But where is he? I need to find him."

Tom pointed a weaving finger at a run down adobe past the far edge of the crowd. It looked like the kind of place a person would only go to after every other place had burned down. "Geez," I said, shaking my head. "Is he drunk?"

"I hope so," said Tom, turning back into

the milling crowd. "I hate to think he acts that way *sober.*"

I hurried on to the dingy cantina, and just as I started for the door I had to step to the side as a big man with a dirty red beard came sailing through it, through a cloud of circling flies, out into the dusty street. Jack stepped into the open doorway and pitched the man's flat brimmed hat out into the dirt beside him. I just stared as the man struggled to his knees with a hand over his nose, then pushed himself to his feet.

I heard a trace of a German accent as the man said: "You'll pay for this with your life." But I saw he managed to keep his hands a cautious distance from his pistol. A stocky Mexican came running up beside him leading two horses. He held out a hand to steady him, but the man slung him away, snatched a pair of reins from him and ran a sleeve across his flattened nose.

"Come back when you can stay longer," Jack called out. He grinned. A tall wild-eyed blonde came up, leaned against him, giggled, ran her hand inside his shirt and nipped at his shoulder. I stood staring as Jack and the tall blonde turned back into the darkness of the cantina; and I watched, turning in the street as the two men rode away.

"Alright, Jack, that's enough," I said, stepping into the darkness of the cantina. "Party's over."

I saw him and the blonde hanging against each other in the middle of the dirt floor, their faces buried in each other's shoulder, swaying back and forth to the sound of a Spanish guitar playing so slow it appeared the music would melt and drip from the air.

At the end of a dirty bar, I saw the young Mexican and Rafe Rafferty look at me. Rafferty's hat was gone and his hair ruffled. His plaid coat lay across the bar — across a puddle of beer. The Mexican shook his head slowly as if forecasting disaster. Jack looked up from the blonde's shoulder and said: "In a second." Then his face dropped back down.

Damn it! I walked over to Rafferty and the Mexican, keeping an eye on the open door. "What was that all about?" Flies snarled above the bar and I yanked off my hat and swiped it through them.

"Aw, señor. You and your amigo must leave this place before it is too late. The man with the beard is Red Fowler, another of Mangelo's men. He is even higher up than Renald. I think maybe —"

"Mangelo," I said. I shoved my hat down on my head. "All I hear is, Mangelo . . .

and his *men.* Why is it that everywhere I go, we keep running into these fellers? Where the hell is Mangelo?"

"I myself have never seen the man, señor, but his men are everywhere. It must be destined for you to have trouble with him." He glanced about and crossed himself. "You come here to take the black stallion. Your amigo has trouble with his men. Santa Maria." I saw a pot bellied bartender amble over and shove some money into Rafferty's hand. Rafferty grinned and shoved it down in his shirt pocket, his pocket already bulging with dollar bills.

"Look," I said to the Mexican. "Let me say this once more, so maybe you'll understand. I'm not here to take away this *Mangelo's* horse . . . or anybody else's. And my friend didn't mean to insult anybody. He's just drinking. Surely Mister *Mangelo* and his men understand how it is to have a few too many. We didn't come here looking for trouble."

"It does not matter now about the *horse,* señor, or about insulting his men. It is already certain you will have trouble with him."

"I'm afraid he's right," I heard Rafferty say. "I only hope I can be of service to you and your friend before it's too late."

I glanced from one to the other. "What do you mean?" The Mexican pointed a finger at Jack and the wild-eyed blonde. "*She* is Fowler's woman."

After a few attempts at getting Jack to leave, I gave up and had the young Mexican go with me to pick up our horses and the mule where I'd left them at the livery station. Rafferty fell in with us, walking a couple of feet behind us, counting a wadded up handful of money, smoothing it out and shoving it into his wrinkled shirt pocket. "If she's this *Fowler's* woman," I said, glancing at the two of them, "what's she doing playing up to another man?"

"Today she is just getting drunk . . . probably to tease Fowler. I think it is a crazy game between the two of them, señor."

"And one that's quite dangerous, if you ask me," Rafferty said.

I looked at the two of them as we walked along through the dry powdery street. Earlier, the Mexican had said his name was Abraham Lincoln Morales. I had to ask him why. It seemed that five years ago he'd gotten in trouble over in El Paso. When a sheriff asked his name, he'd rattled off the first Anglo name that came to mind, hoping it would help if he passed for an American.

It didn't work, but the name stuck. ". . . and the sheriff got such a laugh, he let me go." Abe had shrugged. "So why change it, señor?"

We walked on to the stable through the swirling dust. "What do ya'll know about this Mangelo? Just how *crazy* is he?"

"Crazy enough that he is out to take over Mexico with his army of pistoleros," said Mexican Abe. "He says he fights for libertad for our people —"

"Nothing crazy about that," I said.

"Si, but who knows. Some think he only fights for the money. There is little known about Mangelo — few have even seen him."

"Why does Mangelo think the contesa's stallion belongs to him?"

"Oh . . . Morcillo?" Abe glanced at me as we turned and headed into the livery station. "That stallion is the devil, señor." Abe crossed himself. "I hear that Mangelo worked for the Cortez family back before he became a great leader. He went loco over the stallion." Abe tapped his finger to his head. "He tried to steal it many times, but could not. It is said that he still sits for days at a time on the cliffs overlooking the Hacienda . . . watching for Morcillo. It is crazy, no?"

"Sounds crazy," I said. "Must be quite an

animal." I wasn't about to tell him I'd already seen the stallion or that I would give almost anything to own such an animal myself.

"Si," said Abe, eyeing me suspiciously. Somehow he still had in his head that I was here for the stallion, Morcillo, this 'diablo' caballa as he'd called it — devil horse. I wasn't about to tell him I was here to deliver the fortune in jewels I carried in the money belt beneath my shirt.

"Well," I said, stopping inside the station as an old man came to us wiping his hands on a dirty rag. "I've never seen a horse, or a political cause, *or a woman,* worth going loco over. So maybe Mangelo was just crazy to begin with." I motioned toward our horses and our mule as I took some money from my pocket; and the old man turned to get them. "Either way I don't want any trouble. I wanta get my friend outa here before anything else happens.

"I dare say," Rafferty chuckled, "you two *do* lead a colorful life." He smoothed down the front of his wine-stained shirt. "Makes mine seem rather pale by comparison." I noticed he'd left his plaid coat behind.

I looked him up and down, shook my head and turned to the old man as he led up the animals. When I'd paid him, I turned and left, leading the animals back to the cantina with Rafferty and Mexican Abe behind me. They seemed to have drawn to me like a couple of lost calves. When I spun the reins around a broken hitchrail outside the dingy cantina they stayed right with me.

"Just between us," I said, as we stepped inside, "if this Mangelo feller tried anything with my friend, he could end up with wind whistling through his belly —" I looked over at Jack and felt my face redden. "— Not in the shape he's in now . . . of course."

"Si," said Mexican Abe. "He looks not so good." Jack lay spread-eagle on a dirty table staring straight up through glassy eyes. Sally Dew sat halfway propped on the table with one leg swinging back and forth, holding Jack's head in her lap, curling his hair with one finger and smoking a thin black cigar. She glanced at Mexican Abe and me with a teasing smile, rolled off a fancy garter, stretched it around Jack's hat band and hung his hat on a chair-back. Then she stood up, laying Jack's head down carefully, smiled down at him and left.

"Well, that's that," I said. "Maybe we can go on with our business with no harm done."

"I hope so, señor, but I doubt it."

I looked at Abe, and just to change the

subject, said: "So you're a cowboy?" I nodded at his chaps and gauntlets. I was tired of hearing about Mangelo and his men.

"No, Señor Beatty. I just wear these to look like I have a job. It is hard enough to be a Mexican around here sometimes. Even worse to be an *out-of-work Mexican.*"

"I understand," I said. "Do you know your way around Silver Basin, around Little Sand Hole?" Abe seemed a decent enough sort of person. I figured since he was hanging around anyway, it might be a good idea to have him show us the quickest, safest way. During breakfast, the Kid had mentioned that the Mescalero Apache were slipping on and off their reservation and kicking up a lot of dust along the stretch between here and Silver Basin. Having an extra gun along wouldn't hurt.

"Si, I know the area, señor. It is full of Mescaleros, guerrillas, bandidos, and every other kind of —"

"Wanta ride along? I'll pay you."

"No money, por favor," he tossed a hand. "I would only spend it, then I would be broke. I will ride with you just to see you take that horse away from here. But I will not go near it."

"I told you, I'm not after a horse. I'd like for you to ride along with us —" I shot Rafferty a glance, saw the eager look on his face, and I let out a breath. "— Both of you if you like. But you've got to understand. I'm not here to take anybody's horse. Comprende?"

Their eyes glistened above crafty smiles. "Of course," Rafferty said, and he winked, shielding a smile with a dirty hand.

"Si, I understand," Abe said in a low voice, letting me know I could trust him to keep it a secret.

I just stared at them a second then nodded toward Jack. "Let's get him up and outa here."

We looped Jack's arms over Abe and Rafferty's shoulder and led him out of the cantina to the nearest horse trough. When we'd finished dunking him a few times, he slung us away, staggered around in the dirt and over to his horse. "You don't stick a man's head in a horse trough, for God's sakes," he said. "That's something a damned *cowboy* would do." He slung his hair back and looked at me. "The hell's wrong with you anyway?" Dirty water ran down his face and dribbled from his chin.

"Here." I shoved his hat to him. "There's nothing wrong with me. I ain't the one getting blind drunk and causing all this trouble."

Jack glanced around and leaned against his horse: "What trouble?"

I shook my head. "Come on, we'll talk about it later. I wanta put some miles between us and here —"

"Where's the Kid?" Jack wiped his face and looked around again.

"He's not here," I said. "That's for sure. We'll ride by and see him on our way." I turned to Abe and Rafferty. "Get your horses and meet us at the cantina over by Maxwell's."

They turned, Rafferty looking all around the street as if he'd misplaced his horse; then Mexican Abe directed him by the shoulder and they walked away toward a distant hitchrail. I helped Jack up in the saddle, climbed up on my big chestnut and chucked him out into the dusty street. It was already after noon, and the party-goers had fallen off here and there for siesta by the time we reined up at the cantina across the square from Maxwell's.

Jack stayed on his horse with his head bowed, and I walked past three horses covered with road dust, and into the cantina. No sooner than I entered I saw the Kid sitting at a table in a corner facing me, talking to a feller wearing a tall black Stetson. "Come on over," the Kid said. Halfway there, the man in the black Stetson turned facing me, and I stopped in my tracks when I saw it was the sheriff I'd met in New Orleans the night Quick Quintan went down.

His brows arched, then eased down as he let out a breath and said: "Well, well. Look who we have here."

Instinctively I started to take a step back, then saw Gosset, the deputy, beside me near the bar holding a short barreled shotgun. Beside him stood another man wearing a badge. He looked me up and down and laid his hand on a pistol in his belt. "I hope you try to make a run for it," Gosset said. I just stared as he leveled the shotgun.

The Kid stood up slowly, staring at Gosset but talking down the sheriff across the table. "Call him off, Pat, or I'll start popping buttons off his shirt." Now there was no air of play or excitement about the Kid, only a cold, calm deadly stare; and I saw that unlike the four wild shots at the tin can, whatever he pointed his colt at now would fall, and fall hard.

Gosset started to move the shotgun toward the Kid, but the sheriff raised a hand. "Stand down, boys. We ain't here on business." Then he turned more in his chair and looked at me. "You do get around,

Beatty . . . if that's really your name."

The Kid eased back down, forcing a smile as he drew his eyes slowly from Gosset, and motioned me over. "Don't pay any attention to ole Pat here. He's just got himself crammed full of law these days." He stared at the sheriff and threw back a shot of Tequila. "Right, Pat?"

"Didn't know you two knew each other." The sheriff leaned back in his chair and looked me up and down. "It must be true about birds of the feather."

I just stood there looking down at him, wondering what move to make and reminding myself that there was really no cause for him to be after me for something that happened all the way back in New Orleans. "Didn't know *ya'll* knew each other, either," I said, nodding from him to the Kid.

The Kid breathed deep and poured another shot glass from the bottle. "Aw-yeah. Me and Big Casino here go way back — gambling, charming the señoritas. Stole enough beef together to feed the Persian Army." He threw back the drink and I saw his throat tighten from the sting of it. "Now he's pinned a badge on and come to run me off. Ain't that just the bending diddles —"

"It's between us, Kid," said the sheriff. "I didn't come to talk to this . . . this two-bit *assassin.*" He glanced at me with disgust. I saw the Kid's hand clinch around the glass, ready to slam it down; but he caught himself and lowered it calmly to the table. "Well, Pat, maybe you've gone to keeping things from your friends, but I ain't. Beatty can hear anything you've got to say to me." He grinned up at me: "Might need him for a witness, you never know." He turned back to the sheriff.

"Okay, Billy. I'll keep it short and sweet." The sheriff raised a glass of whiskey and tossed it back. "You're out of the country by the next time I come down from Lincoln, or I'm taking you down. You, Foliard, Bowdre, the bunch of you." He glanced up at me. "And you. I don't want to see you around any longer than it takes you to leave."

"You've got nothing on me, Sheriff," I said. "You know I never shot Quick Quintan —"

"No, but your friend did, and if I knew then what I know now, you'd never left there that night. I know the two of you set ole Quintan up for his wife. I can't prove it. But I know it."

"That's a damn lie!" I felt my neck heat up. "I didn't know nothing about the two of them —"

"I *said,* I can't prove it." He let his hand drift to a watch in his vest. He calmly pulled it, checked the time and put it back, but his hand drifted down near his sidearm and stopped there. "But if you or your *nameless* friend hang around here, I'll find a reason to take you down." He glanced at the Kid with a slight smile, then back to me: "Lincoln County is on a growth spurt, and I propose to see it become a good respectable community."

"So this is how you treat ole friends, huh, Pat? How long we been friends now?" the Kid asked, then stared at him.

"Quit awhile, Kid." The sheriff glanced around, looking everywhere but right at the Kid. "But you've been stepping on the wrong toes. You knew they'd be sending somebody, Billy. So don't act like it's all a big surprise." Then he looked straight at him. "If I hadn't been your friend, I wouldn't made this trip. They wanted you taken straight down. But I told them no. Said, let me talk to him first. Said, I owe Billy that much —"

"*They? They!*" The Kid swiped his hand across the table, knocking his empty glass across the cantina, and snatched the bottle of tequila. "*They* is nothing. *They* is a turd with all the dung scraped off it! Where was *they* when ole boys like Foliard, Bowdre and me —" He pointed with the bottle; tequila sloshed over the edge. "— *And you,* was all the only ones riding the badlands twixt their cattle and the Mexican bandidos? Huh? *They* . . . sure didn't begrudge us a turn of beef back then, did *they?*"

"Times have changed, Kid." The sheriff picked up the cork on the table, corked his bottle of whiskey and slid it inside his duster. "I'm hoping you've got sense enough to change with 'em. If not, my next trip here is strictly business. Think about it."

"Sure, Pat." The Kid threw back a drink of tequila. "Sheriff Patrick Garrett. Gunman for *big business.* What's it costing them to kill me, Pat? Hunh? You gonna do alright on it?"

"Not enough, Kid, believe me. If it was up to me, I'd —"

The Kid cut him off. "What ole Evin Howard always said about you was right I reckon. He always said your mother woulda been better off mashing your head and selling her milk."

I saw the sheriff's eyes flash like hot coals; but he let out a breath and chuckled: "It ain't working, Billy. You're not gonna rile me today." He looked up at me then back at the Kid. "Today's visit is on the house.

Next one will cost you. All of you." He stood up slowly and looked back at me. "And I don't even want you or your friend leaving your footprints in New Mexico Territory, comprende?"

Gosset called out to me from the bar: "And tell your *nameless* friend I'll settle with him myself . . . *personally.*"

"Tell me yourself, *right now,* you wet bag of crackers —" I heard Jack's voice and we all swung our eyes toward him as he stepped out of a storeroom with a short-barreled shotgun. "— I got time to *dust* your wagon." He stepped around and stopped five feet from Gosset. Gosset's face had lost all color.

Sheriff Garrett's hand tensed near his holster. "Easy," I said. The other deputy stepped away from beside Gosset.

Gosset swallowed a lump and tried to look unshaken: "If this here's a shotgun stand-off," he said, his hand tightening on the triggers, "it's even money we'll both die, mister."

Jack grinned: "It would've been . . . except yours ain't cocked."

Gosset glanced down and back up with a sick expression.

"Mine is." Jack reached out, tweaked Gosset's nose with the short barrel, grinned and took his shotgun from his hands. "Now

what is it you want to settle with me — ?"
He broke open Gosset's shotgun; the loads
fell to the floor. He handed it back to him
and smiled again. "— You pig-eyed son of a
bitch."

"What do you want me to do, Sheriff
Garrett?" The other deputy stood trembling.
"Tell me something here!"

"Nothing, Bell," said Garrett in a dis-
gusted tone. "Just try not to soil yourself. If
he meant to kill him he already would've."
He turned to the Kid: "So this is *how you*
treat an old friend, huh, Billy? You set 'em
up from behind?"

The Kid just stared at him.

Garrett turned to me. "Next time I see
either of you *assassins,* I'll just start shooting and figure it's another ambush."

"It won't be an ambush, it'll be an altar
call," I said. Then I said to Jack without taking my eyes off Garrett: "Cut 'em loose,
nameless friend." And I stepped back and
stared at Garrett until he walked out the
door with his deputies backing out behind
him.

"I ain't forgetting you," Gosset said, pointing a shaky finger at Jack.

"Jack grinned: "It's always good to be
remembered."

We stood watching dust stir in the doorway for a second, then I let out a breath, turned slowly, looked at Jack and said: " *'Wet bag of crackers?'* "

His face reddened. "The hell'd you expect? I been drunk two days and dunked in a water trough. Ain't even good and sober yet."

I shook my head slowly: "But still . . . 'A *wet bag of* —' "

"Don't harp on it, okay?" His brow narrowed. He turned facing the Kid as Charley Bowdre stepped out of the storeroom behind him.

Bowdre pointed at Jack: "I woulda shot Garrett if this one hadn't snuck in and grabbed my shotgun."

"Sorry Kid," said Jack. "I couldn't see bushwhacking them like that when the sides were even."

"And you was right," the Kid said to Jack. "I didn't know Charley was doing that." He shot Charley Bowdre a cold stare. "Now Pat thinks I was dead-eyeing him."

"Hell, Billy!" Bowdre spread his hands. "The man's out to get us. I had ever cause to kill him, ambush, dead-eye or whatnot —"

"Not like that," the Kid said. "I don't like backshooting a man unless I have to. Never have. And I don't like Garrett thinking I'd

125

do him that way. The man was my best friend . . . whether he likes it or not."

"It's too late now, Kid," I said. "He already thinks it. Maybe you oughta ride out with us. It ain't far from the border where we're going. You could lay low awhile."

"He ain't running from 'em, are you, Billy?" Bowdre said.

I turned and looked at the Kid. "Heck," he said. Ole Pat talks tough, but he can't shoot me when it comes right down to it, no matter what he thinks. Like I said . . . he used to be my best friend."

Jack pushed up his hat brim. "*Used to be* is the same as *never was,* Kid, once a man pins tin on his chest and says he's taking you down."

The Kid threw back the last drink from the bottle of tequila and pitched the bottle to the floor. "I'll have to try and remember that the next time we meet, I reckon." He walked to the door and watched Sheriff Garrett and his deputies ride off in a swirl of dust.

And he stood watching even after they'd disappeared from sight, watching with an air of loneliness about him, as if hoping that at any second they might turn and ride back, as if upon their return he'd find that the whole thing had been some strange misunderstanding that could all be straightened out among friends. But then his shoulders let down slightly; he ran a hand across his face and kneaded the back of his neck. "Nunca fue," I heard him say under his breath before walking out into the sunlight and dust. *Never was.*

I stood watching the Kid for a second; and I made up my mind then and there that I couldn't ride off and leave him. It was none of my business, but I saw what was coming if he hung around Sumner. I saw it and couldn't let it happen, not if I could stop it. The Kid had played out his string here, and like it or not he had to leave, leave or die.

"Nobody in their right mind would stay here waiting to get shot," I said to Jack that evening.

Jack grinned: "Whoever said the Kid was *in* his right mind?"

I spent the rest of the evening talking the Kid into riding out with us. Even though Sheriff Garrett's warning was clear as a bell, getting the Kid to leave was like pulling teeth. But finally he grinned his bucktoothed grin and said: "Does this mean you're offering me a job riding with the James Gang?"

I looked at him, studied his face in the glow of a low campfire, and realized that anything I could offer him was not much better than what he had. Somewhere there was a bullet waiting for the Kid, no more, no less. The most I could do was try to postpone it. "We'll see, Kid," I said; and I looked away, hoping he couldn't tell I was lying.

CHAPTER 6

We rode out of Old Fort Sumner that evening as red sunlight boiled in the west and the fiesta crowd began to stir and gather back into the streets. Guitar, violin and accordion began dancing in the air above the smell of roasting meats and bakery goods. Jack stared at the row of wine skins on our way out; but he only shook his head and gigged his horse forward when the old man laughed and called out to him.

"Por favor," Jack whispered under his breath, wiping a hand across his sweaty forehead and riding on beside the Kid and me.

Directly behind us, Rafe Rafferty and Mexican Abe rode along, Rafferty riding bareheaded, leading our pack mule loaded with supplies — enough food and water to make the barren crossing to Silver Basin, on into Little Sand Hole. Before we'd left, I noticed Rafferty taking a handful of money

129

from Bowdre and O'Foliard. He'd shoved it into his bulging shirt pocket and shook both their hands. The Kid had asked both men to ride along, but they turned him down, acting a little disappointed that he was leaving them.

We covered nearly twenty miles before stopping that night, owing to the brightness of a full moon that lit the land as clearly as a dim sunlight. A *rustler's moon,* the Kid called it; and when we drew a camp late that night alongside a thin stream running down from a rise of foothills, we did so with no need for a fire.

"Feeling better?" I asked Jack as the two of us watered the horses and the mule. He'd been silent all evening, sweating and working past what looked like a terrible hangover.

"Better than *what?*" He chuckled, kneeled down and sank his canteen and two others into the stream.

"What came over you back there anyway?" I kneeled beside him, sank two more canteens into the water and watched it run in clear dark braids across my hands. "Never seen you go so wild like that all at once."

"Beats me," he said, shaking his head. "I reckon all that talk about this *enchanted land* finally got the best of me." He raised his face and looked around at the black distant horizon. "I see how the Kid has a hard time leaving here. Fiesta all the time, food, drink . . . señoritas. I love this place."

"Yeah, well, I don't know how much it loves you. You've managed to piss off some pretty tough gunmen on both sides of the law. And as far as señoritas . . . you can forget the blonde. She belongs to one of Crazy Mangelo's men. The one you threw out in the street."

"That tall pretty thing?" Jack raised a hand to the garter stretched around his hat band. He took off his hat, looked at it and sat it back on his head. "Where'd she go anyway?"

"Don't you remember anything, Jack? Remember throwing one of Mangelo's men out in the street? Remember her leaving you stretched out across that table?"

"Just bits and pieces. But, *man,* what a woman." Then he looked puzzled, reached up and touched the garter again carefully. "I didn't do nothing I shouldn't, did I?"

"No, not with her I don't reckon —" He looked relieved. "— All you did was drink yourself into a stupor, busted that big feller's nose all over his face . . . then you passed out colder than a wedge of lead."

Jack made a sheepish grin and ran his hand across his face. "Well, it was only our first date."

"Better make it your last . . . from what I hear about these boys they ain't to be fooled with, especially that one."

"Then he shoulda done something right then. He don't own her. Besides, I was just having a little fun. If they don't want people to party, they shouldn't throw one."

"Who's *they*?" I picked up the canteens and capped them. "Is that the same *they* the Kid was talking about?"

"*They,* is whoever gets between you and whatever you most want to do, I reckon. Never seen a man have trouble but what *they* didn't cause it. *They,* is the wind that fans all fires." Jack raised the canteens, capped them and looked at me. "What was Garrett talking about — us setting up Quick Quintan for the contesa? Did I miss something there, or did he say she was Quintan's wife?"

"Aw-boy, Jack . . ." I shook my head and told him the whole story. When I finished, he just stared at me a second and said: "Nothing's ever simple with you, is it? Can't gamble without ending up in a fight. Can't just win money like anybody else — Nawsir. You gotta take on a parcel of jewels and land . . . and end up accused of murder. I swear, amigo — Then you have the gall to say I went a little *wild* for awhile." He shook his head. *"Never simple."*

"It is from now on. I'm going in and out — strictly business — get the money from the contesa, settle up and move on. I'm gonna talk the Kid into going down to Old Mex — keep him from getting his head shot off. I'm worried about that boy."

"I don't know why," Jack said. "He's doing alright."

"Doing alright?" I cocked an eye. "Everybody and their brother out to kill him — his *best friend* out to kill him. You call that doing alright?"

Jack shrugged: "Could be worse, I reckon."

"Worse? How?"

Jack shot me a glance. "He could have a partner who goes around sticking his nose in other people's business."

I let out a breath. "Alls I'm saying, Jack, is that's no way for him to live. Always looking over his shoulder, always on the run, worried that any second he'll hear the bark of a gun. The hell kinda life is that?" I shook my head.

Jack studied me for a second with a puzzled look on his face, then just shook his head and picked up the canteens. "I don't know why I talk to you sometimes," he said.

He stood up and walked away, leading his horse behind him.

I felt my face redden, stood up, and followed him back to the others.

We cut strips of dried shank, ate beans out of air-tight cans and drank cool water from our canteens. As we ate, I watched the Kid in the grainy blue light, saw him pick at his food and stare back toward Fort Sumner somewhere in the deep purple darkness. Finally I said: "So, Kid. I suppose now that you're shed of that place, you'll go on to Old Mex and take up a new life for yourself?"

He grunted, sat silent for awhile, then said: "After I left you boys up in Cimmaron, I came to Lincoln County and took me a job with an Englishman . . . name of Tunstall —" He stopped and sucked his teeth as if considering something. "— Wasn't so bad for an Englishman. Taught me to read some, to write a fair hand. We was pretty good friends, him and me." He let out a breath. "They killed him. The same bunch that Garrett's working for now. It don't seem right, me leaving like this. Seems like I'm letting the ole boy down somehow."

"You ain't letting nobody down by keeping yourself alive," I said. "If that Englishman was still here he'd tell you the same thing . . . if ya'll was that close."

He got quiet for a second, then said: "Yeah, I know. Hell I even went to court and tried to testify to what they did to him. Even told the truth as far as I could. Nothing come of it. Still the same ole hands pulling the ole strings. It just don't set right with me . . . that, and having ole Foliard and Bowdre thinking I'm running out on 'em. Especially now that we know it's my ole buddy Pat doing the running. That's a bitter pill."

"Maybe they knew it, Kid," I said. "Whoever *they* are." I shot Jack a glance. "Maybe they picked him knowing it would keep you here. Maybe they don't just want you gone. Maybe they want you dead. Ever thought of that?"

"Naw. That's too much thinking for me. I do better *not* thinking too much. One reason I'm still running loose is because they spend all their time trying to figure what I'm thinking . . . fact is I ain't thinking or planning nothing at all. I'm just taking it as it comes. They can't handle that. Everything has to be in some kinda order and make some kinda sense to them." He chuckled and spit. "Dang. A man lives like that . . . he ain't really lived at all. The way I see it."

Rafe Rafferty leaned forward, chewing his

beans, and pointed his spoon for emphasis. "There's a certain amount of relevance to what you're saying there, Mister Bonney. If you don't mind my saying so." I saw he'd tied a dirty bandanna around his head. His face bristled of a beard stubble.

"Amount of *what?*" The Kid looked at him in the grainy darkness and scratched his head.

"*Releven*—" Rafferty stopped, wiped a hand across his mouth, then wiped it on his pants leg. "Let's say it this way. The more civilized we become, the more we desire predictability. What they find so unsettling about you, I'm sure, is the fact that they can't anticipate your next move. If Garrett or his leaders could predict your actions they'd be a lot more comfortable about you being alive."

"They know I've got scores to settle," the Kid chuckled. "That's for sure."

"Precisely." Rafferty spread his hands in the darkness. "And owing to your spontaneous nature, it must drive them crazy not knowing when or at what time you might decide to strike." He turned to me. "Would you agree, Mister Beatty?"

I drank from my canteen and capped it. "Sounds like a lot of hocus-pocus *insurance* talk to me."

The Kid laughed: "Yeah, *Alias*. How do you know so much? Is that what you learned selling insurance to businessmen then screwing their widows out of it?"

"Please, gentlemen." Rafferty leaned back against his saddle and smoothed the front of his dirty shirt. A sole was torn loose on one of his Wellington boots and looking like a frog's mouth. "Let's just say that I've been exposed to all kinds of people and their situations in this business."

"Bet that's how he got his nose busted," Jack said.

"Be that as it may . . ." Rafferty dismissed us with a wave of his hand.

"Señores," said Mexican Abe, sitting down his empty bean can. "In my country the old folks tell of how to *see* the wind. A small wind stirs on the desert floor but you cannot see *the wind*, only the dust that spins in it. They say the wind spins and grows because there is nothing there to stop it. As it grows it becomes stronger and picks up many more things — larger, heavier things — and spins them inside it . . . until you think you see the big terrible wind, but you are only seeing what *the wind* has gathered." He shrugged. "Because we know that no one can *see* the wind, eh, señores?"

I glanced at Jack, Rafferty, then the Kid,

137

then back to Mexican Abe and said: "Alright, so . . . ?"

"So. When the wind becomes full and strong and begins destroying what is in its path, you still do not see *it,* only the large contents of it. Then when it is gone, you do not even see its contents, only the destruction it has left behind —"

"There again," Rafferty said, cutting in. "Right back to the unpredictability. The randomness of it —"

"Shut up, Alias," the Kid said. "We ain't talking insurance here."

Abe raised a finger and said: "These men in Lincoln. They have only seen what you have gathered, Señor Bonney, and what you have left behind. For that they fear you. For that they have hired your amigo, Sheriff Garrett — not to chase you away as they have perhaps led *even him* to believe — but to keel you." Abe crossed himself and looked down. "And I'm sorry to say . . . he will keel you before it is over. He will do what no one else can do."

"Why — ?" I looked close at Abe in the grainy light as a coyote let out a long mournful cry. "— Because Garrett ain't afraid?"

"Oh no, Mister Beatty. Sheriff Garrett is just as afraid as the rest of them, perhaps even more. But unlike the rest of them he has known Beely the Kid before he swept across the desert and became so big and powerful." Abe looked from one to the other of us and nodded his head slowly in the dim light of the moon. "Sheriff Garrett knows that he and only he . . . has, *seen the wind.*"

We sat in silence for a few seconds, then I leaned back against my saddle, sipped cool water from my canteen and said: "Well, you can study it and consider it from now on, but the fact is —" I turned my face toward the Kid. "— It makes no sense, staying somewhere where folks want to kill you when you can go anywhere else you please. This is a big world, Kid. Only a fool would hang around Sumner."

"But it's been home," said the Kid, "after a long time without one." Then a silence fell around us that marked his final say on the subject, and one by one we adjusted on our blankets and saddles beneath the stars; and I listened to lingering calls of distant coyotes until I drifted to sleep.

I awoke in the morning wrapped in my dusty blanket on my bed of sand; and as I turned over on my side, I saw Jack standing nearby, gazing toward the horizon, and I heard him say just above a whisper: "We got company coming. Hope they ain't expecting breakfast."

I heard the caution in Jack's voice and rolled up from my blanket, taking up my rifle from my saddle scabbard on my way. I saw the Kid rise up slowly on the other side of Jack. Next to him, Rafferty, then Mexican Abe, putting on his sombrero and drawing the string up against his chin as if anticipating a hard storm.

I gazed out sixty yards at a dozen horsemen riding abreast, slowly, down from the crest of a rise until they disappeared briefly then reappeared closer on a stretch of flat land in a gray morning haze.

"Draw the horses up," I said across to Rafferty without taking my eyes off the riders. Then I said to the Kid: "What do you think? Indians?" I jacked a round up in my rifle and heard Jack do the same. But even as I asked, I knew different. These were white men, some wearing wide, flat brimmed hats with low crowns — a kind more common back before the civil conflict — and some wearing caps with ear flaps loosely tied above their heads, giving them the appearance of some ancient mongolian warriors riding out of the silver morning as if riding out the dark past. Steam puffed from their horse's nostrils and drifted back across them.

"No," the Kid said quietly; and he said no more as he swung a shotgun up, checked it, and let it lay across his forearm with a thumb across the hammers.

"Hola, the camp," said a deep voice from the center of the riders as they drew closer. On either side of the voice, the other riders began spreading out, drawing closer. I felt my neck crawl at the sight of them; and I heard soft rattling sounds as they drew ever nearer. Ornaments of bone and dried hide dangled from around their necks and from their wrists. I smelled something rancid and sour announce them from fifteen yards.

"Hola, yourselves," said the Kid. "If that's you, Turk, you best tell your boys to tighten that line. I hate a son of a bitch fanning out around me before I've even had coffee."

At the sound of the Kid's voice the center rider reined up sharp and raised a hand. The other riders stopped and sat still as stone. "That you, Billy Bonney?"

"It's me. Now draw 'em up before I count to *one,* or I'll just bust two loads of nail heads on you and go on back to sleep."

The deep voice laughed under its breath. "Yeah, it's you alright." Then he said to his men: "Pull back in boys, before Billy gets

141

cross on us. Ain't no hair here worth lifting nohow."

I glanced at the Kid, saw him seem to ease down a little, but with his thumb still across the hammers. The riders drew back into a close line. The lead rider rode up, stopped ten feet back and looked us over. "Morning, Turk," the Kid said, but his voice was less than friendly. "How's the skinning business?"

"Poor to terrible," the man said. "Same as with buffalo. Seems like anything I skin, we run out of." He smiled across broken teeth the color of moss and black tobacco, eyed Mexican Abe up and down, then turned back toward the Kid. "How much you take for that greaser? His hair's black enough."

I heard Abe curse under his breath and take a step forward. Jack waved him back cautiously. "He ain't for sale, Turk," the Kid said. "Ain't you a bit off your graze?" He nodded toward a string of long black scalps hanging from the saddlehorn against the big man's leg. "Thought the Federales quit paying for scalps a long time back?"

"They did." He grinned, reached down, raised the string of scalps and shook them. "But there's a few private citizens buy 'em. Enough to keep my hand in. I'm just making one last sweep. Then I'm changing my occupation. Skinned some out a few miles back, mostly squaws and youngins . . . few old men." He shook the scalps again and dropped them. They swung back and forth against his shin. "Got no coffee made?"

"Got nothing for you, Turk —" The Kid grinned. "— Except these loads of nail heads." He bobbed the shotgun gently. "You know we never did like each other that much."

The Turk spit and ran a dirty hand across his mouth: "I know it. Just figured a little coffee, maybe."

"Not a chance." The Kid shook his head. "And if I see ya flanking us across these flats, I won't take it kindly."

"Hell, now." The Turk grinned. "I wouldn't kill a man over a handful of coffee beans."

The Kid grinned back: "But I would. So don't forget it."

The big man nodded slowly and backed his horse. "Yeah, I reckon *you* would. Been hearing a lot of bad talk about you, Kid. They's saying you're a heartless killer and —"

"It's all true, Turk. Now ride on."

He started to turn his horse, but stopped for a second. "We'll be headed the same direction crossing here. I don't wanta ride in your dust the whole way."

"We'll give you plenty of start," the Kid said. "I don't *want* you riding behind me . . . *ever.*"

"Ole Billy Bonney." He chuckled and shook his head. "We oughta be more friendly when we meet. Time's running out on ole boys like us, ain't it?"

"Is it?" said the Kid. "Hell, I ain't even carrying a watch."

"There's bounty on ya, Billy." He narrowed his eyes beneath the shadow of his hat brim. "I heard about it back in Three Rivers last time through. Mighty tempting, for a man looking to turn a few dollars."

"You'd have to stand in line, Turk." The Kid shook his head slowly. "You don't want to do that."

"Alls I'm saying is —"

"I'm through talking to ya, Turk," the Kid said. "Now ride your stinking ass away from here. You're spoiling the air and spooking the horses." He raised the shotgun and pulled back both hammers.

"Alright then." The man raised a hand in a show of peace, turned his horse, and galloped back to the other riders, the sound of bones rattling against his chest and the scalps swinging against his leg.

"The hell was that?" I watched the riders

until they'd swung wide of us and rode off into the thin line of gray morning, looking like beasts riding into their netherworld.

"That is the devil, señor," said Abe. I looked around and saw Rafferty ease up from among the horses. Jack propped his rifle back over his shoulder, picked up his saddle and walked to the horses.

"Scalp hunters," said the Kid. He shot Abe a glance, then looked back at me. "Never give 'em an inch or show 'em no kindness — they misinterpret it. Been killing so long, they don't know nothing else. They used to hunt down Apaches for the Mexican government. Now I reckon they just do it for fun." He gazed off where they'd disappeared. "Have to watch our backs awhile. Turk's known for turning back on ya." He shot Mexican Abe a glance. "Especially if there's any hair that'd pass for Apache."

"They are animals without souls," said Mexican Abe.

"Maybe. But there was a time when your people sure slept better knowing they were around."

"They were *always* animals," Abe said.

The Kid only grunted, swung the shotgun down, took up his saddle and walked to the horses. Rafferty stood wide-eyed holding all the reins, his lips starting to chap and crack from the sun. His bandanna was pulled down to his eyebrows.

"Either way, that's a hell of a way to make a living," Jack said, pitching his saddle up on his silver gray and taking the reins from Rafferty.

The Kid threw his saddle up also, made the cinch and drew it up. "They was heroes to the Mexican government at one time. Back when nothing else stood between the villages and the Mescalero." As I walked up, he checked down the cinch and said: "Funny ain't it? How everybody wants the meanest bastards they can find till the land's settled, then the same bunch that threw you flowers end up throwing you a rope."

"Times change in a strange way Kid," I said, raising my saddle and pitching it up over my chestnut stallion.

"I reckon," said the Kid, staring off at the void where the riders had vanished. "But the more I see of civilization, the better I like the badlands."

When we'd tended the animals we rode away single file. Mexican Abe took the lead. Rafferty and the Kid rode behind him, and Jack and me brought up the rear leading the mule, watching over our shoulders. In the east, daylight wavered in a stark white swirl, boiling as if in anger, ready to spill down on the earth below.

We traveled quietly, searching the land on either side and glancing behind us, listening for any sound of man, other than our own.

After awhile I rode up beside the Kid. "To be as young as you are, you've sure gotten around. Seems like you know most everybody," I said.

He grinned: "Yep. I've kept busy. I don't wash dishes no more."

"What's this Sante Fe Ring I keep hearing about?"

"It ain't a *what,* it's a who," said the Kid. "And nobody really knows who they are, not for sure anyway. Businessmen mostly. The ones at the top are so damn big, their *names* don't even make it down to where we live. They pull strings, everybody else dances." His grin widened. "Except me, that is. I ain't invited to their *welcome to the world* party."

"And that's who Garrett works for? They're the ones posting bounty?"

"Yep. Them, the big cattlemen, hell! It's a long list. My name crosses more lips than the president. I oughta run for office."

"You oughta run for the border."

"I know it. But I just seem to turn it loose

here. Look at ole Turk back there. Him and his bunch has run wild so long, they'll run wild forever."

"It don't have to be that way for you, Billy. You're young. You can start over."

He grinned: "It might be fun to just hang around and see who gets me."

"Bounty money can turn a lot of heads, Kid."

"You of all people oughta know that, eh, Jesse?" He winked at me. "You and Frank back there?"

"Kid . . . Kid," I sighed and shook my head. "I almost wish I was Jesse James, just so you wouldn't be so damn wrong about it."

"I hear ya, *Jesse* — I mean, *Crowe* — I mean, *Beatty*. Beatty is it?" He chuckled and gigged his horse ahead.

I shook my head again, and smiled, and gigged my chestnut up and cantered along beside him.

CHAPTER 7

We rode for four days upward through a string of low mountains, swinging wide of Lincoln and following an old Spanish trail that winded the Sacramentos and turned downward into a flatland of sand, sparkling in sunlight like new fallen snow. Then we turned south into the town of Three Rivers and took on supplies before heading on to Silver Basin.

I'd noticed that the farther we distanced ourselves from Fort Sumner — then from Lincoln and the long strands of barbed wire that ran in both directions as far as the eye could see — the more the Kid seemed to loosen up, become more like his old self, the way I remembered him from the days in Gris and Cimmaron when he'd quit his job as a dishwasher and stood beside Jack and me to shoot it out with the Quarrels Gang — just for practice, as he'd said.

Since then the Kid had become a young

man with big problems. Like the rest of us, Billy could not go back and change what life had bequeathed him; and I reckon somewhere deep inside he had to know that like the buffalo hunters, the scalp takers, and the wildness of the land itself, his time was closing quickly. Looking at him, I could not help but feel a sadness, for I could not picture him ever being any more than he already was, just a young man with too much wild road behind him to ever settle for a milder path.

"I been figuring, maybe you boys are right," he said, twirling his pistol, reining up beside me as we rounded a turn between a wide stretch of sand and a low rise dotted with scrub juniper and cholla cactus. "There's nothing holding me here." He pushed up his hat brim with his pistol barrel, then spun the gun into his holster. "For a man who can hang his hat anywhere he wants to, I've sure let myself get overly attached to this place."

I grinned: "Now you're talking, Kid. Go where your nose leads you. If they don't want you here — to hell with them. It's a big world, and you ain't seen but a part of it —"

My words were cut short by the crack of a rifle from the edge of the low rise, and I caught a glimpse of gray smoke as I rolled from my saddle and flattened on the ground with my hand on one rein.

"Damn it," I heard a voice say from atop the low rise. I looked around at Jack and the others taking cover on the ground. Then the voice said: "Come on up out of there, Kid. I've got ya all pinned. There's no way out."

I shot the Kid a glance: "Who the hell's that?"

"I don't know," he said, checking his pistol with one hand and holding his horse's rein with his other. "Voice sounds familiar. Just ain't placed it yet."

"Alls I want is you, Billy," the voice called out. "Stand on up and get it over with . . . the rest of ya can go on."

"Aw-hell," said the Kid; and I saw him grin and raise his head slightly. "Is that you Al Delbert? It is, ain't it?" Another shot kicked up sand; the Kid ducked his head.

There was a second of silence beneath a low whir of wind, then the voice said: "Well . . . yeah it is."

The Kid laughed. "I thought so. How've you been, you ole scuttler?" He scooted back on his belly as he spoke, glancing around for any sign of better cover. I did the same.

151

"Not so good, Billy, that's why I'm here. They've got a reward on ya for you killing Buckshot Roberts last year. Saw ya in Three Rivers. Thought I'd come claim it, bad as I hate to."

"Now, Al," the Kid said, tying his loose reins snug around his horse's front leg. "You're an undertaker. You got no business out here like this." He gestured to me with his hand. "Keep him talking once I stop," he whispered. Then he slipped behind a scrub juniper, and I kept an eye on the low rise.

"Times has been hard, Billy. Took to drinking, lost my undertaking business playing Monte. You know how it goes."

"Sorry to hear it, Al. I sent ya all the business *I* could."

"I know, and I appreciate it, Billy. But I couldn't get a square deal in Lincoln. Everything's sewed-up by the politicians. A small businessman ain't got a chance . . . you know that?"

"Yep. That's anywhere you go these days, Al. But it's no cause to go and bushwhack *me*," the Kid said. Then he slid quickly across the ground and behind a dried clump of mesquite. "Never figured you for a ambusher."

"You've got no room to talk, Billy. I spent

many a Saturday evening burying men you shot in the back, remember?"

"Now that's a terrible thing to say, Al."

I saw what the Kid was doing, working a wide circle to get up and behind him. I glanced at Jack, Rafferty and Mexican Abe. Jack saw what was happening and nodded. Then I called out up the low rise. "What about us here? You gonna keep us here if he don't come out? We've nothing to do with this."

"I'm sorry about that, Mister," he called back to me. "If I hadn't missed him the first shot, ya'll coulda been on your way."

"So we're stuck here in the sand because of your poor shooting? That's as bad as you hunting the Kid here because you got drunk and lost your business."

"I ain't blaming nobody for nothing," said the voice. "It's just how things are. I always *liked ya*, Billy. You know that don't ya?"

A silence passed as I watched the Kid scramble out of sight, up and around the rise of sand. Then I called out: "He ain't talking to ya no more. Says if you wanta kill him, you've gotta come down here face to face."

"Now, Billy, you know I can't do that. You said yourself, I've got no business out here trying to —"

153

Two pistol shots exploded from the low rise, followed by a ringing silence. "That'll do it," the Kid called down. I let out a breath, untied his gray gelding and led both our horses up the low rise, followed by Jack and the others.

I heard the Kid and the wounded man talking as I topped the rise, low and matter-of-factly — a cordial conversation between the living and the dying. "Yeah," the Kid said to him, "I heard the Apaches shot ole Jake up pretty bad. Heard the sun burnt him to a cinder before he died." He glanced up at me from beside the dying man with the man's rifle across his knee.

"Yeah, that was a bad way to go," said the failing voice. "Don't know if it was Apaches or scalp hunters, but I thought I'd warn ya. Wouldn't want nothing to happen to ya."

"Thanks," said the Kid. "We already run into Turk and his bunch."

"Damn scalp hunters. There's a bunch you better watch close. I'd hate dying that way." The old man turned his face slightly toward me as I stepped up, then back to the Kid. "Never thought I'd die like *this.*" He tried to laugh but it turned into a deep wheeze. "Reckon there's any chance you'll bury me after while?"

"Not a one." The Kid shook his head

slowly. "Once I kill a man I'm through with him. You oughta know that better than anybody, Al."

"No harm in asking, though, is there . . ." The old man coughed and shuddered.

"I reckon not," the Kid said. He looked off, then back down at the man. "Why'd you do this, Al? If you needed money, I woulda lent you some." The Kid bit his lip and stared at him.

"Yeah, I know —" He winced, rolled slightly onto his side, and I saw the two bullet holes in his back. "— But I hated to ask."

"My goodness!" Rafe Rafferty jerked back a step. "You *just* shot him? In the back? Twice?"

The Kid looked up at Rafferty, started to rise, but the old man clutched his arm. "Don't go blaming Billy here," the old man said. "He done the best he could." He coughed and settled back. "I'd of been no less dead if he'd mailed me a letter first. Right, Kid?" He offered a trembling smile and squeezed the Kid's arm before turning it loose.

The Kid smiled in return, stood up and stepped back jacking a round in the rifle chamber. "That's right, Al. It'd all come to the same turn, I reckon. Just wish you hadn't done it."

"Aw-hell. Think nothing of it." The old man dismissed it with a weak swipe of his hand. "It was just some foolish notion I had. But I want ya to have that rifle, Kid. And be sure keep an eye out for Apaches." He took a shallow breath. "Hope you won't tell nobody how poorly I showed here."

"Don't worry, ole timer," the Kid said. "I won't say nothing." He pointed the rifle one-handed as if handing it back to him; but then, as he took a step, he put a bullet through the old man's forehead and walked away.

"Oh my!" Rafferty jerked his eyes away and shielded them with his hand as a backdraft of blood misted in a cloud of burnt powder. I glanced at Mexican Abe, saw him pin his hat against his chest. A strand of hair flickered in the warm breeze. Beside him, Jack spit and ran his hand across his mouth.

"What was that about Apaches?" Jack asked quietly. I watched his eyes search the distant horizons.

I shrugged, and searched the horizons myself. The Kid turned and walked back to us. "It was them or one of Turk's boys." The Kid nodded down at the dead man. "Said they shot an ole boy named Jake Kelsey. Mighta been Turk, mighta been Mescaleros. Who knows."

The Kid reached down, picked up the old man's hat, opened his bloody coat carefully with two fingers, pulled out a small pistol and stepped back checking it. "Doubt if we've got anything to worry about —" He glanced at the forty-four on Mexican Abe's hip, then turned to Rafferty, looked him up and down and pitched him the gun. "— But here's you some *insurance,* Alias, just in case."

Rafferty caught the pistol, then stepped back holding it away from him as if it were diseased. "You, sir, just *killed,* a *dying* man!" He stared at the Kid with an indignant expression. I looked at Jack and shook my head.

"What would you have done, Alias?" The Kid took a step toward Rafferty with the rifle hanging from one hand and the battered hat in his other. "How long would you have left him laying there with his guts shot up? Huh?" He shoved the dead man's hat down on Rafferty's head, down over the sweat soaked bandanna. Rafferty flinched, but left the hat on. "Would you let him lay there and fry his brains in the sun?"

"*Well* . . . I certainly wouldn't have just —"

"You gotta lot to learn, Alias," the Kid said, stepping past him, cutting him off.

"Now shut up about it. Be glad you got a hat."

Rafferty cowered to the side adjusting the floppy brim as the Kid walked over to his horse. "But we can't leave him here like this. We *must* bury him —" He turned to me. "— Shouldn't we?"

"No shovel," I said quietly, turning, stepping into my stirrups.

"*No shovel?* My God! What kind of people are you?" Rafferty spread his hands, imploring heaven.

Jack spit and said: "The kind that knows *dead* is *dead,* and there ain't nothing gonna change it, shovel or not."

Mexican Abe crossed himself and turned to his horse. Rafferty turned toward Jack and said: "Wait! Please!" as Jack reached for his reins. He started to grab Jack's arm, but Jack shot him a cold stare and his hand stopped.

"*You* stay and bury him," Jack said, mounting up and tugging down his hat brim. "Maybe some Apache, or Turk's men, will show up and help ya."

Rafferty swallowed a lump in his throat, looked down at the dead man and ran a dirty hand across his sweaty beard stubble. "It's not as if I knew him, after all . . ."

"That's the way to look at it," Jack said.

"Just be glad you didn't have him insured."

I shook my head, turned the chestnut stallion and chucked him forward; and we rode away in silence hearing only the wind as it stirred, raising a low swirl of sand before us.

I saw an immediate change in the Kid after he shot the old undertaker. He turned as high strung and as edgy as I'd ever seen him; and as soon as we'd ridden a few hundred yards away from the low rise, just as it appeared he was ready to explode, he gigged his gray gelding ahead and spun it in a wide circle. He raced around, whooping, yelling in Spanish, waving his hat in the air and raising a cloud of dust. "For God's sake," Rafferty said, sidling up beside Jack and me, "is he celebrating killing the old man?"

"Naw," I said, watching the Kid work the killing out of his system on the wide desert floor. "He's just getting it straight in his mind." I glanced at Jack, then Rafferty. "It's a hard thing when the people you know are the ones trying to take ya down."

"Yeah," said Jack, "and it looks like everybody around here knows the Kid. That's a lot of guns pointing at ya."

"But my goodness, gentlemen." Rafferty tugged his reins to keep his roan in check.

"The young man is a desperado. A law breaker, a killer. People like that generally get what they deserve, don't they? It says right in the book —"

"Shove your book, Alias," Jack said. "Nobody made ya come along." He and I shot each other a glance and chucked our horses forward. Mexican Abe caught up to Rafferty, leading the mule; and when they caught up to us we had joined the Kid at the edge of a broad flatland of white sand.

"You doing alright, Kid?" I'd said as we rode up.

He laughed, but it was a dry tight laugh: "*Hell* yes! Twice I shot him! *Twice!* Before he even knew what hit him. Did you see it?" I saw sweat streaking down his face as he looked back and forth between us. We didn't answer. After a second he ran a sleeve across his forehead beneath his sombrero and said: "Well, maybe I ain't doing so good after all."

"I know, Kid," I said; and when Abe and Rafferty caught up to us we rode on in silence through cholla cactus, scrub juniper and scraggly low slung pinon that grew more and more sparse in the east, and ahead of us, west, the endless swells of white crystal sand.

The rest of the day the Kid grew more

and more surly and quiet and had distanced himself from the rest of us. That night while he and Rafferty took their turn filling canteens from a trickle of water coming down from the foothills, Abe, Jack, and I made coffee, heated some beans and jerked beef, and drew around a low fire.

"Poor Beely," Abe said in a quiet voice. "Deep down, I think his heart is right, but I fear he has gone too far to ever change what will become of him." He shrugged: "I don't think his luck is so good. And that is too bad, because if a man's heart is right and he is honest, good luck should follow him, no?"

"I haven't always found that to be the case, amigo," I said. "And I reckon honesty is judged different by each of us. Yours is yours, mine is mine." I sipped hot coffee and saw Jack nod his head in agreement. "As Rafferty would say, *it's all relevant.*"

"Is that why they call you Abraham Lincoln —" Jack tore off a strip of jerky with his teeth. "Because you're so honest?"

"No, señor. As I told Señor Beatty. I got in trouble in El Paso and I told a little lie. I should not have done it but I told the sheriff my name was Abraham Lincoln."

Jack swallowed and nodded again. "Another Alias. What kind of trouble?"

161

"They accused me of stealing something."

Jack grinned: "Is that a fact? Well, I guess we all go astray now and then."

"Oh, but I did not do it."

"Of course not," Jack chuckled, "nobody ever does. How long did you go to jail?"

"I did not go to jail, señor. Once they saw I was innocent they let me go. I kept the name, but I have lied about nothing since then."

"So now good luck follows you?" I smiled slightly. "Because you're honest and your heart is right?"

"Si. And I try to do good things. That is why I will help you take away the devil stallion. The beast is evil, and when he is gone my people will be better off." He crossed himself quickly. "They have suffered much because of the contesa and her devil stallion." Abe looked away for a second and shook his head. "She thinks the stallion is the key to finding the lost oro."

"The what?" Jack's eyebrows arched slightly. So did mine.

"The gold, señors. The devil's oro. The lost gold of Silver Basin? Surely you know of it?"

Jack raised up slightly, cleared his throat, and scooted over beside Abe. I edged closer to the fire straight across from him. "There's gold around there? The shiny stuff you dig up out of the ground?" I thought about the deed to land folded snugly in my money belt as I shot Jack a quick glance.

"No, señors. It is the gold of the conquistadors who pillaged the land of my ancestors and brought such misery —"

Jack tossed a hand. "We know all that. What about the —"

"Come on, Jack, show some manners." I cleared my throat and leaned closer to the fire. "Go on, Abe."

He shrugged and sipped his coffee. "It is said that the invaders buried tons of golden objects stolen from across Mejico. Buried them somewhere in Silver Basin." His eyes glittered in the firelight, moving back and forth slowly between Jack and me. "And it is said that the place is cursed . . . and it is true —"

"Imagine that." Jack smiled, cutting him off. I saw he was about to dismiss the story as one more campfire yarn; but I owned land there, and anything that affected its value was of interest to me. Maybe I wouldn't be so quick to turn over the deed for fifty thousand. I still owed the contesa her jewels, but nothing said I had to sell her back the land.

"So . . . Abe." I tried to sound casual.

"Tell me about the contesa? What do you know about her?"

"Not so much, except that she is evil." Abe's voice dropped low. "She is a bruja, señors." He looked back and forth between us with searching eyes. He crossed himself quickly again.

"Oh," I nodded, "a *bruja.*" I cocked an eye to Jack without the slightest idea what Abe was talking about.

Jack spread his hands. "You know . . . a *brew-ha.* It's like a holy-roller, only they have more fun."

"Oh no, señors!" Abe shook his head with a serious expression. "She is a Bruja —"

"She's a witch," said the Kid, walking up with the canteens over his shoulder. "I've heard them stories myself." His expression was grim, and he pitched us each a canteen. "It's all bull. Just like the legend of the lost gold mine." He sat down and cut a piece of jerked meat. "Nobody knows much about the contesa, so they make her out to be a witch. Nobody know *nothing* about Crazy Mangelo, so they make him out to be a bad-ass killer." The Kid leaned down for a coffee cup. "Everything's makeup and superstition down here. Look at me. If I did everything they said I done, I'd have to be a hundred years old."

"Oh no, señor Beely, it is not the *lost mine,* it is the lost *oro.* Gold objects that rightfully belonged to my people. But it is true about the contesa and it is true about Mangelo Sontag." He looked the Kid up and down. "Of course, only you can say what is true about you. I am not your judge."

"Well, that's real generous of you, amigo," the Kid said with a trace of sarcasm. "I feel better knowing it." He poured a cup of coffee and walked away into the darkness.

Abe looked at me and shrugged. I said in a low voice: "Don't worry. He's just got a lot on his mind. Now what about the gold? What about the contesa being a witch?"

"There is gold, señors. I know there is. And the stallion Morcillo is the key to finding it. It has been said for many generations that Cortez's stallion will lead someone to the golden objects and they will be returned to my people."

"Cortez's stallion?" I shot Jack a glance, feeling the excitement about the treasure starting to ebb. "That would be one truly *old* horse." I grinned and settled back. "Maybe we better forget this little fireside chat. "I won't be able to sleep — thinking about witches and whatnot."

"I know you mock, señor . . . but it is true. The contesa is a witch."

165

"In what way?" I raised my hat and ran back over my hair.

"They say she is very powerful. That she has come back from the dead to rule the living and to walk this earth." He crossed himself."

"Now that's a *long* walk," I said, dropping my hat back on and leaning back against my saddle on the ground.

"And a hell of lot to *rule,*" said Jack.

"Aw, señors," Abe said, waving a finger back and forth. "You know so little about the ways of my people. What is real to them, is *real.* It doesn't matter if it is real to you. To them . . . it is real. And if you are around them it *becomes* real to you."

"Abe, Abe," I chuckled beneath my hat. "How you do carry on."

For the next two days as we traveled, a cloud of brooding tension seemed to hover about the Kid until on the third morning when he'd ridden ahead of us and sat waiting in the skyline atop a rise of sand, I rode on up to him before the others and said: "Kid. I know you gotta lot bothering you. Wanta talk about it some?"

He shook his head: "Naw. Ain't much use in it. What's done is done, I reckon. Now I have to figure what's next." He sat quietly for a full minute, then looked off and nodded toward the far horizon. "I knew that ole undertaker. Knew him better than I know you. See what I mean about the Ring? They pulled the strings, that ole undertaker just pulled the trigger." He waited a second and smiled a weary smile: "Glad I've got no relatives, or they'd be gunning for me next."

"You're right, Kid. And it's gonna get worse for ya before it gets any better. This is as good a place as any to cut out for the border. Abe can lead us from here."

"Abe couldn't lead a fly to a bear's ass."

"Thought you didn't know him?"

"I don't, but he seems a little weak in the stool, with his *bruja* talk, and his religious crap. I reckon on riding in with ya, if you'll have me along."

"Hell, Kid, that goes without saying. "You're welcome along anywhere we go."

"Good." He grinned. "Then I'll go back to Missouri with ya, ride with you and the Youngers?"

A silence passed as I just looked at him, not knowing what to say. I hated turning him down, but I knew it would never work. I'd just started to say something along that line when he held up a hand, chuckled and said: "Forget it. I didn't mean to put you on such a spot there, mi amigo."

"Sorry, Kid."

We watched as Rafferty, Abe, and Jack grew closer, rising up from a low swirl of dust in the wavering heat. I turned back toward him and said: "But you *could* give it a year or two down in Old Mex. A lot of things can settle down once you're away from here awhile."

"It ain't my style down there." He was silent for a second then said: "I *had* to shoot him in the back. You saw that, didn't you?"

"You don't have to explain nothing to me, Kid. Even *he* didn't hold it against ya. He *was* out to kill ya after all." I nodded south across the desert. "So, you come on with us, and when we head back, you can split down to Old Mex, hunh?"

"We'll have to wait and see about the Old Mex part. I don't plan nothing that far ahead."

I smiled. "Sure, Kid."

We waited in silence until Rafferty and Abe rode up to us, then turned our horses on across the sand. "What's over in Silver Basin?" Rafferty asked, gazing in both directions as if searching for a sign. "I mean . . . does it get any better than *this*?" We drew our horses down and looked at him. I could tell he'd been having second thoughts since the Kid killed the ole undertaker.

168

"What could be any better than this?" The Kid grinned at Rafferty. "Thinking about turning back?"

"Well, I have to admit, this isn't quite what I had in mind."

"Then why'd you come along?" I looked him up and down.

"I'm not sure." He shrugged. "The adventure of it, I suppose. But I'm no gunman." Rafferty rolled a hand. "Sure, I like a little excitement, a game of chance now and then. But all this shooting and killing, and leaving a dead man in the desert." He shook his head. "Gentlemen, I'm not sure I'm cut out for it."

"Could've fooled us," Jack said. He grinned: "Ain't much like that paper novel, is it?" He sat watching Rafferty with his wrists crossed on his saddlehorn.

Rafferty's face reddened. "I certainly don't want to get caught up in some legal tangle over shooting someone, or end up *getting* shot . . . or *hung* even."

"You sure waited long enough figuring it out," I said. "And you're a bit far-out to turn back now."

"Then what should I do?" He looked from one of us to the other until the Kid laughed and said: "Ride it out, Cowboy."

"Come on with us, Alias," Jack said. "You

169

know you want to. You're just wanting somebody to talk you into it. And we won't."

"Did I mention there might be whores and gambling in Silver Basin?" the Kid said. Mexican Abe had already started on without us.

Rafferty rubbed his dusty chin with a concerned look, as if we were handing him the reins to a wildcat. "Yes, well . . . perhaps you're right. I'd love to see the place, the people, their customs —"

"I bet ya would." The Kid grinned and turned his horse. Jack and I did the same. "They won't be buying any insurance over there, Alias," I called back; and when we'd ridden a few yards, I said to Jack and the Kid under my breath: "He's just an outlaw in the making, ain't he."

Jack grinned: "Selling insurance is as good a way to start as any, I reckon. If I was him I'd be looking to do anything else I could find, just to keep from blowing my head off."

"I don't believe he really sells insurance," I said in a hushed voice. "*Life* insurance? Who ever heard of such a thing? Everybody dies. That's like insuring that the rain won't fall. Naw, I believe it's something *he* came up with to keep himself in spending money. "Some people will do anything, huh?"

170

"Yeah," Jack said, and he smiled. But I saw a bemused look on his face as we turned our horses.

"Jack, you didn't fall for that speel, did you?" But he didn't answer.

Before us, the desert swirled in dazzling sunlight as our horses cantered silently across sand too fine to strike a hoofprint.

If there was any credence to Abe's story of *seeing* the wind, or any understanding of Rafferty's uncertainty, I felt it there in the dry warm wind and the vast, unending emptiness of the land. We were all nothing more than tiny mortal creatures crawling through the swirl of a blazing universe — invisible as the wind from any great distance, and from one level of uncertainty to the next, I thought, as uninsurable as the toss of dice.

CHAPTER 8

"I'm glad the Kid's riding in with us," I said to Jack as we pressed on through the wavering sunlight across a rolling carpet of fine sparkling sand. Abe was now in the lead, followed by Jack and me, then the Kid and Rafferty farther back — Rafferty leading the mule. "It'll give him time to think things out. Maybe catch his breath for awhile —"

"I see what you're doing." Jack glanced at me, then away. "You're trying to get the Kid to change his ways, only it ain't gonna work, no more than you teach a rattlesnake to chew tobacco."

I shook my head: "Why do you have it in your head that the Kid is destined for some terrible end? Don't you believe there's a chance he could mend his ways?"

"No," he said flatly, "and neither do you, if you'd be honest about it. He's an outlaw, just like us — *worse* than us. He's an outlaw even by *outlaw* standards. Too damned wild to go down by any peaceable means." Jack reined up slightly and faced me. "Hell, I like the Kid, you know that. I'd do anything to help him off this road if he wanted off . . . but he don't. He's on it till it stops. We all are."

"Oh? I don't know about that. I can see a day coming when I might settle down, change my ways, live a tamer life . . ."

"Do you? Do you really see it?"

"Yeah, I do." I nodded firmly. "Damned right I do. I can see a little house someday, a wife . . . maybe even a job."

"Right." Jack chuckled. "And I might someday run for public office."

"I mean it, Jack. I can see an end to this outlawing, someday."

"Truthfully?"

"Yep, you bet."

"Good then. That just proves my point about the Kid."

"How's that?"

"Because you can *see* a good end to it — the Kid *can't.*"

"How can you say what he sees or don't see —"

"I just know," Jack said. "Ask him sometimes." He gigged his horse ahead.

And we rode in a line, up and down across rises of sand until after two hours the land flattened for a ways and we drew our animals abreast. We let them rest as they walked, winding themselves down and shaking out their mane.

For a time, I caught myself gazing all about us at the vast wavering desert, until I realized what a forlorn feeling it was causing inside me, as if all that ever was had fallen off behind us and left us nothing but the stark void ahead. Here, in the wake of ancient conquistadors, on a shifting carpet of living earth, I felt abandoned somehow, given to a foreboding that I imagined had haunted all others who'd passed this way before.

I glanced at the Kid beside me and saw a distant look in his eyes. "*This* is where you've lived since Cimmaron?" I fanned an arm about us, taking in the land.

"No," he said without facing me. "This is just my backyard." Then he glanced around, shook his head and smiled.

I looked across at Abe and saw that his eyes were hollow, fixed straight ahead on some imaginary horizon, as if through some inborn wisdom he'd learned to give himself up to the overwhelming spirit of this land, and to realize the insignificance of his own. When the stretch of flatland once more began to rise and fall beneath us, we fell back into a line, this time with me in the lead. My stallion raised his head into the warm wind, nickered and probed the air as he high-stepped sideways down a swell of sand. I drew the reins slightly. "There's no mustangs around here," I said over my shoulder to Jack and Abe.

"No, señor," Abe said above my stallion's low nickering. "But there could be Apache nearby. "They may grow bolder . . . and want to see what we have."

Hearing Abe's words, Rafferty shoved up the brim on his floppy hat, and drew closer beside Jack as Jack drew his rifle and propped it on his thigh. I also drew my rifle, and glanced down at my shirt, making sure the money belt was well covered. The Kid smiled and said: "No need to worry. We could see them as well as they could see us." He gigged his horse and jumped ahead of us. "If they are around, they might look us over, but they'll think twice before taking us on."

"What in God's name would they be doing in a place like this?"

"It is their land, señores," said Mexican Abe.

I checked my stallion back, leading the mule, and followed the Kid with Jack and Rafferty beside me scanning the sand flats.

Abe pulled ahead.

In less than an hour, we rode into dust devils that stung our eyes, whipped our horses' manes, and tugged at our clothes and hats. We drew bandannas over our faces and pressed on from one whirling cloud to the next, our horses arching their necks against the stinging sand.

Finally we felt the sand grow more and more firm beneath us, and the winds began to dissipate. Ahead, we began to see the crests of mountains rise slowly out of the waves of silver dust, and we pressed on until the wind had died altogether. Except to walk our horses from time to time, we didn't stop until we felt the land slope upwards and hold for more than a mile; and we saw the bulge of rolling foothills on the near horizon.

It was evening when we reached them and the air had began to cool. We walked our animals the last mile up among spills of large rock and dropped to the ground in a clearing surrounded sparsely by scrub juniper and mesquite bushes. Above the sand-flats the air felt cooler, yet below, behind us, dust devils still danced in the hot air on the distant valley floor.

We chewed silently on dried shank, and sipped water from our canteens, and when we'd rested enough to speak, Jack said to me: "I don't know about you, but I'd rather ride back through Old Mex and swim back to Texas before crossing here again. This is the most god-awful, god-forsaken land the devil ever cut off of hell."

Abe crossed himself. "Please do not blaspheme, señor. Not here. Not this close to the contesa and her diablo caballa."

The Kid glanced at Abe, shook his head and said: "Have you spent your whole life afraid the sky's gonna fall?"

"I fear nothing," Abe said. "I have lived an honest humble life. For me there is nothing to fear. It is those whose spirits are not at peace who fear —"

"Yeah, yeah," the Kid cut him off. "Go rattle some beads or something."

Maybe Abe's fear and superstition played a part in it, but beyond that, there was a crushing desolation haunting the sand-flats. Now that we were past it, it felt as if we had overcome a great evil that lay waiting for our return. The land before us lay calm and peaceful, yet something about the valley seemed to cast a pall over our spirits, an omen of something that lay ahead.

"Abe," I said quietly. "Don't take this the wrong way, but the Kid's right, you do have a way of depressing a-body. Could you brighten up just a little? Enough that we don't feel like a big hand is gonna drop out of the sky and squash our guts out?"

Jack chuckled, threw back a shot of water, swished it, and squirted it out on the ground. "Amen."

"Si," Abe said. "I will try."

I squinted at the evening sun and down along the miles of rambling foothills. "So, I suppose we'll be at the Cortez spread by tomorrow evening?"

"Before then," the Kid said, "if we leave here early and make good time."

"I will wait for you in the foothills," said Abe. "I will not go near the contesa."

"What about you, Alias," I asked Rafferty. "You gonna take a chance and ride in with us?" I grinned: "If anybody tries to hex ya, we'll light out most pronto, I promise."

Abe ignored my teasing him. "I will keep enough food from our supplies. There should still be enough run off water in the rock basins. I will be alright."

Rafferty turned and stared at Abe from beneath his sagging hat brim. "What about the Mescaleros? What about the scalp hunters? You'd rather stay out here and take your chances with either of them, than ride into the Cortez spread?"

"Si. The Apache and the scalp hunters

only kill me." He crossed himself and gazed away. "There are worse things than dying, Señor."

We camped there for the night, each of us weary and spent from the day's ride. When we drew around a small fire, we sipped coffee and let the weariness of the day settle inside us. After awhile, Rafferty let out a long breath and said: "So . . . this is how you gentlemen live all the time . . ."

"Yeah," the Kid laughed, "what time we ain't stealing cattle or robbing banks, right amigos?"

"Kid!" I lowered my voice. "That ain't no way to make jokes. People who don't know better might think you mean it."

The Kid ran a finger beneath his nose, glanced at Abe and Rafferty and said: "Sorry. I *was* only funning."

"I should hope so," Rafferty said. He shook his head slowly watching the low flames. "Bank robbery . . . now that's a perfectly stupid thing to do. How much intelligence does it take to stick a gun in someone's face and yell threats at them."

"Oh, I don't know," I said, feeling a bit indignant. "I can see where it takes a certain —"

"You're right," Jack said to Rafferty, cutting me off. "No ill gotten gains takes much —"

"Oh, gentlemen," Rafferty cut in, smiling. "I have nothing against ill gotten gains. I'm simply saying armed robbery is a sucker's game. A smart robber can steal a bank blind, live like a king . . . and never fear the hangman."

I cocked an eye, so did Jack. "How's that?" We spoke in almost perfect unison.

"*Embezzlement,* gentlemen." Rafferty tapped his forehead with a dirty finger. "The *thinking man's* crime. Work for a bank, get to a position of trust, then nip a little here, a little there. Get up a little higher . . . manipulate stocks, bonds, what-have-you. If they *ever* catch you at all, it's usually after you've made some powerful friends, political contacts. At most, you get a slap on the hands — certainly no hangman's noose."

We sat in silence, staring at him for what seemed like the longest time, until I finally cleared my throat and said: "Yeah, but that requires schooling, refinement, social standing. And if I had all that, I wouldn't rob a bank anyway." Rafferty shot me a curious gaze, and I added quickly: "I mean, if I robbed banks in the first place, which I *don't.*"

"What he means is —" Jack jumped in to

help me. "—That's damned deceitful, gaining people's trust so you can steal their money." He shook his head. "No, if I was gonna rob banks — which I *ain't,* of course — I'd feel better just going in and doing it straight up like a robber oughta. Seems more honest somehow."

The Kid threw back his cup, then let out a coffee hiss and said to Rafferty: "Know any slick easy ways to steal cattle — I'm all ears."

"In fact, I do." Rafferty smiled. "You steal them on paper. Get in good with a government agent who requisitions large numbers of beeves for . . . say, the military, the Indian reservations, that sort of thing —"

"Rafferty," I said. "Why don't you save your breath. Those are *rich boy's* crimes. Hell, we're all just day to day —" I stopped myself from saying *outlaws.* "— Working boys," I said instead, sliding Jack a glance.

"Yes, but those are the people making the big money." Rafferty laughed. "The pen is, *indeed,* mightier than the sixgun."

"I'm starting to wonder about you, Rafferty," I said, leaning back and finishing my coffee.

The Kid chuckled: "I ain't. I knew ole Alias here was a grifting snake, first time I laid eyes on him."

Rafferty raised both of his dirty hands slightly: "Just making fireside chat, gentlemen . . . that's all."

I saw the look of shame and disappointment on Abe's face as I stretched back on my blanket for the night.

The next day we followed a winding trail up and down through sandstone, scrub trees and cactus until finally coming to a stop at a sharp rim above a wide valley. Since Abe was going to be waiting for us, I told him the truth about my owning the land around Little Sand Hole, rather than have him thinking I was there to take away Morcillo the stallion. When I told him he only shrugged and made no comment. But the Kid chuckled and said to him: "So, if this was some religious expedition for you, looks like you made the trip for nothing."

"Why would anybody in their right mind want to own land here?" Rafferty asked me, gazing all around. I didn't answer.

At the rim overlooking the valley, Abe rose in his saddle, pointed his hand to the right end of the valley and drew it slowly to the left. "Little Sand Hole starts there, señores, and goes almost to there." His hand stopped a little ways past the halfway point of the valley floor. "Your land must be somewhere up the other side of the valley. Everything from here south belongs to the contesa."

Jack chuckled. "Stopping where, at China?"

I took out my deed and spread it across my lap. A breeze licked at the edge of it as I tried to make sense of the boundary description. It might just as well have been written in Latin. I cleared my throat and read: "At a point starting at the north westerly edge of a place known as Finger Rock and extending for a distance of two and three-quarter miles southwest to a location known as 'Dead Man's Caverns . . .'"

"I like this already," Jack said, shaking his head.

Abe looked surprised. "Your land includes Dead Man's Cavern?"

"So it says." I reached a hand up under my hat and scratched my head. "Do you know where that's at?"

"Si!" Abe turned in his saddle facing me. It used to belong to the Cortez family. I can not imagine anyone ever taking it from them. Many think the lost oro is hidden there."

"Well, I reckon ole Quick Quintan must've had his way for awhile," the Kid said. He grinned, pointed a finger at me and clicked his thumb up and down.

I shrugged: "Maybe that's why the con-tesa was so interested in getting the land. Probably feels like it rightfully belongs to her."

Abe gazed out across the valley nodding his head. "And I agree with her. She should own it. It is a place of evil. Even the Apache do not go there. I am only sorry that you did not come to take away the devil stal-lion."

I grinned, and said to the Kid: "Of all the luck. I own land where a man doesn't have to wake up to a scalping party . . ." I stood in my stirrups and gazed across the valley. "Where is the Cortez spread from here?"

"Don't know," said the Kid. "I've never been all the way there."

"I have." Abe pointed southwest into a swirl of sparkling sunlight. "There is a bend in the valley, out there. Around it you will find the Cortez hacienda. It is a fortress, señor. I will cross the valley with you, but I will go no closer."

I gazed long in both directions, then asked: "What about Finger Rock?"

"Never heard of it," said the Kid. I looked at Abe, saw a puzzled look on his face. "Nor have I," he said.

We winded down across the valley and up into a hill of sandstone and rock overhang.

After setting Abe up with the remainder of our supplies, we took one canteen of water each and rode down along the edge of the valley. I checked the jewels in the money-belt once more before riding off. I raised the handkerchief close to my face, caught the faintest lingering scent of the contesa, then folded it and put it in my shirt pocket. The Kid saw me do it, but only smiled and looked away.

According to Abe, we would follow the lower trail seven miles and turn into a wide pass through the hills. My mind lingered briefly on the scent of the contesa; but I pushed it away. After all I'd heard and unknowingly been a part of, I would take care of business as soon as I arrived and be gone before our dust settled.

By mid afternoon we made the turn and followed a trail of hoofprints up a long low rise for two more miles. At the top of the low rise, we looked down at a high wall of carved sandstone that blocked a wide pass into the valley below. Abe was right about the Cortez spread; the wall surrounded a sprawling fortress of a structure that looked as ancient as the mountains themselves.

We heard music drifting toward us from beyond the walls, and the Kid spun his horse and said: "See how it is? Everywhere

I go there's a party waiting." His face lit up like a schoolboy's.

An accordion whined in the air; and Rafferty stepped his horse forward and gazed at the walls with a look of relief. The tails of his bandanna hung down his neck beneath his hat brim. One of his shirtsleeves was ripped at the shoulder. I watched him and shook my head. A heel was missing from one of his Wellington boots.

"See, there," I said quietly to Jack as the others filed past us to the trail down toward the compound. "The Kid's in better spirits already. You might be surprised what a few days with us can do to change his outlook. A few days away from O'Folliard and the rest of them . . . away from all the violence, seeing us set a good example . . . a more genteel way of dealing with folks. Hell, he could develop a whole new —"

"Why don't you let up?" Jack stared at me. "I coulda stayed in Missouri and gone to a *tent meeting,* if I wanted to hear all that crap."

"Alls I'm saying is it wouldn't hurt us to set a good example for the boy. Show him there's a better way to live, is all."

"I will if you will." Jack spit a stream of tobacco and ran his hand across his mouth. "But you first," he added. "I'm gonna get me a bottle and spin down in it."

We rode down to the wide open doors of the compound, the music stronger, our spirits lifting after the long ride. But just as we started through the gates, two uniformed guards stepped out before us, one on either side with rifles pointed toward us. We reined back, and I raised a hand in a show of peace. "Here's something *else* that seems to happen everywhere I go," said the Kid.

"Who are you people?" One of the guards demanded in Spanish. "What are you doing here?" He poked the rifle barrel at us; my chestnut stallion nearly reared.

"Easy now," I said, righting my horse. I caught a glimpse of the Kid's hand go to his gun butt. "That's not the way to handle this, Kid." He eased his hand away, then I heard him rattle off something in Spanish and nod toward me. The guards eased back a step, and I said: "I'm here to see the contesa." "I'm Mister Beatty . . . James Beatty."

The guards stepped back quickly, lowering their rifles. "Apprendito," said one. "You must excuse us, Señor Beatty. These are troubled times —"

"Si," I said. "I know. But I think the contesa will want to see me."

"Of course! Of course," he said, turning, gesturing us inside with his free hand as the other trotted out of our way. "Por favor by all means. Please come in. I will take you to her straightaway. She has been expecting you."

I shot Jack a smug grin: "So nice to feel welcome. See what I mean?" Jack only grunted.

Once we passed through the open gates, we heard more clearly the sound of music and laughter; and through the crowd, I heard a commotion and saw men race back and forth, barefoot in the dust, scrambling and yelling. Then a woman screamed as the crowd parted, and I saw Morcillo the stallion rear up before the men, pawing out at them with his hoofs. The men jumped back from him, one even dropping and rolling through the dust as the stallion lunged at him.

"Close the gates, quickly!" one of the guards yelled to the other. From thirty yards away Morcillo broke into a run toward us, crashing through a vendor's fruit stand, ripping down a long row of hanging flowers. Pedals flew. Rafferty and the Kid veered their horse away from the gates. Jack's gelding spun in a circle. I dropped from my saddle and slapped my chestnut stallion on the rump, moving him, then spread my arms before Morcillo as he neared. Behind me I heard the gates creak, closing; and from among the men a voice yelled: "Run . . . run away!"

I stood crouched slightly, ready to bolt away at the last second if I needed to. But Morcillo slid down on his haunches in a spray of dust, then reared up, snorting through flared nostrils, and pawed down at me. I jumped a step to the side and snatched up the lead rope hanging from his neck and snapping like a whip in the dust as he spun back and forth.

"He will keel you!" a voice screamed. Morcillo swung toward me. I gathered the lead rope snug, moving with the stallion until I had a firm hold close to his neck. Then as he reared again, I rose up with him, leaning against his neck, hanging on, and planted my boots firmly in the dirt as they touched back down.

"Easy, big feller." I held the lead tight and against his neck, and ran my free hand up onto his muzzled, pulling down firmly as he thrashed his head back and forth. Twice he banged his muzzle into my chest, but I gave with the blows, and the third time he did not hit as hard, and I felt him settle. He rooted his muzzle against my chest, pushing me back, nipping, but settling more as I eased my hand along up his muzzle. "That's it, boy, easy," I said again, letting down with him as if we both worked off the same set of nerves and sinew.

Quick as a snake, I slacked the lead rope, slid it up high behind his ears, ran it down along his jaw, snapped a backing hitch in it, looped his muzzle, and haltered him before he knew it. I caught a glimpse of Jack shaking his head as the men in white peasant clothes moved toward us cautiously. "I can see them writing it on your tombstone someday —" Jack ran a finger through the air. "— *He never thought a horse would kill him.*"

I let out a breath, keeping a firm hold on the rope beneath Morcillo's chin as he struggled gently, now subdued but nipping at my shirt. And my shirt grew wet from him. "They've got him so spooked they can't handle him," I said quietly; and as soon as I said 'they' I thought of the *they* the Kid had spoke of, and of the same *they* that Jack had said, *fanned all fires.*

I shot the Kid and Rafferty a quick glance. Rafferty stared, bug-eyed with fear. The Kid spread a bucktoothed grin as the men came running up, sliding to a halt a safe distance away, barefoot and frightened. I heard Jack chuckle: "You sure know how to make an entrance. I'll give you that."

"Señor," said the closest man, slipping from beneath his straw sombrero, "nosotros testigo un milagro!" He swung a thin and shaky hand across the others. "We witness a miracle . . . a miracle! No one can handle Morcillo except the contesa herself. We have prayed for the day —"

"He's just got ya'll drawn to a standoff," I said, feeling my face redden. All across the wide courtyard, people stood staring as if in awe. The yard turned silent save for the buzz of a large fly and the click of boot heels stepping through the crowd.

"Out of my way!" a voice barked, and a powerfully built man in a tan uniform shoved his way through the crowd. "I will show you how to deal with this beast!" I heard what I thought was a German accent. His face was lit red; his short cropped yellow hair stood up like bristles on an angry dog. I saw a long wooden club swing out at Morcillo, and I jerked the stallion away just in time.

His swing missed and he almost fell from the force of it. "How dare you interfere!" he shouted, drawing back for another swing. I could not tell if it was intended for Morcillo or me. So I pulled the stallion away, still holding the reins; and I caught the man's arm while it was still high in the air, and shoved him back.

Morcillo thrashed against me. "Easy, boy!" I tried to hold his reins and steady him as the man jumped toward me, cursing. He drew back the long club and started to swing it again, closer to me; but this time he stopped when the barrel of my cocked forty-four pressed against his sweaty brow. My other hand struggled with Morcillo's reins.

"I will break you in half!" he hissed through clenched teeth.

I nudged the barrel. "Not without a forehead, you won't. Now drop it! You horse beating son-of-a-bitch."

"Shoot him," the Kid yelled, "and I'll shoot him again before he hits the ground!" I heard his pistol cock behind me. The man stood seething, not giving an inch.

"There's my partner," Jack said, "Setting a *good example.*"

"Shut up, Jack!"

I thought sure I'd have to shoot the man. But then the crowd parted wide and another man in a tan uniform stepped forward and said: "That will be all, Herr Corporal. Release this man and the stallion at once."

Release me? I shot him a glance, then back to the corporal, as he took a step back, still boiling, under control but just barely. "I will see to you another time, you —"

"That *will* be all, corporal!" the other man's voice boomed. "Return to your post at once." Then he rattled something in German, and the corporal smiled — if you could call it a smile. He stepped back, held the long club by each end and strained down on it until it snapped, then dropped it at my feet. I tried not to look impressed as I eased down my forty-four, uncocked it, and spun it into my holster. The corporal turned and walked away.

"I trust you have an explanation for your actions," said the remaining man in the tan uniform.

"None that I care to discuss," I said, with a snap. I stared at him. "Who the hell are you? Where's the contesa?"

"I am Colonel Frothe," he said in a haughty tone. "And the young man who was about to kill you is one of my military advisors to the contesa's liberation forces. Now, who — as you say — *the hell,* are you? And what are you doing here?"

About to kill me? Liberation forces? I started to ask what the hell was going on, but I stopped myself. Instead, I said: "I'm Beatty . . . James Beatty. These men are with me. I'm here to see the contesa on a matter of business."

"I'm afraid that is impossible. The contesa is indisposed —"

"Horse whackle," I said. "The guard at the gate just said she's been expecting me —"

"He is an ignorant peon who knows nothing! I say who can and cannot see the contesa." He pounded a broad hand on his chest. Medals bounced on his tunic and glittered in the sunlight.

"Now let's not keep on like this till one of us gets our feelings hurt," I said in a calm tone. Morcillo tugged on the reins, nudging his warm muzzle against my chest as I raised the forty-four from my holster again, bending my elbow, pointing the barrel straight up, cocking the hammer at shoulder level. The crowd spread away.

I heard Jack chuckle behind me and say: "Pay attention here, Kid. He's fixin to show you a more *genteel* way of dealing with folks."

From across the dirt courtyard, the sound of heavy boots pounded the earth.

CHAPTER 9

Jack, Rafferty and the Kid had slipped quickly from their saddles by the time I saw the contesa step out onto a balcony high above us on the other side of the courtyard. The Kid had pulled back both hammers on the ten gauge; and he said: "Come to Daddy!" to the seven tan uniforms spreading out before us ten feet away. I heard Jack lever up a round in his rifle. The two of them had stepped up, one on each side of me. Rafferty was somewhere behind us. The tan uniforms braced themselves and leveled their rifles toward us.

"Now, Herr Beatty," said Colonel Frothe, "your words and actions have brought about your —"

"Stop this!" I heard the contesa shout from the balcony; but I dared not take my eyes off the tan uniforms. All seven of them could've come from the same litter. Each had blonde short cropped hair, wide shoulders, and a wet sneer on their lips. They wore knee-high black boots. Their uniforms were stained dark with sweat. "Colonel! Stop this at once. I know this man. I have been expecting him!" Beside me, Morcillo tugged the reins, raised his nose in the air and sniffed toward the sound of her voice.

"These men are riff-raff," the colonel shouted back to her without taking his eyes from me. "It is obvious from their appearance and manners. We can*not* have such men around us."

I still had my pistol up and cocked at shoulder level; but I lowered it slowly until it pointed straight at the colonel's face. "They'll get *us,* Colonel," I said. "But they'll be complaining tomorrow about having to bury your bloody ass."

His face swelled red. "Colonel," the contesa yelled again. "This man brings support for our cause. He is valuable to us. *Valuable to them?* I glanced quickly up at her, then back to the seven tense and sweaty faces.

"It's decision time, *Frothe,*" I said. "We ain't got all day." Morcillo tugged again on the reins in my hand.

The Kid stepped forward with the shotgun raised to his shoulder. I could've sworn he was humming something under his breath.

"Stand down as you were, men!" Frothe

barked at the seven bristled blonde heads, and they snapped their rifles up and held them at port arms. They looked disappointed; I felt relieved. I raised my pistol back up, held it shoulder level and uncocked it. The Kid was still braced, with the ten gauge pointed.

"Kid?" I spoke quietly. "Okay, Kid? Let it down, now." But he still stood ready to crank out a round. The men shot Frothe a nervous glance.

"C'mon, Kid, damn it," Jack said. "You can shoot a couple of 'em later on. I wanta get a drink."

I watched him lower the shotgun slowly, uncock it and let out a breath. "Them's some snappy uniforms," he said to the men, grinning. Behind us, I heard Rafferty let out a faint sigh, as if he'd just relieved himself after a long wait.

The riflemen followed us, their weapons still at port arms, half circling us as I led Morcillo into a large barn and stabled him. Then we led our horses across the courtyard and hitched them outside a sprawling hacienda. I glanced up, saw the contesa turn and walk back inside from the balcony, and she stood waiting in the center of a large room when we walked in. Frothe stepped around and stood half between her and me until she said: "That will be all, Colonel Frothe. Take your men and leave."

"But, mine Contesa. Surely you see the manner of men these are. I must *insist* on leaving guards here to —"

"I have entrusted Mister Beatty with something most precious to me, and he has not disappointed me," she said. Her dark eyes looked into mine, and she smiled slightly. "Go now," she said to Frothe, still smiling at me. "Everything will be fine here."

When they'd filed out the door, I turned to the contesa with my hat hanging from my hand. "Sorry for the disturbance," I said. "The guard at the gate said you'd been expecting me. I came to bring you the —"

"Si." She cut me off. "I have been expecting you. You must overlook Colonel Frothe and his men. They are here to train and direct my freedom fighters. But sometimes he forgets his position."

"Freedom fighters? Freeing who? I had no idea you were a part of anything like that." I glanced at Jack and the others; Jack rolled his eyes slightly and looked away. Rafferty and the Kid looked around also; I did the same, taking note of the plush surroundings, polished wood, golden objects, and carpet fit for a sultan's palace.

"Would you not have come, Señor Beatty? If you knew?"

I swung my gaze back to her: "To each their own, I reckon. I just don't picture this as headquarters for a band of rebels. Who are ya'll mad at, if you don't mind me asking."

Her eyes lit and sparkled. "Oh, you like my home, si?" For just a second her expression was that of an excited child; but then she caught herself. "We prepare here for the overthrowal of the Mexican Emperor and his band of murderers and thieves. My army — I mean, *my people's* army trains here and grows stronger every day."

"*Here?* In a territory of the United States?" I rubbed my jaw not knowing quite what to say. "Well now, that's certainly a first for me —"

"We break no laws, if that is what you think."

I started to say something more but Jack cleared his throat beside me, and the contesa turned toward him. "How rude of me. You must be thirsty . . . and tired, after riding across the sand flats."

"I could use a little something," Jack said.

"Miguel," she called out, and a thin, elderly Mexican appeared at once. "Bring wine for these gentlemen. Have food prepared . . . and make ready four guest rooms for them, por favor, at once."

"Don't go to no trouble, mam," I said, glancing at Jack and the others with a smile.

Miguel's boot heels clicked away across the clay tile floor; and he was back in an instant with a silver tray of wine glasses, and chilled bottles of red Spanish wine. The air in the hacienda was pleasantly cool for such a hot day, and I commented on it as Miguel poured and handed us each a long stemmed glass.

"When the Spanish monks decided to build here, they did so because of a vein of natural catacombs that runs beneath us." She gestured toward the polished clay tiles and at metal vents in the floor, one near each wall. I stepped over and looked down through metal grillwork, into a pitch black hole. "It keeps the entire hacienda comfortable year around." She smiled proudly.

I sipped the wine: "That's real nice, mam. I oughta think about doing something like that for myself, back home." I glanced at Jack, thought about my ramshackle cabin in the woods near Kearney, and felt my face redden as he grinned and looked away.

She must've seen what I was thinking. "Yes, well . . ." She swept a hand toward a long hallway. "If your friends would like to accompany Miguel, they can refresh themselves while you and I talk of our business, si?"

I looked at Jack and the Kid. They shrugged. "Sounds fine," the Kid said. I looked around, saw that Rafferty had wandered across the room. He'd picked up a small golden object from atop a long polished table and was studying it closely. He glanced up, saw me watching him with a cold stare, and he put it down. He rubbed his hand on his dirty trouser leg.

As Jack and the others followed Miguel out and down the long hallway, the contesa took me by the arm with an air of urgency and led me away, into another room. When we stepped inside, she closed the door quickly and leaned against it for a second as if to catch her breath.

I saw that we'd entered a game room; and there in the center of the room stood an ornate billiard table, not much different than the one where Quick Quintan had made his last shot. It stood like a shrine, bathed in a stream of sunlight through the windows. I shook my head and looked away from it, across a row of cue sticks standing in a wall-rack like soldiers at attention.

"Thank God, you've come at last!" She stepped forward and took both my hands in hers, squeezing them. I saw fear in her eyes — a different person now that we were alone. She nearly swooned and I steadied her.

"Easy, there," I said. She shook her head, looking down. "What is it? What's wrong," I asked.

"Oh, Señor Beatty. I fear I am in great danger here. I fear for my very life. Because of *him.*" She nodded toward the windows overlooking the courtyard.

"Who? *Frothe?*"

"*Si!* Yes, Colonel Frothe. You must help me. I will do anything —"

"But, he works for you."

"He has been well paid to help my people in their struggle, but since my return from New Orleans he has grown bolder and bolder. I believe he plans to take over what I have built here!"

I studied her eyes, telling myself to move slowly here, not wanting to get too interested in anything to do with governments, soldiers, or revolutions. Something told me that the quicker I could settle up and leave here, the better. I'd gotten tangled up in one war. I figured *one* was enough to last me a lifetime. From what little I knew of the situation in old Mexico, a revolution was long overdue, but I wasn't clear on just how the contesa might take part in such a takeover, and I was pretty certain that I didn't want to know.

"I am frightened. I do not know who I can trust, and who I cannot." She glanced around the small room. "That is why I am so glad *you* are here."

I just looked at her, but I didn't draw my hands away from hers. "Contesa, I wish you luck in whatever it is you're trying to do, but I have to tell you, war is not my favorite pastime. I brought the deed and the —" I started to say *the jewels,* but she reached out with a finger and pressed it against my lips.

"Do not speak of them now," she said in a hushed tone. "Even the walls have ears. We will speak later, *tonight,* in your room." I saw the fear in her eyes, but through it I saw a veiled suggestion. She drew her hand back. "Frothe is worried about you and your companions. I can see it. He will be watching every move you make." She let out a breath. "You must be careful of him."

"I'm here on business, Contesa," I said, and I glanced away again. At the end of the row of cue sticks, I saw one that was inlaid with pearl and bearing a brass nameplate near the bottom end. I leaned slightly, just enough to make out Frothe's name engraved on it, and I wondered just how much Frothe had already taken over.

She studied my eyes as if searching for something more to say. But after a second of silence, she only said: "I must go now, and you must join the others. "Tonight, I will come to you." Her hand touched my arm. "Late tonight, while everyone sleeps, I will tell you everything."

When we'd finished eating, old Miguel showed us to our rooms. "Well, I'll be *stripped*," the Kid said behind me, glancing around at the splender of the place; and I heard Rafferty marvel in a hushed voice.

"Yep, not half bad," Jack commented.

We looked out across the room below as we ascended the stairs to an open upper landing. The walls were draped in rich soft tapestries, highlighted by large, ancient looking gold plates and vases strewn along the floor below them. Above a high arched hearth hung an ancient looking portrait of a Spanish Conquistador. He held a shiny metal helmet under his arm. An old Spanish war axe on an eight foot handle leaned against the hearth beneath the picture.

Miguel stopped and swung open a large door. A young servant girl ducked past us and disappeared down the hallway. Jack shot me a curious glance; I shrugged. Miguel smiled and bowed his head before me. "If you please." He swept an arm into the room.

I stepped in wide-eyed and turned around in a slow circle. There was enough room here to house everybody I knew . . . and their horses. Near a glass paneled door that led to a wide balcony, I saw a bar laid out with a white linen cloth, upon which sat a selection of whiskey, tequila, and red wines in wax sealed bottles. A huge wicker basket seemed ready to spill over with grapes, apples, and exotic fruits I couldn't begin to name. I heard the Kid whistle low.

"I get it," Jack said, grinning at Miguel. "You're God . . . and this is heaven?"

At first Miguel appeared stunned by Jack's blasphemy; but he quickly caught himself and glossed over his expression with a smile. "I hope this is satisfactory," he said to me. He turned back to the others and said softly, "If you'll follow me, please, your rooms are right this way." Jack hesitated; Miguel gestured toward the hall, and said, "Your rooms are the same, of course."

"Of *course,*" said the Kid.

Jack shot me another curious glance before leaving. Beyond the balcony doors, music and laughter drifted up from the courtyard.

In a second I stood alone in the large room and heard Jack and the others walking away. I rubbed my jaw and wished I'd brought my saddlebags. No sooner than I thought of it, I saw near the far wall, a shaving stand complete with razor, mug, toothbrush, a pan of water, and a folded white towel. I stepped over and dipped my fingers in the water; it was warm. Turning a brass handle on a door next to the stand, I pushed it open slowly and saw an ornate bathtub full of water, with steam rising from it.

I backed away slowly, leaned my rifle against the wall, and sat down on the side of a soft bed that smelled of sun bleached linen. On a night stand beside it sat a chilled bottle beside a long stemmed glass. The glass was poured and trickles of water ran down it. I just stared at it for a second, pictured the pool table and thought of Quintan's last words, *Now it's your turn.*

For some reason, I took out my forty-four, checked it and laid it across my lap. Then I looked down at it and felt foolish. The bed felt soft and inviting beneath me. I shrugged, picked up the glass of wine and sipped it, felt the cool sweetness of it pour through me, then threw back another, longer drink. What was I worried about?

I suddenly felt tired to my bones and

flipped the forty-four over on the mattress beside me. I almost laughed at my suspicious nature. I wanted to talk to Jack and the others, but it was nothing that couldn't wait. Laying back on the soft mattress, I gazed up at the ceiling and let out a long breath. The bed seemed to surround me like a mother's arms. I thought of how good another long drink of wine would taste, but I couldn't peel myself up from the bed long enough to pour it. Enjoy this awhile, I thought . . .

Through a veil of sleep, I heard volley after volley of rifle fire from somewhere far away, but I could not tell if was real or dreamed. When I awoke, it was to a soft but insistent rapping on the door to my room; and I heard Miguel's voice saying just above a whisper, "Senor Beatty, may I come in? Mister Beatty?" Setting up on the side of the bed, I rubbed my eyes and looked around at the darkened room, seeing that someone had lit a lamp beside the bar of fruits and drink, and trimmed it low. My saddlebags hung from a peg on the wall. "Mister Beatty?" The doors to the balcony had been opened, their curtains stirring in the night breeze. Soft moonlight spilled across the floor. Somewhere outside, the sound of music and laughter drifted up and through the open doors. "Mister Beatty?" Again the soft rapping, and once again from far off behind the hacienda I heard a volley of rifle fire and this time knew it was real.

"Yes," I said, "come in." I stood up adjusting my shirt, picked up my forty-four from beside me and dropped it in my holster as Miguel stepped inside and closed the door behind him. I was perplexed that I had fallen asleep, uneasy about the fact that while I slept someone had been near me, near enough to have taken my gun and I wouldn't have known it. It was not like me. "Where's my friends?" I asked, hearing the impatience in my voice. "And what's all the shooting about?"

Miguel looked taken back by my questions and apparently by my expression. "Si, the rifles," he responded hastily. "I hope they did not disturb you. I must apologize. I'm afraid these are troubled times for us, and the contesa has hired *proteccion* for the compound." He tossed a hand. "But do not worry, we are safe. Those are *our* rifles — our men in training. As for your friends, we have a small cantina in the compound." He gestured an arm toward the distant music coming through the window. "They went there straightaway. They said not to wake you."

Miguel swept his arm slowly about the room and past my saddlebags. "It was your amigo who gathered your things and trimmed a lamp for you."

"Oh." I let out a breath, feeling better, knowing it was Jack who came in while I slept. "I see. Thank you, Miguel," I said. "I've slept quite awhile?" The music outside was soft and dreamy, Spanish guitars and a woodflute above a deep and peaceful bass. Beyond it, the sound of rifles, distant and obscure.

"Si, you must have been very tired." He gestured a hand toward the distant rifle fire. "I will send a rider and have them stop —"

"No, that's alright," I said. "I was just curious."

"Good then. Perhaps you would like to bathe and refresh yourself? I will prepare something for you to eat."

"Don't bother," I said. "I'll join my friends."

After Miguel left, I opened a fresh bottle of chilled wine, took it with me to the bath tub and sipped it as I soaked and scrubbed. I had told myself I would be in and out, *business only,* and I still meant it, especially after what the contesa had told me; but I saw no harm in hearing what else she had to say. I could enjoy a hot bath, a meal, and some civil hospitality. I would give her the jewels, sign over the land, take my fifty thousand and leave, first thing in the morning, I told myself.

The scent of the soap reminded me of the contesa and I was stirred by the thought of her, somewhere close, waiting to come to me late in the night. I thought of her and wondered just how much of what Abe had said was true, and how much was pure unfounded gossip. I recalled the look of burning hatred in her eyes the night she spoke of Quick Quintan as he lay dead, back on the casino floor. But I had no idea what he might have done over the years to cause such hatred.

The soft music had suddenly turned fast and tense as I finished my bath and dried myself on soft towels. I went back into the bedroom, took clean clothes from my saddlebags, dressed, and shaved for the first time in many days. When I finished, I strapped on my holsters and headed out toward the cantina, the music churning fast and unending. I wanted to talk to Jack and the Kid, tell them what the contesa had told me and let them know that we'd be leaving early.

On the way there I saw two old men lifting a head stone from a grave in a small cemetery thirty yards to my left. I thought it odd to see someone taking a stone *from* a grave, and as I walked on, watching them drop it onto a flatbed wagon, they turned and stared at me until I tipped my hat toward them and looked away.

When I stepped inside the cantina, I saw Jack leaning on the bar, his rifle beside him, licking salt off the back of his hand and cutting shots of tequila with a red-eyed bartender. He turned as I entered and raised a shot glass toward me as I stepped in beside him. "Back from the dead?" He laughed and tossed back the drink as I turned over a glass and the bartender filled it.

"Yeah," I said. Glancing around, I saw the Kid by himself at a corner table. He looked small and stoop shouldered, staring down into a glass of tequila. I glanced around and saw the band playing fervently although there were no other customers. The musicians looked strained, worried. "What's wrong with the Kid?" I asked Jack, still glancing around. "Where is everybody?"

"Kid's drunk," said Jack. "He got drunk and run everybody off. Told the band he'd kill 'em if they stopped playing." Jack grinned. "Reckon your *good example* ain't quite struck home yet." "Where's Rafferty?"

"He's under a table somewhere. We'll be

having company most any time." Jack threw back his shot glass.

"Damn," I said under my breath; and I walked slowly toward the Kid. "Hey, Billy, it's me." I waited a second, then stepped closer. "It's me, your amigo?"

"I'm drunk," he said, "not blind." He barely raised his face. I looked at the band, then back to the Kid. The musicians were sweating, looking exhausted.

"Hey, Kid. I want to talk to you. Why don't I have these boys stop playing for a minute?" I saw that his left hand was under the table and I knew what it meant.

He picked up the shot glass before him, drained it and stared at the table. "I don't think so." I saw the accordion player roll his eyes toward the ceiling; his face glistened red, and wet with sweat as he struggled to maintain the tempo.

"C'mon, Kid. This ain't right. We're guests here you know."

"I'm a guest everywhere I go," said the Kid.

Through the open doors, I saw four uniforms crossing the courtyard carrying rifles. "Naw, Kid. This is crazy. I'm telling these guys to stop." I studied him a second then said: "Alright?"

He raised his face slightly, then dropped

it. I raised a hand to the band, and the guitar player almost fell over when he quit strumming. They disappeared out the back door as I walked cautiously over and sat down across from the Kid. "Going at it a little strong, huh?" I said. "Maybe you oughta slow down some?" Near the bar, I caught a glimpse of Rafferty slip out from under a table.

"Nothing to it," the Kid said. "Just like good snappy music when I drink. No harm in that, is there?"

"Well . . ." I grinned. "There is when the band's about to fall over on their faces." I looked around now as the four uniformed men came through the doors and stopped before us. I raised a hand toward them. "It was just a misunderstanding. It's all settled now. My friend here is a little drunk." They just stared, but with their rifles pointing at us. Past them, I saw Jack step toward us and to the side, flanking the four men with his hand near his pistol. The bartender dropped behind the bar like the floor had fallen from under him.

"That is no excuse for bad manners," said Frothe's voice from the door. He stood ramrod straight, then took a step forward. "There is never an excuse for such conduct." He strolled over calmly, stared down

213

at the Kid, and folded his hands behind his back. "*You* are Billy Bonney."

"I already knew that," the Kid said, spreading his bucktoothed grin.

Frothe's face swelled red. "I heard this from one of the old peasants. That you are a criminal and a killer."

"I knew that too," the Kid said, still grinning. "It's hard to be one without being the other." I heard his chair creak a little.

"Easy," I said. I raised slowly, thinking of something to say that might lighten the air. "He ain't done nothing, Frothe, and we're leaving come morning. We're not looking for any trouble here. He's been drinking a little —"

"You are indiscriminate in your choice of friends, Herr Beatty. We will escort Herr Bonney somewhere where he can consider the consequences of his actions." He gestured at the four uniforms and they started to step toward the Kid.

"Wait!" I crouched, my right hand on my forty-four, my left still raised. "That's a bad idea," I said. I'd heard Jack's pistol cock and knew that any second somebody was going to die. The Kid raised his face in a crooked grin. I knew his gun was drawn and cocked under the table, knew it had been all along. Our second standoff with these men in one day, I thought.

"Where we come from, you don't haul a man off just for getting a little feisty and chastising the band." I spoke quietly, but hoped my message was clear.

"Where you come from, Herr *Beatty* —" Again the tone. "— Being an outlaw is perhaps a symbol of status, but it is not so, here."

He looked back at the Kid: "Now, do you come along quietly? Or must I have them shoot holes through you and carry you out?" By the bar, I saw Rafferty stand up slowly with the small pistol cocked and pointed, his hand trembling but determined.

"Let's shoot it out, *Fritz,*" said the Kid, leaning forward, his hand still under the table. "I like the odds."

I felt like smacking the Kid in the mouth, shaking him, and asking him what the hell he meant, *liking the odds;* but instead, I felt my hand tighten on my forty-four. My thumb slipped across the hammer, tight, ready.

"That will be all, Herr Frothe," said the contesa, from the door. Hearing her voice, I eased up on the hammer.

But Frothe snapped her a glance, then back to the Kid. "No, that will not be all, my contesa. I will have this man in detainment until —"

"I *said,* that will be all, *Herr Frothe.*" This time as she spoke, her voice took on the sharpness of tempered steel. I almost flinched as she came across the room and stopped two feet from the colonel. "You were supposed to go to the training camp to meet the new men. Why have you not done so?"

Frothe's wide jaw tightened as he faced her, but behind her in the doorway stood three young Mexicans with rifles of their own. He looked at them, then at us, then eased down a bit. "I was on my way there when I heard there was trouble here."

"But as you see, there is no trouble here." She glared at him as the three Mexicans stepped inside and stood watching him and his men.

"As you wish," he said, but his heart wasn't in it. He snapped his head toward the guards, then toward the rear door, and in a second they were gone. I stood facing the contesa, letting out a tense breath.

"I see that you and Colonel Frothe are becoming better acquainted." I read the message of warning in her eyes. By the bar, I saw Rafferty drop down in a chair with the pistol hanging from his hand. Dirty sweat streaked his forehead. I noticed he had neither shaved or bathed since I'd seen him earlier. I shook my head as Jack walked up beside me.

"Things got a little out of hand, Contesa." I shot Jack a dark glance. "I reckon *I* shoulda been here looking after everybody."

Jack chuckled, reached down and pulled the Kid to his feet, the Kid's double action colt still hanging from his hand. "Sorry, Kid," he said. "But now I gotta go dunk your head in a water trough — it's the rules." He shot me a scowl.

"Do, and I'll kill ya," the Kid said as they walked away.

The contesa stared after them and said to me: "Then he *is* Billy Bonney, si? Billy the Kid. A killer of men." She shook her head slowly.

"He's made a couple of mistakes," I said. I shrugged: "But he's a polite young man once you get to know him — a good boy — a good friend of mine."

The contesa seemed to consider something for a second, then said to me: "Why do you travel with such a man as this Billy the Kid? I hear of him — that he is wild and lawless. That there is a price on his head."

"I've know him for awhile," I said. "Back before he got into trouble. I don't turn away from a friend just because he's made a couple of bad turns. He's treated me alright. That's the only way I judge a man."

"I see. So it does not matter to you what he has done, only how he has treated you."

"Something like that, I suppose. Once I side with somebody, I don't drop 'em just because things might get a little tough."

"I see. So, you would risk your life for a friend?"

I smiled. "Well, I sure wouldn't risk it for an enemy."

"That is no answer." She returned my smile. Then she leaned forward toward me again. "Am I your friend, Señor Beatty?" Again, I saw the slightest suggestion in her eyes.

"I'd like to think so," I said.

She leaned close and said in a hushed tone: "Tonight then, we shall see."

CHAPTER 10

I waited for her in my room late that night, knowing, yet not quite knowing what to expect. I had not mentioned to her that I knew she'd been Quick Quintan's wife, or that *some,* particularly Sheriff Garrett, seemed to think she'd wanted her husband killed. Nor had I mentioned the rumors of her being a witch — a bruja — like Mexican Abe had told me, or about the rumors of the lost *oro* that to him was all so true.

If I had mentioned these things to her, I might've also told her that the more I was near her, the more I wanted her, far more than I had wanted a woman in a long time. Yet the nearer I came to her, the more clearly a voice inside me cautioned me to stay away. And it was as these thoughts were trying to sort themselves out in my mind that I heard the quiet rapping of her hand on the door, and I turned from the balcony where I stood listening to the music from the cantina.

"Yes?" I said, and I stood in the moonlight. For a second there was no response, then slowly the door opened and I felt my breath almost stop as the contesa stepped into the dim-lit room and pressed it closed behind her.

She stood against the door for a second, her lips slightly parted, the soft gold light of the lamp illuminating her dark eyes and the soft glow of her skin. I felt I couldn't speak, so I didn't try. The breeze across the balcony nipped gently at the white satin gown she'd changed into, pressing it against her. I saw the fullness of her breasts as she breathed in. "So, now at last, we are alone, where ears cannot hear us, or eyes see us."

Her voice trailed as she released her breath. Lamplight flickered on her as she took a step forward. I reached to turn up the lamp. "No, don't," she said, and I watched her move toward me, expecting. "Let us enjoy the darkness."

"Of course," I said. I waited, waited to hear her tell me what she'd started telling me earlier, about Frothe, about her fear of him. But she didn't mention it.

"You do not know how I have waited for you to come to me — how I watched for you every day since the night in New Or-

220

leans — the night you handled Morcillo as if he were your own. At times I felt foolish, but something told me you would come." She stepped closer."

"There are some who would've bet against it," I said softly, managing a smile.

"Si, but *I* knew. I knew you were a man of honor." She tossed her head gently; her long hair swayed back over her shoulder as she stopped close to me and gazed into my eyes. Her hands reached out to my waist and I felt myself shiver as her fingertips slipped over the edge of my trousers and unbuttoned them.

I could not move. Her eyes stayed fixed on mine as she opened my trousers and slid her warm hands around my waist, then tugged gently at the moneybelt. I'd felt myself begin to stir at her touch, felt lost in the closeness, the scent, the heat of her. I started to raise my hands to her shoulders, to lean forward, to draw her against me. Then it dawned on me — the belt, the jewels; and I stopped myself, let my hands relax at my side as her fingers toyed with the leather ties on the side of the belt.

"Oh, yes, the jewels . . . the deed," I said, letting go a tight breath. "I have them here. Held them in good faith, just like we said."

Her eyes stayed on mine as she smiled,

her fingers working softly as she loosened the ties and let the belt fall to the floor. Then her hands caressed me gently where the belt had been, and she pressed herself against me. There was nothing more to say, or think. I knew why I'd ridden across the badlands and the sand flats, through the heat of the burning sun. We both knew.

Outside, the music played on and on; and somewhere in the distance, above the music and the wind and the faint volley of rifle fire, I heard Morcillo the stallion neighing, long, wild, and powerful in the desert night.

Near dawn, I drifted out of a trance and felt her sleeping against me. Lifting her arm gently from across my chest and her warm leg from across my waist, I eased out of bed and stepped over to close the doors to the balcony. A thin line of sunlight cast a gray glow on the horizon. I stepped out naked on the balcony and let the desert air surround me. The music had long since stopped; a silence hovered like a cloud over the vast and sleeping land.

Just as I shivered in the chill of morning, I felt the contesa press herself against my back; her breasts were burning coals. She stirred against me, warm against my naked back. I leaned my head back, felt her breath against my throat, and put my arms back and around her. It had all come about so quickly, the way she'd swept into the room and into me, and surrounded my senses; and my need for her had been overpowering, as I somehow knew it would be if I ever held her. Was this the magic Abe had spoke of? If it was, there was nothing dark and evil about it, unless evil is born of man's desire and his wantonness spawned from a dark hunger inside him.

"I wanted last night to be something special — something you've never known." I heard her take a bite of a fresh apple, then she held it around to my face with her free hand.

"It was," I said. I licked at the juice as a drop of it fell on my chest. I took a bite and tasted the sweetness of it.

"Is that all you have to say about it?"

I turned and looked into her eyes, but said nothing more, until finally she stepped back.

"Then I will have Miguel prepare us something," she said, and she turned and walked back to the bed. I followed her as she pulled loose the sheet, wrapped it around herself, and turned toward the door. I caught her arm gently. "Wait. Won't he know . . . I mean, that we've been together?"

She glanced at my hand on her arm — I turned loose. She tossed back her hair and smiled. "Of course he'll know. He knows already. Does that bother you?"

"But you were worried about Frothe —"

"He left for the training camp last night. Miguel will tell him nothing."

"Well . . . it's just not the way we do things in Missouri. I thought maybe you should dress first?" I felt myself blush.

"In my own home? Don't be foolish," she said with a coy smile. "Modesty is for peasants and fools. Look at me." She opened the sheet and posed. "Should I be ashamed?" She ran a hand down her naked body.

I stepped forward, ready to pull her against me once more. "I'm not used to letting people know my private life," I said.

"Yes, I know. You are a very private person." She stopped me with a hand against my chest, and smiled, as if she'd been waiting for just such an opening. "That is why you have so many different names —" She watched my eyes closely. "— Mister Miller Crowe."

I stood speechless watching her eyes, planning what move to make, what words to say. She slipped away from me, wrapped the sheet back around herself, and tossed back her hair. "Or is it Mister *Jesse James*?"

"It's neither," I said. "I'm Beatty . . .

James Beatty." I stared at her.

"Do not worry," she said as if reading my mind. "I will say nothing. I knew who you were the night we met in New Orleans. You are known as the man who supplies horses for the Bandidos — the James Gang, si? I heard this earlier that night from the bartender. Is it not so?"

Damned bartenders. I just stared, running it through my mind as she continued. "You are a man who will go to great lengths to make money. And yet you are a man of honor — who can be trusted, as you have proved by coming all this way." She gestured toward the belt full of jewels. "I have searched for someone like you for a long time."

"You lured me here? Is that what this was all about?" I thought about Quick Quintan, saw his face in the puddle of dark blood. "What about the killing? Did you plan that, too?"

"Of course not. And I did not *lure* you here," she said. "You followed your own desire. As for that pig, si . . . I am glad you killed him, because if you hadn't, he would've killed you."

"That *pig* was your husband," I said. "I found that out later, and not from a *bartender.*"

She searched my eyes for a second, then said: "If that was troubling you, why did you not mention it *before* we made love?"

I didn't answer as I started to put on my trousers. She reached out and stopped me. She tried to step back against me but I stopped her with a raised hand. "Yes, he was my husband. But you cannot know what an animal he was. Cruel, abusive! I am not ashamed to say it — *I am glad he is dead!*" Now she stepped back on her own.

I shook my head. "I never should have let this happen." I hurried my pants on and reached for my shirt. "This whole thing has had me confused from the start. I really don't know why I came here. Something just drew me. I've heard things about you. Things that should've kept this from happening —"

"What you hear are the rumors of peons who know nothing —"

"Yeah? Well, maybe not, but I decided before I got here that I would settle up and move on. And that's what I'm going to do. I'm sorry this other thing happened —"

"Oh? You are sorry you made love to me?" She tilted back her face, and added: "No. Of course not . . . but it offends you that I wanted something else from you? Or simply that I wanted to make love to you but did not allow you to lead me into it like some village virgin?"

"I don't know," I said firmly. The more I listened to her the more unsure I became, until all I could do was shake my head and say: "This is all going too fast for me. Whoever you thought I was, whatever you thought I'd do —"

"Do not act like an injured child. You wanted me more than the land or the jewels. You came here to have me, to taste me. And now you *do* have me . . . and you will still have me, for as long as we want one another. But make no mistake . . . you can not ride away like I am some foolish peasant girl — someone for you to laugh about with your friends."

I shook my head. "We've sure managed to throw a quick chill on a warm afterglow."

"Si, you are right." Her voice turned smooth and soothing as she stepped against me. This time I let her, felt her body warm through the sheet. "Listen to me. I did want you here for a reason. I want to make you rich. There is wealth beyond your wildest dreams hidden in the caverns in Little Sand Hole. *I* must have the land of my fathers, but we will share the wealth that is on it. Is that so terrible?"

"For all I know, that's just one more myth —"

"No! It is there. And you must get it for us." I felt her breath against my neck, smelled the essence of body. "Morcillo will lead you to it. It is *meant* to be. No one else can ride him. No one has gotten close to him but you." Her words aroused her as she spoke, and she clung to me, her words rushed by the heat inside her. "I saw how he let you near him. I did not believe in the legend until I saw you handle Morcillo after so many have failed. You are the man the ancient ones spoke of —"

"What about you? He lets you close to him." I pressed myself back from her lips, her hands.

"He must be ridden by a man . . . a *warrior,* with blood on his hands! For him the stallion will *fly*! In order for the gold to be found, a man must lead *the stallion* into the dark land beneath the earth . . . then Morcillo will lead *him* to the treasure. There, the man must wrench the treasure from the hands of the ancient conquistador who lays in wait . . ."

I only half heard her as my body trembled in response to her hands, her mouth touching me, warm and wet.

She raked her nails down my chest. "Be

strong for me. Be like the big stallion we heard throughout the night. You must be ruthless and brave like the conquistadors of old." She clenched her fingers like claws, her nails pressing into my chest. I flexed my body against the sharp thrill of it. Then, just as I abandoned myself to her, she let go of me and stepped back. "Now, *you* must decide."

She let the sheet slip from around her and gather around her feet. "Will you take me . . . and the gold of the conquistadors?"

When we'd finished eating from the bowl of fruit, she sat propped up beside me on a pillow and laid the bowl out of reach. "The treasure is the gold of my ancestors. It has been hidden and sought after for two hundred years." Her eyes shined in anticipation and excitement as she spoke. "Morcillo is the direct descendant of the first Morcillo . . . the great black stallion Hernandez Cortez rode when he conquered Mexico and took all the gold?" She paused for me to respond.

I shrugged. "History ain't my strong suit."

She glanced around and leaned forward as if in secrecy. "The first Morcillo was wounded and had to be left behind in the care of Indians, along with some other horses. They thought the stallion was a god. Once a year they bred him to a mare . . . but they would kill the offspring until there was one who was identical to Morcillo. Then they did the same thing over and over, century after century. Because Cortez rode Morcillo into the caverns where the treasure was hidden, legend has it that only Morcillo's descendants can find the cavern."

I said: "And you *actually* believe all this?"

"No, but it does not matter what I believe. It is something the peasants believe strongly. These are times of uncertainty, and they need someone to follow, someone who will lead them in the direction I choose. They will follow the person who rides Morcillo and finds the lost oro. That is why it is important that you ride him —"

"Hold it . . . hold everything," I said, raising a hand and stopping her. "You mean all this . . . your whole venture, is just something to keep the people hanging onto some far-flung legend? Something you've concocted to keep them supporting your plans?"

"No. It is something to keep them hanging onto their dreams."

"Dreams, legends." I shook my head. "There's no way they could've brought along Morcillo's bloodline, and kept it pure that long. Any of them are smart enough to know that."

"They know what they *want* to know, as do we all. It is only important that they follow me. It is the only way for them to be free."

She took my hands, squeezed them in hers, her eyes wide and shining. "Listen, por favor! I am a direct descendant of Hernandez Cortez. It is his picture hanging over the mantel downstairs. It was made after his return to Spain. Hidden in the back of it was a map to one of the caverns. The golden bowls and goblets along the wall . . . they came from one such cavern. Morcillo led the way. But since then no one has been able to ride Morcillo . . . until now . . . until *you.*" She reached out and stroked back my hair. "You can. I am certain of it."

"Then you *do* believe all this *lost oro* stuff?"

She looked confused for a second, then said: "After seeing Morcillo let you near him, I do not know what I believe, except that the people must have something to hold them together. I did not believe the legend until I saw how he is drawn to you. I have kept him wild, and mean, to keep the peasants afraid of him. Their respect is born of fear. But now, I see something unexplainable happen, and I have to wonder."

I looked at her dark full breasts and recalled the warm taste of them only moments ago. Perhaps the contesa herself was treasure enough for any man, enough of a reward to justify riding a wild horse across an arid land in search of someone's illusion. I let out a breath and laid my hand in her naked lap. "Who else has tried to ride the stallion?"

She hesitated a second. "Only one man . . . and only for awhile did Morcillo allow him close to him. That man's name is Mangelo Sontag . . . they call him *Crazy* Mangelo. He is the leader of a band of —"

"I know who he is." I perked up. "So that's why he thinks the stallion belongs to him? That's why he would kill anyone who tried to take Morcillo away?"

She cocked her head. "Where did you hear this?"

"It doesn't matter," I said. "But I've heard different versions of this lost treasure. First I heard it was golden objects, then I heard it was a lost mine. Somebody needs to get their legends straight."

"You must tell me where you heard these things."

"Never mind." I wasn't going to mention Mexican Abe or his stories of her. "But I can't ride your stallion, if it's just to deceive a bunch of people into fighting a war. This is the kinda thinking that gets innocent folks killed. I want no part of that. Maybe it's still that way over in Old Mex, but we've learned our lesson here."

"You are worried about Mangelo?"

"No, I'm not worried about Crazy Mangelo. I don't even know if he's real. Nobody I've met has ever seen him.

"Oh, but Mangelo is real. I have seen him, many times . . . he is very real. He is a monster and a brute! He is the one the people will follow if I cannot show them a better way."

"Still, I don't think I'll get involved in this. Although I truly do appreciate your hospitality." I was, after all, laying in the bed of a Spanish contesa, eating fruit from her fingertips. I moved my hand slowly around her lap, felt her tremble at my touch, and heard her breath turn hushed. "But I'll pass on the gold and the revolution." I whispered near her: "Now, what about the land. What about my fifty thousand?"

"*I* must have the land," she said, her voice affected by the slow, steady searching of my hand. It was a part of a grant from the Spanish government, still honored by the

Americanos when they took over the territory."

"Sentimental reasons, huh?"

"Si, if you choose to say it that way. I had a new title drawn up. You can have the money or you can even keep the jewels, whichever you desire, but you *must* deed me the land."

"Sure . . . sounds fine to me." I let out a breath, seeing that I'd soon be on my way home, fifty thousand richer, bred, fed and so much the better for experience. I reached for her.

"Then sign it for me now," she whispered, drawing little circles on my chest with her fingertip.

"As soon as I get the money," I whispered, running my hand down the length of her warm back.

"Of course." She shivered slightly and pressed herself against me. "Meanwhile, go see my black stallion. See how he lives. Look into his eyes, then tell me you will not ride him for me."

CHAPTER 11

When I finally staggered from the bedroom and into the tub of clean, freshly warmed water, sunlight played through the curtains on the closed balcony doors. I heard the contesa slip quietly from the bedroom as I bathed, dried and dressed. I didn't bother to shave; I wanted to check on my horse and take a look at Morcilo while I was at it. I'd told myself that come morning I would settle up and leave, but now I knew I wasn't going to, not yet. On the way across the dirt courtyard, I heard the Kid call out behind me, and I turned as he came trotting up beside me. His eyes were bloodshot and he smelled of rye whiskey, salt and tequila. "Don't you ever sleep, Kid?" I shook my head.

"Sleeping's just a cheap way of dying," he said; and wiped a shaky hand across his face and grinned. "I passed out a couple hours last night. That oughta hold me awhile. I thought we's leaving early."

We walked on as I said: "Early's already been here and gone." I glanced around. "Where's Jack and Rafferty?"

"They're rigged and ready to ride. I just came to get you."

"I just wanta check on the black stallion first. Then get settled with the contesa."

"Ouch." The Kid spread a knowing grin.

"It ain't what you're thinking, Kid," I said. And on the way to the barn I told him about Morcillo and the legend of the lost ora. We stopped outside the barn when I'd finished, and the Kid looked at me and said: "So, now she's even got you believing in the treasure, no different than Mexican Abe or the rest of these —"

"I haven't made my mind up yet," I said, cutting him off. "Besides, I'm not sure she really believes there is a treasure."

"Then that's real dandy. She wants you to ride out and pretend to hunt for it?"

My face reddened: "Like I said, I ain't decided yet —"

He chuckled: "Sure you have."

Inside the barn, we saw the same old man I'd met that stormy night in New Orleans. He was walking quickly back from a closed stall carrying a water bucket, glancing back over his shoulder as if pursued by the devil.

236

When I called out to him, he stopped with a startled shudder, then, seeing us, he let out a tense breath. "Sorry," I said, walking on toward him. "We didn't mean to scare you . . ." I looked past him toward the stall he'd been watching.

"I did not see you come in, señors. You should let someone know you are there — just good manners." He cut a hand through the air. He seemed embarrassed that we'd caught him hurrying from the stall. "Next time, we'll come ringing a bell," the Kid said.

"I'll just see to my horse and we'll be on out of your way," I said.

"No . . . it is alright," he said with a tired smile. "It is the stallion, Morcillo that frightens me. Always it makes me nervous to be around him. Please stay, if you will . . . I would feel much better."

From the closed stall, I heard a deep, strong rush of breath, like hot air from a bellows, and a powerful hoof slammed the ground. The old man cringed and almost hid behind me. "He must think he's some holy-terror," said the Kid, "the way he keeps everybody bowing and scraping." But the old man's eyes shined of fear and dread.

"Do not make jest of him, señor . . . please. I think he knows what you say —"

"Aw, come on," the Kid said. "He's just a four-legged animal, like any other."

"I didn't have any trouble with him yesterday, or the night in New Orleans." I glanced from the old man to the Kid.

The old man looked at me as if I had blasphemed an angry God, but then his expression changed and he said: "I know. It was a miracle I saw that night, and I have spoke of it many times." He crossed himself.

I saw my chestnut stallion poke his head over a stall door at the sound of my voice, and I walked over to him as the old man followed me closely. "I have been feeding and watering your horse . . . and your amigos, señor. I always see to the others first . . . to put off feeding Morcillo as long as I can."

"Then it's no wonder he goes around with a mad-on all the time," the Kid said.

I reached up and rubbed my chestnut's muzzle, saw that he'd not only been fed and watered, but washed and curried as well. We looked away toward the closed stall of Morcillo as we heard a long nicker and the thud of a hoof. My stallion craned his neck out of the stall, laid his ears back and snorted like a bull. "Two stallions in the same barn, might not be a good idea," I said, rubbing the chestnut under the chin.

"If Morcillo could get to your stallion, he

would keel him, señor." The old man crossed himself quickly.

"Don't sell this boy short, my friend," I said, feeling mildly and strangely offended by his comment. "This chestnut ain't no silk-shirt when it comes to standing his ground."

"I'm sorry, señor. I did not mean to —"

"Don't worry about it," I said. I felt a little embarrassed that such a simple comment had struck me the wrong way. I looked at the old man and saw the dread in his eyes as he stared at the closed stall at the end of the barn. It appeared that for him, walking down the long rolls of stalls to Morcillo would be like walking past a row of cells on his way to the gallows. "Want me to feed and water him for you?" I said it off-handed, not wanting to shame the old man.

"Oh . . . would you, señor?" The old man swept off his hat and a swipe of white hair stood up.

"Sure." I shrugged and nudged the chestnut's head back into the stall. He stepped back and shook out his mane. From the far end of the barn Morcillo let out another long nicker and stomped the floor. My stallion replied, slamming a hoof against the wall so hard the stall trembled.

"Bless you, señor," the old man said. "Let

me fill the bucket for you." He hurried quickly to a long trough and dipped the bucket in it.

"He must think he's something special, requiring that much stall," said the Kid, as we walked to the far end of the barn. The barn width stall was large enough for six horses. The door was still closed solid, as it had been the day before, with no place for the stallion to see out into the light. "Who takes him out to stretch his legs and keep him from going crazy?"

"Oh, no, señors," the old man said in a hushed voice as I took the bucket from his hand and slipped the bolt on the stall door. "No one takes him out but the contesa. You saw what happened when he got loose. Even if they could do so without him keeling them, it is forbidden." From inside the stall, I heard Morcillo's heavy, powerful breathing, not like the ordinary breathing of a large, dumb animal, but like the measured breath of some sinister intelligence, waiting and reasoning, making judgement before executing a plan.

I hesitated for a second listening to the unnerving sound, then reminded myself that I'd already handled this big stallion once before — stopped him at a dead run; and that I'd broken and trained some of the wildest, meanest horses twixt hell and Texas. They could be dumb, kind, cruel or crazy, but in the end they were all subject to man's dominion.

Maybe the old man's fear spooked me for a second. Maybe I was weak, and my thinking not as steady as it should be after making love all night and half the morning. "How old is he," I asked as I swung the door open slowly.

"He is seven years old, señor." The old man and the Kid hovered close to my back as I stared once again into the pitch black stall and felt the heat of Morcillo, near, but unseen.

"Seven years? And never allowed out in the sunlight?" I looked around, searching in the darkness. There was not so much as a small window, only the light through the slash we'd created by opening the door.

"No wonder he acts the way he does," said the Kid. This poor sumbitch is bound to be loco —"

His voice stopped as Morcillo lunged out of the darkness and stopped within a foot of me, as if testing me, seeing if I would cower. I held firm, reached out a hand and slapped him across the muzzle, not hard, but soundly enough that he pulled his head back. The old Mexican gasped; I heard the

241

Kid laugh under his breath.

Then Morcillo slung his head back and forth, nickered and poked his nose gently against my chest. "Señor, again my old eyes see a miracle. Nobody has ever treated him in such a manner! Why is it that he does not keel you? Why does he let you do these things to him?"

"Because he's met the one person he can't push around," said the Kid.

Morcillo sniffed me up and down, nudging me and blowing out his breath now and then. I smiled, knowing why. Morcillo had learned to care only for the contesa. He smelled the scent of *her* on me. Even though I'd bathed, I knew the scent of the contesa was still here, on my clothes simply because they'd been in the same room with her, and in my hair and deep in my flesh, because my flesh had been so deep in hers. Before, it had been the scent of her on the handkerchief, now, *her* scent permeated me.

"What should I do, señors?" The old man's voice trembled.

"Go get some rope," I said, without looking around. "Get it and weave it across the doorway. And get some more lanterns. Hang them right outside the door." I touched my hand gently against Morcillo's damp muzzle. He flinched once, then stood still as I ran my hand up between his eyes and rubbed him. "Make some light," I called out quietly as the old man scurried away.

"Yeah," the Kid called out. This stallion's been in the dark long enough." I heard him laugh, and I felt his hand slap me on the shoulder.

I sent the Kid to tell Jack what I was doing, and I stayed in Morcillo's stall for the next hour, rubbing him, Indian style, all over, getting him used to human hands, letting him know that I would not be bullied, but that I would handle him gently. When I asked the old man, Paco, how they had managed to keep the horse so well groomed, he leaned near and whispered as if ashamed, "Medication, señor, but do not say that I told you."

I shook my head. "What about all the vaqueros around here? Surely somebody could've broke and handled this stallion."

"I will not say, señor. It is not my place. But the contesa has allowed no vaquero near him." He shrugged, "I cannot say why."

I had the old man bring me a sliced apple and I fed it to Morcillo by making him lean closer to me with each slice. On the last slice, I did something that should have taken a month to do with a high strung, mishandled animal. I stood against his side and reached my arms up around his neck, held him firm and gentle for awhile, then slowly raised half my weight up on his back, stroking his neck and chanting quietly to him all the while.

When he made only the slightest attempt at stepping sideways to shed my weight, I soothed him a few seconds and slipped quickly but ghostlike upon his back, before he had time to resist or even think about it.

Setting high atop the big animal, I glanced up and saw the loft rafters dangerously close, if he decided to go loco all at once. I wondered for a second why I'd done something so foolish here in this closed area, but he stood beneath me munching a fleck of hay as if I'd been riding him for months. "Oh, señor," said old Paco. "You are one who could handle the devil . . ."

"A horse ain't the devil," I said softly, still rubbing the stallion's withers, and up and down his shoulder. "And I don't think much of a spread that would allow a fine animal like this to get in such a sorry state of mind."

By the time I left, Morcillo was ready to follow me out of the stall. I nudged him back and closed the stall. Down the line of stalls, my big chestnut poked his head over the door, nickered and stomped, and shook out his mane. Behind me, Morcillo blew out a deep breath. "Tomorrow, I want you to get that stallion into a regular stall, one with a split door . . . and a draw window if you can. If the contesa asks, tell her I said for you to do it."

"I don't know, señor," he breathed softly. "There could be trouble over —"

"Just do it," I said firmly. I leaned near the door, "See you tomorrow, Morcillo, mi amigo." I felt him lean his muzzle against the door and let out a powerful breath.

I walked back to the hacienda, and on the way there, I saw the same two old men who'd lifted the headstone from a grave the day before. Now they were carrying it from the wagon and into a small building behind the barn. I walked on, watching them struggle with it, then when they turned and stared back at me, I tipped my hat toward them and looked away.

As soon as I stepped inside, I saw the contesa in front of a long mirror, slipping on a flat brimmed riding hat and drawing the string up under her chin. She swung toward me, the hem of her riding skirt swaying against high topped riding boots; and she smiled, posing, as if asking my approval. I nodded, looking her up and down.

"Come, ride with me. I must show you something very important." She lowered her voice. "Something that will make you change your mind and ride Morcillo for me."

I started to tell her that I had already changed my mind. After seeing the way the big stallion was being treated, I'd decided there was *one* thing that would get me to ride him for her. I would ride him only if she would give him to me afterwards.

She turned back to the mirror for a second as an old man came hurrying up, holding out a pair of riding gloves. She took them, looked at them: "These are the wrong ones!" She drew them back. For a second I thought she would slap them across his face, but she stopped herself as he cowered away. She let out a breath and turned to me. I stood there staring, stunned by what I'd seen.

"I cannot tolerate servants who are bungling and lazy," she said. "I am sorry you had to see this." She turned back to him, sliced off a few words in Spanish, then said: "Go now, pronto! Bring Señor Beatty's chestnut stallion, and for me, a riding mare." Again she turned to me with a smile as the old man scurried away.

"They are *so* like children, these poor peasants. One must be firm with them or they wander and grow inattentive."

I bite my lip to keep from saying something.

"You will be excited by what I have to show you," she said, ignoring the look on my face. I stopped, watched her step over beside me and loop her arm in mine; and the scent of her caressed my face and my senses. Her manner disarmed me. "You will change your mind. I am sure of it."

"Where are we going?" I hesitated a second, feeling my anger subside in her urgency and excitement; but she moved me along toward the door somehow, effortlessly.

She patted my arm looped in hers. "No questions now, por favor." We stepped out on the porch and she smiled up at me.

I saw Jack, Rafferty and the Kid atop their horses near the hitch rail, and I saw Jack smile and shake his head slowly. "The Kid tells me you've taken a shine to the black stallion," he said. They sat watching me. Standing there beside the contesa, I felt a little awkward, a little embarrassed in their gaze.

"You must come with us," the contesa called to Jack.

Jack nodded and tipped his hat; but then turned back to me.

"Sure," I said. "Ride with us. We won't be long."

■ ■ ■ ■

We rode out through the sunlight and sand for well over an hour, across a hot flatlands dotted with clumps of gramma grass, trotting the animals now and then at a brisk pace until finally slowing long enough to let them blow and rest. I patted the chestnut stallion's neck and checked him down as he shook out his mane and cantered sideways, playing toward the contesa's bay mare and kicking up sand. Jack and the others rode up beside us.

"How far does your land run?" I spun the chestnut and reined up beside the contesa on the crest of a rise that dropped for a long ways before us.

She pushed back her hat and let it fall to her shoulders, then shook out her hair, unbuttoned her blouse and fanned it against her breasts. I glanced at Jack, ducking my head slightly, and saw him and the Kid tug at their hat brims and look away. Rafferty stared bug-eyed.

"My land runs forever," she said, lifting her face into a breeze, her eyes closed, and the breeze playing back through her raven hair. "As a child, I used to dream of owning the world. Now it appears that I do."

I stepped my chesnut stallion closer to the contesa, breaking Rafferty's stare. "Where is Finger Rock?" I asked her. Her eyes searched mine, and I added: "On the deed, it says the land starts at a point known as Finger Rock and extends to a —"

"Oh," she waved it away. "It is a long way from here, out across desert. The land is so vast, there must be a way to define the boundries. Finger Rock is more of a place than an object."

"I see. It's a big land. There's no denying that," I said, not knowing what else to say to someone who dreamed of owning the world. Jack walked his horse past us, tipping his hat to the side; the Kid and Rafferty followed.

"Yes." She looked at me with a proud tilt to her chin. "And I must have someone to help me rule it."

"Rule it? I don't know about ruling —"

"Si, of course, it must be ruled. What do you think the big cattlemen do. Do they not rule a kingdom? Do they not make the law? Do they not enforce it, like some feudal landlord, some ruler who is both feared and revered by those with whose lives he is entrusted?"

I watched as Jack and the others rode on and stopped a few yards ahead. The Kid gigged his horse and ran in a narrow circle, then slid to a halt and reared, playing.

"They might think they rule it." I grinned, just to lighten the air. "But in case you haven't heard, this is the United States of America . . . a territory of it anyway. This is a free country now. Nobody here is a *ruler.*" I gazed out across the land, sparkling sand the color of gold, shimmering in the sunlight like silk.

"At times you speak with the innocence of a child, my brave pistolero," she said. And she laughed playfully. "I think I like that about you." She drew her hat back up and tugged it down on her head and I saw her expression turn serious once more. "But, there are only two kinds of people on this earth. Those *served,* and those who *serve* them." She gazed ahead, watched the Kid prance his horse and raise a low swirl of dust. Then she tapped her mare forward gently and I fell in beside her.

"Maybe in other parts of the world," I said, "maybe in old Mex still, but not here. It'll never happen here."

"It has *always* happened here, as it happens everywhere." She swung her arm taking in the whole of the rolling land. "Because this is now Neavo Mejico Territory, instead old Mejico, you think the people simply take the responsibility of their freedom? After centuries of being ruled by others, you think they even know *how* to think for themselves? To make their own laws and know how to live by them?" She shook her head. "They are peons still, no matter which side of the border they are on. They know nothing but how to serve. It has been bred in them for too many years to change. For them to live any other way only confuses them."

"That's a hell of a way to think. Is that why you think you came near slapping an old man for bringing you the wrong gloves?"

She stopped the mare cold and stared at me, then said: "Yes, and he loves and fears me for it . . . enough that he would die for me if I asked it of him. It is how people are. I did not make them that way."

"Maybe *your* people are that way . . . mine ain't. We're Americans. Too many died for freedom here. They'll never go back to lords and peasants."

"In time they will," she said matter-of-factly, as if it was something to which she'd given much thought before finally resolving for herself. "When shrewd men are through taking their profits . . . and there is nothing left of the land and its resources, the peasants will have nothing to do but provide *service.* And *they* will elect through this so-called *democratic process,* the very ones for whom they will serve. It is only human nature. All the peasants of the world can hope for is that their ruler is benevolent. Then, when they are hungry, the ruler's dreams will fill their belly — that when they die, they will have *served* well, so they will not rot in the ground but go on to *serve* in some much greater kingdom."

I sat staring, speechless for a second, then said: "I don't know about all that. But there is one service I've decided I'll provide for you. I've decided I will ride Morcillo for you —" I raised a finger. "— But on one condition."

She smiled. "Oh? A *condition?*"

"Yes," I said, trying to ignore her tone of voice. "I want you to give him to me afterwards."

I studied her eyes as she considered it. I said: "The stallion doesn't mean much to you. If he did, you wouldn't be treating him the way you do. Give him to me. I'll take him home and get the madness out of him." I waited, watching her think about it.

"Si," she said, after a pause. "I will give him to you after you search for the lost treasure. You will ride him out in the basin. And when you come back you will be carrying my jewels, and you will say you found the treasure of Cortez." She raised a gloved finger and leaned nearer. "And you must never, *never*, tell anyone about this." She stopped and gave me a lingering gaze, then a smile crept across her face. "Then you will sign over the deed to me."

"Of course," I said, "as soon as I get the money."

She buttened her blouse and we rode up to Jack and Rafferty. They sat watching the Kid run his horse out across the sand, zigzagging, cutting and turning in a wake of dust. "Your Billy Bonney is reckless and foolish," the contesa said as we reined up near Jack. "If the Mescaleros were near, they would see him tire his horse out, then they would attack."

The Kid had slid his horse to a halt, turned and galloped back toward us. "I'm sure he knows that," I said. "The Kid ain't stayed alive this long by being stupid." I glanced at Jack, then out across the endless flatlands. I heard Rafferty pull the cork from a bottle of whiskey he'd taken from inside his dirty shirt. "Si, I'm sure you are right," said the contesa. Her voice lowered as her gaze slid across Rafferty and back to me. "I should say nothing bad about your friends . . ."

CHAPTER 12

When we stopped the horses again they were winded and well lathered. I'd dropped back beside Jack as the contesa rode ahead of us a short distance. Rafferty and the Kid rode a few yards behind us passing the whiskey bottle back and forth. "I know what you're thinking," I said to Jack. "But she's got no hold on me. I'm just being courteous. She's shown us a lot of hospitality, after all —"

"Um-hmm." Jack spit a stream of tobacco. "More to some of us than others."

I saw the Kid and Rafferty gig their horses up toward us as I said to Jack: "So? Are you saying I done wrong, turning down what's offered?"

"*Hell* no! I'd be worried about you if you did. But the Kid tells me you're gonna ride the black stallion out and search for the lost treasure."

I felt embarrassed: "Yeah, I think so. But

she's agreed to give him to me for doing it. Jack, that big stallion needs to be somewhere besides here. It's a damn shame, keeping a big animal like that penned up —" I nodded toward the Kid as he and Rafferty reined up beside us. "Ask Billy, he's seen the way Morcillo lives here."

"Don't ask me nothing," the Kid said. "I'm just along for the ride — dodging a posse, drinking, talking to crickets." He spread a grin. "Ain't life grand?"

"I just don't trust her," said Jack. "She wants too much. I can see it in her eyes."

"Lord-God," said Rafferty, wagging the whiskey bottle in his dirty hand. "The way she threw open her blouse — just pitched them puppies right out there —"

"Watch your mouth, *Alias,*" I said, hearing Jack and the Kid muffle a laugh. "She's a fine woman. She's just got peculiar ways."

"Sorry," said Rafferty. "I'm just amazed at the life you fellows live. I wouldn't have missed this for the wo-orld" He belched, threw back another shot and licked his lips.

"It's just one party after another," the Kid said. He took the bottle from Rafferty and threw back a shot. "Sometimes it's bullets whistling past your ass —" He gestured the bottle toward the contesa, ahead of us and topping a low rise. "— Other times you just fall into the lap of royalty."

I shook my head. "Kid, are you ever gonna straighten up? Don't you ever want anything more than this?"

"Here we go," Jack said just above a whisper.

"Naw-sir," the Kid said. His voice was beginning to slur. "All I ever want is three things: To ride a fast horse, sleep with a pretty woman, and not let no sumbitch tell me what to do." He nodded, as if settling it in his mind.

I'd started to say something more, but ahead I saw the contesa turn in her saddle and wave a hand. "We'll talk about it later," I said; and I gigged my chestnut stallion forward.

I rode up quickly beside the contesa, and when I reined up, I looked out across a valley and felt my breath stop in my throat. Beneath us, I saw rows of army tents, a large remuda of horses, and a column of men on horseback riding out, twenty horses strong, away from us and across the flat valley floor.

"Who the hell is this?" I gazed down at them, saw some of them wearing the tan uniforms like Frothe and his men, and others of them dressed as I, in road clothes, and carrying rifles with bandoleers across their chests. Along the perimeter of their camp, I saw four field cannon, and behind them a stack of cannonball and kegs of powder shaded by a heavy canvas tarpaulin.

"Boy oh boy," I heard Jack say quietly beside me as he reined up.

"This is my army," the contesa said quietly, almost in awe at the sight beneath us. I looked at her and saw the proud expression, like that of a general reviewing the troops. "This is the army that will free the people." She turned toward me, her eyes riveted on mine. "Together *we* will lead them across Mejico. We will overthrow Mejico City and make the country ours."

"Not meaning to bust your bubble, mam," said the Kid, "but somebody tries that about every six months or so."

She snapped her eyes to the Kid. "Señor Bonney. You know nothing of these things. If you did not come here with Señor Beatty, you would be in chains right now. So do not presume to —"

"Easy, now," I said.

I glanced between her and the Kid. He grinned and swept off his hat. "Yes man, and I want to thank you kindly for not allowing that to happen."

I watched her eyes for a second, saw her seething, then watched as she yanked her mare around and pounded away down the steep rise of sand. "Damn, Kid, couldn't you just let it go? I told you she's a little peculiar."

The Kid shrugged; Jack said: "You call wanting to start a war, '*A little peculiar?*' I call it stone crazy."

I just looked at him and turned my stallion down the steep rise behind the contesa. *Stone crazy,* I thought, as I followed her down into the valley; and just my luck, I'd only come to the realization only after getting tangled into her dreams, her obsessions, her illusions . . . and her sheets. As two men in uniforms came up and took our reins, I reminded myself to go along with whatever I had to until I could figure a way to make a clean break, take Morcillo if I could, and leave so fast that we'd be back in Fort Sumner before our dust even settled.

As we stepped down from our horses, I saw Herr Frothe and another man come walking up from a row of tents. Frothe looked past the rest of us as if we weren't there, but clicked his heels and nodded curtly for the contesa. The other man stood with his thumb hooked in his belt, and seemed amused by Herr Frothe's posturing. Frothe said: "Permit me, my contesa, to introduce you to Herr —"

"I'm Wolf Paterson, mam," the man said,

258

cutting him off. "Call me Wolf —" He shot Frothe a cold glance. "— Forget all this *Herr* stuff. I ain't no gawddamn *rabbit*." He glanced at Jack, then Rafferty, then at the Kid: "Howdy Billy," he said. The Kid tipped his hat. Then with a proud grin, Wolf looked back at the contesa. "No, of course not, Señor Wolf," the contesa said quietly. "I am honored to have you and your men join my forces. I hope you have found everything to your —"

"What the boys and me wanta know is when do we see some gawddamn money."

"How dare you talk like this to —" Frothe's words were cut short by the contesa's raised hand. I saw Jack watching Frothe with a guarded smile, but it was not a friendly smile.

Wolf Paterson turned his head, spit a long stream and rolled a cud of tobacco around in his jaw. I wanted to step forward and smack his chin up around his eyebrows, but I held still.

"Soon, Señor Wolf," the contesa said, again quietly. "You will get everything that is coming to you. Be patient, por favor?" She slid a glove from her hand, smiling.

"Patience my ass! We'll kill and skin anything that wiggles, but first let's get some coins rolling in my direction." He rubbed his thumb and finger together in the universal sign of greed. "We could always hook up with the opposition, you know. Them federales would pay for our services same as you . . . maybe better." He cocked his head toward the Kid, grinned: "Right, Billy?" Then he turned back to the contesa.

"Bad idea," I heard the Kid say to me under his breath.

"I see," the contesa said to Wolf Paterson. "You would leave me and join the federales? Join my enemies? Betray me?"

Wolf squinted his yellow eyes and spread an even broader, somehow dirtier grin. "That's right, mam. Fact is —"

Bang! The contesa shot him.

Wolf's mouth stopped and fell open as the loud pop of a derringer rang in my ears; and where his right eye had been only a second before, there was now a bullet hole, as a string of blood snapped out of his eye and splattered down his cheek. He sat straight down as if he'd been wanting to rest all day and decided right then to do it. Then he rocked forward once and fell back in the dust.

"There went Wolf," the Kid said.

I heard the contesa say beside me: "Again I must apologize. I'm sorry you had to see this unfortunate —"

"You just *killed* him?" As soon as I'd said it, it flashed across my mind that I sounded a lot like Rafferty the day the Kid shot the old undertaker. I stared at her as she neatly wiped the derringer with her glove, slipped the glove on and shoved the derringer in the palm of it. From across the camp, men came running, sliding to a halt, cautiously, staring down at the dead man. "Damn," somebody whispered.

"Si," she said, facing me. "He is dead, no?"

I swung a stunned glance to Jack; he nodded and crossed his arms on his saddlehorn. "Deader than he ever thought he'd be," Jack said. I looked back at the contesa.

Herr Frothe stepped in between the men and the body on the ground. "This does not concern any of you," he said raising his hands. "He insulted the contesa. Let this be a warning to anybody who doesn't want to conduct themselves in a loyal military manner."

Shoving his way through the crowd, I saw the scalp hunter, Turk, who we'd met on the trail across the basin. He stopped and looked down at the body, then up at the contesa. "There's one of my best men —" I saw fury raging in his eyes as he glanced at me, then Herr Frothe, then back to the contesa. "— One of my cousin's only son!"

261

"Then you must bury him," said the contesa, calmly. "Was he here speaking for you? Are you concerned about your money? So much so, that you would abandon the rest of my soldiers and become a traitor?"

"Traitor?" Turk swallowed hard and looked all around at the faces watching him.

"Watch what you say, Turk," the Kid chuckled.

Turk swallowed hard again: "Well, no . . . I'm just saying, I'm gonna miss him, is all. What'll I tell Cousin Luchian?"

"Tell him he died quickly and did not suffer, señor *Turk.*" She took a step toward him. "You and your men are new here, but you must learn quickly that you are no longer roaming the desert on your own. You are now a part of an organized effort. You no longer do as you please, but like all civilized men, you now obey orders. It is too bad this man did not realize it." She gestured toward Wolf Paterson's body. "So let his death serve as a reminder. You are now part of something much larger than yourselves."

"Don't that make you proud, Turk?" The Kid spread a grin and stared at him. Once more I noticed a rancid smell drift in on the breeze.

"The hell are you doing here, Billy Bonney?" Turk looked at the Kid.

"Beats the hell out of me, Turk." The Kid shrugged. "If this is the new career you was talking about, you shoulda explained all the drawbacks to ole Wolf first."

"He always had a big mouth," Turk said, sliding a cautious glance at the contesa.

I looked around, took note of Turk's men, and other assorted border riff-raff and hard-cases. Beyond them, I saw young Mexican boys, clean faced and wearing uniforms a bit too large for them, carrying rifles still smelling of packing oil. They were the con-tesa's true believers, I thought — the ones who would follow blindly and die willingly.

Turk and the others would kill for money and ride away afterwards. But these young ones would fight for her cause, and her cause alone. As I thought this, I saw Frothe watching me as if reading my mind. He smiled faintly.

She stepped back and addressed the crowd. "I bring good news for everyone today. All of you will soon have your money. Señor Beatty and his amigos are here to help us. He will ride Morcillo for me, and he will find the lost treasure of the conquis-tadors." I heard muffled excitement ripple through the young Mexican soldiers. I saw Jack shoot me a look of warning, the same blank look he'd given me the night in New

263

Orleans.

Turk's men and the other mercenaries just stared, the same as I would have done, had I been standing on their side listening to promises of lost treasure.

"When this is done," the contesa went on, "Perhaps they will join our forces. These men know much about fighting *guerilla* style." She gestured a hand past Jack and me.

She turned to me as if I should say something. I looked around at faces toughened and burnt by the desert sun, at the scalp hunters and gunmen hired to help this woman carry out her madness. The faces looked back at me, eyeing me the way a pack of wolves eye a strange lobo. I saw a couple of them smirking, whispering back and forth. I looked over and saw the Kid's crazy grin, and the stunned look on Rafferty's dirty face.

I stepped away, tapping the contesa on the shoulder. "Uh, Contesa," I said in a low voice. "I think we need to talk here for a second."

"Now, all of you go back to your duties," I heard Frothe say to the men as I nudged the contesa.

"Why did you say such a thing?" I spoke between the two of us. "I told you I didn't want to be a part of —"

Her eyes riveted to mine. "You have agreed to ride Morcillo. You are already a part of it."

"In for a penny, in for a pound," I heard the Kid say.

"Will you *please* shut up, Kid!" I turned back to the contesa and said: "I agreed to ride Morcillo, but nothing more." I shook my head.

"I have trusted you, señor Beatty. I have shared my home, my bed, my *body* with you. Does that mean nothing? Did you think you could fill yourself with me, then ride off into the sunset?"

I just stared at her, knowing that I was being pulled in by the oldest trick in the book; but I also knew that the derringer in her glove still held one more round.

The contesa had suggested we have a look around at the training camp while she attended to some business with Frothe in the command tent. Turk fell in beside the Kid like a lonesome hound, and the Kid kept shoving away because of the terrible smell that surrounded him. "Sorry, Billy," he said, creeping back up after the Kid shoved him away. "But don't you think it's about time we threw in together on something. I've always said, ole boys like us —"

"Turk," the Kid told him. "If you don't keep your stinking body down wind from me, I'll shoot you till there's nothing left to shoot at."

We walked on down a wide path between two rows of cannon, Turk's men pressed close around us, and farther back, the young Mexicans carrying their training rifles. The Mexicans stared at us in awe, as if we were indeed legendary warriors come to help them win their war. I saw Rafferty pull two of them to the side, and he began fanning a deck of playing cards. I shook my head and walked on between Jack and the Kid, past rows of Black Betty hand grenades stacked like cannon balls, their wicks cut short for quick delivery. "Now them look like the kinda toys I could play with for hours," the Kid said quietly. "I better ease me out a few of 'em."

"Wait, Kid." I tried to stop him, but he stepped away quickly toward them.

"Let him go," said Jack. "They *could* come in handy." Inside an open top wagon, a Gatlin stood with its barrels tilted upwards. I glanced at it, then at Jack. He looked at it too, then smiled and added: "In fact, it probably wouldn't hurt to get our hands around that little sweetheart. You ever fired one?"

"No, I haven't," I said. "But I don't think we've got anything to worry about."

"That's probably what that ole boy Wolf thought, right before the hammer fell.

"He *was* a little rude," I said.

"Yeah, well, maybe I better scout around and see what we can *procure* out of here, in case one of *us* happens to forget our manners." Before I could stop him, Jack swerved away and disappeared into the throng of young Mexicans surrounding us.

Damn it. I started on to the tent, but three of the young Mexican soldiers stepped in front of me and swept off their hats. "Señor, we want to tell you how grateful we are that you will ride Morcillo and find the treasure for us. It is all the hope we need in order to march victoriously against our oppressor and —"

"Hold it," I said. "Have any of you ever had to shoot a man? Have you ever had a gun fired at you?"

"No, señor. But we are not afraid. You are the great warrior the ancient ones spoke about. Nothing can stop us."

I looked down at their bare feet in the dust and shook my head.

CHAPTER 13

I sat watching a fly spin and dart beneath the flapping ceiling of the command tent; and I thought about some of the same things I had thought about on and off since the end of the great civil conflict. Only now as I thought about them, I had a clearer form of reference. Here I was, watching evil struggle to be born, kicking in the womb, and crying out in the shadows of man's dark nature. All it takes is one crazy person with the power to influence the ignorant, I thought, and there is born the evil that will *live* long and prosper as all else dies around it.

The contesa had that influence — had it in spades. She had the ignorant young, the powerful backers, the ruthless killers, and me, I thought . . . whatever I was.

She had the ignorant young men, the ones essential to any act of war, the ones who would share in, and follow her illusion —

the promise of some legendary treasure delivered by some mythical stallion — something that would change their lives and the lives of their people forever. She had the support of a powerful foreign government who cared less how many died, so long as they profited in the end; and she had the hired guns, the mercenaries, the stone cold killers who would do the dirtiest of the dirty work, the things that would turn the stomach of decent folk. Turk and his men fit that bill to a T.

Bruja, I thought to myself, a witch . . . a witch indeed. Not of the kind Mexican Abe had imagined, but one far worse. One who had within her power the ability to cause much death and destruction, all in the name of some noble cause —

My thoughts were interrupted by Herr Frothe as he stepped into the tent flanked by two of his German advisors. "So," Herr *Beatty,*" he said curtly. "We have met again. And I see you are still under the protection of my *Contesa.*"

I looked up at him, noticing he used the same tone in *his Contesa* as he used in saying my name.

"I'm under my own protection," I said. "Always am." I took my time noting the bulky Swedish pistols on their hips, fastened snugly in military holsters, and I laid my hand on my chest near the big sleek lined American made Colt, strapped loosely under my left arm.

"And where are your comrades?" He looked around as if he'd missed them when he came in.

"They're out and about, looking things over. The messenger said the contesa wanted me to meet her here."

"It was I who sent for you, Herr Beatty."

"In that case," I said, "say what's on your mind, so I can get out of here."

He heard the contempt in my voice, and said to his men: "Take a good look. Here we have the *American Outlaw* — Arrogant, ill mannered, unbathed —" The men stood rigid but each with a subordinate scowl. "— The kind of trash we would sweep off our streets in the Fatherland. The kind of low criminal who would —"

"Did you want something in particuliar, Frothe? Or are you just tired of the heat and want to get put out of your misery?" I raised slightly from the army folding chair. His two soldiers tensed.

"No. Wait." He raised a hand between the soldiers and me. The soldiers eased down. So did I. "I come here under my Contesa's request. She said I must apologize for the way I acted toward you and your *Mister Bonney* in the cantina last evening."

"And you're doing a fine job of it, so far," I said. As I eased back down I noticed that each chair in the tent was marked U. S. Army.

"I will tell her I apologized," he said, leaning closer, "and you will confirm it. But between us, *Herr Beatty,* I will tell you once and once only. I demand that you leave here, you and your outlaw friends, and never look back. You are meddling in the affairs of another nation, and I will not tolerate you. Too much is at stake here to have you and your criminals around."

"*Another* nation?" I glanced down at the dirt, then all around. I felt like telling him that nothing would suit me better than to leave right then and never look back; but instead I looked back up at him and said: "Tell me if I'm wrong, Herr Frothe . . . but when I took a piss this morning, I believe it was *American* soil I saw splattering back at me?"

"I honor the borders of no country that does not honor its own. The American border here is for sale to the highest bidder. At present, that is us. But I am not here to banter with you. We prepare here for a great undertaking in Mexico, and you *will not*

271

interfere in it."

I studied him for a second, letting it sink in that the contesa was only a puppet here, a puppet whose strings were wrapped around Frothe's fingers. He'd only recently begun to pull. Yes, she had the power to influence, to persuade for a time, but standing before me was the real power — the power to control, afterwards, and for a long time to come. "Tell me," I said, lowering my tone, knowing that power of this magnitude had to reach somewhere into the United States in order to risk massing an army right here, right smack on the free soil of Nuevo Mejico Territory. "Who turned over the rock — ?"

He looked puzzled by my words. Then I added: "The rock you crawled out from under. I might be just a two-bit horse trader, but I see well enough to know that you boys didn't just show up one day, swim the Rio and set up housekeeping. Who do you know?" I rubbed my thumb and finger together in the same sign of greed that Wolf Paterson had used before the contesa stopped his clock. Frothe looked surprised, even smiled slightly: "You do have perception, Herr Beatty." He stood in silence for a second, then said: "There are businessmen in Sante Fe who . . . how should I put it

— ?" He smiled, if you could call it a smile.
"— Share our beliefs on law and order.
They invested their venture capital with
Quick Quintan in the overthrowal of the
present Mexican government in order to
establish a more favorable regime. Now that
you have so conveniently orchestrated his
demise for us —"

"The Sante Fe Ring," I said flatly. "The
same bunch that worries about protecting
ranchers from a nickel and dime rustler like
the Kid." I shook my head at the irony of it.
"Why?" I said. "For the gold in old Mex?
The Silver?" I looked up at him. "Or just to
mess somebody around — flex their muscles
so to speak. Show you boys in Europe that
they can roll as high as the rest of the
world."

"Ha! No one would be impressed by this
fledgling *Democratic Government.* There are
men in my homeland who would buy this
wilderness with their pocket change. And
they will, someday —" He shot a smug
glance at the soldiers. "— And when they
do, it will be at a discount." Then he looked
back at me. "But yes, it is the same men
who want your friend Billy Bonney dead.
And they will have their wish. I sent two
men to Las Cruises yesterday to inform the
new sheriff of Lincoln County that your

friend is here —"

"You rotten bastard!" I bolted up from the chair; he jumped back a step. The two soldiers threw their hands to their pistols. But just then the contesa stepped into the tent, and I stopped, stared into Frothe's eyes from two feet away. We stood like two pit bulls waiting for a bell.

"I trust all is settled between the two of you?" She glanced back and forth. I knew she had to hear me shout at him before she stepped inside the tent, but her question was more of a command. "If so, Señor Beatty and I will be leaving now. We have much to do, and time is of essence."

"Yes, my Contesa," Frothe said, staring into my eyes, warning me. "I think Herr Beatty and I each understand the other's position." I noticed the tone was gone when he said my name. He'd given me what amounted to a slap on the wrist. What happened from this point on was of no concern to him. If I got in his way, he'd just kill me, flat out; and I took a certain amount of comfort in the simplicity of it. He knew that my next move would be to warn the Kid, then ride out as quick as we could . . . if I was smart.

I stared right back at him for a second; but then I nodded, almost humbly, giving him every reason to think he'd won something. I would heed his warning to do whatever I could to get my friends and myself out and away of this madness. But what he didn't know — what he couldn't have possibly seen in my eyes before the contesa and I turned and left — was this: if the Kid went down because of him, there wasn't enough *power,* or *control,* or any amount of *resource* or *influence* on this wide green planet, between the Alps and the Rockies, to keep me walking back up to him, face to face, and blowing his brains out.

That evening, Jack, Rafferty and the Kid rode on ahead of us as the contesa and I argued about revolutions and young men dying for lost causes. I'd told the Kid about Frothe sending for Garrett's posse but it didn't seem to bother him, although by my calculations Garrett would be here within a couple of days, even quicker if he pushed it. I'd been silent for a few minutes, and when Jack and the others were out of sight, I said: "Contesa, we really need to just settle up and let me go on my way." I raised my hat and wiped sweat from my brow. I glanced around to say more, but she was no longer beside me.

Now what? I reined around and saw her

step down from her horse and gaze off into the red and purple sunset. She swept off her hat, and as I turned back to her, I saw the wind lift her dark hair from her shoulders and sweep back through it. Her blouse clung to her breasts and billowed at her back.

"Come stand with me and feel the wind," she called up to me, as if what we'd been arguing about was already forgotten. I reined up near her; and even as I warned myself to stay away, I stepped down and over beside her, my reins dangling from my hand. "Isn't it lovely out there?" She gazed into the western horizon. I felt her hair play in the wind and against my shoulder, standing there, close to her.

"I never think of it as *out there*," I said. I like to think of it as here. Here, there, everywhere I suppose . . ."

"Si, you can do that," she said. "But I see it out there, out there in Mejico . . . mi Mejico," she whispered. "I dream only of being there again . . . someday."

I looked at her. "But, aren't your people from Spain? Hasn't this been Cortez land for generations?"

She turned to me: "Enough talk . . . hold me." She reached out with her arms, but I took a step back. "I am sorry we quarrled so about the war."

"Look." I raised my hands chest high. "We *need* to talk about some things. There seems to be some real strong obligations to holding you, contesa. I don't want you feeling misled by anything I've said or done —"

My words stopped short as her arms slipped through my hands, and around me, and her lips covered mine. I tried to pull away from her for about the first split second, thinking if I didn't do it right then, I could not do it at all. And I was right. Once her lips found their place on mine, there was no amount of force imaginable in my mind that could pull me away from her warm mouth; and I melted against her, knowing I'd be sorry, and soon . . . but for the moment not caring.

"Contesa." I whispered into her hair as the wind drew it around my face like soft silk. I wanted to whisper, why do you have to be crazy? Why do you want to rule Mexico? But I said nothing more as she held me, her face against my chest. I felt the shape of the derringer in her glove as she moved her hand around on my back; and it served as a warning, a cold reminder of all that was involved in holding *this* woman.

It was one of the hardest things I'd ever done, pushing her back gently from me, but

I did it somehow. "What is wrong?" She stood a foot from me, her hair in the wind still caressing my face, and the scent of her drawing me toward her. She glanced at the bulge in her glove: "Oh . . . I see." She peeled it off and shoved the derringer down into my belt. "You keep it."

"It's not just that," I said. "It's a lot of things, things we need to talk about —" I started to say *right now.* But I saw her fingers work fervently at the buttons on her blouse, saw it come off and blow across the gramma grass when she turned it loose in the wind. *Aw-Jesus.* She pulled the tie loose on her riding skirt; my whole body shivered with heat as she stepped out of it. She was naked beneath it. The wind whipped through her hair.

"Take me . . . make love to me here, now! Here in the sand and the grass in the colors of the evening."

In a second, I caught a glimpse of my shirt chasing her blouse across the patches of grass, dancing up, billowing and rolling across the low rise. All better judgment blew away like smoke in the wind, and we fell upon one another on the ground, on her spread riding skirt; and we spent our passion on one another in the long shadows of evening with sunlight streaking across the sway of the land.

When the wind lessened and the evening cooled in the shadows of night, and the sun melted behind the thin line of distant mountains, I lay beside her, listening to our breathing, already wanting to curse myself for being drawn farther in.

"You wanted to talk," she said softly. "Now we can talk."

I glanced around at the darkening land, at the clumps of grass and the sand surrounding us. "There could've been rattlesnakes here," I said, for some reason.

"That is what you wanted to tell me?" Her voice sounded as spent and dreamy as my own. "That there could have been rattlesnakes?"

"No," I said. "But it's something we mighta considered before —"

"Shhh." She reached over and placed a finger on my lips. "Let's enjoy what *is* instead of thinking what might have been."

I turned on my side and looked at her face, into her eyes, and realized that no man in his right mind could blame me if I fell chin over elbows for this woman laying naked beside me. As if reading my thoughts, she said in a soft whisper: "Come with me. after you ride the wild stallion, come with me to conquer Mejico. Give up everything for me . . . and in return, take everything I have. We will live like king and queen." Her eyes searched mine.

I thought of all I'd be giving up: living out of my saddlebags, sleeping on the ground, at times dodging a posse or slipping out of nameless towns, being shot at by nameless lawmen . . . It didn't seem like a lot.

"Contesa . . . Contesa." I shook my head slowly, looking into her eyes, feeling all warm and misty there, naked and near her. But just before I plunged off the edge of reason and allowed myself to fall into her fantasy, I snapped back to reality and said: "Can't you see what's happening? Don't you know that all you're going to do is get a bunch of dumb boys killed before their next birthday?"

"Of course a few must die, but it is for the good of all." She stirred and raised up on an elbow. "You will still ride the stallion, like you said —"

"Yeah. I'll ride the stallion like I said. And I'll bring back your jewels and make it seem like I've found your lost treasure. But I'll do it only to save Morcillo from the darkness." I shook my head at the craziness of it. "Lord knows . . . something should be saved from all this."

"I should not have killed Wolf Paterson in

front of you. It has turned you against me. I see that now." She lowered her eyes.

I just stared at her for a second. The contesa was a hard woman to discern. I rubbed my temples: "I'd love to tell you that had something to do with it, but that's only a small drop in a large bucket. This whole thing is wrong from all directions. The only ones who'll ever come out ahead on this, is Frothe and his leaders, and a bunch of businessmen. They'll make their presence felt, and the Mexican government will have to deal with them for a long time to come. All you'll do is show the federales that they have enough unhappy people to start a war. That a wealthy nation can throw enough money around to stir up a revolution anytime they feel like it."

She snapped to her feet; I snapped up with her. "No! That is not true," she said. "I know I cannot trust Frothe, but I trust my people. They will fight for me until the present regime is unseated. Then it is I who will lead the country through those I appoint —"

"Listen to me." I held her by her arms, both of us standing there naked . . . naked and small, and arguing about overthrowing a whole country. *Now it's your turn,* I heard Quick Quintan say in my mind, but I shook

281

his words away. "I know that right now I'm holding one of the most beautiful women I'll ever hold in my life. And if I thought there was anyway in the world I could live with you and hold you from now on . . . I'd do it, do it in a second." I let out a breath. "Even if you are a little, well . . . *peculiar,* I'll say, for lack of a better word." I glanced down quickly, making sure the derringer was still laying on my trousers, out of reach. "Peculiar? That means crazy! How dare you —" She struggled against me but I held her. "Because I am a woman? Because I want a better life for my people? Because I want a man to share this with me? A man like you *could be,* if only you would believe as I do! For this, I am crazy?" I saw her eyes glisten with tears.

"Well —" I cleared my throat. "— Yeah, Contesa, you really are. I hate saying it, but from what I've seen . . . you're crazy as a june bug. You might want a better life for your people, but only if you're still holding the reins. That makes you no different than any other two-bit generalissimo who thinks their ass was made to fit a throne. And you want these people to follow you, but instead of leading them on the truth, you drag up this lost oro legend just to keep 'em fed full of bull diddle, so they'll think you're a part of some kind of legacy left by Hernandez Cortez." I turned her loose but stayed between her and the derringer. "I think he was sort of a dirty bastard anyway . . . to be honest about it."

"Oh," she said in a resigned tone. "But then, history is not your strong suit, si?"

I reached down, picked up my trousers and stepped into them, shoving the derringer into my pocket. "I'm sorry. I've just seen too many good people die over this kind of crap. I reckon I get a little mouthy about it."

She stooped, picked up her riding skirt, shook it out and wrapped it around herself. "I am not used to being talked to in this manner." But her voice had lost its haughty confidence, the way a person will when caught with their pants down and slapped with a handful of cold reality. She stood silent for a second, her arms folded across her naked breasts, biting her thumbnail and gazing down. Then she threw back her hair and said: "But you will search for the lost treasure? The lost treasure of the conquistadors?"

I stared at her. *Now it's your turn.* I shook my head and let out a breath. "Yes," I said. "I'll do it. Then I'm gone. Can you give me my fifty thousand tonight?"

"You heard me tell them that I will have money when you find the lost treasure. Until then, I have none."

"*Jesus!* You don't even believe in the lost treasure. How can you say that you'll pay me when I find —"

"I do not know what I believe anymore!" She turned to me, her fists clenched at her sides, tears running down her face. "The stallion has taken to you in spite of all I've done to keep him crazy and wild. Perhaps it is true that a man will come who will ride him and bring back the treasure! I'm so confused!" She sobbed and held her fists to her face.

I stepped over and drew her against me. "Please," I said. "Take it easy here." I could've mentioned the reason the stallion had taken to me was because of her scent on the handkerchief, but I decided against it. Instead I said: "Mangelo rode him, right? He brought back some treasure? Who knows, maybe there is something to it."

She sniffed and held her face against my chest. "It was made up, the same way I must make it up about the jewels you will bring back. I thought you would have known. Mangelo worked for my husband. My husband bought the gold plates and vases in Mejico. Mangelo rode the stallion for me —

because at the time . . . he and I were lovers."

I thought about it. I wanted to say something about Mangelo, about Quick Quintan, about the army she had gathered and the war she wanted to wage. I wanted — for some strange reason — to tell her I loved her, and that I would straighten things out for her somehow. That I would take her somewhere far away, somewhere to an island in the sea where we would spend our years making love and teaching parrots to talk. Yet when all these things came together at once in my mind, I opened my mouth, and all I could really say was: "So . . . I suppose I won't be getting my money?"

"Your money? After what we have shared together, and all we could share together in the future? This is all you think about? *Your money?*" I felt her nails clench into my arms. I thought about the derringer laying safely in my pocket, feeling better that it was there. "Can't you see?" She pushed back slightly from me and looked into my eyes. "That I have . . . have fallen . . . in love with you?" She spoke haltingly, her expression one of surprise, as if she'd only realized it herself as she said it.

There it is, I thought, for the better or the worse, whether she meant it or not . . . she'd said it; and I, in my weakened state right then, came close to saying the same thing in return. And had I said it, I would've meant it, right then standing there, still feeling her body against me in the colors of the desert night. But I took a deep breath, breathing in the scent of her, and softly in her ear I whispered: "Then, forget about the money —" And ever gently I buried my face in her long dark hair. "— I'll just keep the deed to the land."

CHAPTER 14

I almost didn't recognize Rafferty from behind. When I walked into the cantina that evening, he was leaned on the bar with his dirty hands spread along the edge, his dirty shirt hanging loose from his belt, his floppy hat pulled low and the tails of the bandanna hanging beneath it. "Actually, I'm a *final needs administrator,*" I heard him say to the red-eyed bartender as I walked over to Jack and the Kid sitting at a table in the corner. The bartender huffed his breath on a shot glass and rubbed it on the front of his shirt. "Sure, and I'm Andy *fucking* Jackson," he replied, "just here for the climate." I just shook my head.

When I stopped across the table from Jack and the Kid, they looked up at me. Jack threw back a shot of tequila and said: "So, how's the courtship going? It sounded a little shaky when we rode off." He grinned: "You look a little frayed."

"Aw-Jack." I pushed up my hat brim and rubbed my forehead, not knowing just where to start. I'd taken the contesa to the hacienda, then led the horses to the barn and gave them over to the old Mexican there. He'd looked at me through sagging eyes, full of sympathy and curiosity, as if knowing the contesa had just left my mind screwed to a pinwheel. She and I had bickered and bartered all the way back. There was no saving this *courtship,* as Jack had called it.

I picked up the bottle from the table, and before turning it up I said to the Kid: "Billy, I reckon you need to get out of here and wait for us with Mexican Abe, before Garrett shows up. We'll light out of here as soon as we can."

The Kid looked at Jack and shrugged: "I told ya, Garrett can't shoot me when it comes right down to it."

"But one of his posse can," said Jack. He reached over and took the bottle from me. Rafferty came walking over to us with his head cocked sideways, listening. I saw the pistol butt sticking up from his belt. Jack pointed the bottle toward an empty chair. "You better take a seat and wash the heat out of your head." He turned to the Kid and said: "See how he gets?"

Rafferty propped his foot up on an empty chair and hooked his thumb on the pistol butt. I looked at him, shook my head and sat down.

For nearly a full minute they just stared at me, then as if coming out of a deep trance, Jack cleared his throat and said: "So, does all this mean you won't be getting the money?"

I shook my head. "Money ain't everything. But I'm keeping the land. I'm taking Morcillo —"

"Why? The stallion ain't got a lick of sense." Jack leaned back and propped a boot on the table.

"He might have . . . if I get him away from her." I glanced back and forth among them, and said: "Ya'll saw how she shot that ole boy in the eye."

"I think what's bothering you about it," said Jack, "is knowing that somebody you've been bumping your roscoes with is capable of dropping a hammer on a man. You figure it mighta just as easy been you getting your eye popped."

I looked at him. "Well . . . that might be. But come morning I'm settling up and getting into the wind. I'm giving her back her jewels and keeping Morcillo . . . as soon I make my little trot out into the desert and *find* the lost treasure." I shook my head. "I don't know how I get into this kinda mess."

The Kid grinned: "I ain't leaving till the rest of ya do. As far as that revolution crap goes, you're taking it too serious. I told you, everybody takes their turn with old Mex. It's just a good place for other countries to go to and stir up a little trouble." He grinned.

"But they're training right here! Right on American soil. That ain't right."

"So?" The Kid shrugged. "Gotta train somewhere."

"Write your congressman," Jack said. "Since when did you get so patriotic?" He threw back a drink.

"I never like to see a bunch of dumb kids get killed over somebody's scheming, greedy, crazy-assed ideas —"

"What do you think *any* war is?" Jack cut in.

"— Not if I can do something to keep it from happening."

"But you can't," he said. "So forget about it. Relax. The band'll be here anytime."

I stood up. "No, I'm turning in early. I'm settling up tomorrow and getting outa here."

"You keep saying that," Jack said. He spread a knowing grin, as if saying I had trouble pulling away from the contesa and her *enchanted land.* "But I'm thinking that stallion ain't the only one she's driving nuts here."

"Not me, she ain't." I picked up my hat and put it on. "I'm clear of it, and staying clear of it."

"So . . . I reckon you'll be sleeping alone tonight?" Jack grinned and threw back a shot. I felt my face redden.

"That's personal," I said, "but yeah, I reckon I will." And I turned and walked out.

I heard the Kid laugh, saying to Jack: " 'Bumping his *roscoes?*' I like that, that's a good one."

I walked from there to the hacienda, and along the way, I heard a hushed voice call out my name from the shadows between two adobe huts. "Señor Beatty," the voice said again as I turned toward it. "Who's there?" I stepped over with my hand on my pistol butt, until I saw the drooping eyes of the old stable tender looking out from the shadows.

"It is I, señor. Por favor, be quiet. She might hear you." He leaned out a bit, looked up toward the balcony of the hacienda, then ducked back into the shadows, motioning me closer. I stepped over to him. "Señor. It is at great jeopardy, that I come here to tell you this." His drooping eyes turned up to

291

mine: "But I think you must know."

I too, spoke in a hushed voice. "Know what?"

He held onto my sleeve as he spoke. "Listen, por favor. Tonight, when the hacienda is asleep . . . go to the hovel over there." He nodded toward the adobe building where I'd seen the two old men carrying in the tombstone. "You will see something there for yourself. Something that no amount of my words can explain to you."

"I don't like guessing games. What is it?" I gazed into his eyes.

"I must go now," he said. "But you will see for yourself. I tell you this because you are a good man, and because Morcillo likes you, the same as he liked Mangelo Sontag. Mangelo himself is a good man . . . it is *she* who has made him crazy."

"How?" I said; but he was already backing into the shadows. "Wait," I called out in a whisper.

"No, señor. Go! Go tonight and see for yourself." And in the next second he'd melted into the darkness.

Damn. I glanced over at the adobe building, then up at the light glowing from a window of the hacienda. *Alright, I'll wait. I'll see what the old man's talking about.* Then I walked on to the hacienda and inside.

Miguel appeared beside me from out of nowhere as I took off my hat. I jumped, startled at the sound of his boots clicking together. He reached for my hat but I snatched it away. "The contesa will not be joining you for dinner tonight, but I will prepare for you a dish —"

"Gracias, but that won't be necessary." I saw a bottle of chilled wine in a silver bucket on a tray near the stairs. "But that will." I hooked the bottle on my way to the stairs.

"Si, of course," I heard him say as I ascended the stairs. "It was there for you, señor."

"Then gracias," I called back over my shoulder.

Inside my room, I pulled the cork from the bottle and threw back a long sip. I plucked up some fruit from the fruit basket and walked into the bathroom where I saw steam rising up from the tub. I shook my head, not knowing if I did so because I grew weary of such pampering, or if I knew that staying with the contesa and giving into her world and her ways would insure such pampering from now on.

While I ate fruit, bathed and shaved and sipped the wine, I thought of the frightened drooping eyes of the stable tender and wondered what awaited me in the adobe building. Whatever it was, I figured it had something to do with the tombstone. *Why not?* But it didn't matter. Come morning, I'd ride out on Morcillo like some noble conquistador — if conquistadors were noble — traipse a few miles across the sand, come back with the sparkling jewels and . . . What? Make a big to-do of it? Dazzle a few peasants? Get them worked up in a full head of steam, steam fueled on bull squat. *Viva el revoluccion!* I shook my head.

To hell with it, I thought. Jack had made his point before I left the cantina. If I wanted nothing to do with all this, why was I, as he would say, *bumping my roscoes,* with the woman who was behind all the madness. I sat the wine beside my bed, walked over and propped a chair beneath the door handle, trimmed the lamp and went to bed. "So there," I said to myself, "it's done," and I threw the satin sheet across me and went to sleep.

For about five minutes.

Then I was awake, sitting on the side of the bed, wondering where the contesa might be, wondering if she'd tried my door but I hadn't heard her there. *Was she already gone?* I felt a deep hunger inside me, a craving for the woman, the scent, the feel, the taste of her. *Damn it.* I stopped myself from thinking about her, took a sip of the luke warm wine and went back to bed. Then I was up again and pacing back and forth; and that is what I did until around midnight when I heard the door creak against the chair.

I stood silently, wondering how long she would try the door before giving up and going away. Not long I hoped, because I knew if she stayed there long enough, talking, pleading, luring me, me hearing her whisper across those warm lips . . . But after three or four seconds when the door did not creak again, I knew she'd turned and walked away.

I bounded across the room and slung the chair against the far wall, knocking over the basket of fruit. Grapes flew. "Contesa, wait!" I yelled in a hoarse whisper, springing into the dark hallway as the door behind me jarred against the wall. She turned, her face aglow in the flicker of the candle she carried.

"It is alright," she said, bowing her head. Candlelight glistened, played in her hair. "I understand. I will go away and leave you be." I could not believe how humbly she stood there. Then she nodded slightly and started to turn away.

"No, please —" I stepped toward her. "— We need to talk. Just talk," I said.

"Si," she said. "That is why I came here tonight. Just to talk with you, nothing more. No lovemaking —" She shook her head slowly, stepping toward me. "— Just talk." Another step toward me, this one quicker.

"Good," I said. I stepped toward her, also quicker. "Because we really need to talk, more than we need to —"

We lunged into one another; the candle hissed and turned black between us, and we fell to the floor. Hot wax spilled down my bare chest as we pulled and tore at one another's clothes. And somewhere in the whirl and the heat of it, we were back in the room, crawling there over one another, rolling there together, then standing, clawing, stepping backwards through spilled fruit. Grapes squirted free of their skin; and we fell upon one another across the bed — not talking . . . not talking *or* thinking right then; but devouring each other, growling, gasping, purring.

I eased up from the bed in the dark hour of morning, looked down at her laying there, naked, on her back with a hand dropped over the edge. *Well . . . no talking done there.* I shook my head, ran a hand across my face — *now it's your turn* — and quietly searched the darkness until I found my trousers.

When I found them, I slipped into them, felt and made sure the derringer was in my pocket, then picked up the empty wine bottle and crept out into the hall, the soles of my feet sticky against the floor.

Through the dark hacienda I crept like a phantom of the night, out through the door, easing it shut behind me. I hurried barefoot past the fountain, and across the sand to the adobe building, crouching, holding the empty wine bottle and edging along the side of the building until I went around a corner and came to the side door. The wine bottle was my alibi if stopped by Miguel. *Just looking for the wine cellar here.*

I was prepared to force the door open; but when I tried the handle, it made a low groan and swung open an inch on its own. *So far so good.* I slipped inside and left the door cracked an inch behind me. In the first hint of grainy morning light through a dirty window, I saw before me a wooden coffin atop two sawhorses. Before stepping over to it, I glanced around and saw the tombstone propped against the wall with a blanket over it, the bottom edge of it clinging to dirt and sand, and the roots of some small plant life.

Then, cautiously I stepped over beside the coffin, smelling the sour smell of flesh curing by the arid heat of the desert. It was the same smell I'd smelled the morning Turk and his men rode up to us through the swirl of morning. I hesitated for a second, tried the lid and saw that it was laying there loose. Then, taking a deep breath and holding it, I raised the lid, looking in. Grainy light slid across a naked chest full of bullet holes — bullet holes turned purple, the color of bruised fruit. *Jesus.* Quick Quintan, *still* not yet in the ground. *Now it's your turn,* his drawn and shrunken face seemed to say.

Was this what the old man had wanted me to see? Why? Nobody knew better than I that Quick Quintan was gone down for the duration. I'd seen it, had taken part in it, I thought, and now was shamelessly *bumping my* — No! Was now . . . *making love, yes making love,* to his fiery widow.

I rolled my eyes toward the dark ceiling, still recalling all the explosions that had pounded him against the wall where he'd left a smear of blood as he hit the floor. "Well, ole buddy," I said softly, down to his hollow, purple cheeks. "If it's any consolation to you . . . wherever you are, I'm learning the hard way —"

"— Yiii!!" Something screeched, flew up from the coffin, slapped my face and batted away. I stumbled backwards, spitting, rubbing my face, ready to screech myself; and I stepped on the edge of an empty bucket and fell back groping for something to break my fall. I clutched the blanket covering the tombstone and felt it pull loose and fall on me. I scrambled to my knees, slapping dust from my chest. *Son of a bitch!* Still spitting, I scurried back on the dirt floor and stood up holding the blanket, my knees rattling against my trembling pants leg.

I stood for a second letting my heart stop thumping, then reached out to throw the blanket over the tombstone. In the dim light, as I spread the blanket, I saw the letters on the stone, and before the blanket settled on it, I whipped it back off and fell to my knees, staring, my mouth open and my fingers trembling as they felt across the rough chiseled words.

Son of a Bitch! I turned all around there in the darkness, back and forth with my arms spread, as if needing someone to slap me and make sense of it. *Son of* — I glanced at the lid to Quick Quintan's coffin laying on the dirt floor, started to pick it up and put it back as I'd found it. Started to pick up the blanket, cover the stone, run from here, get Jack, the Kid, Rafferty and the horses, and leave here, leave this crazy place while I still had enough sense to do so. *Now it's your turn* — leave without even my *boots,* my pistol, my hat . . . Just *leave!*

But I didn't, couldn't, wouldn't . . . *hunh-uh,* not just yet.

CHAPTER 15

She moaned softly in her sleep and tried to move, and I raised up just enough to let her turn over on her back. Then I eased back down astraddle of her there on the bed, where we'd made love — No! Where I'd *bumped my roscoes* only hours before. Her lips parted slightly, her eyes opened once, then closed. She raised a hand and laid it across her sleeping face, but I took it gently and laid it down on the pillow. I leaned forward, closer to her, my dirty feet sticking to the satin sheets, sticky with wine, moist with sweat. My heart pounded in my chest. My chest heaved. I wiped a dirty hand across my sweaty face and cocked the forty-four.

Her eyes snapped open, fluttered, then opened wide, looking up the barrel, then into my face.

"Who . . . in the *hell* are you, *lady?"*

She tried turning her face away, but I

pressed the tip of the barrel between her eyes and eased her face back toward mine. I glared down at her. "One more time," I said through clenched teeth. "Who in the living, breathing hell, are you!" This time it was not a question but a demand.

"Are you going to shoot me?" Her voice was soft, resolved, almost serene, I thought, for somebody about to die. She had no way of knowing I wouldn't kill her. The expression in my eyes said in every way that I would. But even in my shaky, enraged condition, I knew I wouldn't. Not for the world.

"You better believe it!" I tensed my hand on the pistol. "I'll blow your pretty, scheming head right through that pillow if you don't tell me what the hell's —"

"You *know* who I am. I am the Contesa Animarcic—"

"Naw-you're-not!" I turned halfway around, my pistol out arm's length, felt it buck in my hand and belch fire in the grainy morning darkness. "There *she* is!" I held the smoking pistol pointed at the tombstone leaning against the wall. Flecks of sandstone showered down on us from the pistol shot; and in the first dim rays of morning I saw the bullet hole right above the name: Contesa Animarciclo Cortex. "You ain't her!" I jerked back around and pointed the pistol at her. "Unless you're seventy years old and been dead for *five* years — you sure don't move like it."

I heard footsteps running in the hall. I'd jammed the chair back beneath the door when I lugged the heavy tombstone in.

"Let me up!" She bucked beneath me, but I held her down.

"No! Now who are you?" I heard someone jiggle the door handle.

"Contesa," Miguel cried out through the heavy door. "Are you alright in there?"

"Si! Go away! Please!"

"Let me in!" He pounded on the door; I turned and fired a round into it. It thumped like the blow of a hammer. Then there was silence, until through the window I heard excited voices stirring in the courtyard.

"Now tell me. Who are you?" I didn't bother cocking the gun again, because by now she must've known as well as I that I wouldn't kill her.

She let out a breath, gazing up past me and into the ceiling as if it were miles above us. "I am Flora Hablena." Then she offered nothing more.

"Oh," I said, not knowing what else to say.

"Now get off me. You are hurting me." She bucked again beneath me, and I eased off her. I saw her eyes glisten with tears. "I did not want you to see the tombstone. Now you have spoiled everything . . . everything beautiful I have planned for us, you have ruined."

For one flash of a second I felt strangely compelled to apologize. I had to shake it from my mind. Once I did, I said: "Okay Flora Hablena. From the top. Who are you and what's this all about?" I glanced at the pistol in my hand, frowned and shoved it down in my waist. Outside I heard the voices quieten down. I didn't consider it a good sign.

"To them —" She nodded toward the courtyard beyond the balcony doors. "— I am their contesa. But as you now know, I am not her. The contesa was Quick Quintan's wife . . . but he murdered her." She watched my eyes for any sign of belief on my part. I stared poker faced. He purchased me from my family in Sonora and hid me out until he killed her. Then, when her body had laid in state for many weeks, he slipped me inside the funeral bier, and when I walked out of there the next day, I became the contesa *incarnate.*" It is how they believe." She shrugged. "I had no choice in the matter."

"But you sure haven't done much to

change it since Quintan's death," I said. "And you sure didn't mind leading me on —"

She waved an arm: "All this was bequeathed to me. I could either take this, or go back to a life so poor that a father must sell his daughter in order to feed his family. You tell me, señor *Beatty,* which would you have chosen?"

I just stared at her.

"Even though he bought me, I did not lay down for Quick Quintan like some two dollar *puta.* No! I spent my time watching, learning, and I turned myself from being the *used* to being the *user.*" She stood up, naked beside the bed. "I made him love me with this —" She ran a hand down her body. "— But I destroyed him with this." She tapped a finger against her head. "Quintan is dead because of me. And I am proud of it." She tossed back her hair. "I took everything from him — everything *he* took from the Contesa Cortez. So I *did* become her . . . with a vengeance."

I stood up also, and stepped back. "And all this revolution, it's all just you wanting more? More power? More control?" I heard voices through the balcony door. "And what you've said to me, and what we've done together — all show? Doing to me the same

305

as you did to Quintan?"

"No." She yanked the satin sheet from the bed and wrapped it around her. "You cannot come from such poverty as I have come and not feel compassion for your own people. I long to see them free, and fed, and happy. I learned from Mangelo Sontag, that no *one* can be free unless everyone is free. I will lead them."

"I'm starting to see why you're the way you are," I said, stepping over toward the balcony doors. "You want to *free* them, but you don't want to give up anything you've managed to wrap your hands around. Maybe you want them to have *something,* but you still want to have *it all. Your peasants.* That's all anybody is to you . . . I see it now. Is that what drove the wedge between you and this *Crazy* Mangelo? You both wanted a revolution, but you want to keep control by playing on the people's ignorance and superstition." *Stallions . . . lost treasure,* I shook my head. "All I've been is one more game to play."

I gazed down and across the way, at the courtyard where I saw old men with rifles gather out front of the cantina. I knew Jack, Rafferty and the Kid had spent the night there, drinking. I shook my head. *Damn it.* They could've been sleeping here in soft

306

beds. They would've been beside me right now, armed, ready for whatever was about to happen.

"It is not true. I want to free my people." I heard her voice waver. "And it is not true about you. Yes, it started out that I wanted to use you. But I meant what I said, that I have fallen in love with you."

"Sure, *Contesa.* The way you love the stallion. How long was you going to keep *me* in the dark? Keep me waiting. Keep my flesh quivering for the slightest touch of your hand?" I thought of Morcillo, how he longed to be near just the scent of her . . . if only on a handkerchief in a stranger's pocket. "How crazy did you need to make *me* before *I* became the symbol of your power?"

I turned back toward her. "Well, luckily I stumbled onto the tombstone. It's over now. I'm gathering my friends and we're getting out of here." I drew the pistol and let it hang down my side. "You better pray that bunch of old men don't try to stop us."

"You did not stumble onto the tombstone. I am no fool. Someone told you of it —"

"Think what you want to think." I motioned the pistol barrel toward the door. "It's over, let's go. If they try anything down there, it's your life for my friends."

307

"No, it is not over. They have disarmed your friends by now. I will have them shot if you do not carry out our plans. I wanted you with me, the two of us as one on this. But since it cannot be, you will still ride Morcillo for me. You *will*."

"You don't know my friends," I said, almost smiling. "They don't *disarm* very easy . . . or very often. If you wanta see a bloodbath, just tell them old men to try and stop us." I again waved the gun toward the door. "Let's go." And we left the room, her before me, and me with the pistol fanning back and forth as we walked along the hall and descended the stairs.

"Are you alright, my Contesa?" Miguel asked at the bottom of the stairs, then moved away cautiously when she nodded her head.

We stepped across the floor and out of the hacienda, into the early light. The contesa held the sheet wrapped around her, gathered above her breasts. I stood beside her one step behind, still barechested, still barefoot, a hand on her shoulder and the pistol raised slightly toward the group of old men with cocked rifles. They stood in a semicircle around Jack, Rafferty and the Kid, with the rifles pointed at them. Without turning their rifles, they turned their faces toward the contesa and me.

"There you have it," I said to the contesa, seeing that Jack and the Kid had their hands poised near the pistols on their hips. "Say the word, and we'll turn this place into a buzzard's holiday."

"What gives here?" I saw Jack offer a flat grin as he turned slowly toward us. "These boys told us to hand over our guns. We told 'em we're a little bashful about that sort of thing."

I glared at Rafferty. He stood wide-eyed, his belt empty and his pistol butt sticking up from the waist of one of the riflemen. He shrugged. "I didn't know. I'm new at this. If somebody would've told me —"

"Shut up, Alias," said the Kid. "We know you're stupid." He took his hat off slowly and held it out arm's length. "But if anybody's a little *bashful* about getting this ball rolling, I'll just drop this hat and we'll let her fly." He watched my eyes for any kind of sign.

"Okay, Contesa," I said. I let out a breath. "Looks like that's the end of it. We'll just gather our horses and —"

"Then drop your hat," she said to the Kid. "We are not afraid to die!"

I saw the Kid's bucktoothed grin, saw the hat leave his fingertips. "Whoa now!" I yelled as I jumped forward. But quick as a cat, the Kid's fingers snapped down and caught the hat before it had dropped two inches. Jack's hand had already closed around the handle of his La Facheux. It froze there. Rafferty's eyes were open so wide they appeared to be crossed. The Kid waved his hat back and forth slowly, taunting, ready to drop it again.

I said to the contesa: "You'll get these men killed just to play out this crazy game?"

"Si," she said without the slightest hesitancy.

"Well, I won't." I stepped forward. "Listen to me, you men," I said. Their faces flared. "Do you realize that this woman has been deceiving you? She is not the contesa come back from the dead! There is no lost treasure of the conquistadors! This is all just a ruse dreamed up by her and her dead husband. It's all about her controlling your lives. Don't let this happen!"

"Say the word, Contesa," said a voice from among the old men. "We will do whatever you say."

I glanced at the contesa and saw the glazed look in her eyes. Had it been a poker game, I would've bet she was bluffing; but while this was a game, it sure wasn't poker, and from the looks on everybody's face, one word from her or me either one would turn the morning red with blood.

"Jack," I said as quietly as I could, least even a quick word be misinterpreted and bring forth the killing. "Will ya'll be alright here if I ride out on that stallion?"

"We're alright either way," he said. "Right Kid?"

"Fine as can be," the Kid grinned.

I turned to the contesa. "Okay, you'll get your horse ride. But that's it and nothing more. When I come back, we're riding out, if we have to do it with everybody's blood on our boots. You comprende?"

"I understand," she said softly. I saw a drift of wind spread a strand of hair across her face; and her eyes watched me through the dark veil.

When I'd dressed, strapping the moneybelt beneath my shirt, I walked to the barn, picked up my saddle and walked back to Morcillo's stable. I noticed the old stable tender was nowhere around and I wondered if he might have got frightened and left as soon as he told me about the tombstone. I shook my head, thinking of what was happening, thinking of how, had someone told me only two weeks ago that I'd be doing what I was now doing, I would've laughed

311

in their face.

With the contesa's handkerchief in my shirt pocket, I eased the bit into Morcillo's mouth and bridled him. Then I eased the saddle and blanket on his back and watched his muscles quiver beneath the skin. I rubbed him, soothed him, made the cinch; and after a few seconds stepped into the stirrups and up on his back.

I was prepared for anything. But after a few nervous sidesteps, Morcillo slung his head against the newness of the reins and the bit in his mouth, and pranced out into the sunlight as if he and I had been riding together for years.

I heard and saw a deeper hush fall over the already quiet gathering of men outside the hacienda as I rode up and looked down at Jack, Rafferty and the Kid. Some of them took off their sombreros as if witnessing a holy event. Jack stepped forward, started to lay a hand on Morcillo, but drew it back when the big stallion snorted and slammed a hoof on the ground. I leaned down to him and said: "You're sure ya'll be safe here?"

Jack grinned: "Safer than they'll be, if they start anything. You just worry about getting back. The Kid and I can handle this bunch. Once you're gone, I figure they'll keep a watch on us, but other than that nothing'll be any different. Atmosphere might be a little strained, but there'll be wine and music. Who could ask for more?"

I nodded, turned Morcillo and headed for the front gates. The contesa smiled as I rode past her, but I looked away. All I wanted from her was a clear road out of here once I brought back the jewels, the *lost treasure of the conquistadors,* and dropped them in her lap. If these people were bent on dying for her *cause* or her craziness, so be it. Who was I to try and stop them?

I rode out of the narrow valley and did not look around until I'd topped the crest of the rise where we'd stopped and heard the music three days ago coming in. Only three days, but now it seemed like years; and the silence of the desert closed around me, there alone, looking back on the ancient walls of the compound.

From where I sat, no one could guess that beyond those walls lived an insane, beautiful young woman, whose life had started out in a poor village somewhere in the hills of Sonora, and in a strange turn of events now stood on the verge of challenging the Mexican army.

There atop this fine big stallion, I thought about the contesa and the illusion she'd painted for herself. I was her make-believe warrior riding out to find her make-believe treasure. Perhaps in the spin of things she had fallen in love with me as she'd said, but if she had, it was only more illusion, drawn from the fact that the stallion *had* allowed me close to him. Perhaps that fact and that fact alone now had the contesa actually believing the legend of the lost oro — gotten caught up in her own yarn like a cat in a ball of string.

I shook my head. If that was the case, everything happening here, and everything that had happened since the night in New Orleans was born on the essence and aura of her . . . the smell of a handkerchief, and the illusion of fools.

I rode straight to where we'd left Mexican Abe, but when I got there, the camp was empty and looked as if it had been a day or two. I dismounted, searched around for signs and saw a trail of dried blood leading off to the scrub juniper where we'd kept our horses tied. There were two bullet holes in the juniper, and I ran fingers across them trying to get a picture of what had happened here. From where I stood, I saw the hoofprints of many horses leading off and into the rocks.

It looked like a band of riders had surprised Abe, that he had perhaps made it to his horse, wounded, and got away. How far? To where? Was he still alive?

I stood looking all around, wondering if other eyes were looking back, then I mounted Morcillo and struck out following the hoofprints as the trail led upwards, higher and higher into a world of silence, tall rock and sunlight.

It was afternoon by the time I reached a clearing atop a plateau overlooking the valley below. I'd lost the hoofprints a half mile back across solid rock, but I'd continued on, hoping to catch a sign of any kind. As far as the lost treasure — the jewels lying snugly in my moneybelt around my waist — I could turn back at any time and play out the contesa's crazy game. But if there was a chance of finding Mexican Abe, alive, I would stay out overnight, search for him as long as I could before riding back to the compound.

I saw a thin line of dust rising up in the distance on the valley floor, and I led Morcillo behind a shelter of rock and stayed low as I eased back and looked out. The three dots at the front of the rising dust were riders, but other than that I could tell nothing about them from this distance. *Damn it.* I never thought to bring my saddlebags, and with them my field lens. So I laid there squinting in the evening sun, hoping the riders would draw close enough to give me a better look.

I must have been watching them for a quarter of an hour or more, attending to them steadily until my eyes ached and watered, when I heard Morcillo let out a low nicker from the shelter of the rocks behind me. "Easy boy," I said, glancing over my shoulder then back to the valley. Then as I realized what I'd just seen glancing back, I spun around, slapping my hand against my pistol butt, and looked squarely at Turk and three of his men, standing there, grinning, with their big horse pistols pointed at me.

"Looky here, boys," Turk said, working a jaw full of tobacco. "It's the man what's gonna teach us to fight *guerilla* style."

"Yeah," said the one nearest him, "I can't wait to learn."

Turk stepped forward and stopped, saying: "Now just ease that ole pistol out and pitch it away —" He grinned across broken teeth. "— *Guerilla style.* And let's hear what you've found out about that lost city of gold."

"The what?" I stalled on slipping my gun from my holster, looking for an edge, a way to turn things a little more in my favor. I thought about the derringer in my boot. But it only had one shot left in it.

"Don't play dumb. I was there when the contesa told us you was gonna find it, remember? Now ease that gun out and lay it on the ground."

He'd gone from *pitch it away* to *lay it on the ground,* and each time he mentioned the pistol he was one step closer. I stalled.

"It's not a city of gold, or a lost *mine,* or *golden objects* —" I shook my head. "Hell, it's not anything." I kept my hand on the pistol but didn't raise it, still stalling. "It's all something she made up to keep all you *soldiers* in line." I said the word soldiers with the same tone he'd used saying *Guerilla style.* "There ain't nothing out here but sand — you can have my share of that if you want it."

"We ain't as stupid as we look," said Turk. "If there's no city of gold, how the hell you plan on explaining it to them old Mexicans when you get back?"

I wasn't about to mention the jewels in my belt. "If it *was* a city of gold, I don't reckon they'd expect me to drag it in on the end of a rope, now would they?"

He glanced around at the other two, grinning, and said: "Hear that, boys, I was right. It *is* a city of gold!"

I just shook my head. He turned back, snapped his free hand open and closed toward me. "Now get that pistol on up and give it over to me . . . lay her right in my hand, easy like. Don't go trying no fancy border-roll on me or I'll shoot your damn head off.

His big horse pistol was pointed at my face from three feet away, but it was a single action and it wasn't cocked. "Alright. I guess you got me." I drew out my forty-four slowly, making sure he watched, but instead of handing it out to him, I held it dangling from my hand above the holster, making him lean for it. Then to keep his mind off what I was doing, I said: "What now? Are you gonna shoot me . . . because if you do you'll never find the lost city."

"Naw, I won't waste a bullet on ya. Your hair's not black enough to be worth anything. I hate killing a man less I can make something for his scalp. Lost money on that Mexican friend of your'n. Kilt him, but he fell off a cliff before I could skin him down." He leaned forward for my gun as his words about Mexican Abe sank in.

"You son of a bitch!" As he took the pistol from my hand and leaned back, I'd slipped my hand in and out of my boot. His neck stiffened when he heard the derringer cock and felt it shoved into his ear. "You killed him? You and these egg sucking dogs?" I caught a glimpse of the others stepping back and forth, trying for an aim, but not getting it as I spun Turk around between me and them. He smelled worse than a buzzard's breath. "I'll clean your ears out *guerilla style* from one to the other, you stinking son of a bitch!"

"Don't shoot!" he bellowed, either to me or his men, I wasn't sure which. "You need us! We need you! Don't shoot me! Damn it to *hell*! Don't shoot me!"

I reached around and took my pistol from his hand. "Now ya'll pitch them guns out, pronto!" I said to the other three, farther back. "I can't stand smelling this stinking bastard."

"Personal remarks are uncalled for," Turk said.

"Shut up!" I pulled the derringer away and jammed my pistol under his chin. The three men stalled in pitching out the guns the same way I had. "Don't even think about trying something smart. I won't wait another second." I cocked the pistol with a snap of my thumb.

"Do what he says," Turk yelled. "Can't you see he means it?"

"How will we *know* he means it, if we

throw down our guns?" said one. He stepped forward with his horse pistol still pointed at us.

"You'll know for *damn sure,* if you don't," I yelled back. The other two spread out beside him, and the three of them stalked toward us slowly. With my free hand, I reached around, picked up Turk's pistol off the ground, ran the hammer down his buckskin sleeve, cocking it, and pointed both guns at them from around him. The smell of him rose around me like a thick rancid cloud. I didn't know how long I could hold out without breathing. I'd have to kill 'em and kill 'em quick.

"One more step, and it'll be your last," I said, trying to hold my breath and talk at the same time.

"He's bluffing," one said to the other two; and he was the first one I shot. The big horse pistol bucked like a shotgun and the man seemed to disappear backwards in a streak of fire. Then the other two started shooting at the same time I did, Turk screaming as a bullet nipped his ear. One man went backwards and down, the other crouched low and fanned the big pistol. White fire exploded in the sunlight. Then a bullet from my forty-four hit him in the chest and he sank down and fell forward.

I shoved Turk to the side. "I'm hit all over!" he bleated. I stood up, staring at the three men with my pistol smoking. I took a cautious step forward, heard Morcillo nicker behind the rocks; and all around us the world drew still and silent save for the wind whirring through the rocks, making eery sounds there among the dead.

"You kilt 'em all," Turk said, "and I'm wounded all to hell and gone."

I turned and looked at him. He raised a hand and said: "Not that I'm blaming ya, or fostering any hard feelings —"

Stand up, you stinking bastard," I said.

"Can't. I'm shot all to hell here. Won't make it. Won't live to see tomorrow —"

"Then I'll finish you off, right now." I pointed the big horse pistol.

He bounced from the ground. "I'm up, here. See, I'm up."

I saw the spot of red spreading on the front of his grimy buckskin shirt, and saw blood running down from a nick in his ear. "Not nearly as bad as I thought," he said, working his arm at his shoulder joint.

"Now, where did you weasels kill Mexican Abe?" I stepped toward him. "Where's his body?"

"His body's over the side of the cliff there, 'bout a hundred feet down." He pointed toward the rocks behind us. "Got his horse right back yonder with ours. Look for yourself. Hell, you can even have it if it makes ya feel better."

"You killed him for his scalp —" I clenched my teeth. "— Which you didn't even get." I cocked the forty-four and stepped closer, with it pointed at his chest. His eyes widened. "You killed a fine, decent, God fearing man like Abe —"

"Hell, he was just a Mexican, there's millions of 'em." Turk shrugged, as if to ask what real harm had been done. "But if you keep shooting that pistol you better get ready for some company pretty quick." He nodded toward the rise of dust still streaking on the valley floor. "That's ole Garrett down there, come to kill your amigo, Billy Bonney — You too, 'less I miss my guess."

I squinted, glanced out and down at the valley, then back to him. "How can you tell from here?"

"Can't, from here. But I saw him yesterday through my field lens. Him and two deputies, riding smack toward the contesa's place. You better let me go if you know what's good for ya. Won't look so good . . . you killing me and all."

"I'd probably get a medal for it," I said. But I lowered the pistol anyway. If it was

Garrett and his deputies coming down there, Turk knew something I didn't. He knew the back way into the compound where the troops were gathered. The best way — maybe the only way — to avoid Garrett, was to ride around him, slip in the back way and warn the Kid.

He saw me lower the pistol, and said: "So, you ain't got the stomach to kill me straight up?"

"I ain't got the stomach to *smell* you straight up," I said. "But make no mistake, I'll kill quick if you make one wrong move. You're leading me back to the compound the way you came out. Now, let's go."

"Well now." He grinned and sat down with a hand pressed against the wound in his side. "Maybe I better think about this. See I kinda got me a notion that you and I —"

I started shooting at him; the first round hit an inch from his feet, the second knocked his hat off, the third nicked his trousers right in the crotch as he scooted back across the dirt, throwing his hands up. "Alright! Now! Damn it!" He sprang to his feet, cowering back with a hand raised. "I just thought we might partner up on finding that *golden city*, is all."

"I owe you a bullet for killing Mexican

Abe," I said. "Don't push me again or I'll kill you and leave you lay."

"Alright. Damn it. I never seen a man so touchy about one dead Mex. It ain't natural."

"Move it," I said, glancing back at the rise of dust, then shoving him from behind as he ambled toward the horses. Dust and stench bellowed from his back. I almost gaged.

I untied Morcillo's reins and led him, following Turk to the other horses. When I'd turned Abe's horse and the other men's horses loose, I slapped their rumps and sent them running back down the trail I'd rode coming up. Then we mounted and headed out on the trail Turk and his men had used. It curved down through the rocks at a dangerous angle, but it spilled into the valley much quicker than the one I'd used, and it left a tall mountain of rock between us and Garrett's deputies.

At the foot of the mountain, Turk led around a tangle of spilled rock and up and down across land swells and ravines that could stagger a mountain goat. Morcillo held up better than any animal I'd ever seen, considering he spent most of his life in a darkened stall. I decided as we traveled into the dark shades of evening that if I came out of this with nothing else — and that appeared to be the case — I'd keep this big stallion, take him back to Missouri with me and show him what life was supposed to be.

We made a dark camp for a couple of hours that night in the light of the moon, throwing down our saddles beside a rock basin of run off water, just long enough to rest and water the horses before pushing on. Turk pulled his buckskin shirt open, and I held my breath long enough to look at the wound in his side. It was a flesh wound, in and out across the top of his hip bone.

"Jeez," I stepped away and let out a breath. I fanned my free hand back and forth and motioned toward the basin of water with my pistol. "I can't stand it anymore," I said. "Get in there and wash . . . scrub some of the stink off you, before you start drawing buzzards."

"The hell I will." He tightened his jaw. "You ain't about to fire that pistol now, not out here, not without knowing where Garrett and his boys are."

"You're right," I said, and I stepped in quickly and cracked him across the forehead with the barrel.

"Alright! Damn it!" He stepped into the

water holding his head, and sat down slowly until the water was just at chin level. "I've tried washing before, you know. It don't do no good. I've stunk this way long as I can remember." He grinned, but I saw a look of regret behind his expression.

"Just stay there till we get ready to leave. At least the water will keep it confined awhile." I shook my head and walked over to the horses.

"Truth is," I heard him say behind me, as I stared off across the darkness. "I came west in forty six, just because I smelled so bad nobody could stand it in Georgia." I heard him splash water and splutter it from his face. "Mayor of the town said, *'go west you stinking polecat,'* so I did. Been here ever since, stinking to high heaven. Happy as a coon in a corn crib."

"Is that a fact?" I gazed out and across the land. "I've heard all kinds of reasons for a person coming west . . ."

A flash in the distant darkness caught my eye, and I stood silent, watching until once again I saw it, then saw it grow, then realized someone had just built a fire. I heard Turk babbling on behind me, but I no longer listened to him as I watched another fire flare up a short distance from the first. Then a short distance from there, I saw another. "Turk, come up here. Tell me what you think of this."

In a second I heard his wet clothes slosh up beside me. I stepped away from him and pointed at the fires in the black night. "What do you think, Garrett and his two deputies?"

"Not likely," he said, "unless they've got mad and ain't speaking to one another."

I shot him a cold stare; he raised a hand in a gesture of peace. "Apaches?" I turned and looked out again.

"Naw, they wouldn't be building fires, being off the reservation and all. They got better sense." He studied closer as another fire flared up, then in a few seconds, another. "It's a large group though. They're spread out aways."

"Army?" I craned my neck as if it would help me see better.

"Naw. If it was army, they'd be hunting Apache. They sure wouldn't be building no —" He stopped. "Aw-hell. It's Federales. Nobody else would be brazen enough to do such a thing. Yep, it's Federales alright. I'd bet on it."

"Federales? Here? In New Mexico Territory? I don't think so."

"Why not? Don't you think they can swim the Rio, same as the rest of us?" He grinned and rubbed his hands down his wet face.

Now he wasn't just stinking, he was stinking and wet. "I don't know where you young fellers get the notion that anybody on either side gives a damn about *borders*. Nobody I know ever did."

"But what the hell would they be doing here? Trying to start an incident? Get the whole U. S. government down on them?"

"Wolf Paterson," Turk said under his breath. "That sneaking son of a bitch." He slapped a wet fist into his hand. "Why didn't *I* think of it first?"

"What are you talking about?" I looked at him, seeing the distant fires sparkle in his dark eyes.

"He said he could make money working for the other side." Turk ran a hand back across his wet, stinking hair. "That bastard sold us out. He told 'em what we was up to." He pointed a wet finger at the fires. "Don't you get it? They's headed the same place we are, sure as hell. They're going in the back way and kick the hell out of the contesa's revolution."

"You're out of your mind," I said. "They wouldn't do that. This is the United States of America — Would they do that?"

"You can bet a bite of Sweet Lucy's they'd do it. Ain't no troops around to stop 'em. Hell, even if there was, they might just give 'em free rein. What does the government care about a handful of guerilla — Mexican guerilla at that."

"Come on," I said, turning quickly toward our saddles.

"*Come on,* why? What the hell do we care if they bust up the party. We could go find that city of gold while they're killing each other."

"I got friends there," I said. "Come on!" I waved the pistol toward our saddles on the ground.

"Why-*hell!* I got a dozen of my boys there. Best scalp hunters ever lifted a set of braids. But they was all gonna die sooner or later anyways. That's just nature." He spread his hands. "If we was smart, we'd get to looking for that city of —"

I cocked the pistol, the sound of it sharp and clear in the quiet of night. "Get your saddle and get your stinking ass on that horse. I don't know if it's Federales or not. But you're leading me in tonight, just as fast we can get there."

In a few seconds we were saddled, mounted, and stretching into a gallop across the desert night, Turk in the lead with a hand pressed against his flesh wound and the fringe of his buckskins bouncing in the night air. I could smell him six feet in front

of me as we kicked the miles behind us
beneath our horse's hoofs.

CHAPTER 16

Riding back the way I came would've taken till midnight. Riding wide, and around to the back of the compound where the encampment stood would take until morning or longer; but it kept us from running into Garrett, and it showed me the way to get the Kid out on the back trail once I got there.

We rode hard, taking care to walk our horses down every few miles, least we spend them and end up afoot. By the gray hour of morning we made what Turk called the last stretch before coming back into Cortez land. It was a narrow crease deep between two rock walls, sheer and steep, littered with rock spills — perfect country for an ambush, I thought, as I glanced around in the silver haze.

Our horses were lathered and steaming. I didn't like the idea of not keeping Turk in front of me, but I found it easier to ride *beside* him than have his smell drifting back on me. I heard the slightest clicking of his bone necklace, and I glanced over at him. "Keep that thing quiet," I said in a hushed tone. "There could be Apache around here."

"Who are you telling about Injuns?" he said, his voice too loud in the stillness. "I've kilt more Injuns than my sister had friends in the navy."

"I don't care. Just keep them from rattling." I glanced at the long string of bones reaching down to his waist. "What kinda bones are they anyway?"

"Them's finger bones, my boy." He grabbed them, shook them, then grinned.

"Finger bones?" I looked at them, then looked away, shaking my head.

"Yep. Been collecting 'em for years. Injuns mostly . . . a few Mex. Might be a white preacher or two in there. You know how it is. Once you start collecting something, it's easy to go *hog-wild.*" I heard him chuckle and rattle the bones.

I stared ahead into the silver haze, studying the spills of rock before us. I saw what the Kid meant about Turk. It would be easy to drop a hammer on him if the reason ever came up. In fact, if a person had never shot anybody before, but wanted to just to see if they had a knack for it, Turk was a good

332

place to start.

Deep into the narrow crevice as the haze began to lift around us, I heard a shrill bird-call from high above us, then in a second I heard the call answered from lower on the other side. *Uh-oh.* I stopped and tensed, with my hand on my pistol, and listened for the slightest sound. The clicking of bones beside me stopped, and I wondered for just a second if I should give Turk back his big horse pistol. "What do you think," I whispered, "Apaches?" But Turk didn't answer, and I realized he must've been as tensed and listening as I.

"Turk?" I whispered again, still staring ahead. Again he didn't answer. I sniffed the air and noticed it smelt cleaner all of a sudden. *Damn it!* I swung around, but Turk was gone, seemed to have vanished. *Now what?* After a second, I slipped down from Morcillo, led him forward silently and over to the cover of a rock spill, drawing my pistol and scanning the crevice high and low. I heard a dull whistle from the silver haze above us and saw an arrow shatter against the rocks ten feet away. I flinched as I heard another strike the ground behind me, then swung around and saw it sticking between two rocks, quivering, no closer than the first one. They were above me, still blinded by the rising haze, taking pot luck shots, hoping I'd fire back and give them something to shoot at. I wouldn't.

Quiet as a ghost, I led Morcillo forward, hoping, praying he wouldn't nicker or strike a hoof on a rock. There wasn't a doubt in my mind that ahead of us more Apache lay in wait; but if I stayed here until the haze lifted I'd be a sitting duck. Turk had pulled back and disappeared in one direction. I figured my best move would be to head forward, get mounted and make a run for it.

I stepped up on Morcillo and sat there breathing slow and evenly, clearing my mind, coaxing myself to make a strike with my spurs. Behind me came the whistle of an arrow, then another farther back in the silver haze. A picture of me as a young man slid across my mind, then a quick glimpse of my folks, then Jesse and the boys. Somewhere in there — Quiet Jack, smiling, throwing back a shot from a canteen; and I braced myself and nailed Morcillo in the flanks. The big stallion bolted straight up, letting out a long nicker as he pawed the air. Breath from his powerful lungs exploded, swirled in the haze, and my shoulders snapped back for a second as he hit the ground and shot forward like a comet. I hunched forward, low, and felt his mane strike my face like a serpent's tongue, giving him rein, feeling him swerve past rock only visible at the last second in the thick haze.

He lunged up and over rock piles that I dare not look at least I try and check him down, and in so doing kill us both. Arrows spit across my back like angry hornets.

Ahead, where the haze thinned, I saw two figures jump into the narrow path, saw them go down into a crouch; but no sooner than one arrow sliced past my face, we were upon them. They leaped, one to either side as Morcillo shot between them, head down and stretched out, his hoofbeats sounding like a fast drum roll against rock and sand. I heard them yelping behind us like coyotes.

In a few seconds, the narrow canyon opened onto a stretch of flatland. The air became less hazed now. Streaks of silver lay in patches above shallow draws. I ventured a glance back and saw horses pounding down toward us from both high sides of the narrow canyon. They came in a spray of dust, descending from the rising haze, their horses stretching out toward us. I heard them yelling in a frenzied tone that tightened the tendons in my neck and turned my skin to ice.

At first I could hear them gaining ground. I felt something sting me just above the knee, but I only flinched and stayed low on Morcillo, not even risking the split second it would take to throw back my pistol and fire a shot. Then, as the land ahead lay more clear, I glanced back and saw they were fading back, winded against the pace of the big stallion, I thought.

Patches of scrub grass streaked past us. I looked straight ahead. At a distance of fifty yards I saw an eagle flying low; and I saw him shoot down as if into the earth. But then I saw the big wings raise back up, and I felt a chill run through me.

"Whoooa!" My eyes flew open wide. I let out a yell that would curl rope as I swung the reins, sitting back on them, standing in the stirrups as the stallion dropped down on his rear haunches, pawing backwards, then sliding sideways and stopping less than four feet from a yawning split in the earth that seemed to drop straight to hell.

I came out of the saddle, stepping back, snatching the reins as Morcillo righted himself and reared up, pawing his hoofs out toward the open air. The eagle soared down and hovered beneath us. My knees quivered against my trouser legs; cold sweat beaded my brow. I looked quickly right and left, saw no end to the split in the earth, and looked back at the horses speeding toward us from two hundred yards. I glanced down and ran a hand over the arrow sticking out of my leg, but it didn't seem important right then. Soon there would more arrows sticking out of me, perhaps a spear or two. "Jesus!" I shook my head and started to raise my pistol toward the spreading line of horsemen, but then I realized it would be of little consequence.

Morcillo thrashed and reared toward the wide open chasm as I clutched the reins. I glanced once across it, then refused to look across it again as I slipped back atop the big stallion and raced straight toward the thundering hoofs coming at us. At fifty yards I saw the lead rider raise a rifle over his head, yelling something; and I wondered for a split second why he hadn't fired that rifle. I didn't even want to think about what I had to do.

I turned Morcillo back and spurred him once more toward the bottomless ravine. Once more I saw the eagle rise and fall as we raced toward it. *It's up to you, Morcillo.* Then I held my breath as the thunder of his hoofs turned silent. And the earth disappeared from beneath us as he shot out off the edge, his body stretched out and sailing through thin air.

I felt myself raise slightly from the saddle, and time dropped back a notch and moved slowly, like a running man in a bad dream. I caught a glimpse of the eagle shooting up past us as we sailed by, near enough that I could see its eyes — eyes that asked what we were doing out there, hanging in the air where man and horse surely didn't belong.

But we only hung there for a precious second.

Even as the other edge drew closer, I felt the depth of the ravine pulling us down. We sped out and down, Morcillo writhing, struggling in midair, reaching, willing himself forward. And I lunged forward pushing — as if pushing would help. What a beautiful jump this must look like, I thought . . .

Behind me, somewhere up there, I heard the warriors shouting. Something crashed beneath me. I felt a hard jolt and saw a blur of sand spew up beneath Morcillo. *Made it! We made — !* But then I was once again sailing through the air, then tumbling, rolling and sliding in a tangle of scrub grass and Morcillo's tail and hoofs until we stopped in a veil of rising dust. Only when I pushed myself up from the ground did I feel the pain in my leg.

I stood, dragging my left leg and looking around for Morcillo in the cloud of dust. The arrow shaft had broken, half of it hanging down the back of my calf dripping blood. I saw Morcillo roll up from the dust and stand, stiff legged, with my saddle spun down around his belly. He shook himself off like a dog and scraped a hoof on the ground. Then my heart sank as I watched him turn and bolt away in a wake of dust.

Behind me I heard a loud yell, and I turned like a man in a trance. Above me on the other side of the ravine, I saw a warrior on a spotted horse sail out off the edge. I just watched with my mouth open as his yell turned into a scream. A heavy thud jarred the ground when he dropped out of sight and slammed into the side of the ravine. *"My God!"* I winched, hearing man and horse tumble and bounce until the sound of them dissipated down into the void.

I stood dumbstruck with my hands spread, looking over and up at the warriors on the other side. They appeared as stunned as I, gazing down and back at me in disbelief, until finally the leader raised his rifle over his head, waved it, and with a blank expression motioned the others back from the edge. Still, I just stood there as they left, stunned and staring. In a second, the leader reappeared at the edge, looked over and down at me for a second, shook his head and rode away.

Once I accepted the fact that I was still alive, my first thought was to find cover somewhere, least the Apache know of a way to cross the ravine at some other point. Yet I saw nowhere where a man could hide there on the barren stretch of flatland that reached a good mile before it stopped at what I could only figure was another ravine. Apparently I had jumped into a long land fault — a slice of earth a mile wide that had collapsed and dropped a good twenty or more feet beneath the surface.

After breaking the arrow shaft the rest of the way off, I dusted myself off and limped along near the edge of the ravine. I had no idea how to get back across. The ravine would be a hand and toe climb, down at least two hundred feet, then back up. Not on the best day of my life, I thought, let alone with a wounded leg.

I must've walked for over an hour, taking what appeared to be a gradual downward direction, stopping every few minutes and sitting down on the ground to relieve the pressure of my wound. I'd tied my bandanna around my thigh above it, and with the broken shaft still through my leg, bleeding was no problem. But I could already feel dizziness creeping up on me, and I knew the danger of infection, not to mention the fact that the arrow could've been dipped in poison.

I'd just stood up and started to walk on, when I heard something above me on the other edge. Apache? I drew my pistol and stood silently until I saw Turk step to the edge and look down at me. "Don't shoot," he called out, trying to keep his voice quiet as it resounded across the wide gap between us. I let out a breath, shoved my hat up on my forehead and looked across the ravine, up at him.

I watched Turk walk his horse along the higher edge, keeping up with me. He looked back and forth in both directions, and after a few seconds he shook his head and called over to me: "How the hell'd you get out there? If ya don't mind me asking."

"I jumped," I said, and I glared over at him, there atop his horse. "I oughta shoot you for cutting out on me like that, you son of a —"

"Now what the hell was I s'posed to do? It was me they was after anyway. They're all the time trying to kill me. I figured on drawing 'em off — giving you a chance." He swung an arm. "I came back for you, didn't I?" I heard his voice echo down along the ravine.

I considered it for a second and let out a breath. This was no time to argue. "Next time, let somebody know your plans," I said.

"Next time?" He cackled. "Now that's damned optimistic of ya, all things considered." I saw him look down into the ravine.

"How do I get back over there?" I asked, still limping along.

He scratched his head beneath his hat brim. "I don't think you *can* get here from there," he said. "Where's the stallion?"

"To hell and gone," I said, tossing a blood smeared hand.

"Well, at least he saved ya from that bunch."

"Yeah," I said. "Now all I gotta do is take up a homestead out here."

"I gotta rope," he said.

I felt myself perk up. "Yeah?"

"But it won't reach," he added. He gazed down the ravine, then back over to me. "How far you reckon it is across there?"

"I don't know . . . sixty, seventy feet maybe?"

"*Lord*-God! That stallion jumped it?"

"The drop helped," I said, not really wanting to talk about anything but getting back across. "You could heave that rope over to me. Maybe I could climb down with it and back the other side —"

"You don't give up easy," he said, chuckling. "But I can't risk throwing this rope over there. It was give to me by a friend. If it don't make it, I'd never get it back. You're more than likely dead anyways. That leg'll kill ya if it don't get attended pretty quick."

I felt my jaw tighten and I clenched my fists. I knew he was right, but I also saw how much he seemed to be enjoying my situation. "Listen, Turk . . . ride back to the compound, tell my friend where I'm at and —"

He shook his head slowly: "I don't know. That's a long ride, and I can't see anything in it for me —"

"I'll pay you! Just go tell him!"

"Ahhhh-now. I'd think an ole *trained* guerilla fighter like yourself would be ashamed to —"

"*Turk!* You rotten son of a bitch! If you don't go back and tell —"

"Now, you just hold it," he yelled. "I come back to help ya. But if you're gonna be abusive, I'll just say, *Adios.*" He reined his horse slightly.

"No! Wait! Don't leave —"

"Sorry, too late," he called out. I saw him

343

pull back from the edge, and in a second I saw a drift of dust from his horse's hoofs.

I stood there clenching my fists for a few seconds, then looked all around at the desolate land, took a deep breath and walked on. I had no idea what to do next, except to follow the gradual sloping land until someone found me or I dropped on my face. By mid afternoon, I knew I had wandered farther and farther away from the edge, but for some reason, it mattered less and less to me as I staggered along, no longer able to feel anything in my left leg. I had stopped and dropped down on a flat rock to try and regain some strength and clear my mind, when up ahead I saw a short line of horsemen rise up from the swirling sunlight. I squinted against the glare until I could tell it was the same band of Apache that had chased me over the edge. *Good enough.* I stood up slowly on wobbly legs and raised my pistol from my holster. At least I'd take a couple with me, I thought.

"Do not point that pistol at me," the lead rider called out in clipped English. Once again, I saw his arm raised, waving his rifle back and forth. They rode slowly toward me from fifty yards as my hand weaved back and forth like a drunkard's, then dropped toward the ground. I tried raising it with both hands. "I will not tell you again to point your pistol away from us," the lead rider called out. He sounded a bit perturbed, but not all that bad for a blood thirsty warrior, I thought.

"Don't come any closer," I called out, stunned and not sure if I could trust my own senses.

"If we wanted to kill you, I could have shot you with my rifle." I saw his hand moving in sign language as he spoke.

Light-headed though I was, I saw that each of the seven of them carried a rifle across their laps, and I realized he was right. Their bows hung across their chests like an afterthought. I lowered my pistol as they rode closer and spread half around me. "Then why were you pelting arrows at me?" I squinted, trying to clear my blurry mind.

He stared down at me as I wobbled back and forth. "We thought you were the stinking one. It was hard to tell in the dust and the haze. We saw you were not him once you neared the ravine, but by then you had been shot and he had gotten away." He shook his head. "If you had stopped, I would have told you it was a mistake. I have never seen anyone loco enough to make such a jump." His hand sliced the air in sign. "I have never seen such fright, even in a white man."

I heard a chuckle from the others and felt my face redden. "You speak English, huh?" I stood looking at him, still squinting.

He closed his eyes, shook his head again slowly and said: "What do you *think* I have been speaking here?" He turned to the one nearest him, reached out a hand, took a battered army canteen from him and pitched it down to me. "I am called Monralite."

"I'm called Beatty . . . James Beatty." I turned up a shot, swished it and spit it out, then took a short sip and patted my blood crusted hand against my numb leg. "Which one of you did this?"

"That had to come from Na'tiche. He got too excited. It was he who tried to jump the ravine behind you." He sat silently staring at me, then added: "He was my woman's brother. Now I must tell her what happened here. She will probably blame me for it. It will be days before I see any peace because of this. You should have stopped, instead of jumping. We would have made talk, and Na'tiche would still be alive."

I could already feel the water start to clear my mind. "Sorry," I said, "but when people start shooting arrows at me, yelling, *chasing* me, I get a little tense — just figure right off that they seriously intend to kill me —"

"We *seriously did* intend to kill the stinking one. I can not leave this world knowing I had a chance to kill him and did not do so. But we saw you take him captive and shoot the other two, and I said to my warriors, now there is a white man who makes sense. This is a man we can make talk with. Someone who will tell us why an army is gathering on our land."

"Your land?" I took another sip, looking from one to the other of them. One of them wearing a ragged straw sombrero eyed my boots closely; but I saw no intent of malice, and I eased my pistol back into my holster. "So, you fellers are really on the level?"

"The level?" He glanced among the others then back to me.

"Forget it," I said. "Just a figure of speech." I sat down on the ground and let out a breath. "Any chance I could get a horse from you?"

"After we talk," he said, "we will see what you have to trade. First we must get the arrow from your leg." He glanced at my leg. "Na'tiche was riding my best horse." His brow furrowed thinking about his dead brother-in-law. "My woman and I have just gone through a dark and ugly time. She says it is because I am never there — that I am always out trying to know what the white man is doing here." He gazed off across the ravine; a breeze licked at his hair. "Now this had to happen . . ."

It was nearly dark when we'd reached the bottom of the gradual fall of the land. Riding behind one of Monralite's braves, I noticed the slice of sunken land narrowed as it declined until at the base of it the two ravines came together at a point, still high, but now accessible to the flatland by way of a narrow path.

When we'd winded down the path, we made a camp beneath an overhang of rock, and two of the braves removed the arrow stub from my leg. They poured a finely ground red powder into the wound, packed it with a sticky green substance, and bound it with my bandanna. "So, the arrow wasn't dipped in any poison?" I touched a hand carefully against my leg and wiggled my bare toes. They were swollen some, but were coming back to life.

"Would you be alive now if it was?" Monralite had a way of making anything I said sound foolish.

As we dined on rattlesnake and stale flour crackers, I told him all I could about the contesa's band of revolutionist training on the land far back behind the compound.

He seemed relieved that they were not preparing to bring war on his small band. From what I could gather, his was a band of Apache that considered themselves under no treaty with the United States or the Mexican government. They roamed back and forth across the border at will, yet considered all the land around the basin as their own because it had been since, as he put it, *the beginning of time.*

"When the Jesus followers came onto our land, they taught many of us the language of the white man. Then, in Mexico, the holy men in robes taught us the Spanish tongue and how to make signs on our heart, the way the Mexicans do. Never did any of them learn to make *Apache* sign or speak *Apache* tongue. Still they say the land is theirs."

I watched him stare into the low flames. He seemed confused, and I took out the deed to my land and decided to explain to him how things worked. I said: "This is called a deed." I spread it out and handed it to him. He sniffed it and examined it in the firelight. "The only way to own land now-days is to have something like this with your name on it —"

He said something to the others in Apache, and turned back to me as they all grunted in what could've been a weak laugh. "How can you put the land on this small piece of paper? How can you ride on it, hunt on it, or breathe the air that blows above it?"

I thought about it, scratched my head and reached for the deed, realizing it was a waste of time explaining. "It takes some imagination," I said.

But he drew the deed back an inch; the expression in his eyes took on a crafty gleam. "Would you trade your paper land for a horse? So you can ride back to the place where they prepare for war?"

I leaned a little closer, reaching, but he drew it back another inch. "The land is worth a thousand horses," I said.

"You cannot ride a *thousand* horses. But you can ride one, if I trade it to you for the paper land." He watched my eyes.

I thought about it for a second. It would've been easy to lie to him, but I decided not to. "The truth is, I could trade you the land for a horse, but the white man's law would not honor it. As an Apache you can't own land, unless it's allotted to you by the government."

"I know this," he said. "I wanted to see if you would speak the truth." He nodded toward the others, then looked back at me.

"But what *will* you trade for a horse?"

I bit my lip, thinking of the federales riding onto the contesa's land, ready to spill the blood of a bunch of young Mexican boys, who were waiting like a litter of dumb rabbits for me to ride back with the lost treasure of the Conquistadors. I thought of Sheriff Patrick Garrett riding in the same direction to kill my friend Billy Bonney, if I didn't get back to warn him.

"Okay," I said, and I let out a breath as my hand went inside my shirt and loosened the catch on my moneybelt. "I've got something here I'll trade you for a horse." They all watched as if I were pulling a snake from inside my shirt. I drew out the belt, laid it across my lap, emptied out the jewels and pitched the belt near his bare feet. "There now, that's something you can be proud to wear for a long time to come."

I forced a smile and watched him pick it up on the end of his finger. "What would I do with this?" He bounced it up and down slightly, examining it, while I hastily scooped up the jewels and dropped them in my shirt pocket.

I reached out, slipped the deed from between his fingers and leaned back with a wider smile. "Well . . . you can carry *important* stuff in it, maybe give it to your wife to

351

ease the bad news about her brother's death."

"I see," he said, "*important* stuff," and he dropped it and gazed back into the fire as he spoke. "And what about the things in your pocket? Are they *important* stuff?"

I patted my pocket. "These? Important? Naw, nothing you'd be interested in." I pointed a finger: "But that belt, I'll tell you what. You could —"

"Let me see them," he said flatly, still gazing into the fire.

"But why? What could you possibly do with —"

"What could an Apache do with a fortune in jewelry?" He once again shook his head as if tiring of my ignorance. "Well . . . let me see." He tapped a finger against his forehead. "Maybe take them up the mountains, to the pueblo traders at Taos. Maybe trade them for rifles, blankets, food for my people?" He turned and faced me. "I could give some of them to my woman, to *ease the bad news about her brother's death*? I could give her some of them and tell her how we saved a man's life by trading him a horse instead of leaving him out here to die?" He leaned back slightly and watched me, the way one poker player watches another when a bet has just been raised.

I looked at them, from one to the other, watching the firelight flicker on the dark and somber faces. I cleared my throat and said: "Well . . . Yeah, I suppose you could do that with them." Slowly, I reached inside my pocket and raked up the contesa's jewels already wondering how I would explain it to her. I reached out and dumped them into his cupped hands. The others nodded among themselves.

Monralite laid them in his lap and looked away, back into the low flames, and said: "Next time an Apache wants to talk with you, it would be cheaper if you stop and listen."

I awoke the next morning, still a little weak, but feeling better after having water, food and a night's sleep. My toes were not swollen, and the pain in my leg was considerably less than the night before. When I'd stood up and looked around, Monralite and his warriors were gone without a trace. So were my boots and my hat — I'd slept with one hand on my pistol and the other on my glades knife.

At the edge of the cliff overhang stood a spotted mustang tied to a jut of rock. On the rock lay the flattened straw sombrero the older brave had been wearing. I leaned down near the ashes of last night's fire and picked up the empty moneybelt. *Another day another dollar,* I thought, wryly; and I put on the sombrero, slipped atop the horse, and gigged him forward with my bare heels.

By mid morning I'd ridden high up the other side of the ravine, past the narrow canyon where I'd first ran into the warriors, and up to the top of a high cliff overlooking the flatland. I sat there for a long time resting the horse. Somewhere close the federales would be swinging wide around the jagged cliffs and headed toward the unsuspecting Mexican rebels, but I could do nothing more than to push on atop the small horse and hope to get there in time to warn them.

On the far side of the flatland, I saw a huge clump of boulders with a tall slender rock sticking up from the midst. I studied it awhile, then turned my horse and started down a steep path to the flatlands. To my right would lay the back boundary of the contesa's land, to my left, the jagged running ravine that circled as far as the eye could see and disappeared into the far mountains. By the time I'd weaved down the path to the flatlands, I could see a wide curtain of dust drifting up on along the far horizon. That would be the federales, I thought, five, six hours behind me at the most. Not much time to prepare the contesa's army for anything but a hasty retreat — a mad rush was more like it, I thought.

At the foot of the path I turned the horse and gigged it out across the flatland, pacing it, to keep from wearing it out and once more being afoot. Crossing the valley, I thought I heard the deep powerful voice of Morcillo the stallion calling out from across the distant ravine. But the voice could've been real or imagined — seeming to amplify up from the land itself, so I just glanced around and pressed on.

Crossing the stretch of flatland, I looked around now and then at the huge clump of rock with the slender rock stick up from the middle. There was something nagging and ominous about it, something I couldn't quieten within myself. It seemed to sit there like a large fist, with a finger raised to heaven, as if telling god what he could do with his *enchanted land.* Thinking about it, I smiled, reached back with a raised fist and made the same sign toward it, pumping my finger up and down as I rode on.

I dropped my hand and turned forward on the bare back horse. Then it struck me all at once — *Finger Rock?* I stopped, turned, looked at it again. *Has to be!* I jerked out the deed, spread it and ran my hand across it. *Jesus!* My land started at Finger Rock. *From a point known as Finger Rock,* I read aloud, *extending to a point known as Dead Man's Cavern!* A sharp jolt of realization stiffened my back. *This is my land!* The beginning of it anyway. I looked all around, getting my bearings on the lay of the land as I gigged the horse forward. If that was Finger Rock — and how could anybody mistake it — according to my calculations, the contesa's compound lay smack in the middle of *my* land. Everything she had lay on *my* land! I thought about it, kicking the horse faster across the flatlands, folding the map and stuffing it in my shirt as I rode. *My* land! The Federales, Garrett and his posse, Frothe and his mercenaries, Monralite and his warriors — one of them wearing *my boots*! "Thank you Morcillo," I yelled. "Thank you Turk!" I glanced back at the big finger sticking up, insulting the universe. "Thank you Jesus!" I shouted there on that barren earth. They were *all* on *my* land. And I wouldn't stand for it.

CHAPTER 17

It was evening when I rode the spotted Indian horse across the last stretch of flatland. I could see the tops of tents flapping in the wind and cannon tilted high as I came within a hundred yards of the camp. Just as I wondered if they'd even posted guards, I heard a voice call out in a German accent and I slid the horse to a halt. One of the young men in a tan uniform seemed to rise up out of the sand with a rifle at port arms. "It's me, Beatty," I said, watching him step forward in the grainy light of evening.

"I see who you are. What are you doing back here? We heard you were riding out on the black stallion." He eyed the Indian horse.

"It's a long story," I said. "I need to get to Frothe and the contesa real quick. There's a column of federales six hours behind me."

"Sure there are." He grinned, a flat, sarcastic grin, and motioned me on with his rifle. "Ride slowly to my horse, and I'll escort you in."

He trotted along beside me a few yards over the crest of a low rise, took up the reins to a horse there and followed me into the camp. "Colonel Frothe is not in camp tonight. He is at the compound, but I will take you to the corporal." Then he added in a crafty tone: "He'll be most happy to see you."

"I don't have time to stand around arguing my way through the chain of command. I need to see Frothe!" He only smiled and nodded toward the tents.

A handful of young Mexicans drew around us, looking at me and the spotted horse when we reined up near the command tent. One of them asked about Morcillo as I stepped down, but I raised a hand cutting him off, and walked quickly with the tan uniform beside me. The corporal was seated in a folding chair with a boot propped on a small desk when we entered the tent. He stood up smoothing down his shirt. "So, Herr Beatty. At last we meet again. This time without the contesa around to —"

"We'll have to recall the good times later," I said. "I just rode here ahead of an army of federales. You need to get these soldiers and get the hell out of here —"

"Federales?" He glanced at the other soldier, then back to me. "Do not insult my intelligence, Beatty. This is American soil. They would not dare to come here!"

"Jesus!" I swiped a hand across my forehead. "Why does every son of a bitch out here think he's the *only* son of a bitch with no regard for the border. They're coming, Corporal! Count on it! Now, send out a scout or whatever you've got to do to confirm it. But meanwhile get these boys ready to move out."

"I will do nothing until I have orders from Colonel Frothe." He dismissed the notion with a toss of his hand. "If such a thing were to happen, we have a plan of defense." He turned to the soldier beside me. "Where did you find this man?"

"He came in from the west, riding an *Indian* horse," said the young soldier.

The corporal turned back to me. "Oh. And yet I understand that you left here on the contesa's black stallion?" He clucked his cheek, moving his head back and forth slowly. "Tell me, Herr Beatty. Have you misplaced Morcillo?" He glanced down at my bare feet. "Did he leave you sitting in the sand, and now you have come back with some concocted story of —"

I felt my neck heating up. "There's no

359

time for this!"

He slammed a hand on the desk. "Of course there's time! I'm in command here. We will tell Colonel Frothe your story in the morning when he arrives —"

"You'll be on a burial detail, if you don't get word to him tonight. Do you think I would make up something like this?"

"You are an outlaw, Beatty. Nothing you say should be taken —"

"Damn it!" I yanked off the battered straw sombrero and slapped it against my leg. "Then I'll ride in and tell Frothe. At least it'll save a couple of hours."

"You are not going anywhere, Beatty. Colonel Frothe is at this moment having to deal with your *comrades* because they have gotten drunk and stolen our Gatlin gun. I certainly will not let you join them!" He turned to the soldier. "Escort Herr Beatty to the surgeon's tent and post a guard on him."

"They did what? Stole what?" I batted my eyes. At first was to choke Jack and the Kid if they'd done such a thing. But as it sank into my mind, I almost smiled. Whatever Jack had done, he'd done it for good reason. And with all that was about to happen, I couldn't think of anything more comforting than a warm Gatlin gun.

"Yes, Herr Beatty, a Gatlin gun! We took it to the hacienda for a demonstration — it disappeared! Along with boxes of ammunition and several of our hand bombs. Your friends are thieves!" He slapped the desk again.

"Then I'm damned disappointed in them," I said. "But you've got to believe me about the federales —"

"You disgust me, Herr Beatty." He snapped his head toward the soldier. "Take him out of my sight."

"Wait Corporal!" I started to step toward him but felt the rifle barrel nudge my ribs. The soldier nodded toward my holster. Okay, I thought, no point in arguing. I raised my pistol with two fingers and laid it in the young soldier's hand.

No sooner than we headed to the surgeon's tent I started right in on the young soldier by saying: "You think this is something?" I grinned, waved an arm taking in the camp. "Hell, this is child's play." I eyed him closely, looking back at him as he prodded me on. "I fought in the great civil conflict, you know." Before he could say anything, I added: "Yep, sure did. Now you wanta talk about a war, there it was." I waved an arm: "Cannon crashing, columns of men colliding head on . . . blood, guts." I shook my head. "Now *that* was a *war.*"

"I heard of it," he said, stopping and pulling back the flap on the tent for me to enter. "I was only a schoolboy, but I heard of it."

"Yeah?" I leaned and entered the tent, then turned as he followed me. "All the way in Germany?"

"I am not from Germany. None of us are except Frothe. But we heard of it everywhere in Europe. And I was interested even then in becoming a soldier."

"No kidding? That's interesting. I fought along the Missouri border myself. Ever heard of Missouri?"

He smiled; I saw a flash of excitement in his eyes. "Yes! Yes I have heard of it. It was called the bloody border war, wasn't it?"

"Man!" I smiled, pushed up my hat, inching closer to him. "You sure know your military history."

"Oh yes, I do. I had once thought of —"

I hit him once, hard, right in the nose. Before his head even bounced back, I snatched his rifle, stepped back, and butt smacked him with it in the side of his head. "Never talk to a prisoner," I said down to him in a quiet tone. But he didn't hear it.

I looked down at his boots, sizing them, then bent down, slipped them off, and shoved my dirty feet down in them. I stood and wiggled my toes. *Close enough.* I took off the battered sombrero and dropped it beside him.

I took my pistol from his waist and stepped to the rear of the tent. There was still too much evening light to make a clean escape, but I couldn't wait. I slipped the glades knife from inside my shirt, slashed it down the canvas and peeped through it, toward the string of horses in a small corral a few yards away. I smiled to myself, realizing how many times I'd done this sort of thing before — how well I knew *this* part of any game.

Two young Mexicans were knelt down sipping coffee with their rifles across their laps. I raised my fingers to my forehead as if scratching, and walked right past them to the corral. There, I glanced around once, crouched down, stepped through the rails, and slipped quietly in among the horses. I patted them gently, moving through them, keeping them settled until I came to a big roan. I cupped my hand under his chin, led him to the rear of the corral, slipped the rails and stepped him out.

Yep. This part was second nature. Once atop the roan, I laid low on him and rode quietly, keeping the corral of milling horses between me and the camp. I figured with any luck, it would be an hour before the soldier woke up, a couple more minutes while he lay there realizing he'd been butt-stroked and boot stripped, then a few more minutes while he explained it to the corporal. I could've spooked the corral of horses away, but I didn't want to leave those boys stranded come morning.

I slipped away silently, then glanced back from atop a low rise a hundred yards out and saw no commotion in the grainy light of dusk.

For the next hour, I stretched the roan out across sand, stopping every few minutes to let him blow and rest. Night was light by a full moon — at least the elements of the heavens were on my side. I could ride fast and see well ahead. It would be a three hour ride, pushing hard, which meant that even if Frothe believed what I told him, it would be nearing daylight by the time he rode back and took action. I shook my head. *Where the hell would Jack and the Kid hide a Gatlin gun?*

I had just cleared a low stretch of scrub grass and slowed, topping a rise, when something slammed into the roan from the side and sent both the horse and myself rolling sideways, then backwards back down the rise. I covered my head against blows from thrashing hoofs as we rolled, then I kicked out away from the horse, snatching for my pistol. But as I pulled it up, I felt a hard blow against my wrist and saw the pistol fly away. I spit, shaking sand from my face and trying to see through the heavy puff of dust. "Freeze, Señor!" a voice called out; and I did, hearing a rifle cock very close behind me. *Jesus! Now what?*

As if answering my thought, a tall Mexican stepped around before me pointing his rifle and said: "You are being liberated by the army of Mangelo Sontag."

"Great," I said through clenched teeth, more to myself than him, "Just what I needed." I braced my feet, ready to lunge at him.

"Nada, nada, Señor!" He smiled as two more riflemen stepped in beside him in the dusty haze. "It does not work that way."

I took a breath, raised my hands, and said: "Alright listen to me. You guys are rebels, right?" I looked from one to the other, then added. "There's a whole army of federales descending on this place in about five hours. I'm headed in to warn —"

"No, no." The man in the middle shook his rifle back and forth. "We know who you are. You are going nowhere. We are here to take over the contesa's army — those of them who *truly* want to fight for their freedom."

"Then take me to Mangelo," I said. "Unless somebody makes a move, there ain't going to be a *Contesa's Army* left come morning."

"I've seen this bird," said a voice from in the dust. I watched the man named Fowler step closer. "I know his amigo. He's the one who free-handed my woman back in Sumner." He shot me a dark stare. "Where is that son of a bitch?"

I let go a breath. "Oh, him?" I shrugged. "Hell, he's gone. Took off right after that. Said he was sorry the whole thing happened —"

"I bet." The feller spit and nodded toward the darkness. "Alright, let's take him to Mangelo —" He grinned at me. "— See how he wants him killed . . . fast and bloody, or slow and with a whole lot of —"

"Listen to me," I said; but someone pulled my hands down and behind me, and I felt a strip of rawhide loop around my wrists. I let out a breath and let my shoulders slump. "It never gets easy around here, does it."

We rode for nearly half an hour, ever closer but more to the right of the compound. If I could get away, I could still make it there and warn Frothe — not only about the federales, but now about Crazy Mangelo as well. Damn, I thought, talk about the bearer of bad news! "I've got to stop and relieve myself," I said, as we rode along through the moonlit night.

"Tough," the man on my right said flatly. "Keep running your lip and I'll relieve you with a bullet through your kidney."

I turned to the Mexican on my left and said: "Does he have to talk to me like that? I mean . . . I ain't *done* nothing. I'm a veteran myself." He glanced at me, and I added: "Yep. Fought the great civil conflict. I suppose you heard of it?"

"Señor." He let out a breath. "There is no way for you to escape. So relax and enjoy what time you have left."

"Gracias," I said.

"Had it been up to me," said the man on my right, "I'd killed you and your friends back in Sumner. But, *noooo*. Mangelo said leave them be for now. Said, they might even be of service to us once they get to the contesa's. Said, who knows they might even —"

"Why don't you shut up, Fowler," the Mexican said, leaning forward and looking across me at the other man. "You know better than to talk to a prisoner."

"That's true," I said, nodding to the

Mexican. "One thing I learned back in the civil —"

"You shut up too," he said. "You gringos . . . always the talk, talk, talk."

I turned to my right. "They all call us gringos, huh?" I shook my head. "So, that night back in Sumner. Why'd you want to kill us? Just because my friend danced with —"

"No! That was just part of it. We rode there that night to take over Sumner. But there was you, your friend, the Kid and his bunch. It spoiled our whole plan —"

"No kidding? You mean Billy the Kid and us . . . saved Sumner? That'll never make the newspapers." I chuckled: "That really rips it." I glanced back and forth, then said: "You boys don't seem like the types who'd make a man wet himself in the saddle. Why can't I just slip down real quick —"

"Si, why not," said the Mexican; and I already thought of my glades knife stuck down in my boot. *All I have to do* — The Mexican raised a boot and kicked me from my horse. I heard them laugh as I stood up spitting sand. "Piss where you want to piss, señor. We have arrived."

Where we had arrived was just a low spot in the sand, partly lit by a low fire that was built down in a hole with a bank of sand around it. Four Mexicans and the two wild looking Texans I'd seen in Sumner walked up and looked us over. From behind them, I heard Turk's voice say: "Beatty, it's you! Will you tell these fellers I'm just a stinking ole sumbitch who means no harm?"

I glanced around at him, then back to Fowler and the Mexican beside me. "I'll give you five dollars if you'll untie me long enough to choke that bastard to death." I was still just trying to work up an opening for myself — keep everything stirred up until I could make a break.

The other man said: "Thought you had to piss so bad?"

I snapped him a glance. "No, I just wanted to give you a reason to unbutton my —"

His face swelled red as the Mexican laughed out loud. Then he lunged at me, swung his fist. I ducked as the Mexican caught him around the shoulders and pulled him back. "Facile! Easy, mi amigo," he said to the man from behind. "Can't you see he is only trying to rattle everyone?" He turned Fowler loose, patted his shoulder, and said to the others, "Put him with the stinking one until Mangelo gets here."

"Don't make me sit beside him," I said as two of them dragged me away. They shoved me over beside Turk, just out of the dim circle of firelight. I sat up as they walked away, back to the others around the fire. Fowler and the Mexican who'd brought me in talked for a second then mounted up and left. Now there were four left.

"You didn't mean that about choking me, did ya?" Turk spoke in a meek voice. I turned my face away and tried not to breathe too deep.

"Jesus, Turk. Somebody oughta, just to put you outa your misery." I scooted a foot farther away and looked back at him. "How'd you end up here?" I looked him up and down, saw a bloody welt on his forehead.

"It was pitiful," he said. "I was riding in to tell Frothe about the federales, you know? — figured it would be worth a few dollars. Damned if I didn't get took by this bunch." He looked me up and down. "How'd you get out of your predicament?"

"Apache," I said. "A real serious feller by the name of Monralite?"

"They're all *real* serious —" Turk nodded. "— But yeah, I know him. All the time in trouble with his ole lady? Thinks this is still *their* land? Hates me?"

"That's him. He traded me a horse —"

"Now, see there," Turk said. "If that'd been me, he'd kilt me sure as hell. Gives you a horse!"

"I'm just glad he showed up," I said.

"It's getting where you can't take a squat-down without somebody showing up. I remember when there weren't nobody out here but us ole —"

"Where is this Crazy Mangelo?"

"I don't know. I've never seen the bastard. But he'll be here. He'll kill us, sure enough — me anyways. He might give you a horse." Turk looked down at his boots.

"You up to cutting out of here?" I asked him in a lowered voice.

He turned his head slowly toward me: "Hell. I'll go anywhere with anybody for any reason. What ya got in mind?"

I scooted my black boot over near him and nodded toward it. "Took these off a soldier. There's a knife in it."

He looked at me curiously: "*All* of 'em have one?"

"Turk, damn it," I hissed. "I'm gonna scoot around where you can reach it, you're gonna cut me loose. Got that?"

"Don't get snippy with me," he said. "I ain't had no better day than you, you know."

"Sorry." I turned slowly, watching the men as they talked around the fire. As soon as I felt Turk's hand slip the knife from my boot, I straightened around and put my tied hands back against his. The smell was terrible.

I breathed easier when I felt the cool air on my wrists, and felt the rawhide strip drop loose. I reached over, took the knife from Turk's hand and cut him loose. I was all set to lean near him and tell my plan — tell him that we'd wait until they sat down and relaxed. But as soon as he was free he swung his hands around, rubbing his wrists, and said: "Now we'll see who's gonna bust who in the head!" He jumped up before I could stop him. The men snapped their faces toward us. They'd already grabbed their guns.

"Jesus!" I rolled away as Turk let out a squall and plunged into their midst. Bullets slapped the ground, following me. I caught a glimpse of Turk raise one gunman over his head and throw him in the fire. A cloud of ashes and sparks billowed up. Two men had hit the ground when Turk charged into them. Now they'd rolled to their knees, pointing their pistols.

I sprang up and dove into them. "Damn it, Turk!" I scrambled for a loose pistol, snatched it up and fired into one as he aimed at Turk's back. Then I waved the pistol back and forth, scanning for a target. But it was over. One man had grabbed a

372

horse and disappeared into the darkness. Turk stood with his arms spread like a grizzly, snarling at the downed gunmen. The one he'd thrown crawled away from the fire with smoke rising from his back.

I ran to the horses. Turk let out another squall and leaped on the man's back. I ran back leading two horses, and saw Turk snatch a knife from the man's waist. He raised the knife with one hand and grabbed the man's hair with his other. "No! Turk! No!" I ran and grabbed his arm just before he sliced the knife across the man's head. "That's not part of it!" I shoved him off the man. "Just one!" Turk's eyes were glazed, wide, shining like a wolf's. "Just one for my trouble? He's the one hit me in the head!"

"No!" I kicked at him as he crawled back toward the man. "Let's get outa here. He's still alive for God sakes!"

"So. That don't mean nothing. Ain't no rule says you can't —"

"Come on, Turk —" I reached down, snatched up a pistol and cocked it at him. "— Let's go."

We rode hard toward the hacienda, keeping a good ten foot of breathing space between us. I could feel time slipping like water down a drain spout for the young Mexicans back at the camp; but if I could reason with Frothe, he could still get there in time — tell them to retreat — get the hell out before the lead started to fly. Just as we started across the last few miles of flatland, I heard a voice call out my name, and I saw a figure off on our right, waving at us through the moonlit night.

Who the hell? I reined up, drawing the pistol from my holster, and called out: "Who's out there?"

"Shoot at 'im," Turk said.

"It is me, Mexican Abe," said the voice; and I saw him riding toward us, leading a horse behind him.

"Thought you said you killed him?" I glared at Turk, but felt a relief in hearing Abe's voice.

"I also told ya I was lying about it," said Turk. "Don't blame me because you choose to believe the worst."

"Abe," I said as he rode up. "It is you!" I saw he was leading the man who'd escaped us back at the campfire. I bolted my horse up close and grabbed his outstretched hand. "You're alive!"

"Si," he said, and he crossed himself. "No thanks to that stinking pig." He nodded at Turk. "And no thanks to this one." He jerked the reins of the horse he was leading

374

and swung it up near me. The man sat staring down with his hands tied behind him. "This is one of Mangelo's men, Señor Beatty. They are everywhere tonight. I saw them coming in and knew I must warn you."

"I know," I said. "He got away from us a few miles back." I glanced from the man, back to Abe. "A lot's going on here. But thank God you're alive."

"Si." He looked past me and stared at Turk with eyes full of threats and deadly promise. "I do not believe in taking a life. But this one —" He pointed at Turk. "— For this one I could make an exception. He and his friends threw me off a cliff and left me for dead."

"Don't start belly-aching about it," said Turk. "You still got a full head-a-hair, ain't ya."

CHAPTER 18

I didn't have time to properly tell Mexican Abe how glad I was to see him — to know he was still alive. But as we rode the last stretch toward the hacienda, I filled him in on all that had happened since we'd left him to wait for us in the hills.

I told him about Frothe, and about how the contesa wasn't really the Contesa Cortez, but a peasant girl — Flora Hablena — who'd been played into Quick Quintan's tangled game. I told him how the treasure was nothing but a legend based on superstition, but it was being used to control the young Mexicans who were foolish enough to fall for it. I told him how I'd ridden Morcillo out and jumped the ravine, and lost him; and I told him about Finger Rock and how I actually owned the very land we were riding on.

I even told him about the contesa having an affair with Crazy Mangelo Sontag —

which might explain *why* he was crazy. "Boy oh boy, Abe," I said when I'd finished. "This has been the damndest, I mean *damndest!* mess I've ever been in . . . in my whole life. And all because I won a game of pool."

"No, Señor Beatty," he said after a second of silence. "It was not because you won a pool game. All these things were waiting to happen with or without you. It was just the pool game that brought you into them."

"Maybe," I said above the horse's hoofs as we galloped along. It felt good talking to Abe, sort of like talking to some holy man — a preacher or such, but one who might *actually* know what he was talking about — who might even *believe* what he was talking about. He was silent again for a second while Turk and I just glanced at him as we rode along. Finally he said over to me: "But at least the devil Morcillo . . . he is gone? For good, si?"

"I'm afraid so," I said.

"But that is not a *bad* thing, Señor. You have done *some* good, if nothing else. Perhaps he will die out on that desolate slip of land. He is evil." Again he crossed himself.

"No," I said. "He's a fine animal. He's just been mishandled and misunderstood. It ain't his fault. He was just a part of the crazy game."

"Only you would say such a thing. It is the same way you speak of your *Billy the Kid*. But you are wrong. There is such a thing as *pure* evil, and no one can excuse it, or justify it. It does not matter *why* it is evil, or *who* conjured it, or even *how* it came to be. If it is evil, it must be stopped, whether it is evil created by demons who prowl our world or demons who prowl our mind." He tapped his forehead.

I scratched my head, knowing he'd just spun a full notch higher than I could reach; and I reined down to a walk, seeing the dim distant lights of the hacienda. "I reckon we all see evil differently, Abe. To me, evil is a bunch of dumb boys back there ready to get their ass shot off, because they've been pumped full of other people's bull whackle. That's *pure* evil, if there is such a thing — and if evil runs any deeper than that, I reckon it'll take somebody smarter than me to fathom it."

Turk chuckled: "If ya ask me —"

"I didn't," I said. "So keep quiet. You're easier to get along with when you don't say anything."

"See," he said, "your friend shows up, all of a sudden you get testy with everybody else."

I just looked at him, let out a breath, turned back to Abe and said: "Alright. We're riding in. I know you don't want to get around the contesa, but with Mangelo's bunch around —"

"I will wait here for you." He gestured toward Mangelo's man. "I will gag him with a bandanna so he cannot call out. Mangelo and his men will not find me. But I will *not* go near the hacienda and its *evil* contesa." He crossed himself quickly.

"Okay," I said. "Be sure and lay low." I grinned. "Now that I know you're alive, I don't want nothing happening to you." I turned to Turk. "Are you going in?"

"I told ya — anyplace with anybody for any reason." He shot Abe a glance. "I ain't picky like some."

Abe glared at him, then turned his horse and led the prisoner out off the trail into the night. I shook my head and gigged my horse forward.

When we'd ridden a few yards ahead, Turk glanced back in the darkness, then said in a quiet voice: "The hell was he spouting off back there? Evil this, evil that. If that's all folks got to talk about, I'm glad I stink so bad nobody wants to get around me."

"Abe's a religious sort of feller," I said, gigging my horse.

Turk ducked his head. "To tell ya the truth, as many scalps as I've lifted . . . all the other ugly dross I've pulled in my life, I just as soon not hear all that kinda stuff. Gives me the willies."

I looked him up and down. "I can't imagine why," I said.

We rode right past the two Mexican guards who turned and trotted along beside us to the hacienda. I noticed the place seemed deserted and I asked one of the guards about it. "All the older folks and the little ones are gone. Only Miguel remains. They will return once you have led the army to victory." I just sighed and went on.

I heard Quiet Jack's voice as soon as we'd hitched our horses and started through the door. "You shoulda looked after your stuff a little better, Colonel," he said; and he looked over at Turk and me when we walked into the room. I stopped and looked around the room.

Jack, Rafferty and the Kid stood behind a long table turned on its side; empty bottles and cigar butts littered the floor. Jack's pistol hung from his hand, as did the Kid's. Rafferty leaned against the wall beside the hearth with a shotgun hanging from his hand.

Frothe turned from facing Jack across the upturned table, and glared at me through glossy red eyes, clutching a big Swedish pistol. Beside him stood two tan uniforms in tall black boots. Their rifles swung toward me. "Easy now," I said to Frothe as the contesa came running to me from the bottom of the stairs. "A missing Gatlin gun is the least of your worries right now."

"Oh?" he bellowed. "And how did you know it is missing? Is this a conspir—"

"I heard it from your corporal." I saw him and the two soldiers eye my shiny black boots. "I had to break away from there to tell you that you've got big trouble coming —"

"Trouble? What trouble? Is this more of your outlaw —"

"Where is Morcillo?" The contesa cut him off. "Have you found the lost treasure?" I saw the desperate hope in her eyes, as if in spite of it all being a ruse, she actually believed I might've found the treasure. I shot Jack a glance. His eyes told me that he was not as drunk as the colonel might think. I also saw that he now owned a Gatlin gun, hidden somewhere close by.

"There's no treasure, contesa," I said.

"Ha!" Frothe took a step over toward me. "You sent a thief to look for gold? What did you think he would —"

"Shut up!" She spun toward him, then back to me, her eyes searching, desperate.

"Not only that," I said, "Morcillo's gone too."

"No, no." She shook her head slowly, swooned, and I caught her by her arms. She caught herself, swallowed and said: "Then my jewels. I must have them to —"

"This gets worse," I said; and I glanced from one to the other about the room, then told her everything.

She backed away as I finished, and holding her stomach, she sat down slowly in a wing backed chair." I knew something terrible had happened. All evening I kept hearing Morcillo call out to me, over and over . . . and somehow I knew . . ."

"One more thing," I added, taking the deed from my shirt. "This is *my* deed, my land, my hacienda —"

"This cannot be!" Frothe bounded over closer; I put the deed away. The contesa buried her face in her hands.

"It sure is," I said. "There are federales riding down on your training camp. By morning they'll turn it into a shooting gallery. You've got a precious few hours to ride your ass out there and get *your* army off *my* land." I glared at him, then added: "And keep an eye out for Crazy Mangelo. His men are swarming in like hornets.

The contesa's eyes snapped open toward me. "Mangelo? Is here?"

"See there," said Jack to Frothe, "it's probably his men who stole your stuff."

"Yeah," the Kid said. "But here you are blaming us." He spread his grin; Frothe fumed.

"Yes, contesa," I said to her, thinking it strange how even though I knew she was not really a contesa, I still called her one. "I had a run in with his men. They said they're here to take over your army. Mexican Abe is holding one of his men captive right now."

"*Abe?*" Jack looked astonished. "Where'd you run into him?"

"Out there," I said, gesturing toward the door. Turk and his men threw him off a cliff. But he's okay."

Turk had stood quietly gazing about the lavish hacienda, but he shrugged when Jack shot him a dark stare. "I didn't know ya'll was that gooda friends," he said.

The contesa shot Frothe a pleading expression. "He straightened his shoulders and said: "Mangelo will do no such thing. I will have my men ride them down and kill them." He turned to the two uniforms beside him. "Go quickly, get us horses at

once. We ride to find Mangelo and kill him."
He turned to me. "I will finish with you and
your thieves later. And I will personally
examine the deed —"

"You've got a busy night, Frothe," I said.
"Why don't you quit threatening everybody
and go do something." It struck me that
nothing I'd said about the federales coming
to kill his men had seemed to bother him,
not nearly as much as my telling him I
owned the land — not nearly as much as
the contesa's pleading gaze when I told him
Mangelo was out to take over. "You're off
my land by morning —" I couldn't help but
grin at what I said next. "— Or I'm bringing in the *law.*"

I let out a breath as he and his men
stomped out of the room in their shiny
black boots. "Follow them," I said to Turk;
and he spun around and disappeared behind
them.

"Do you really own *this parcel* of land?"
The contesa stood and rushed toward me.
"I must see for myself."

Again I opened the deed, held it out to
the side as I walked over to Jack and the
others. The contesa followed the deed like a
pup following a meat rhine. "But how can
this be? There are three parcels and three
separate deeds. Quintan would never have

384

gambled the main parcel — not with the hacienda on it."

"Read it and weep, *sweetheart.*"

I held it out for her as I said to Jack: "Good work. I figure they've already torn this whole compound apart searching. So, where's the Gatlin gun?"

Jack and the Kid turned to Rafferty. Rafferty smiled, leaned out from the wall, glanced in both directions and tapped his battered Wellington boot on the floor. I looked down at the metal grill of the floor vent, then back up at Jack and smiled. "You're kidding. That's the first place I would've looked."

I kept the contesa near me reading the deed, and when Jack and Rafferty lifted the heavy floor vent, I snapped the deed closed and watched the Kid tug at a rope tied to a metal loop on the bottom the grill work. He raised it hand over hand a few times until I saw the ugly steel barrels of the Gatlin gun raise up from the darkness. Behind it on a rope tied to the tripod came a box of ammunition, then another and another. "Plus," said the Kid, "I carried off so many Black Bettys my britches almost fell."

"Way to go, Kid." I grinned, turning to Jack, helping him and Rafferty hoist the gun and tripod out and spread it on the floor.

"Ya'll did all this while you were being watched by the whole damned place?"

"And drunk too," Jack said. "Once the Kid gets ta stealing, he can't stop." He nodded at the contesa. "But she helped too."

I turned to her. "I told you I did not trust Frothe," she said. I must not be left at his mercy — especially not now, now that the federales are coming." She turned her face from me and looked away. I'd started to say something when I heard a slight, ever so faint sound come from the open floor vent. I glanced at Jack and the others, busy with the Gatlin gun and ammunition, like school children with a new toy.

"Anybody hear that?" I cocked my head, listening.

"Hear what?" Jack spoke as he adjusted a leg on the tripod.

I waited a second, then shook my head. "Nothing," I said, and I started to lean down near the Gatlin gun. Then I heard the sound again, this time a little clearer — the sound of a horse nickering? From down in the vent shaft?

"Everybody be still," I said. We all listened until finally I heard it again.

"Yep," said Jack. "I heard that." He looked at the contesa. "Is that the sound you've been hearing all evening?"

"Si," she said in a whisper. Her face had gone pale as she stared at the open black hole in the floor. "It is the ghost of Morcillo come back to claim me for causing his death out in the —"

"Jesus!" I shook my head, knowing what she said was crazy, but not having much of an explanation myself. "But it does sound like him." I looked at Jack.

The Kid chuckled: "He musta got wet and shrunk, if he's down in there."

"Quiet, Kid," said Jack. I saw the strange look on his face as he and the rest of us stared into the void. Rafferty stepped to the hearth, picked up a long sulphur match, struck it and held it out over the vent shaft. The draft from the vent pulled the flame down a bit. "You ain't gonna see nothing like that," Jack said.

"I know," Rafferty replied, "but it shows the direction of air through the shaft." Again we heard the faint sound of a horse nicker, and though I didn't want to come out and say it just yet, it *did* sound an awful lot like Morcillo.

"So?" Jack stared at Rafferty. "What does that do for us?"

Rafferty didn't seem to hear him as he rubbed a dirty hand across his jaw, gazed at the contesa. "Sound travels on air. This shaft is to draw air back down into the shaft." He asked the contesa: "Are some of these shafts to let air in and some to draw it back down?"

"Si, it circulates throughout the hacienda."

"And if we're hearing this in the shaft drawing air down, we'll hear it better through a shaft coming *up.*" He raised his brow toward me as if I should understand. I shrugged.

"I know what he means," said the Kid; and he turned to the contesa. "Where is a shaft that flows up?"

The contesa searched our eyes in confusion for a second, then took a breath and said: "That would be in the wine cellar, beneath the cooling room."

In moments, there we were, the five of us, carrying candles and torches, standing in a circle around the large black hole in the floor of the wine cellar. Jack and Rafferty had brought the Gatlin gun; it lay at Jack's feet. The Kid had taken bottles of wine from a wall full of bottles, and stuffed them in his trouser pockets, shirt pockets, and down in his waist. He carried one opened in his free hand. Through the large grill work on the dirt cellar floor, the sound of Morcillo the stallion drifted up, more clearly now, riding the flow of cool air.

"Gentlemen," Rafferty said, after a few seconds of stunned silence, "it appears we have a horse beneath us."

They all looked at me; I scratched my jaw. At that second, all I wanted was a horse beneath *me*. One headed for Missouri. I'd done all I could to save the young Mexican soldiers. I'd sent Frothe to give them orders to leave. What more could I do? I wanted to pick up Abe, take my deed and my tired and swirling mind, and beat a path back to my cabin near Kearney. But I looked at Jack and said: "How the hell could this happen? Can you imagine something like this?"

"No." He shook his head. "But I couldn't imagine *Finger Rock* sticking up in the air either. That Indian didn't give you any cactus to eat, did he?"

I looked at the Kid. "This is your part of the country. Could there be caverns running far enough that Morcillo could be headed back here *underground*? I mean . . . it's a day's ride from where I lost him."

"Might not be as far, though, as the crow flies —" The Kid looked down. "— Or as the mole rolls. There's caverns under this country that'd run from hell to Texas," he said; and he threw back a swig of wine.

I spoke low, almost to myself as I stared at

the large hole in the flicker of torch and candlelight. "A horse could follow a scent — a scent of something familiar. I glanced at the contesa and thought of her handkerchief, of how Morcillo had let the scent of her draw him to me. It crossed my mind that if the scent of her had drawn me from across the desert, what was a few miles through a dark cavern . . .

I felt my feet aching raw in the black shiny boots, and I said without looking up: "Anybody got any clean socks I can borrow?"

"What's he talking about?" I heard Rafferty ask Jack in a whisper.

"Socks," Jack said flatly. "The man needs some socks."

"But why?" Rafferty's voice was almost a whine.

Jack chuckled. I saw him reach out a hand and take the bottle from the Kid. "Because we're fixin to go down that hole."

CHAPTER 19

Rafferty and the Kid had gone to the stables and came back, each carrying a shoulderful of hemp rope. I'd gone with the contesa to get a pair of socks while she'd changed into boots and jeans. The pain in my leg caused me to wince as I'd put on the socks. She took note of the bandage around my leg and reached to touch her hand to it: "You are hurt. We must do something."

But I drew away and said: "I've been hurt before — you've *done* enough already."

"I know you hate me now, but I must —"

"No," I said. "To hate you, I'd heave to think of you *period.* And from here on I don't plan to. I'll tell you the same as I told Frothe — tomorrow, you're off my land."

"How can you do this? After all we have shared, how can you toss me aside? I know I have made mistakes, but only because my feelings for you have had me so confused."

I just stared at her, slipped on my shiny

black boots, stood up and wiggled my toes in them.

When we all gathered back in the cellar, we quickly tied three long ropes together, tied an oil lantern to the end of it and lowered it into the black hole.

The four of them watched as I lowered the lantern slowly, getting a good look at the rough and jagged walls. I glanced at the contesa, leaned over, staring down intently, a strand of hair loose hanging past her face. The glow of the descending lantern glowed in her eyes. She looked different somehow — more vulnerable and more real — now that she'd become Florena the peasant girl, or was it perhaps because I now owned the hacienda with its fine tapestries and its gold vessels and polished woods.

I'd expected a long drop to the cavern shaft, but at the distance of less than thirty feet, I saw the bottom, then felt the lantern jar to halt on it. "And there we are," I said quietly. I looked at the others, and started raising the lantern quickly. "I'll go down first," I said. "I'll see what it looks like."

"Then I must go next," said the contesa. "If Morcillo is there, I must see him." She looked at me, and I saw the desperate hope return to her eyes.

"No," I said. "Jack goes next, then you.

Kid, I want you and Rafferty to lower the Gatlin gun down to us, then come on down. Until we leave here, let's keep that gat at arms reach." I looked around at them in the lantern light as I raised it over the edge. They nodded in unison. And I untied the lantern, tied the rope around my waist, and stood up as Jack and the Kid tied the other end around a heavy wooden beam that supported the wine rack.

All three of them fed me slack as I stooped down and slid into the black hole. With one hand on the edge, I hooked the lantern in my other and leaned out with my shiny boots against the wall. "Be careful," the contesa said. I almost said, why start now. But instead, I only nodded at the others and felt them lower me slowly as I braced out from the wall and walked down it.

Beneath me, I felt the cool air drawing upwards and heard the distant sound of the stallion nicker and what I thought was the scrape of a hoof echoing along a long tunnel. "You alright down there?" Jack called down to me, but before I could even answer I felt my boot heel bump the bottom, and I stepped onto it cautiously, lowering the lantern for a closer look.

"I'm down." I called up to them and felt the rope go slack at my waist. I untied the rope, yanked it twice and turned it loose. It twirled up and away; I turned and ventured forward with the lantern out before me.

I'd crouched slightly and crept along ten feet into the shaft when I heard Jack call down: "Hey. Are you gonna give me some light down there?"

"Sorry," I said. I turned and walked back toward the bobbing light of a candle, and saw Jack's boots feel toward the bottom, then settle down on it. I held the lantern out for him. "Afraid of the dark?" I asked as he untied the rope from his waist.

"No. Just afraid of being left in it." He turned the rope loose and jiggled the candle stand. "This is all I've got," he said. The candle flame stood thin in the glass shield, drawn by the updraft.

I sat the lantern on the dirt floor and turned the wick high; and we waited until the contesa came walking down the wall, then helped her the last step. She looked around and out along the pitch black shaft. "The treasure is down *here*! All this time, it has been right under my feet! I know it's here."

Once more the sound of the stallion came from the shaft. I glanced at Jack, then back to her. "Don't go getting your hopes up, Contesa," I said. "If we can get the stallion out of here, I'll settle for that." I watched the rope twirl upwards.

"No, it is here somewhere!" She clutched my hand and held it up. I saw the dry crusted blood from my leg wound. "Don't you see? You rode the stallion with blood on your hands. You led *him* to the land where no one goes, now he leads you, *through the darkness that runs beneath the earth!*"

"You don't know how to quit, do you?" I just stared at her until I saw Jack reach a hand up toward the Gatlin gun as it came down into reach. I stepped over and helped him let down the gun and the boxes of ammunition, then untied the rope and watched it twirl upwards. Rafferty came down next, then the Kid let the rope hang from the wooden beam and he climbed down it on his own.

We followed the long shaft of cool air, feeling it descend gradually deeper into the belly of the earth; and quietly we gazed around in the dim lit tunnel, moving single file, crouched slightly beneath the low, rough ceiling of stone.

At a spot where the tunnel narrowed, we had to leave the Gatlin gun. We turned sideways, and with our backs against the wall, continued on, careful of the torch flames. I was in the lead, and behind me I heard Jack say: "Does it get any better up there?"

"Not that I can see," I said; and I inched on through the narrow space, hearing once more the sound of Morcillo calling out from the darkness ahead.

At a point where the tunnel once again widened, I stepped into a small room of stone about the size of a horse stall and held the lantern up as the others stepped in. "Now what?" Jack and I both looked around at the small clearing, but I saw no way to go any farther.

"Follow the draft of air," said Rafferty. So I did, across the small clearing while they watched me, but it seemed to stop against a wall of stone. We'd apparently come to a dead end in the winding shaft — yet from beyond the wall there was the sound of Morcillo breathing, as if he were trapped inside the stone itself.

I searched, running my hands across the wall of stone. "This makes no sense," I said over my shoulders to the others. But then I leaned with the lantern, felt the cool air grow stronger near the bottom of the wall; and there at the bottom where the draft was strongest, I saw a crawl space no more than ten inches high. From within it I heard

Morcillo blow out a breath and scrape a hoof.

"Damn," I whispered. I looked back at the others, at Rafferty holding a torch. I held the lantern toward him and said: "Here, take this and give me the torch."

"You're going *under* there?" He stared down the slash of darkness as he handed me the torch. I didn't answer. I lay flat and held the torch back under the crawl space.

I bellied under and followed the torch through sparkling sand for five or six feet, feeling my back rub against gritty sandstone, until I saw the firelight flicker on four milling hoofs, and saw Morcillo sniff at the ground along the edge. "There you are big feller," I said, inching forward faster now that I saw the end of it.

I held the torch to the side, away from him, and felt his wet muzzle run across my face when I came out crawling out like a rock lizard. I stood up quickly and gazed into Morcillo's eyes, eyes that said he was glad to see me — perhaps to see anyone right then. He stomped a hoof and blew out a breath in my face; and I patted him, then stepped aside and raised the torch cautiously. The torch flickered.

"Easy, boy," I whispered softly, running a hand along him as I gazed past him into the darkness. I tensed up for a second as the glow of the torch drifted across the outline of a man sprawled atop a pile of stones that appeared to be crawling with snakes. But then I let out a breath as I saw it was not a man, but a skeleton, a skeleton wearing armor breast plates and a metal helmet. "Holy-God," I whispered, and again I caught my breath and felt a shiver run up my spine as I realized it was not a pile of stones he was laying on, but a pile of golden vessels.

The torch glistened as I stepped forward, realizing it was not crawling snakes I'd seen surrounding the man, but glittering strings of jewels that seemed to writhe in the glow of the flame. I stood dumbstruck, staring, moving the torch back and forth slowly, until I heard Jack's voice muffled by the wall of stone between us. "You okay, in there? Hunh? Tell us something here." "It's no myth," I whispered to myself. My voice was breathless. I stepped carefully over to the skeleton and saw his bony fingers clutching a dazzling necklace of gold and jewels. I reached out, pried it from his hand and dropped it around my neck. Then I stepped back when Morcillo once more slammed a hoof on the dirt floor and a stream of sand fell from the ceiling, twenty feet above us. I looked up and saw another stream of sand drop, this one closer to me. Behind me I heard Jack's muffled voice, and again the sound of Morcillo stomping a hoof.

"I'm coming in," I heard Jack say.

"No, wait." I called back to him in a loud voice, and felt the sound swirl around the stone ceiling. Another stream of sand poured and raised a puff of dust on the skeleton. I stepped back slowly and lay down at the crawl space. With the torch beneath it, I could see Jack's face on the side, in the glow of the lantern. "Don't come in," I said, trying to keep my voice low. "It ain't safe over here."

"What're you doing?" he called back.

Behind him I heard the contesa say: "Have you found Morcillo?"

"Yes," I said keeping my voice low. I wouldn't mention the treasure, not yet. I didn't want her and everybody else charging in and bringing down the ceiling.

"Why does he speak so softly?" I heard the contesa ask Jack.

"I don't know," he said.

I called out in a low voice: "I'm afraid the noise will cause the —"

"What? What did he say?" I heard the contesa ask.

Jack's voice boomed across the crawl

399

space: "What did you say?"

I felt myself tense up as I heard another stream of sand fall behind me, heard Morcillo let out a long neigh. "I tried to stay calm, and said quietly: "I'm afraid the noise will —"

"What's wrong with him?" Now it was the Kid's voice.

"I can't hear a damn thing he's saying," said Jack.

"I said — !" I yelled so loud my throat ached. "— I'm afraid the damn place will fall!" No sooner than I shouted, I heard a large crust of sandstone crash on the floor behind me. "Jesus," I whispered. Morcillo shied back against the wall; I tried to calm my voice. "Jack, it ain't safe over here. I'm going to try and find a way out for Morcillo, then I'll crawl back over there. Okay? Can you hear that?"

"Yeah, I hear. What's over there anyway?"

"Jack, it's just a big empty cave. Keep everybody over there till I get back."

I looked Morcillo over good, but saw no injury from the jump we'd made; and he nudged me with his muzzle as I turned and led him, stepping through mounds of treasure like a man witnessing a holy event. With the reins in my blood-crusted hand, I touched my fingertips gently across the mound of gold and jewels to assure myself that they were real. When Morcillo nudged me again, I had to shake my head to take my eyes off the sparkling mountain of treasure. *It's not a myth.* Here was the lost treasure of the conquistadors, found by a man with blood on his hands, who'd ridden the stallion into the dark — All I could do was stare.

I turned and looked closely at Morcillo, even decided that perhaps he was a descendant from the very first Morcillo, the one who'd stood on this spot ages ago and watched the treasure being hauled in by Indian slaves. Morcillo's eyes glistened in the glow of the torch, and for just a second I had to remind myself that no matter his lineage, he was only a horse. "But a damn fine one," I said, stroking his muzzle.

I led him around the cavern, staring at the endless mounds of treasure and searching for a passageway out. But I saw none, other than the crawl space I'd used coming in, only rows and stacks of golden goblets, large plates and sculpted figures that revealed themselves to the torch as we neared them. We were lost in a cavern of riches, an endless sea of bounty that staggered my mind. I reached out, ran my hand through a mound of golden trinkets and let them spill.

Searching the floor of the cavern until I found Morcillo's hoofprints, I followed them until we came to the mouth of a long corridor. Behind me I heard another crash as a large slab of sandstone cracked loose from the wall and pitched over a mound of jewels. "Okay, big feller," I said, "looks like this is as much as I can do for you." I took off the saddle and reins, stepped back behind him and slapped the reins across his rump. In a second I watched him bolt off into the yawning darkness, then I heard his hoofs clicking against rock until the sound faded away.

Walking back toward the crawl space, it dawned on me that this cavern of jewels was on *my* land. There was really no reason for me to mention a word of it to anybody. All I had to do was let things settle down, get everybody out of here, and claim what was legally mine. And there was no hurry, at that. It had been here since the days of the crusaders; I could come and get it any time I pleased. I would see to it the contesa got a healthy share — there was no point in being greedy — but I could share it with her without ever telling her where it was hidden. The rest was mine, *all* mine . . . and Jack's of course . . . and the Kid's, Rafferty's, and Abe's too, since they were in on it.

At the crawl space, I leaned down and said: "I'm coming through, Jack." I heard no answer as I held the torch out before me and snaked my way into the crawl space. "I sent Morcillo on his way. He should have no trouble getting out." Still I heard no answer as I crawled. I saw the torch reach past the edge before me, and I said: "Okay, give me a hand."

Then I felt my back stiffen as hands gripped my wrists and jerked me forward. "Of course, señor," said a voice. But before I could pull back, I was dragged to my feet and grabbed by another pair of hands, then slammed against the wall as a pistol cocked beneath my chin.

"We've got company," said Jack, from across the small area. I glanced at two faces near mine, saw the sly grin of Fowler and the Mexican who'd captured me earlier. *Mangelo's men. Damn it.*

"This time you will not escape," the Mexican said in my face. Fowler reached down, pulled the pistol from my holster and pitched it away. "Now tell your amigos to drop their holsters."

"They won't do it," I said. I let out a breath. Jack, Rafferty and the Kid stood against the far wall, their hands chest high, but their pistols still in their holsters. The contesa stood in the center of the area holding a torch. Beside her, a short Mexican stood holding the Gatlin gun like it was a rifle, the tripod hanging down his leg. His face looked strained from the weight of it. "And if that ole boy pulls the trigger on that Gatlin, we'll all die from the ricochet." I looked back in his eyes. "So there," I said.

"What do I do now," said the short Mexican holding the Gatlin gun, his voice sounding strained.

"Shut up," said Fowler. "We wait for Mangelo. He said not to kill them." He shot Jack a glance, saw the garter around his hat brim. "Got that from my woman didn't-cha?"

"You wouldn't *believe* everything I got."

"Son of a bitch!" He started to step forward but the short Mexican with the Gatlin gun staggered between them. "I *cannot* keep holding this —"

I heard the Kid chuckle. "Need some help? I'll hold it for you."

I saw a flicker of light coming toward us through the narrow crevice, and the Mexican with the pistol under my chin said: "Everybody freeze. Here comes Mangelo now."

"He is here?" The contesa spoke in a hushed voice. I slid a glance past her and thought it strange that she raised her free hand and patted her hair.

We watched as one gunman stepped in holding a torch, then another. Then I felt the skin tighten on my neck, and I saw a sombrero raise toward me as a figure stepped into the small area. I'd expected to see a monster straight from the bowels of hell; but I let out a breath of relief when I recognized the face. "Abe," I said, almost smiling.

"Mangelo! Mangelo!" the contesa shouted, dropped her torch, jumped toward him and flung her arms around him. "Thank God! How I have prayed for this day!"

I stood watching, stunned, my mind racing back and forth like a horse caught in a burning barn as he pushed the contesa back and looked around at each of us. I looked at Jack, saw him slump his shoulders, spit and shake his head. The Kid spread his grin. Rafferty looked like a man who'd just been goosed. I looked back at Mexican Abe as he stepped toward me. Now that he was Crazy Mangelo, I thought it strange that he somehow looked bigger than he had before.

"You didn't have to lie," I said, glaring at him. He motioned for the Mexican to lower the pistol from beneath my chin.

"Of course I had to lie," he said, half smiling in the glow of flickering torches. "A Mexican of *purpose* must always lie to you gringos. Otherwise you see us as either stupidos or criminales."

I spit near his feet. "Says you." I leveled my shoulders and lifted my chin, offended, but knowing he was at least partly right.

He leaned, lifted the glades knife from my shiny black boot without taking his eyes from mine. "Si, says I." He jiggled the blade back and forth in my face. "Who better to say it than I? I, the simple out-of-work vaquero who you trusted after you heard me say that if I had money I would only spend it." He nodded his head. "Me, with my religion, my peasant superstitions, my fear of evil —"

"He is an animal," I heard the contesa say to Abe. I heard Jack chuckle as she stepped forward and added: "He has used me, tried to take what is mine —"

"Look at me, Abe," I said; still calling him *Abe,* although I now understood that he was the monster, Crazy Mangelo, who everyone had heard of but never seen. I spread my arms, my blood crusted hands. "*You* tell *me* who's been *used* here!" My shirt was ragged, dirty, my trousers stained with blood from my leg wound, a bandanna tied around an Apache poultice that smelled like a wet dog.

"Si, she is a handful, this one." He nodded at the contesa, then back to me. "And you — you look as bad as Rafferty, and you smell as bad as Turk." He leaned closer. "I had faith in you, you know. I thought you were just a simple horse thief who would come here, take the stallion and leave. Then I would take the stallion from you. But noooo, not you. You decide to go along with her *lost treasure,* and to keep these foolish young fighting for her." He shook his head. "Now they are out there ready to die if my men cannot stop them. I am disappointed in you."

"Why don't I go ahead and shoot him," said the man with the beard stubble.

"Why don't you just *try,*" said the Kid.

Abe raised a hand. "No! I will not kill any of you. You are just fools meddling where you do not belong. I want only Morcillo. With him I can lead the contesa's army."

"So you're not above spreading a little myth yourself," I said. "To free my people —" He shot the contesa a dark scowl. "— But not so I can live in a grand palace."

"We want the same things, Mangelo," said the contesa. "And now we can have them. Was I so wrong to want a small taste of the good life . . . after living in such squalor? After being *bought* by Quick Quintan like some beast of the fields?"

As Abe turned toward her, I heard a heavy distant explosion and felt the earth beneath us tremble.

"Cannon," Jack said. "Looks like the federales got here a little early."

Mexican Abe glanced quickly around the small area, at each of us, then said: "There is no time to waste." He looked at me. "Where is Morcillo the stallion?"

I nodded toward the crawl space along the floor. "I just slapped his ass and sent him running. Maybe he'll show up somewhere out near Finger Rock."

He ran a hand along the smooth wall of stone. "What lies beyond here?"

"I believe he has found the treasure on the other side —"

"Shut up, Florena," he snapped at her. "I have men who will soon be dying out there. If the federales caught them by surprise, they will be heading this way!" He turned back to me. "So do not lie to me. There is no time. I can send a man under there." His eyes searched mine as I bit my lip for a second; then I let out a breath and said the one thing that I knew he'd never believe.

"She's right," I said. "Send a man over

and see for yourself. There's a cavern full of gold — the lost treasure of the Conquistadors."

"Mangelo, por favor!" said the short Mexican holding the gatlin. His knees trembled. "This thing, it is too heavy to hold."

Abe leaned down with the torch and looked along the crawl space, then ran a hand back up the stone wall. Another explosion rumbled in the distance; again the earth trembled. Dust fell from the ceiling above us. "This wall was made to raise up and down," said Abe, gazing at the top edge where the wall met the ceiling. "You were lucky it did not fall on you."

I stepped over slightly in spite of the pistol aimed at my stomach. "Jesus," I said softly, getting a mental picture of *me* squashed flat and left for eternity, or until someday when someone raised the wall and peeled me from beneath it — me, with the golden chain around my neck, only a few yards from the conquistador with his skeleton jaws yawning up at the darkness. "I had no idea," I said.

"Of course not," Abe said with a sarcastic snap. "Yet you would tell me of lost treasure in hopes I would investigate?" He grinned toward his men. "I don't think so, senor."

A deep tremble rocked the small area, following another powerful explosion. Dust fell; we looked up, then at each other. I smiled at Abe and thought of the treasure beyond the wall, of how it would wait for me, for now . . . or forever. "Can't blame a man for trying, can you, *Mangelo*."

CHAPTER 20

Streams of dust showered down on us as we slipped single file along the narrow crevice back toward the vent shaft. Abe and his men split up, two in front and two behind us, with their guns drawn, covering us, although it wasn't likely we'd start shooting it out with them, and we sure couldn't make a run for it. I followed Abe, watching him in the flicker of torch light while explosions rumbled above and the earth rocked and trembled below; and as I watched him, I had to ask myself, what was he doing here? What had he really come here for?

I asked him in a hushed voice as we squeezed along through the narrow crevice. He waited a second, then said back to me, "I told you, I came for the stallion."

"No," I said. "You already knew I'd lost him, so don't —"

"I also came to take you prisoners. To

411

make you sign over the deed to the land, so my people can live here in freedom —"

"Nice try," I said, cutting him off again. We'd slowed down as we spoke, and behind me I heard Jack say: "Is this something you could talk about later? The damned place *is* falling down!"

I pushed along behind Abe, talking as he moved along and tried to ignore me. "It was for her, wasn't it? You came back for the contesa. For all the talk you spread about how evil she is, you still want her. I'm right, ain't I?" Dust showered stronger from above us, and I thought I felt the crevice actually tightened around us.

Abe didn't answer until he'd stepped into the main shaft with me right behind him. Then he said: "I should kill her! She has placed the lives of my people in danger just to suit her own selfish indulgences."

I chuckled under my breath, dusting off my shirtsleeves. "*Crazy Mangelo.* Mangelo the *monster.* Mangelo the *madman!* All of it is rumors, rumors started by you. A reputation built on smoke and magnified on fear." I looked him up and down, pretty sure he wouldn't kill me. Whether he knew it or not, there was a part of him that *really was* Mexican Abe. Some essence of that person had to be there, somewhere inside him, in order to play the part so well. "Now your men will die, because they followed *your myth,* no different than the contesa's myth of ancient black stallions and lost *oro.*"

"This is not true," said the contesa, stepping out of the crevice as if materializing out of the earth and stone. "Mangelo has done what he must, in order to lead his —"

"Don't even start," I said to her. "I've seen you take more twists and turns than a snake on a griddle." I caught a glimpse of the Kid appear out of the crevice and stand beside Jack; and it struck me that for all his short comings, he was the only honest one of the bunch. Like Morcillo the stallion, his life had been molded and cast by those around him to suit their gain, tangled into the tapestry of time and circumstance, here in this enchanted land.

He stood shaking dust off his sombrero and slapping it against his leg. I saw him pull out a cigar and light it from the flame of a torch held by one of Mangelo's men. He winked at me and patted the front of his shirt. *A Black Betty!* Behind him came two more of Mangelo's men — one of them the short Mexican toting the Gatlin gun. His face was blue from struggling with the weight of it.

I looked for Rafferty but didn't see him,

and I thought for a second of the treasure back there in the earth, wondering if he was at that moment crawling back toward it. Then, as the ground trembled harder, I looked from one to the other of them and said quietly: "You people talk about freedom, but you don't even deserve what little you've got. There ain't a one of you who's not welcome here in this land, but instead of seeing that and pulling together to protect each other, you've all split up and ran amuck in your own direction. Now the ones that you fear the most — the ones whose tyranny you think you guard against, is right up there, ready to kick your ass up around your collar bone." I glanced up as dust poured from the trembling ceiling. "And you've all got it coming as far as I'm —"

"Shut up, Beatty," shouted Mexican Abe. "You know nothing!" He waved his pistol toward the rope leading up to the cellar. "Fowler, you go up. We will follow." He glanced at me and added: "I said I would not kill you, and I won't unless you force me to. But when we get out of here, you and your outlaw amigos must leave this place and not look back. That is my *order.*"

I shoved Fowler aside and took a hold on the rope: "Not on your life," I said. "You ain't telling me what to do! "This is *my land.* I'm sick of you son of a bitches turning it into a battle ground." I turned quickly to the Kid, saw the gleam in his eye, and I said: "Light it up, Kid. We'll all ride it out of here together." His hand streaked in and out of his shirt, and as quickly as he would've drawn his pistol, he snapped the Black Betty up close to his face and stuck the four inch wick to the tip of his short cigar.

Abe and his men ducked as if it had already gone off. I jumped forward, snapped my hideaway pistol from inside my shirt and swung it toward the others. "Drop 'em fast, or we're all dead!"

I heard the wick sizzling, and hoped the Kid was quick enough to snap it out when I told him to. The Gatlin gun hit the ground with a thud and Jack snatched it up. The others shed their pistols as if they were red hot — all except Abe who jumped forward and shouted: "They are bluffing! You fools!" But I grabbed his gun from his hand.

"Okay, Kid! Snap it off!" I shouted, seeing the wick sizzle down close to the canister; but he only grinned, and I shouted louder: "For God sakes! Kid!" Then I tensed, clenching my teeth as the wick flared against the canister. I braced myself for the blast that would carry us away in a spray of rock and blood. Then I heard the Kid let go a laugh as the wick fizzled and went out on its own.

I heard Jack chuckle, saw him run a hand across his face, keeping the men covered with his pistol. "Damn, Kid," he said. "I just sucked the seat of my pants plumb up to my rib cage."

"Had ya going, didn't I," said the Kid. His pistol was out now and helping Jack cover the others.

I felt my trousers quiver against my knees. I reached over and snatched the canister from his hand. "That wasn't a damn bit funny! You coulda let me know you'd disarmed it!"

"Yeah, but then I wouldn't have seen the look on your face," he said.

I let go a breath and pitched the canister back to him. "Alright," I said to Jack, seeing the contesa swoon near the wall, her face ashen and her hand to her throat. "I'll go up. You send the others —"

"Where's Rafferty?" Jack cut me off, glancing about the small area, still covering Abe and his men with his forty-four.

"Never mind," I said. "He'll be along." The ground trembled, this time more violently; and I looked at them again, shook my head, took a firm grip on the rope and raised myself above them.

I didn't realize how long we'd been under-ground until I'd walked out of the hacienda and saw the first grainy light of morning on the horizon. We'd quickly thrown up a pile of furniture for a barricade; and when we finished, I stood behind it and glanced up at the Gatlin gun mounted on the balcony outside my room — the room where I'd been fed grapes from the fingers of Florena the peasant girl poised as the contesa. It seemed like many years ago.

Across the courtyard, I saw the smoked and ragged outline of wounded soldiers leaning against the wall near the gates. They'd drifted in two and three at a time, drawn to the hacienda as if it were the giver of life — a holy shrine, sanctuary from the killing madness that its very inhabitants had bequeathed them.

I heard them bleating softly like wounded sheep. While the others — Frothe, the con-tesa, and Crazy Mangelo — had worked hard to scheme, deceive, prompt and pro-mote the spilling of blood, here before *me* lay the fruits of their labor, at my doorstep, dying in the thin morning light.

I ran a hand across my clammy forehead. I needed sleep and food, having had neither since the Apaches had stolen away in the night and left me to pursue this march of folly. I rubbed my eyes, turned to the Kid beside me and said: "Billy, you don't owe me this. Why don't you cut out of here . . . while there's time?"

"In for a penny, in for a pound," he said. I heard him spin the cylinder on his forty-four. "Besides, I can't wait to see ole Garrett's face if he rides in here about the time the shooting starts."

I smiled a tired smile. "You know, Kid. Seems like every time we run across each other, I get you involved in a shoot out of some kind."

"I've noticed that myself," he said; and he grinned.

I added, glancing away: "Strange thing is, I was telling Jack all the way here how we both oughta try to set a good example for you."

"Yeah? Well, I appreciate that." He spun the pistol into a shiny blur that ended in his holster. "*Strange* thing is . . . in some way or another, I think maybe you have."

"Really?" I looked at him. "You mean . . . ?"

"Yeah. Maybe I ain't said it, but I see that you boys mean well, most times anyway. You can't seem to keep from stepping in dung.

Fact is you kinda remind me of that Englishman Tunstall I was telling ya about. Ya give
a damn about a lot of things whether ya
admit it or not."

I just looked at him, and he spit and said:
"You boys don't ask for trouble, it just
seems to come to ya. I've never seen nothing like it. Hadn't been for that civil war, I
reckon you'd be turning dirt somewhere,
worrying about your crop of corn." He
grinned.

"Nothing woulda suited me better, Kid,"
I said, gazing out across the mist of dawn,
seeing the wounded straggling in from it
like ghosts. We stood in silence for a second,
then he said: "You know, Jesse, I always
imagined meeting ya someday, even when I
was a little boy stealing wallets off drunks."

"Kid . . ." I shook my head slowly. "I don't
want you to die here thinking I'm really
Jesse James —"

"Sure." He spread a grin. "Who ya want
me to think you are? Miller Crowe like
everybody else thinks?"

"Well, Kid. I'd like to think that Miller
Crowe's just as good as —"

"He's only the horse-man for the gang,"
he continued. "And let's face it, that ain't
much of a position. I know he ain't nearly
as smart . . . or as brave . . . or near as

bold . . . I know he don't have what it takes to really —"

"Alright, Kid, I get your point." I shrugged. "I'm Jesse. Just keep it between us."

"Sure will. You'll always be the top gun in my book," he concluded.

I thought about it a second. "Thanks," I said.

"But, me? Now that's a different story." He let out a breath. "I've never been nothing, and I never will. I was born bad, and I'll die the same way." He shrugged. Somewhere closer an explosion lit rose-red on the horizon, followed by a rumble beneath our feet. "I reckon that's why I don't much give a damn about nothing."

"Now, Kid. That ain't a healthy way of looking at it."

"But it's the damned truth. I grew up killing and been killing ever since. If I lived to be a hundred now, it wouldn't matter. The rest of my life, all I'm doing is paying for what I've already done."

"Anybody can change. You oughta know that."

"Still wouldn't matter. I've snuffed the light out of too many eyes — I'll owe for it from now on."

I gazed at him, then at the wounded as

they limped in and collapsed by the wall. In a hushed voice, I said: "Killing costs us all, Kid. I can't deny that."

But he seemed not to hear me as he went on: "Yeah, I was born to killing — caught up in it at an early age. It's all I know. It's only fitting that my best friend is out to kill me. What better way to pay for what I am. They call me Kid, but you know something? I don't remember ever being one. All the fiesta, the drinking, the whores and that —" He shook his head slowly, staring at the wounded as we heard them wail softly. "— It's all that comes with being *Billy the Kid.* Just the glossy trappings of a troubled soul."

"I know, Kid," I said, somehow realizing that not another person had ever heard what I was hearing; and I realized that Jack had been right. The Kid saw no good end, and for that reason there was none coming. "We all take what we can — what we think we need — to make up for the things we know we'll never have." I scratched my head, wondering if that made any sense at all.

I watched him take a deep breath and smile, a peaceful smile for a change as he gazed up and out across the endless rolling sand. "So, I take what I can get, *here* and *now,*" he said. "A cool breeze, a bottle of good drink, feisty music when it's around."

He gigged me with his elbow and laughed. "*Fast horse? Pretty woman?* No sumbitch telling me what to do? Hunh, mi amigo? Push it hard till hell slams it shut?"

"Sure," I grinned, "why not? If that's all you really want."

"It's all any of us want, one way or another," he said. "Look at you. That's all you've done since you've been here." He pulled a bottle of wine from inside his shirt and popped the cork.

I wasn't exactly sure just how he meant it, but I watched him throw back a shot, and I realized that at the point of all reason where truth sinks deep and touches nerve and bone, in his own cock-eyed way . . . the Kid was absolutely right.

I shook off the strange feeling a person gets at that hour of morning when cannon splits earth in grim reckoning of what's to come; then I thought about it a second, laughed, and snatched the bottle from his hand. "You ain't as dumb as you look, kid."

He laughed with me as I threw back a drink. "I told you I didn't *like* to think about stuff," he said. "I never said I didn't know *how.*"

"Hate to bust up your party," Jack called down from the balcony, from his perch behind the Gatlin gun. "But we got riders coming, a thousand yards out. Ya'll might want to pay attention here."

Thirty or more wounded Mexicans had taken refuge in the courtyard by the time the battalion of federales spread out atop a rise and sent four riders down toward us under a flag of truce. The Kid had lined up seven Black Bettys along the ground at his feet behind our barricade of piled furniture. Above and behind us, Jack sat behind the Gatlin like a captain at the helm of a ship. I walked over beneath the balcony with the bottle of wine as the four riders drew closer; and I said up to Jack: "Wanta drink Jack? Might be your last chance for awhile." I held the bottle by the neck, ready to pitch it up to him.

He shook his head back and forth slowly: "Been meaning to quit," he said. His expression was resolved, his eyes fixed above the Gatlin, seeming to have blocked out all around him, save for the federales on the distant rise. "If they make it to the barricades," he added without looking down, "you and the Kid get inside as fast as you can."

"By the time they make it that close, I guess you'll be ducking inside with us, right?"

I gazed up at him as he took pause for a second, then: "We'll see, when the time comes," he said.

"Now wait a minute, Jack. We'll make our stand, but if it comes to *dying* here —"

"Shoulda mentioned it sooner," he said cutting me off, gazing straight ahead. "The only *stand* to make is the one you'll die for. I'd as soon it be here as anywhere else." I saw him reach out a hand beneath the Gatlin and make a half turn on the crank. "I had nothing else planned for the day."

I pitched the bottle down in the dirt and walked to where we'd tied Abe and his men. Their eyes widened as I pulled the glades knife from my boot, then settled as I pulled Abe forward and cut the ropes from around his wrists. "Your horses are where you left them," I said. "Ride out through the back, gather what's left of your men if there are any, and get the hell out of here." I jerked him to his feet as he rubbed his wrists. "If I see you again, I'll kill you on sight."

"What about my men here?" He nodded down at them.

"Take them with you. Untie them once they're out of my sight."

"I'm still gonna settle with your friend for free handing my woman," said the one with the beard stubble.

I snapped out a shiny black boot and kicked him in the ribs. "You ain't learned a thing, have ya?" The others gave him a stare of contempt.

"What about her?" Abe nodded toward the contesa where she kneeled among the wounded with a pan of water and a bloody towel.

"She can go or stay," I said. "Maybe it'll do her some good to clean up the blood she's spilled."

"Do you love her?" Abe's eyes fixed into mine, and I had to take a deep breath before answering.

"If I do . . . it's in a way she'd never understand —" I glanced away, at her as she touched the wet towel to a young boy's forehead. "— Me neither, for that matter." Then I held his gaze and asked: "Do you?"

He turned rigid. "Of course not! I only came to take her army, her stallion . . . the land. Do not even tell her I am gone."

"I understand," I said; and I gestured the glades knife toward the rear of the hacienda. "Now get the hell out of here." I watched as he led the others away with their hands still tied. He slapped dust from the seat of his trousers. Then I turned, walked back to the barricade, crossed it and walked over to the contesa there among the wounded. "There's four riders coming," I said. "Maybe you better get inside."

She seemed not to have heard me. I caught her wrist gently as she dipped the towel into the pan of water. "Contesa?"

She looked up at me. "They are *children*, only children."

"Didn't you see that when you started bringing them here?"

"No . . . I —" She hesitated, looked about at them, then back at me. "I do not know what I saw."

"You saw power. You saw something noble and proud. But once they're shot full of holes — all soldiers look alike. And they all look like children." I stared at her. "I've seen many of them die. Most of them calling for their mother. So take a good look."

But she hung her head and held the bloody towel against her bosom: "I did not know it would be like this."

"Well . . . now you know. So from now on, when you start feeling how badly you were wronged, how rotten you've been treated by all the faceless *'Theys'* in this world, remember what you saw here today."

Her hands trembled around the bloody towel. "Then you say no one should rise up against their oppressor?"

"Not until you've counted the cost," I

said. I stood up, drew my pistol, checked the action on it, and slipped it back in my holster. I gazed out through the open gates as I heard the four horsemen drawing closer.

CHAPTER 21

Old Miguel had closed the gates, and the Kid and I stood on the cat walk inside the wall. As the four riders came forward I could see that only three of them were federales. The fourth rider was Turk, with a rope around his neck, his hands tied behind him, being led by a skinny little officer with hair hanging beneath his cap. Turk wobbled in the saddle. I saw dried blood down the corner of his mouth. "That sumbitch sure covers a lot of ground to never get anywhere, don't he," said the Kid. I just nodded.

"Greetings." The skinny officer called out, looking up at us. He lifted his cap and spread a convincing grin. "My Generalissimo sends you his regards, and wishes for nothing but goodwill between you and him."

I shot the Kid a curious glance, saw him shrug as he puffed on a black cigar. I looked back down at them, saw Turk wobble. "I wish only the same," I said. "But tell your Generalissimo that he is on my property, engaged in an act of war, and in violation of goodwill with the United States of —"

"No, no, no, Señor." He waved a gloved hand back and forth. "You have misunderstood us. We do not blame you for what has happened here. We know you have only recently acquired this piece of land — Señor Foam informed us."

"You mean Frothe?" I stared down at him, watched the other two as they looked around, taking in our position.

He shrugged. *"Foam . . . Frothe.* What is the difference, Señor? He is a *nice* man as it turns out. What is important is that we straighten out this misunderstanding among us, so we do not have to bother the United States Army with it. That is what my generalissimo *really wants."*

"I bet," I said. "But it's too late. I sent a couple riders out two days back, when we first heard you was coming. They're probably headed back here now with the U. S. Cavalry." He had no way of knowing it was a lie. "It's gonna look pretty bad on your government —"

He raised a gloved finger. "Señor, we simply lost our way and ended up here. Imagine our surprise when we found ourselves attacked by an encampment of our enemies right here in Nuevo Mejico! But make no mistake, señor, we are not here on behalf of our government. We are here on our *own* behalf." He shook his finger for emphasis.

"Ain't we all," I said; and I stared at him a second, then added in a resolved tone: "The morning's passing, and I ain't liking you a bit better —"

He raised a hand. "We want to leave here with no ill feelings, señor. That is why I bring your friend to you — to show good faith." He raised a boot and kicked Turk from his saddle. "He said you would be happy to see him."

"That ain't exactly true," I said.

Turk staggered to his feet and stared up at me. "Now, listen, Beatty," he called out in a nervous voice. "I'd have been out of here, if I hadn't followed Frothe like you told me to. If that don't make us friends, I don't know what the hell does!"

The skinny officer raised a pistol from beneath a holster flap and cocked it at Turk. "I can keel him for you, Señor. He smells awfully bad."

"Naw, don't kill him," I said. "He'd just smell worse." I looked down at Turk and nodded toward the gate below me. He hurried to it as Miguel opened it enough to let him in. "Tell your generalissimo there are no ill feelings here, so long as ya'll clear out and don't come back."

"Gracious, Señor," he said, again lifting his cap and dropping it. "But there is *one* thing I must ask you. Is the desperado, Crazy Mangelo Sontag, here? I'm afraid I must take him back with me. I'm sure you understand why." He shrugged, as if it was no big deal.

I returned his shrug and said: "I understand, but he's not here. He was, but I ran him off last night. He's a big, ugly son of a bitch —" I raised a hand above my head. "— Stands about this high, this wide. You ever seen him?"

"No, I have not. But he is a monster, Señor. That I know."

"Well . . . if he was here, I'd sure give him to you."

"What about the woman? The contesa who started all this?"

"That old woman's dead," I said. "I can show you her grave, her tombstone. Didn't Frothe tell you?"

"No." He shook his head. "Only that he and his men were misled into training a group of soldiers for her. Frothe is a *nice* man. I think he will come back with us to

431

Mejico and work for *us* now."

"It's always good to be employed," I said. "Now, if there's nothing else I can do for you —"

"Oh, wait señor —" He tapped his head as if he'd just remembered something. "— There is *one* more *little* thing." He grinned. "But it is not much to ask. My generalissimo asks that you give us the soldiers who came here this morning."

"Why? They're beat all to hell. They're no threat —"

"Si, I know. But my generalissimo must have them. He is a proud man, and must have his way on this one *little* thing." He pinched his thumb and finger together to show me how little he asked. "We will take them off your hands, si . . . por favor?"

I looked down behind me, at the wounded young men, at the contesa as she stood dabbing the bloody rag against Turk's chin, holding her face back from him as she did so. I looked out across the sand and up at the federales in the distance atop the rise, then back down at the skinny officer as he stared up at me. "You ain't gonna kill them on my land," I said quietly.

He shrugged again and grinned. "How far does your land run?"

"It starts at Finger Rock," I said slowly,

raising my middle finger and bobbing it toward him to show him what Finger Rock looked like. He looked offended. "But that don't matter. They're staying here till they're well enough to travel." For some reason I kept my finger bobbing toward him.

He braced up in his saddle, his attitude going sour, and he jutted his chin. "I see. Then I must tell you. We will not leave without killing them!"

"That's the spirit," I heard the Kid say beside me just above a whisper. I saw his hands go down behind the wall; and I saw him cut the wick of a Black Betty with a pocket knife.

"You must know, señor," the Mexican said. "We could have came here and rode right over this place of yours. How can we be good neighbors if you do not do as we tell you? My generalissimo will be disappointed if I do not take him something."

"Take him *this,*" said the Kid. And before I could stop him, he touched the short wick to his cigar and pitched it down at them.

"Jesus, Kid!" I ducked away as the Mexican officer leaped from his saddle and hit the dust — the other two spun their horses just as the wick flared against the canister. I slumped against the wall as once again I saw the wick fizzle and go out. *Got me again.*

The officer raised his arms from across his head and peeped out through a puff of dust. The other two stared up at us and backed their horses away slowly.

"So! It is games you want to play!" The officer stood up slapping dust from his shirt and mounted quickly. He pointed up at the Kid. "I know who you are! You are William the Child, a murderer . . . a desperado!" He jerked the reins high pulling his horse back as he continued: "Now we cannot be friends! Now I must tell my generalissimo the bad news! That you are not to be dealt with! It sickens me . . . what I must see when I return here. I will have to see your blood spilling in great pools, you're mangled bodies laying in pieces all over the ground! I will have to witness your eyes being picked out by the —"

"I'll spare ya the ordeal, *Earl,*" I heard the Kid say; and I heard his Colt explode beside me, saw the Mexican fall with a bullet hole in his forehead, and watched, stunned, as the other two spun their horses and fled in a cloud of dust. *"Remember the Alamo!"* the Kid yelled.

"Now you've done it," I said, turning to him. He flipped out the spent cartridge and shoved in a new one.

"Yeah . . . well, I just get tired of hearing

all that barn dribble, don't you? You weren't about to do what he wanted, was ya?"

"Naw, but —"

"Then what's the problem? You wasn't gonna compromise, *he* wasn't gonna compromise. Why stand up here scratching our dogs about it?" He nodded down at the dead officer in the dirt below. "Besides, we're already *one* ahead, and the fight ain't even started yet."

I turned and looked over at Jack, back there on the balcony, just high enough to have seen the whole thing. I raised my hands and shrugged; Jack squeezed the bridge of his nose between his thumb and finger and shook his head.

As quickly as I could I raised the few wounded soldiers who still had rifles and could still walk, and I positioned them along the wall. Once there, one of them had turned to me and said: "But we must hear from Colonel Frothe. He will tell us what to do." I just checked his rifle and handed it back to him. "Don't count on it," I said; and I scrambled back down from the cat-walk and walked over to Turk.

"Why didn't ya give up these damned dumb-ass soldiers. They'll get 'em anyway." Turk looked up from where he sat in the dirt. "Was that so much to ask?"

I didn't feel like wasting time trying to explain it to him. "I don't like no son of a bitch telling me what to do," I said. "Now, tell me what you saw out there. How many are there?"

Turk sucked his teeth. "Well, there's about forty up there and another hundred or so back at the camp. They rode right over Frothe and his *revolutionist* army. Last I seen him, he was pouring a drink for him and the generalissimo. Son of a bitch landed on his feet like a cat."

"That kind always do," I said. "What happened to your men, the scalp hunters?"

"They cut and run, I reckon. Can't blame 'em. They ain't never got paid yet. They're gonna be mad at me, just watch. And I ain't done a damn thing to nobody!"

I shook my head. "What about Mangelo's men? Any of them make it?"

"Far as I know they all made it. Only ones took a beating was these soldiers. There's a bunch of them laying back there. If I'd had a few minutes and a good skinning knife, I coulda —"

"Listen to me, Turk. You're gonna have to help us out here. We're gonna make a stand as long as we can hold out. Then we're gonna blow up the hacienda and slip out of here through a tunnel. It'll get us out to Finger Rock. From there we're on our own. You up to it?"

"Tunnel hunh? How much ya paying?" He looked at me with his brow raised.

"Are you serious?" I glared at him. "They're gonna kill ya, all of us, Turk. This ain't no job for wages. This is to save our necks."

"I ain't doing nothing less I'm getting paid. I've learned my lesson about all this *free* labor. If a man's gonna get killed he just as well make something for it."

I kicked him hard on the shoulder. "Get your stinking ass up, and get up that wall!"

He cowered away, then stood up dusting his seat. "I just want what's due me. I'm a mercenary now, ya know, just like Frothe."

"Yeah?" I turned, walked over beneath the balcony, and called up to Jack. "If he tries to get down off that wall, Jack, I want you to *empty* that Gatlin on him, alright?"

"My pleasure," Jack said.

"Alright!" Turk yelled and swung his arms. "I'll go up there. But if we make it out of here, I think you oughta give me something for my services, is all."

I walked away and to the contesa where she sat beside a wounded soldier, brushing his hair from his face. "Start getting them

437

inside," I said. "Get them started down through the cellar and out the tunnel."

"But what about you . . . and your amigos?"

"It's a little late for you to start concerning yourself about us," I said. "Just get moving. Get these boys outa here."

I heard a snappy bugle call, off atop the distant rise; and I ran over, scrambled up beside the Kid on the catwalk, and looked out as the stream of riders descended like ants down an anthill. "Okay, Kid, here we go," I said. I stood up and raised my hand high in the air. "Everybody hold their fire until they're close enough —"

"What the hell's going on here?" I heard a shaky voice from below us on the path leading down from the high rocky edge on the right of the compound.

I looked down just as I heard the Kid chuckle: "Hell, it's ole Pat! The hell you doing here, Pat? Can't you see we're fixin ta kick the hell out of the Mexican army?"

Garrett and his two deputies sat staring back and forth from us to the blaring bugle off atop the distant rise. "What the blazes have you done now, Beatty?" Garrett yelled as he pulled his horse back. "None of your business, Sheriff," I said. "You and your idiots just showed up in the wrong place at the wrong time."

"I'm here ta take the Kid in," said Garrett. "Don't try to stop me, or I'll arrest every damn one of you!" The first round from a cannon whistled in and kicked up a spray of dirt fifty yards away. Sand showered down like rain. *"Damn!"* Garrett ducked his head.

"Good timing, Garrett!" I yelled above the first volley of rifle fire, then heard the bullets thud against the wall beneath us. "We'll surrender to you right now, if you'll guarantee our safety!" I saw bullets spit up sand around their horses' hoofs. Garrett and his deputies reined around as their horses spooked beneath them. "Maybe we'll come back later," he shouted.

"Good idea, Big Casino," the Kid yelled back.

"Why don't you shoot him, Kid," I said, as Garrett and his men ducked back toward the high trail among the rocks.

"I can't shoot ole Pat like that," the Kid yelled. "I'll have to wait till we can face off fair and square."

"That's admirable, Kid," I said, nodding; and I looked out at the federales fanning out as they closed down on us. Bullets thumped against the wall. "Alright all you *rebels,*" I yelled out to the young soldiers huddled against the wall. "Get them rifles over the wall and try to hit something!"

I saw Turk gigging and poking them with a rifle barrel until a couple of them raised and fired, then another, then a couple more. Then Turk raised up with a loud yell, aimed and fired, and a federale spilled backwards from his saddle and rolled on the ground. The Kid and I raised our rifles at the same time, fired and dropped as two more federales fell. I turned around, waved my arm toward Jack, up on the balcony, and saw the Gatlin gun start bucking in his hands.

Turk flinced when Jack's bullets started whistling over our heads. "I hope he don't shoot *us*!"

"He won't," I shouted. "Just keep low." Then I saw the heavy Gatlin fire sweep across the riders like a wheat sickle, and I fired round after round from my rifle as the riders reined short and tried to spread out. Jack's firing followed the ones left of us; the Kid and I fired at the ones breaking to the right. Turk and the soldiers fired in both directions. From atop the distant rise, a cannon exploded, and I looked up at it as smoke rose and drifted above it. Then I heard the sound — air being ripped — as the ball rumbled in low and crashed into the wall like an angry fist.

The nearest soldier tried to bolt, but I

grabbed him, threw him back against the wall, and yelled at the others: "Don't run! Keep firing!" And I glanced down behind us and saw the contesa helping the line of ragged soldiers into the hacienda. "Faster," I bellowed down at her. "Get them moving!"

She actually stopped, turned up toward me with a hand on her hip and shouted: "I am doing the best I can here!"

I heard the Kid chuckle beside me above the sound of him cocking and firing his rifle. I heard the next cannon round whistle in, and ducked against the wall as it pounded up a spray of shattered earth near the gates. I leaned and took aim on the distant rise as the riders circled and gathered for another charge. Behind us, Jack ceased fire and waited for them to ride back into range. "The hell are you aiming at?" I heard the Kid ask me as I raised up the rear sight on my rifle and ran a thumb up it.

"They're going for our gates," I said. "I've got to keep them off it as long as I can."

I concentrated, squinted hard, took aim at the tiny specs on the horizon, and squeezed off a round. I waited, recocking, watching until I saw a puff of dust rise up fifty yards short. Then I raised the rifle higher, too high, I thought, locked it onto the rider skylighted on horseback near the cannon crew as they worked quickly preparing another round. *Here goes nothing.* I squeezed off the round, then watched for a puff of smoke. But none came. Then the tiny dot seemed to jump from the horse and run in a wide circle as the others chased after him.

"Kid!" I yelled. "I *hit* that son of a bitch! Did you see that?"

"No, I'm a little busy here," he said. I glanced at him, saw him reloading. I shook my head, glanced out again, saw two tiny dots meet with the one running, and watched them pull the runner down. "That'll keep the cannon crew busy awhile," I said, mostly to myself. I grinned, even as the riders gigged toward us for the next charge. "Jack," I called out over my shoulder. "Did you see me hit that son of a bitch?"

"Naw . . . I wasn't paying attention," he said.

I glanced at Turk and he said: "I saw it. Saw something anyway. Saw the generalissimo come down off his horse —"

"The gen— ?" I glanced out at the distant rise as the riders' hoofs pounded back into firing range. "—You mean, I shot the main man himself?"

"Don't know what you did to him," said

Turk. "But he came off that horse like he'd been poked in the ass with a hot pot-hook."

"Damn! I can't believe it!" I scratched my jaw, and stared out at the rise.

"Here we go," Jack yelled; and once again the Gatlin gun started spitting out rounds as the riders neared.

CHAPTER 22

Charge after charge we held them back, until after awhile there were more dead federales scattered along the ground before us than there were on horseback. But I knew our luck couldn't last. If Turk was telling the truth, there were still over a hundred somewhere between here and the training camp. I looked back at Jack on the balcony, saw him hold up his last box of ammunition for the Gatlin gun and shrug.

I looked down at the Kid, behind us now and placing the last of the Black Bettys in a small hole he'd scraped out under the corner of the hacienda's foundation. I thought of the treasure down deep in the cavern and wondered how much would be left once the contesa and the soldiers passed through, not to mention all that Rafferty had probably taken on his way out. *Easy come, easy go.* I couldn't have lived with myself, letting the soldiers die just so I could keep the treasure a secret.

I turned to the last three soldiers on the wall and nodded toward the haceinda. "Ya'll get going while the shooting's stopped. The contesa and the others are safe by now. Go to the cellar and down the hole. Follow your nose from there."

"We will never forget what you have done for us, Senor," said the last soldier as the other two scurried down from the catwalk. You have fullfilled the prophesy and set us free. You rode the black stallion out into the —"

"Yeah," I said, brushing him off. "Just get going." And I watched him turn and disappear down the wall. He didn't know the half of it. I'd rode the stallion, but just to deceive him and his fellow soldiers. I'd found the treasure, but purely by blind luck, and only because a stallion was as stricken by the scent of the contesa as I was, enough that he followed that scent through the dark catacombs beneath us. I'd freed them from the tyranny, but I wasn't quite sure just who the tyrant was. The contesa? Frothe? The federales? Perhaps it didn't matter in what way I'd fulfilled the prophesy, only that it had been fulfilled.

"They're forming up out there," Jack called over to me. I looked out at the federales as they moved together for a second then spread out slightly. There were no more than two dozen left now; and as they galloped forward, I noticed they did so not nearly as quick or as bold as when they'd started.

"Start lighting the wicks, Kid," I called down. "Then get the hell down through the cellar, pronto!"

"I hear ya," he said, and I saw him touch the cigar to the longest wick of the bunch — the one beneath the front corner of the foundation. He'd cut the wicks at varied lengths to make them go off at about the same time. I had my doubts, but it was no time to question his work.

I heard a loud shriek and the thunder of hoofs as the federales charged. "Alright, Jack, empty the gat on 'em and cut out with me."

"Right," he yelled, and the Gatlin began its terrible dance. A cannon round whistled in as I climbed down the catwalk with Turk beide me. I had to hold my breath as he passed me and jumped to the ground.

"Hurry up!" He hit the ground swinging his arm, motioning toward the hacienda. I jumped down and had started running behind him when the cannon ball shattered the gates and sprayed us with splinters and chunks of wood. But we only ducked our heads and kept running. The Gatlin gun fell silent as rifle shots slapped against the hacienda where Jack stood. I saw him duck inside.

He ran down the stairs holding his head as I passed him. A wick sizzled somewhere in the large room. "You hit?" I yelled at Jack.

"Nicked," he said, and we followed the Kid and Turk toward the stairs down to the cellar. I saw two more wicks sizzling, and heard the federales' horses thunder through the shattered gates. Rifles popped behind us.

Just as the Kid started to jump down the cellar stairs, I heard the contesa's voice and saw her shove him back. "Get back!" she screamed, running toward me. "The crevice is closed! It has caved in! They're trapped down there! Run!"

"Aw-naw!" I shot the Kid a glance, saw him turn and run to the nearest window — Turk right behind him. I grabbed the contesa, ran to another window as a rifle shot spit past my head. I saw Jack draw and fire his pistol. "Get out, Jack!" I yelled; and I saw the federales charge into the hacienda just as I saw Jack disappear through a window in a spray of broken glass.

There was a second, just as the contesa

and I hit the ground with glass showering down on us, when the world seemed to stop. I heard the rumble of many boots in the hacienda behind us, heard a rifle shot, and heard someone curse. I heard one of them laugh; and as if trying to run in a barrel of molasses, I snatched up the contesa, ran toward a water trough, and hurled us both over it as the earth came to life and seemed to drop from beneath us.

The blast seemed to run like lightning through every bone in my body. Then there was a second when the earth fell still, and we lay there lost in a heavy swirl of dust and debris. Pieces of furniture showered down, splattered into the water trough and down on us. I covered the contesa and held my arms back over my head. Water sloushed over the side of the trough, down my neck and back. Then, following the explosion, the earth seemed to rock back and forth, then settled grudgingly like an old man easing down in his chair. I coughed and waved my hand in front of my face. "Are you alright?" I asked the contesa lying beneath me. Her voice was muffled into the ground.

"Si, get off of me. I cannot breathe."

"I rolled off of her, stood up and pulled her to her feet. We staggered, choking, unable to breathe until we found a spot outside the heavy cloud of dust. Then we both fell to our knees gagging. I glanced beside me as someone else dropped on their knees there. It was one of the federales, but neither of us could do anything but hold our throats and gag at each other with our tongues out.

Finally, I managed to raise my pistol from my holster; but I only dropped it as he stood and stumbled away into the brown swirling cloud. I tried to call out Jack's name but my voice only sounded like a braying mule. "Come on," I rasped. I pulled the contesa along behind me until I found the wall and felt along it to where I thought the gate would be. When we came to the opening, we fell through it.

I crawled, pulling her with me along the outside of the wall. Within a few feet of the gates the dust had lessened, most of it still rising above the confines of the wall and showering down a few feet out from it. Wind drifted it out across the land and up the rise. "I've got to go back and get Jack," I said, coughing and wiping my face on my sleeve. Wait here."

But as I crawled back toward the gates, I saw Jack crawling out on his belly; and I took his arm and guided him along with me back to the contesa. We leaned up beside her against the wall and stared blank-faced into the swirling dust. After a moment, Jack pulled out a bottle of whiskey from his shirt, wiped it, uncorked it and handed it to me. "Found it rolling around in the courtyard," he said. "Couldn't leave it."

"Thought you was thinking about quiting?"

"I still am," he said.

"Good." I threw back a shot and felt the contesa's hand pulling the bottle from me. She coughed and threw back a drink. "Think the Kid made it?" I asked no one in particular.

"If he did, I oughta kill him," said Jack. "How in God's name did he cause such a blow?"

"I don't know." I shook my head. "But that shoulda done it for the federales."

"I found three kegs of gunpowder," said a weak voice from above us. We glanced up as the Kid dropped like a sack of flour and landed beside Jack. "Put them all in the center of the game room," he said. "Was that one hell of a blast or what?" He spread his crazy grin.

"Jesus, Kid." I shook my head, took the bottle and handed it over to him. "Anybody got any guns on 'em?"

"I do," said Jack. "Why? You gonna shoot the Kid?"

I coughed and spit. "I figure there's bound to be a couple of stragglers coming out. Reckon Turk made it okay?" I looked around as if he might be there somewhere.

"We'll smell him soon enough if he did," the Kid said.

I shook my head slowly and stared out into the haze of dust. "All those poor soldiers," I said. "They died because of me. All the while I was trying to save them from everybody else, I ended up killing them —"

"I doubt it," said the contesa. "They all made it as far as the crawl space where you found Morcillo. The pounding of the cannon had slammed it shut. But they should be alright down there."

"Oh? I suppose so, if you call being buried alive alright."

"We can dig our way to the cellar and let them out once the dust settles," she said.

I'd started to say something to her when I heard the slow clop of horses' hoofs coming toward us from out of the dust. We watched as Colonel Frothe, his corporal, and a Mexican in a high hat with a plume atop it came riding up. Behind them marched a half dozen more federales on foot carrying rifles. "Do not try to run, Herr Beatty," said Frothe's voice as they approached us.

451

"I don't intend to," I said. "This is my land."

"Want me to shoot him," Jack whispered beside me.

"Let's see how it goes first," I said. "I think they've had enough." I stood up, along with Jack and the Kid, dusting the seat of my pants and waving a hand back and forth in front of me.

"You look no worse for wear," I said to Frothe as he and his corporal rode ahead of the others who'd stopped ten yards back.

"Why should I? I lead the war, I do not fight it. It is not expected of me —"

"Say what's on your mind," I said. "I've got no casual conversation with you."

"Very well," he said. "I now represent the generalissimo. He has come to ask you one last time to give up the soldiers to him."

"Jesus, Frothe. How can you shave yourself without wanting to cut your throat. They were *your* men, following *your* lead! You'll just hand them over to be killed?"

"It is a tough business I'm in. I am a mercenary. I fight only for the money."

I looked at the corporal and said: "You oughta pay attention here, boy. The day might come when it's cheaper to let you die than to —"

"I trained him, Herr Beatty. He is just like

me. He fights for the highest dollar, nothing more. None of your sentimentality."

"Alright, Frothe," I slumped and let out a breath. "But the soldiers are dead. Tell your generalissimo to see for himself."

"I can speak the *Ingles*. I am a learned man," I heard the generalissimo call out. "Are you the asshole gringo who shot me?" He gigged his horse forward slowly, glaring down at me as the dust swirled away on a breeze. The foot soldiers followed him.

"Shot you?" I leaned and looked over at Jack and the Kid. "See? I told you I hit somebody." I saw Jack's thumb hooked behind his pistol. The kid had taken out a cigar, lit it, and puffed it with his crazy grin, watching the federales. *Uh-oh.*

"Do not get full of yourself, Herr Beatty," Frothe said in a tone of contempt. "You only ruined his boot."

I looked at the generalissimo's right boot and saw half the sole hanging down from his stirrup. He nodded toward the broken gates. "Show me the dead soldiers, Senor. I will settle with you afterwards."

Two federales staggered past us as we walked inside the walls, followed by Frothe, the generalissimo and the others. The dust had settled considerably, and we stood staring at the pile of rubble that had once been the hacienda of the Contesa Cortez, then Quick Quintan, then Florena the peasant girl, then mine, Jeston Nash, aka Miller Crowe, aka James Beatty. Now it belonged to the earth once more, and the wounded soldiers trapped beneath it. I hoped the contesa was right, that they were still alive, and that we could get rid of the others and dig them out.

The generalissimo laughed, turned, and said something in Spanish to his men. They laughed also but it didn't sound like their hearts were in it. I looked up at Frothe, and he said: "The generalissimo thinks it's funny that you, the great *conquistador,* the one sent to conquer their oppressor, have buried them likes the vermin they are."

I felt my neck heat up. I looked at the Kid puffing his cigar, at Jack smiling his smile of warning, like a wildcat showing its fangs. "I'm glad you son of a bitches find it so amusing. Now, unless you wanta start fighting all over again, get the hell off my property!"

Frothe turned to the generalissimo, and rattled back and forth in Spanish, too fast for me to understand. I heard the Kid chuckle as he listened. Then Frothe turned to me. "He says you must pay for ruining his boot."

454

I just stared at him. "After all the federales we killed, he wants revenge for a lousy *boot*?"

"Si. That is exactly what I want. What do I care about my soldiers? Soldiers are fools. The mountains are full of young fools who will replace those you've killed." He turned to his men on foot and laughed. They laughed with him, but again their hearts didn't seem to be in it. "What concerns me is *boots*! Senor —" He pointed at my shiny black boots. "— Get them off!"

I looked at Jack and the Kid. "It's your call," Jack said just above a whisper.

I let out a tense breath. *Damn it.* I sat down and wiggled the boots from my feet. When I stood up, I lifted them by their tops and pitched them over in the dust beside his horse. A foot soldier came forward, picked them up, dusted them and started to hand them up to him. But the generalissimo waved him back, stepped down from his horse and walked over to a pile of debris as the soldier followed. Frothe and his corporal dismounted and walked over, watched the generalissimo change boots and stand up stamping his feet in the dirt.

He grunted and grinned, then looked at the contesa as she cowered behind me covered with dust. "Who is she?"

"She's —"

"I am the Contesa Cortez, the one who —"

"She's a peasant girl by the name of Florena. She's not the contesa."

"Not the one who started all this?" He eyed her closely.

"No. That woman is dead," I said, shooting Frothe a glance to see if he would say anything. He only stared at me. "I can show you her tombstone." I glanced around at the debris. "It's here somewhere." I caught a glimpse of the Kid puffing the cigar.

"Ahhh." The generalissimo waved a hand. "This one is no contesa. She has the feet of a peasant —"

"What is wrong with *my* feet?" she snapped at him.

"Will you shut up?" I felt like popping her on the head.

"I have no time to look at tombstones." He stepped close to me, eyed me up and down, and I said: "You are lucky I do not kill you." He looked down and wiggled his toes inside my shiny black boots. "But I take these boots for my trouble —" He looked all around. "— Since there is nothing else worth taking back with me." He turned to walk toward his horse and I let out another breath knowing it was over.

But then I heard the sizzle of a wick and I snapped around toward the Kid. "Ah-yeah? Well take *this* with you!"

"Kid! Don't!" But he'd already pitched it near the generalissimo's feet as I jumped to stop him. Everyone tensed, but then settled as a sly grin swept the generalissimo's face.

The generalissimo looked down at the wick sizzling at his feet, leaned down and picked it up. "I heard what you did. Do I look as stupid as the ones I sent here earlier — that you think you can fool me?"

"Damn it, Kid. That's starting to get a little old." I shook my head and stepped forward to take it from the generalissimo.

The Kid shrugged. "Anything for a laugh."

The generalissimo stepped toward his men with the sizzling wick drawing close to the canister; they shied back. One took off running, then the others broke and followed. "Your friend, Herr Bonney does not know when to stop —"

"I've had it with you, Kid," I said; but then when I looked toward him, I saw him dive over a mound of rubble. *Oh hell!*

I glanced quickly toward the generalissimo, saw him raise the canister near his face. *"Booooom!"* he called out in a wild laugh; but Jack had already seen what was happening. He grabbed the contesa and made a dive for it as I dropped into a ball with my arms over my head.

I stood up slowly, my ears ringing, staring at the rise of black from the foot deep hole in the ground where the generalissimo had stood a second before. Now pieces of uniform, bones, and a boot sole showered down on us. I looked at Frothe as he and his corporal stood splattered with blood. "You fool!" Frothe screamed. He pointed at me and yelled to the soldiers. "Kill them! Kill them all! This instant!"

I dived over the rubble beside the Kid, saw him holding his sides, laughing. I looked up over the debris cautiously when I realized there was no rifle fire. "I order you to kill them. They have murdered your leader!"

The federales stood looking at the hole where the leader had stood. "Si," said one of them. "But I heard what he said about soldiers. That we are fools — who mean no more than a pair of boots." He leaned and spit at the hole in the ground. "Let him avenge himself in hades."

I stepped up over the rubble, picking up a long oak stair balustrade on my way. I saw the soldiers step away from the hole in the ground. They turned and walked away, out through the gates, and away into the dust.

The Kid stood up also. "I love these damn hand bombs, don't you?"

I didn't answer him. Instead I looked at Frothe and said in a low quiet tone: "You're running out of buddies." I slapped the oak club against my palm. "Now get those boots off and pitch them over here."

I watched as Frothe rode away barefoot beside his corporal, then Jack, the Kid, and I worked for two hours getting the debris pulled away from above the cellar. I wasn't about to forget about the hundred federales still off in the distance, heading this way for all I knew.

When we tipped over a large piece of floor, I saw dust-caked faces peer up at us, then we jumped down near the opening and began lifting them up. I looked up and saw Turk standing at the top of the rubble above me. "The hell's going on?" he called down to me. "The hell's it look like? We're getting these soldiers outa here."

He started to step down, but I held up a hand. "It's too close down here, Turk. Stay up there. Round up some horses for us. We could be getting more company any minute, if we don't hurry."

"Alright," he said. "I'll do what I can. I

got knocked plumb over to the barn, you know."

"Too bad," I said, helping the soldiers. "It's been a rough day for everybody."

No sooner than the last soldier crawled up out of the ground, I heard the sound of hoofs and looked around just in time to see Mexican Abe and a half dozen riders come through the gates. "That's good timing," Jack said; and he quickly picked up a rifle and took cover behind a pile of rubble. "Say the word and I'll start chopping at 'em."

"Easy, Jack," I said, as the Kid stepped over beside him. "There's been enough killing here."

I saw Turk scramble behind the debris as Abe and two of his men reined up ahead of the others and stopped in front of me. "What do you want now, *Crazy* Mangelo?" I stared at him with a hand on a pistol I'd shoved down in my waist.

"What do I want? I want these soldiers, of course." He waved a hand toward the wounded men who'd gathered, dusting themselves off near the wall. Some of them looked up, others just sat slapping dust and coughing.

"You are not taking them," said the contesa, walking forward with a dust covered rifle pointed at him. "*I* brought them together and *I* will disband them."

"You are finished, Florena," said Abe, jutting his chin. "You and *your* revolution. You have done nothing but get many people killed. Now you can go back to your hovel in shame! You can spend your days thinking about what you could've done if you had beeen blinded by all of *this.*" He gestured toward the great waste of rubble and dust where the hacienda once stood. Then he turned back to me as the contesa let the rifle slump in her hands. "You have done us a great favor by destroying this place. It is the *only* reason destiny brought you here."

"Glad I could help," I said with a sarcastic turn to my voice. "But I didn't go to all the trouble saving these boys just so you can take over and get them killed."

"Oh? And what will you do when the rest of the federales get here? Can you lead them out of here? And if you can, what then? Do you have a place for them? A way to feed them?" He shook his head and grinned. "Senor Beatty, there is more to freeing people than just *setting* them free. Tomorrow always comes, and with it the needs of the living. You have nothing more to offer —"

"That may be, but it'll be up to them what they do. They're free enough to make up

461

their own minds."

"Then we will ask them." He turned in his saddle and called out to the soldiers: "Who will come with me? Beatty has struck the first blow by killing the federales. He has saved many of you, saved you take up the fight for those who have fallen. I go now to prepare for the liberation of the people of Mejico! Those who follow me will ride like the wind! We will fight . . . and die if need be. But no one will tell us how to live our lives again. *Si?* Now who will follow me? Who will let *me* lead them? Who will do as *I* say?"

I stood stunned as the wounded soldiers slowly came forward, one and two at a time, some helping the others with their arms looped about their shoulders. I watched them form up a ragged line near Mexican Abe on his dust covered horse. "Jesus," I whispered under my breath. I turned to Jack, Turk and the Kid, who'd stood up from behind the rubble and watched.

"Let it go," said Jack. "They're all free to choose."

"No!" I turned toward them with a hand in the air. "Listen to me! Can't you hear what he's saying? He's telling you to follow *him. Him,* instead of following your own minds. Is that what you want? Is that any better than what you had?"

They looked at each other and scratched their heads. They looked up at Abe who only shrugged and smiled. Then they turned to me, and one of them said: "We are grateful that you have pulled us up from the dark hole, that you have fought the federales to spare our lives." He shook his head back and forth slowly and said with a sad smile: "But we must all follow *someone* . . . until we know for ourselves where *we* are going. Si?"

I just stared at him.

"Si," I said.

Chapter 23

I still stood there, just watching until Abe led the foot soldiers out of sight, watching as they disappeared in the wake of their own dust. I heard the sizzle of a wick burning beside me, and I turned as I heard the Kid say: "Quick! Hold this for me!" But I just took the canister with a patient smile, and watched as the wick sizzled down, sputtered, and went out. I pitched it back to him. "You're getting to where you ain't no fun," he said, catching the Black Betty, grinning and pitching it up and down.

I looked at him, at his bucktoothed grin, and I had to grin myself. "Anybody ever tell you you're stone crazy, Kid?"

"Yeah, but you know how people lie," he said. He tipped his hat and backed away as if leaving a theater stage.

"Do I *ever*," I said, glancing back out at the wake of dust.

I stood watching, and in a second I heard

the contesa clear her throat beside me. I looked around at her, with the dust streaked on her face, her hair matted but now pulled back and tied by a ragged strip of ribbon. "Now that I have nothing left, I suppose you will be leaving too?"

I stared at her as a thousand thoughts raced through my mind; but all I could finally say was: "You can count on it. Just as fast as my horse will carry me."

She nodded as if to say she understood. She glanced at the dust on the horizon, then back at me. "So, you were only lying to Mangelo about finding the treasure down there, right below my hacienda?"

I thought about it, then said: "Yep. I didn't find nothing but the stallion and a cave full of dirt. It'd be stretching it pretty far to think the gold was there all along, wouldn't it?"

"Si, perhaps. But things have gotten so strange since you came here, I would not have been surprised. The soldiers would have believed you. They would have stayed if they thought the treasure was there —"

"Just another way of deceiving them," I said. "There was nothing unusual about any of this."

"But the way Morcillo took to you. I saw it with my own —"

"It was you he was trying to get close to."
I reached into my shirt and searched for the scented handkerchief, but couldn't find it. "Anyway. It was the scent of you on the handkerchief I carried. That's what drew him to me. He was crazy about you. It was the scent of you through the caverns that brought him there. He was following you blindly. Anything he had to do to be near you."

"That is preposterous," she said.

I shrugged: "Think what you will."

She gazed out across the land at the fading wake of dust. "He needs me, you know. He does not know it, but he will need me to tend to him. To cook for him, mend his clothes, take care of his needs —"

"Sort of like you did for Quick Quintan?" I stared at her. She lowered her eyes, but then raised them back to mine.

"Another time . . . another place," she said softly. "It would've been wonderful . . . you and me . . . with nothing of the world to interfere with us."

"I know," I said in a gentle tone; and I meant it as I recalled the scent, the warmth, and the taste of her — things I could recall but knew I could no longer experience.

She lay a hand on my arm and I saw a spark of something in her eyes, but not the same spark I'd seen before when we'd burned for one another's touch. "This place of yours in Missouri. It is a —"

I pressed a finger to her lips, shaking my head slowly. "Don't," I said. "It's just a cabin, nothing more."

She gestured about the courtyard. "But you now own this. You could rebuild a home here, with fountains and great —" She stopped and looked into my eyes. "You have lots of money, si?"

"All I have is standing here before you." I waited a second, perhaps hoping she would tell me that was enough. But then I caught myself and said: "Anyway, there's been too much killing between us, too many things to get *over* before we could ever get *on.*"

She let out a sigh and dropped her hand from my arm. "You are right, of course."

"You can still catch up to him," I said.

She looked up at me again. "You know why I must, do you not?"

"No," I said, but it don't matter."

She started to turn away and go toward the horses Turk had led out and prepared for us, but then she looked at me one more time. "I really meant it when I said I love you. Do you believe me?"

"Sure," I said, "why not." And as she walked to the horses, I took out the deed from inside my shirt, along with the new transfer she'd had drawn up. I signed the transfer, folded them together, and held them out to her as she rode back past me. "Someday, maybe *you* will rebuild here," I said. She took the papers but rode on slowly, reading them as she neared the shattered gates. Then she looked around, held them up near her face and tipped them toward me. "Via condios," I whispered.

In a second Jack walked up beside me. "Did I just see you give her the deed to the land? After all we went through here?"

"It was hers, Jack. I held her jewels in good faith. Wasn't her fault I lost them. Whatever else she's done, she did act in good faith as far as the land, the jewels and the stallion. I reckon if I ever found him, he'd still be mine, far as she'd care."

"Well, since you gave her the land, I reckon it's safe to assume that you was just blowing smoke when you told Abe the treasure was down there?"

"You're a pretty good gambler, Jack. You tell me, what's the odds that the treasure — if there ever was one — would be right smack under the contesa's hacienda?"

His face reddened slightly. "I never thought it was. I was just checking."

"You ready to ride?" I looked at him, then

at the Kid and Turk over by the horses.

"I been ready," he said.

We mounted up and the four of us rode out through the back, swinging wide of the training camp least the federales still be there, and around past Finger Rock. When we stopped at the path that went upward into the rocks, Turk looked all around the flatland and said: "Bad as I hate to leave good company, I think I better head south from here. See if I can't work up another crew and commence gathering some scalps."

"Thought you was giving it up?" We all stared at him.

"I was. But hell, you know how it is, old dogs — new tricks. Hell, ole Monralite wouldn't have nothing to do but stay home and fight with his ole-lady if I ever went out of the business." We just watched *him* as he rode away.

"That has to be the worst smelling son of a bitch to ever fall off the gut wagon," said Jack. "What'd ya suppose makes a man smell so bad?"

"Hell, I don't know, Jack. I reckon we can't all smell alike."

I noticed the Kid got quieter and quieter as we rode upward through the rocks; and as we descended the other side, he too reined up and said: "This is it for me too, boys. If I'm right, ole Garrett'll be waiting just about a mile around that next turn. I'll take leave here and head down to ole Mex."

"Jesus, Kid, just like that?" I looked at him there atop his horse with the sunlight dancing about his shoulders. "You're just heading off?"

"Yep." He spread his bucktoothed grin. "How else can a person leave 'cept *just like that?'* " He snapped his fingers for emphasis. "I figure you boys got banks waiting to be robbed, trains to be looted, payrolls to be —"

"It ain't like that, Kid. Mostly we just hide out . . . and wish we didn't have to. You're welcome to ride along. We could always duck past Garrett."

"Naw, that'd just hurt his feelings, and piss him off at ya."

"So what? He already said he'd take us down too, first chance he got."

"He was blowing off, is all. Ole Pat ain't gonna bother ya unless you're with me. That's another reason I'd just as soon leave. It ain't right getting ya into my trouble."

"Now that's a hell of a thing to say, Kid, after me getting you into all of my trouble."

He grinned and raised his chin. "What trouble?"

■ ■ ■ ■

In minutes we'd said our goodbyes to the Kid and headed on into the long winding path through scrub grass, chola and mesquite bush. Just as he'd predicted, as we topped a low rise and started down, I saw Garrett sitting beside the path, in the dirt, leaned back against a short spur of rock. His reins hung in his hand and his rifle lay across his lap. His deputies leaned against another spur of rock a few yards away. They watched us as we rode up cautiously and stopped.

"If you're waiting for the Kid," I said, "he's dead." I studied his eyes to see if he believed me. "Yep. The federales beat you to him. Nothing more to do now but pack it in, I reckon." I shook my head. "Sure gonna miss that boy. It was a hell of a thing, the way they shot him — kept shooting him, over and over. It made us both sick seeing —"

"Give it a rest," he said. "I bet it was as bad as the way a bunch of Cheyenne skinned and gutted ole Miller Crowe, wasn't it?" He glared at me, and I felt the skin tighten on the back of my neck. Jack stepped his horse away from mine and lay his hand

471

on his pistol.

"Don't worry," said Garrett. "I got no quarrel with ya. I'm only a county sheriff. Anybody hunts the James Gang, it oughta be the ones that made them what they are." He looked back and forth between me and Jack, pulled a bottle from under his duster and held it out. "You boys got time for a drink?"

Jack and I shot each other a glance, climbed down and walked over slowly toward him. Gosset called out to Jack: "I want ya to know, I done forgot any misunderstandings between us, okay?"

Jack only nodded without looking toward him. Gosset added: "I'll tell ya the truth, I nearly darkened my trousers the day we —"

"Shut up, Gosset," Garrett said. "He's not gonna kill ya."

"How you know?" Jack smiled, stooping down and taking the bottle from Garrett's gloved hand.

"Because I figure about all you want right now is to get on back to Missouri." He waved a hand taking in the badlands. "This country ain't your play. It's the Kid's — but not yours." He watched Jack pass me the bottle, and he leaned back again as I threw back a shot and stooped down beside Jack. "I also figure the Kid just left ya about two

miles back and headed down to ole Mex."
He squinted at me and reached for his
bottle.

I handed it to him. "Then why didn't you
come get him?"

He shrugged: "That's all I wanted . . . was
him in ole Mex, stay there a year, two
maybe. The Ring wants him dead. But hell,
they can't expect me to cross the border for
him."

"Don't be so sure," I said. "It was the Ring
who paid the tab on that little bloodletting
back there. They put up the money for a
rebel army under a band of mercenaries just
so they could —"

"Careful now," he said. "They're some big
boys."

"I don't give a damn," I said. "They did
it . . . you can believe that."

He shook his head. "No I can't. Can't
believe it, can't hear it. Don't want to think
it. This is a wild territory here. Only ones
can tame it are those who are as wild as the
ones they're taming." He threw back a shot.
"It'll settle. Then someday we'll all look
back and deny whatever we had to do. But
for now, it is what it is, crooked, wild . . .
crazy. That's what the Kid can't understand.
For all his short comings, the poor bastard
is too honest to abide with all the treachery,

deception — the *politics* of taming a land. Strange ain't it?"

"Strange?" I stood up and ran a hand across my mouth. "What's strange is that you see all that and still want to dirty your hands with it."

"I won't justify myself to you," he said, standing also and brushing the seat of his pants. "But I do want you to know that I ain't out to kill the Kid . . . not if I can keep from it. That boy's like a younger brother to me. But hard talk's all he understands."

"Maybe not," I said. "Maybe if you ask him like he was still your friend he'd stay away just to help you out. It'd be worth a try wouldn't it? I've always found him willing to do anything for a friend."

"You don't know him," Garrett said. "You might think you do. But you don't. Talking to the Kid's like farting in a tornado. It's gone before ya can smell it. Ten-to-one he'll be back in Sumner within a month, *hell,* within two weeks."

I spit and ran my hand across my mouth again. Jack glared at Garrett, and I saw what ran across his mind. Jack had him cold, here and now, a sure way of keeping him from ever killing the Kid. But for some reason I reached out and tapped Jack on the arm. "Let's go, Jack." I looked back at Garrett and saw that he too had seen what had just gone through our minds. "Thanks for the drink," I said.

We mounted and rode on, but less than a mile from where we'd left Garrett and his deputies, we made another turn around a low stand of rock, and there, smack in the middle of the trail sat Frothe and his young corporal. "Nobody takes my boots, Herr Beatty," Frothe said, there atop his horse, barefoot and seething. Beside him the corporal sat with his horse turned slightly to the side, a rifle cocked and covering us. I saw no weapon on Frothe as I reined closer looking for an edge. Beside me, Jack's hand lay poised on his pistol.

"Easy, Jack," I said cautiously. "If boots is all it takes." I stared at Frothe as I spoke, and raised my right boot up across the saddle. "I'll give 'em up. But I have to tell you, I never thought you'd be petty enough to chase down a pair of boots." Then I looked at the corporal and added: "Is this what he'll pay you to do from now on? Find his boots for him? Now *that's* loyalty."

"Shut up, Beatty," said Frothe. "I've told you, my followers are not groomed on loyalty. They work for the highest payer." He spread a wet sneer. "Something your sentimentality would never abide."

"Oh?" I pulled off the boot and let it fall from my hand. And I raised my other boot and said: "So, if I was to offer him *more* to turn that rifle around and put a bullet through *you,* you'd be disappointed if he turned me down?" I slipped off the other shiny boot, dropped it and heard it plop in the dust.

"Stop your foolishness," Frothe snapped. "You have no knowledge of the ways of the world —"

"Not so fast, Herr Colonel," I heard the corporal say in a quiet tone; and as I looked at him, I saw Jack's hand relax on his pistol.

"Nonsense!" Frothe shouted. "Even if that were the case, you have nothing to offer —"

"Let me show you something, Corporal," I said, cutting Frothe off. I ran a hand beneath my shirt collar, drew up the jeweled necklace and let it dangle down my chest. I sat watching the corporal's eyes take on a different expression, then I heard Jack chuckle as I eased my horse forward, pulling off the necklace and holding it out. "Start with . . . let's say, a bullet through the arm, just to get his attention?"

"This is Absur—" Frothe's word stopped as the sound of the rifle shattered the air.

I coaxed my horse forward slowly, dropping the necklace in the young corporal's hand without looking at Frothe. "Then maybe one through each leg? Maybe clip off an ear or two?" I leaned slightly as I passed him and said in a near whisper: "Just take your time here . . . get creative."

We rode east for aways, along the wide ravine. Behind us we heard the echo of the rifle now and then above the churn of the wind; and I wiggled my bare toes in the stirrups, feeling the air between them. I started to tell Jack that this was the ravine where I'd jumped the black stallion and lost him, but as I looked out across the width of it, I had a hard time convincing *myself* that I'd actually done it. I gigged my horse and rode along looking out across it until I thought I saw Morcillo the stallion far off on the horizon. I squinted into the sunlight and studied closely, finally seeing *not only* the stallion, but atop him, none other than Rafe Rafferty!

"Jack, quick! Look at this," I shouted. He spun as I pointed into the sunlight. "There! Way out there! It's Rafferty! Riding the stallion!" Starting out, I swore I could see him top a rock ledge, rear the stallion up and wave something toward us. But how could he have seen us, when I could barely make him out in the glint of sunlight.

"I don't see nothing," Jack said. He cocked a brow at me. "You feeling okay? I got some water here —"

"So help me God, Jack! Look out there." And I'll swear to my dying day that I saw Rafferty waving something from atop the stallion. If I was pressed to say what it was, I'd say it was the contesa's handkerchief; and he waved it high as the stallion reared. Then as Jack squinted and rubbed his eyes, the stallion spun, dropped and rode away behind a stretch of sprawling rock.

"We're gonna have to get you over to Sumner," said Jack. "Get you a steak, some wine, a little music — this place has got you goosing butterflies."

"I know what I saw, Jack, damn it. If you hadn't fooled around you'd seen it too."

"Sure," he said. "But I've seen plenty. More than enough of your *enchanted land.*"

"It's been a strange one, ain't it?" I looked at him.

"Oh?" He grinned. "I hadn't noticed."

"You know what gets me about this whole mess?" I went on before he could say anything. "What gets me is that every damned one of them people sounded *right* in some way or other." I rubbed my temples. "I mean, the contesa in her own way sounded right, Frothe — rotten bastard that he was — even made a lot of sense, as far as how things work. Abe, Garrett, the Kid. Even that stinking scalp hunter made a little sense. Every one of them made *some* kinda sense if you listened to them."

Jack spit and chuckled. "But sounding right don't make ya right. Most dangerous son of a bitches in this world are the ones who think they're right. Main thing is, *we* wasn't wrong, was we?"

I thought for a second, then said: "No. I honestly don't think we were. Not this time anyway."

"Alright then, *they* were."

"*They?* You mean the same *they* that fans all fires?"

"Yep. *Theys* are the ones who keeps the graveyards full."

"Yeah, but think what a fine land this could be if all of the *'theys'* ever got together and put aside their own interest long enough to pull together for a change."

"They might someday, when they see that something like Frothe has slipped in and caught them with their pants down. When something big enough threatens everybody's interest, they might. Until then, I'd as soon not think about who's right and who's wrong. Do enough of that and it'll drive ya nuts, you know."

"Yeah, well. What the hell do we know about anything? We're just outlaws."

"Outlaws, revolutionists, patriots," Jack chuckled and spit again. "I reckon it's a very fine line between all three. Depends on who's left standing once the dust settles."

"Yep," I said, and sooner or later the dust *always* settles." I thought about it all for a second, then tried to put it out of my mind. I wiggled my bare toes and shook my head. "Anyway," I said, "I don't want to stop at Sumner. If it's all the same, I'd sooner go on to Residue Point, where a man can enjoy a little peace and quiet away from all the __,' "

"Then you can go there by yourself," said Jack. "Ain't nothing worries me worse than a quiet peaceful place after a hard ride. I couldn't cope with it."

"Well, look at it this way . . . at least we didn't rustle no cattle."

"Not *yet,*" he said.

I laughed; and we rode on into the long barren sand flats where our spirits would feel the desolation, the hollow smallness as we gave ourselves over to the vastness of the land.

Due east we rode, the sun behind us larger than the earth and sinking blood red, our shadows and that of all around us, cast long and dark like slices of night fell to earth.

I rode silently beside my amigo, Quiet Jack, and wondered to what depth he'd seen all of what we'd been through; and I wondered if he gave any thought to how deeply I'd seen it.

"I've got to ask one thing," he said after the long silence. "Where did you get that necklace back there?"

"It was the contesa's," I said.

"No it wasn't. I never saw it before," he said.

"Alright then, Jack." I let out a breath. "It was from the treasure — the lost treasure of the conquistadors."

"Smart-ass," Jack said. He spit, ran a hand across his mouth, and gigged his horse forward.

I would never tell anyone of the lost treasure deep down in the bowels of the earth, for what would it profit a person to know of such a treasure so near, yet just beyond the grasp of their hands. Treasure, like freedom, I had somehow come to know, only torments, and makes fools and monsters of those who know of it but cannot have it; and who can know of either without craving it . . . or who can know that either is near without risking their all to have it?